LAURENT BINET

Civilisations

TRANSLATED FROM THE FRENCH BY
Sam Taylor

VINTAGE

1 3 5 7 9 10 8 6 4 2

Vintage is part of the Penguin Random House group of companies whose addresses can be found at global.penguinrandomhouse.com

Penguin
Random House
UK

First published in Vintage in 2020
First published with the title *Civilizations* in 2019
by Éditions Grasset et Fasquelle, France
First published in Great Britain by Harvill Secker in 2021

penguin.co.uk/vintage

This book is supported by the Institut français (Royaume-Uni)
as part of the Burgess programme.

INSTITUT
FRANÇAIS
ROYAUME-UNI

A CIP catalogue record for this book is available from the British Library

ISBN 9781529112818

Printed and bound in Great Britain by Clays Ltd, Elcograf S.p.A.

The authorised representative in the EEA is Penguin Random House Ireland, Morrison Chambers, 32 Nassau Street, Dublin D02 YH68

Penguin Random House is committed to a sustainable future for our business, our readers and our planet. This book is made from Forest Stewardship Council® certified paper.

MIX
Paper from
responsible sources
FSC® C018179

'Art gives life to what history killed.'

Carlos Fuentes
Don Quixote, or the Critique of Reading

'Because of the confusion and discordance in which they lived, their conquest was very easy.'

Inca Garcilaso de la Vega
The Royal Commentaries of the Incas

Part One

The Saga of Freydis Eriksdottir

1. Erik

There was a woman named Aud the Deep-Minded, daughter of Ketill Flatnose, who had been queen. She was the widow of Olaf the White, the warrior-king of Ireland. Upon the death of her husband, she travelled to the Hebrides and on to Scotland, where her son, Thorstein the Red, in turn became king. Then the Scots betrayed him and he perished in battle.

When she learned of her son's death, Aud took to sea with twenty freemen and travelled to Iceland, where she colonised the territories between the Day-meal and the Giantess's Leap rivers.

With her were many noblemen who had been taken prisoner during the Viking expeditions to the west, and whom she treated as slaves.

There was a man named Thorvald, who had left Norway after committing murder, and his son Erik the Red. They were farmers who cultivated the earth. One day, Eyiolf the Foul, a relative of one of Erik's neighbours, killed some of Erik's slaves because they had caused a landslide. Erik killed Eyiolf the Foul. He also killed Hrafn the Duellist.

So he was banished.

He colonised the Isle of Oxney. He asked his neighbour to look after his beams, but when he wanted them back, his neighbour refused to return them. They fought and other men died. He was banished once again, this time at the Thorsnes Thing.

He could not stay in Iceland, nor could he return to Norway. That was why he chose to sail towards the land glimpsed by the

3

son of Ulf the Crow one day when he had navigated too far west. He named this country Greenland, because he reasoned that people would want to go to a country with such a beautiful name.

He married Thorhild, granddaughter of Thorbjorg the Ship-Chested, and together they had several sons. But he also had a daughter by another woman. The girl's name was Freydis.

2. Freydis

Nothing is known about Freydis's mother. But Freydis, like her brothers, inherited her father Erik's wanderlust. So it was that she embarked on the ship lent by her half-brother Leif the Lucky to Thorfinn Karlsefni so that he could find the way to Vinland.

They sailed west. After a stopover in Markland, they reached Vinland and found the camp left behind by Leif Eriksson.

They found it a beautiful land, with forests not far from the sea and white sand along the coastline. There were many islands and shallows. Day and night were of a more equal length than in Greenland or Iceland.

But there were also Skraelings there: beings that resembled small trolls. The legends were wrong: they were not unipeds. But they had dark skin and were fond of red fabrics. The Greenlanders swapped all the red cloths they had for animal skins. They traded. But one day, a bellowing bull belonging to Karlsefni escaped its enclosure and frightened the Skraelings. So they attacked the camp and Karlsefni's men fled in fear, until Freydis furiously berated them for their cowardice, picked up a sword and prepared to defend herself from the enemy. She tore her shift open and beat the flat of the blade against her breasts while insulting the Skraelings. Seeing this, her countrymen were ashamed and turned back to help her, while the Skraelings, terrified by the vision of this voluptuous, ferocious woman, ran away.

Freydis was pregnant and bad-tempered. She got into an argument with two brothers. She wanted to take their boat because it was bigger than hers, so she ordered her husband Thorvard to kill them and their men, which he did. Freydis killed their women with an axe.

Winter was over and summer was coming. But Freydis didn't dare return to Greenland because she feared the wrath of her brother Leif once he found out that she was guilty of murder. However, she felt that the others distrusted her and that she was no longer welcome in the camp. She fitted out the brothers' boat, then set sail with her husband, a few men, some cattle and horses. Those remaining in the Vinland colony were relieved when she left. But before going out to sea, she said to them: 'I, Freydis Eriksdottir, swear that I will return.'

They headed south.

3. The South

The wide-sided knarr sailed along the coast. There was a storm and Freydis prayed to Thor. The ship almost crashed into some rocks. The terrified animals thrashed so violently that the men were on the verge of throwing them overboard for fear that they would capsize the ship. But in the end, the god's anger abated.

The journey lasted longer than they had expected. The crew could find nowhere to land because the cliffs were too high, and when they did come across a beach, it was defended by Skraelings with bows who shot stones at them. It was too late to sail east and Freydis did not want to turn back. The men survived on the fish they caught, but some of them drank seawater and became ill.

One day, when there was no north wind to help swell their sails, Freydis gave birth in the aisle between the benches of oarsmen. The baby boy, whom she wanted to name Erik after his grandfather, was stillborn, and she gave him to the sea.

At last, they discovered a cove where they could anchor.

4. The Land of the Dawn

The water there was so shallow that they were able to walk to the beach. They had brought all kinds of animals with them. The land was beautiful. They immediately began to explore.

There were meadows and airy forests. There was an abundance of game. The rivers were full of fish. Freydis and her companions decided to set up camp near the coast, sheltered from the wind. They did not lack provisions, so they thought they would stay there for the winter. They guessed that the winters here would be milder, or at least shorter, than in their homeland. The youngest among them had been born in Greenland, while the others were from Iceland or Norway, like Freydis's father.

But one day, exploring more deeply inland, they discovered a cultivated field. There were neat rows of crops, like ears of yellow barley but with crunchy, juicy grains. So it was that they knew they were not alone.

They, too, wanted to grow this crunchy barley, but didn't know how.

A few weeks later, some Skraelings appeared at the top of the hill overlooking their camp. They were tall and well built, with oily skin. Their faces were painted with long black lines, which frightened the Greenlanders, but this time nobody dared run away in case Freydis accused them of cowardice. Besides, the

Skraelings seemed more curious than hostile. One of the Green-landers wanted to give them a small axe as a peace offering, but Freydis forbade him, and instead she gave them a pearl necklace and an iron brooch. The Skraelings appeared to greatly appreciate the brooch: they passed it from hand to hand and fought over it. Then Freydis and her companions realised that the Skraelings wanted to invite them to their village. Freydis was the only one to accept the invitation. Her husband and the others remained in the camp, not because they were afraid of the unknown, but because they had almost died before in similar circumstances. They named Freydis their emissary and delegate, which made her laugh because she understood that none of them was brave enough to accompany her. Once again, she insulted them, but this time the shame had no effect. So she went alone with the Skraelings, who coated her white skin and red hair with bear fat, then they all got into a boat carved out of a tree trunk and rowed across a swamp. The trees were so tall in that land that ten people could easily fit in a single boat. The boat moved away from the shore and Freydis disappeared with the Skraelings.

For three days and three nights they awaited her return, but nobody went off in search of her. Even her husband Thorvard didn't dare venture into those swamps.

Then, on the fourth day, she returned with a Skraeling chief, who wore brightly coloured jewellery around his neck and in his ears. He had long hair that was shaved on one side, and it was difficult to imagine a more physically imposing man.

Freydis told her companions that this was the Land of the Dawn and that these Skraelings were called the People of the First Light. They were waging war on another people who lived further west, and Freydis believed that the Greenlanders should support them. When her companions asked her how she had been able to understand their language, she replied, laughing: 'Well, maybe I'm a seeress too?' She summoned the man who had wanted to give the Skraelings an axe, and told him to give it to the sachem (as the Skraelings called their chiefs). Nine months later, Freydis would give birth to a girl. She would name her daughter Gudrid, after her former sister-in-law, Karlsefni's wife, the widow of Thorstein Eriksson, whom she had always hated (but there is no point going on about people who will play no part in this saga).

The little colony moved close to the Skraeling village. Not content just to live together peacefully, the two groups began helping each other. The Greenlanders taught the Skraelings to extract iron from peat and to transform it into axes, lances and arrowheads, helping them to be more effective in battle against their enemies. In exchange, they taught the Greenlanders to grow the crunchy barley by pushing the grains into little piles of earth, alongside beans and marrows, so that they could wind themselves around the tall stems. This enabled them to build up stores for winter, when there would be less game to hunt. The Greenlanders were eager to remain in this country. As a mark of friendship, they gave the Skraelings a cow.

After a while, some of the Skraelings became ill. One caught a fever and died. Soon after that, they began dropping like flies. The Greenlanders grew frightened and wanted to leave, but Freydis forbade it. Even though her companions told her that sooner or later the epidemic would start killing them, she refused to abandon the village they had built. This was a fertile land, she pointed out, and if they went elsewhere there was no guarantee that they would find any other friendly Skraelings with whom they could trade.

But then the imposing sachem caught the disease. Returning to his house – a dome made from arched posts covered with strips of tree bark – he saw the corpses of strangers strewn across the threshold, rising like a giant wave to sweep away his village and the Greenlanders' village. When this vision faded, he lay down with a burning fever, and summoned Freydis. When she came to his bedside he whispered a few words into her ear, so that she was the only one to hear them. But in a voice loud enough for everyone to hear, he declared that happy were those people who were at home all over the world, and that the gift of iron made to his people by the travellers would not be forgotten. He talked to Freydis about her situation, telling her that she would have a great destiny, as would her child. Then he collapsed. Freydis watched over him all night long, but in the morning his body was cold. So she went back to her companions and said: 'It's time to load the animals on to the knarr.'

5. Cuba

Freydis still dreamed of voyaging further south. For weeks, they sailed the coastline, and soon they had no provisions left and had to drink rainwater and eat fish from the sea. But whenever they thought that a particular land looked promising, Freydis always refused to stop. At first this made the crew nervous, then suspicious; in the end, they became angry. Freydis said to them: 'Do you want to risk your lives again? Do you want a uniped to shoot an arrow through your belly?' (Because this was how her half-brother, Thorvald Eriksson, had died, and she knew that everyone would remember that gruesome incident.) 'We will continue our journey until its end or we will die at sea, if such is the whim of Njörd or the wish of Hel.' But nobody knew what end Freydis was talking about.

At last, they came upon a land that was perhaps an island. Freydis, sensing that she could not contain her companions' impatience much longer, agreed to berth there.

The knarr entered a magnificent river. All along the shore, the water was perfectly clear, and the land itself more beautiful than any they had seen before. Close to the river, there were only trees, each with its own fruit and flowers. The fruits tasted wonderful. Many birds and their chicks sang very softly. The leaves of the trees were so large that they could be used to cover houses. The ground was very flat.

Freydis jumped ashore. She came to some houses that she thought must belong to fishermen, but the occupants fled in terror. In one of the houses, she found a dog that didn't bark.

The Greenlanders brought their animals ashore and the Skraelings, intrigued by the horses, reappeared. They were naked and short, but muscular; their skin was dark and their hair black. Freydis advanced towards them, thinking that they would not be frightened of a pregnant woman. She let one of them mount a horse and she walked the horse around the village. The Skraelings were all thrilled and amazed. They offered their guests food and welcomed them into their homes. They also offered them rolled leaves, which they burned and brought to their lips to inhale the smoke.

So Freydis and her companions moved in with them, and the Skraeling village became their village. They built their own houses, round and covered with straw, just like their hosts'. They also built a temple to Thor, with wooden pillars and beams. The Skraelings showed them how to get water from the large nuts that grew in the trees with the big leaves, because that water was delicious. They taught them the names for things: for example, the crunchy barley was called *corn* in their language. They showed them how to sleep on nets hung between two trees, which they called *hammocks*. It was so warm all year round that they didn't know what snow was.

It was here that Freydis gave birth. Her husband Thorvard treated Gudrid like his own daughter, and Freydis was touched. She began to think less harshly of him.

The Skraelings became good horsemen and they learned to forge iron. The Greenlanders learned to recognise different animals and to shoot arrows. There were turtles and all sorts of snakes, as well as lizards with scales of stone and very long jaws. In the sky flew red-headed vultures.

The two groups mixed so well that other children were born. Some had black hair, others blond or red. They understood both their parents' languages.

But once again the Skraelings came down with a fever and died. As the Greenlanders were spared, they realised that they had nothing to fear from the disease, but that they had brought it with them. They realised that they were the disease. The men from the north gave the dead graves on which they carved runes. They prayed to Thor and Odin. But the Skraelings kept falling ill. The Greenlanders understood that if they stayed, their hosts would all perish and they would be left alone. They took pity on them and, reluctantly, decided to leave again. They dismantled the temple to Thor and took it with them, but left the Skraelings a few animals as a farewell gift.

After their departure, the fever did not end. The Skraelings kept dying, until they were almost extinct. Taking their animals, the survivors dispersed over the rest of the island.

6. Chichen Itza

As for Freydis, she now travelled west, hugging the coastline, with her daughter Gudrid, her husband Thorvard, and their companions. Once they discovered that the land they were leaving behind really was an island, Freydis wanted to head south again. But her companions refused to sail a single day longer without knowing where they were going, so Freydis suggested that they throw the beams from Thor's temple into the sea, allowing the pieces of wood to show them the way. They would land wherever Thor took the beams, she declared. As soon as they drifted away from the boat, the beams headed towards the land far in the west, and it appeared to the people on the boat that they moved less slowly than might have been expected. After that, a sea breeze arose; they sailed west past the cape of an island that they named the Isle of Women. Then they reached a large landmass that they thought must be the mainland and entered a fjord. They saw that the fjord was inordinately wide and long, and bordered on each side by very high mountains. Freydis named the fjord after her daughter. After that, they explored the area and discovered that Thor had landed the beams on a headland jutting into the sea at the north of the bay.

There was a shallow river that the knarr was able to navigate due to its low draught. They sailed up the river until they came to a village. It was late and, since the sun was about to set, Freydis led her people to the sandbanks on the opposite shore. The next day, several Skraelings arrived in a small boat; they brought with them some red-headed chickens and a small amount of corn – barely enough to feed a few men – and told the foreigners to take this food and go away. But, this time, the Greenlanders wanted to stay because Thor had brought them here. So the Skraelings returned, dressed for war and armed with bows and arrows, lances and shields. Too weary to flee, the Greenlanders decided to fight. But they were soon overwhelmed by the sheer numbers of Skraelings. Ten of the Greenlanders were wounded and all were taken prisoner.

Had it not been for an unexpected event, they would all have been killed. One of the Greenlanders fell from his horse. This terrified the Skraelings, who began making strange cries. They had thought that the rider and the horse were a single being. After conferring, they lined up the Greenlanders and tied them together before leading them back to their home, along with their animals and their weapons.

They crossed forests and swamps in sweltering heat. The humidity was so high that the men from the north felt as if they were melting, like snow on fire. Then they came to a town, the likes of which they had never seen. There were stone temples and tall pyramids and statues of warriors lined up in colonnades. There were also some impressive sculpted serpent heads that reminded them of the prows of knarrs and longships, except that these serpents had feathers.

They were led into an H-shaped arena, where some kind of ball game was taking place. Two teams faced off, each in its own half of the court, and hit a large ball made of a strange material, at once hard and supple, which bounced very high. The aim, as far as they could understand, was to knock the ball back into the opponents' half, while keeping the ball in the air and without using hands or feet – only hips, elbows, knees, buttocks or forearms. Two stone rings were hung on the walls of the pit, at the intersection of the two halves, but at that point the Greenlanders had no way of knowing what they were for. Terraced seating allowed a large number of spectators to watch the game. When it was over, certain players would be sacrificed by having their heads cut off.

Twelve Greenlanders, including Freydis and her husband Thorvard, were thrown into the pit. On the other side of the court were twelve Skraelings, dressed only in knee and elbow pads. The game began and the Greenlanders, who had never played this game before, kept losing points for failing to return the ball or, when they did return it, for breaking a series of rules that they didn't know about. As the game went on, they grew more and more afraid, because they realised that the losers would be sacrificed. But suddenly the ball hit one of the stone rings, without going through it, and this caused a murmur in the crowd. So Freydis encouraged her teammates to aim for the ring. And it was Thorvard, her husband, whose knee the ball hit, before – by a stroke of incredible luck – rising into the air and curving in a perfect arc through the ring. The spectators stood and cheered. Immediately afterwards, the game ended and the Greenlanders were declared the victors. The captain of the losing team was decapitated. What the Greenlanders did not know was that, in certain exceptional cases, the best player of the winning team was also executed, which was considered a great honour. So it was that Thorvard's head was cut off before the very eyes of his wife Freydis and his adopted daughter Gudrid, who wept in her mother's arms. Freydis told her companions: 'We are at the mercy of Skraelings more ferocious than trolls, and if we want to survive, we must win them over by doing everything they demand of us.' Then she recited a poem in old Norse:

And so I learned that in the south
Thorvard breathed his final breath
The witch was cruel to me and Odin chose
Too early which side was his

Her song rose into the air, to the great astonishment of the Skraelings, before falling like an arrow.

Do not imagine I am furious
I am waiting for a better opportunity

Thorvard's body was ceremoniously thrown into a lake at the bottom of an abyss. The other Greenlanders were spared, but at first they were treated as slaves. Some worked in open-air salt mines or cultivated cotton, which they had, in the past, seen brought from Myklagaard by Swedes; these tasks were the hardest. Others worked as servants or took part in ritual ceremonies in honour of the many Skraeling gods, among the highest of which were Kukulkan, the feathered serpent, and Chaac, the god of rain.

One day, Freydis saw a statue of a man lying on the ground, leaning on his elbows, legs folded, a crown on his head. The Skraeling jarl for whom she worked explained to her with sign language that this was Chaac, the rain god. So she went to fetch a hammer and placed it on the statue's belly. She told the jarl that she knew this god by the name of Thor. A few days later, a violent storm hit the city, bringing an end to a long drought.

Another time, Freydis's daughter, Gudrid, was playing with a Skraeling toy that had small wheels. Freydis was surprised that, other than this toy, the Skraelings had no wagons or ploughs. But they did not see the point of such large vehicles, too heavy to be pulled or pushed by human arms. So Freydis asked her companions to build a wagon and then to fetch a horse, which she attached to it. The Skraelings were very pleased with this innovation, but they grew even more so when they discovered that a plough with an iron ploughshare and pulled by a horse or an ox could help with tilling and greatly increase cotton production. So it was that Freydis contributed to the prosperity of the city, since it traded its cotton with neighbouring cities for corn and precious stones.

As a token of their gratitude, they granted Freydis and her companions the right to drink chocolate, a much-prized foamy beverage that Freydis found rather bitter.

At the same time, the Greenlanders ceased to be slaves and were treated as guests. They were allowed to watch the ball games and to take part in the ceremonies around sacred wells. The Skraelings taught them the science of the stars and the rudiments of their writing system, including drawings that were similar to runes but far more elaborate.

For a while, it seemed as if Loki's daughter had finally forgotten them. But Hel never forgets. The first Skraelings fell ill. They were given large amounts of chocolate to drink, but in the end they died. Freydis knew that, sooner or later, their hosts would guess that the foreigners had brought the disease with them. She quickly organised the group's escape. One moonless night, they left the city with their animals and took the road to the coast, intending to find their ship. The mare that had pulled the wagon they built was now pregnant, and she was slowing them down, but they didn't want to abandon her. In the morning, they heard the roar of voices from the city and they knew that the Skraelings would pursue them. They hurried. The knarr was waiting where they'd left it.

But the Skraelings from the neighbouring village had seen them returning and they got it into their heads to try to stop them, so the Greenlanders boarded as quickly as possible. The pregnant mare had been trailing behind and when everyone else was aboard, she was still advancing laboriously along the beach. The Skraelings had already appeared and were uttering war cries as they ran after her. The Greenlanders urged her forward: although the horse was exhausted, she was only a few strides from the gangway. But, having waited until the very last moment, the crew had to cast off to prevent the Skraelings from boarding their ship. The Greenlanders watched as the Skraelings held the mare by her neck, as they'd seen the foreigners do.

They headed south without a word.

7. Panama

Who knows how many leagues the knarr travelled? Perhaps three hundred, perhaps more. When the sea raged and they could not raise their sails without risk of capsizing, the Greenlanders rowed, heads down. Days followed nights. The lowing of the cattle and the wailing of the newborn babies were the only signs of life on board.

They berthed the ship in driving rain. They were dirty, hairy, starving. Before them was a verdant land that they sensed would be hostile. Many birds of all kinds flew in the sky. They killed several with their bows. But most of the Greenlanders didn't want to risk exploring a land that they feared would be inhabited by other Skraelings even more ferocious than those they'd encountered. Instead, they thought they should stock up on provisions and, after camping there for long enough to recover their strength, sail north, back to their homeland. Freydis was fiercely opposed to this plan, but one of her companions spoke to her thus: 'We all know why you refuse to go back to Greenland. You're scared that your brother Leif will punish you for the crimes you committed in Vinland. I can promise you that none of us will say anything, but if Leif happens to find out what you did, you'll have to submit to your brother's judgement or be tried by the Thing.'

Freydis said nothing. In the morning, however, her companions discovered the knarr half-sunk and lying on its side. The group was stunned. Nobody dared overtly accuse her of scuttling their ship, although they all thought it. But she spoke to them thus: 'As you can see, we cannot sail away from here now. None of us will ever return to Greenland. My father called the country that to attract Icelanders like you, in order to increase the size of his colony. In reality, the land wasn't green; it was white most of the year. That so-called green land was far less welcoming than this one. Look at all those birds in the sky. Look at all that fruit in the trees. Here, we don't need to cover ourselves with animal skins or make fires to keep us warm or shelter from the wind in houses made of ice. We are going to explore this land until we find the best place to start our own colony. Because this is the true Greenland. Here, we will finish the work begun by Erik the Red.'

Some cheered, but others remained silent and stricken because they were afraid of what else this land had in store for them.

8. Lambayeque

They crossed swamps, forests as dense as tangles of wool, snowy mountains. They felt the bitterness of cold again, but nobody questioned Freydis's orders. As if, in removing all hope of a return home, the loss of the knarr had also broken their will.

Here and there, they encountered Skraelings, who came to trade gold or copper jewels for iron nails or bowls of fresh milk. They discovered a sea to the west. They built rafts. The further they navigated down the coast, the more elaborately worked became the jewellery that they were offered. One day, a Skraeling gave Gudrid a pair of earrings representing a priest holding a severed head, and her mother was pleased by this. Freydis decided it would be a good idea to live among goldsmiths. Furthermore, these Skraelings had cultivated fields stretching all the way to the horizon. Canals criss-crossed the plain. She knew that the name of this land was Lambayeque.

The Skraelings regarded the iron and the draught animals as gifts of providence. They saw the visitors as envoys of Naylamp, their god. So it was that Freydis was honoured as a high priestess, covered with gold and granted great powers. Her hosts sacrificed prisoners to her with their ceremonial knives: the handles carved into effigies of Naylamp, the blades shaped like half-moons. They were a people of böndis, highly skilled in metalwork. Soon after the Greenlanders' arrival, they were forging iron hammers in every size. They were fascinated by Freydis and her red hair.

However, as she knew what would happen next, she prophesied that a disease would strike them down; so, when they did start falling ill and dying, her stature was only increased. She urged them to sacrifice more prisoners and to intensify their

harvests. The Greenlanders, with their animals and their knowledge of iron, acquired privileged positions in society. Moreover,
as they were spared by the disease, the Skraelings grew ever more
convinced that they must be of divine origin.

At last, one of the Skraelings who went down with the fever
survived and recovered. This was followed by another, and gradually, the disease brought by the foreigners lost its power. So the
Greenlanders knew that they had come to the end of their
journey.

9. The Death of Freydis

Years passed without a winter. The Greenlanders learned to dig
canals and to cultivate strange vegetables: red, yellow, purple,
some juicy, some floury. Freydis became queen. She married the
jarl of a neighbouring town named Cajamarca, and the banquet
organised to seal this alliance was magnificent. The akha – a
corn-based beer – flowed freely, and the guests ate grilled fish,
alpaga (a sort of slender sheep), and cuys (silky rabbits with small
ears, which, when roasted on skewers, had tender, tasty flesh).

Freydis had several more children, and by the time she died
she was weighed down with honours. Her body was buried with
her servants, her jewellery and her plates. She wore a gold tiara
on her forehead. A necklace with eighteen rows of red pearls covered her chest. In one hand, she held an iron hammer, and in the
other a half-moon knife.

Gudrid had grown and, although she did not have her mother's red hair, had gained an eminent position among the
Lambayeques. So, when violent storms swept the region and everybody was lamenting their lost harvests and flooded fields, it
was Gudrid who convinced the Skraelings that Thor was trying

to tell them something. She was in no doubt that they should leave and – very much her mother's daughter – she travelled south, leading a large number of Skraelings and Greenlanders, who were now one people. It is said that they found a great lake, but this saga must end here because nobody knows for certain what happened afterwards.

Part Two

The Journal of Christopher Columbus (fragments)

Friday 3 August
We departed on Friday 3 August 1492, at eight in the morning, from the bar of Saltes. We proceeded under a strong sea breeze until sunset, travelling sixty miles, which is fifteen leagues; then south-west, and west by south-west, which was the course for the Canary Islands.

Monday 17 September
I hope that the Lord God, who holds in his hands all victories, will soon give us sight of land.

Wednesday 19 September
The weather is fair and, God willing, we will see all during our return journey.

Tuesday 2 October
The sea still calm and smooth, may God be praised.

Monday 8 October
Thanks be to God, the air is very mild, like April in Seville, and so sweetly scented that it is a pleasure to be here.

Tuesday 9 October
All through the night, we heard birds flying past.

Thursday 11 October
At the second hour after midnight, land appeared, two leagues distant.

Friday 12 October
We reached a small island, which, in the language of the Indians, is called Guanahani. Naked people came, and I left the ship with Martín Alonso Pinzón, captain of the *Pinta*, and Vicente Yáñez, his brother, captain of the *Nina*.

Arriving upon land, I took possession of said isle in the name of Your Highnesses.

Immediately, many people from the island gathered in that spot. So that they would be bound in friendship towards us and because I knew that they were people who could be more easily freed and converted to our Holy Faith through love than through force, I gave a few of them some red hats and some glass beads, which they put around their necks, and many other objects of little value in which they took great pleasure; and they became so thoroughly ours that it was wondrous to see.

It was obvious to me that these were people lacking in everything. They go about naked as the day they were born, even the women.

If it please Our Lord, at the moment of my departure, I will bring six of them with me to Your Highnesses, so that they may learn to speak. I saw no beast of any kind on this island, except for parrots.

Saturday 13 October
As dawn broke, many of these people came to the beach, all of them young and handsome. They are a remarkably beautiful people. Their hair is smooth, not curled, and coarse like horsehair.

They came to the ship in their boats made from tree trunks, some so large that forty men could fit inside.

They gave up everything in return for any trifle that we offered them. I was very attentive and did all I could to find out if they had gold. By employing signs, I was able to understand that in the south there was a king who had a vast amount.

And so I decided to head south-west in search of gold and precious stones ...

Friday 19 October
What I wish is to see and discover as much as I can before returning to Your Highnesses in April, if it please God.

Sunday 21 October
Flocks of parrots darken the sun.

I wish to leave for another island, very large, which must be Cipango if I am to credit the information of the Indians I am bringing with me, and which they call Colba.

Tuesday 23 October
Today I would like to head for the island of Cuba, which I believe to be Cipango, based upon the descriptions these people have provided of its size and wealth. I do not wish to stay here long since I can see that there is no goldmine.

Wednesday 24 October
Tonight, at midnight, I weighed anchor and set sail for the island of Cuba, which, from all the Indians have told me, is very large, with much trade, an abundance of gold and spice, regularly visited by large ships and merchants. I think that if it is as the Indians have signalled – since I do not understand their language – it must truly be the island of Cipango, of which there are so many wondrous stories, and which, on the globes that I have seen and on the paintings of world maps, is located in these parts.

Sunday 28 October

The grass here is as tall as in Andalusia in April. I declare that this island is the most beautiful ever seen, full of mountains that are high and handsome, though not particularly extensive. The ground is of an elevation similar to that of Sicily.

The Indians say that there are goldmines on this island, and pearls. I have indeed seen a likely place for their formation, and mussel shells, which are signs of them. I believe I understood that large ships belonging to the Great Khan come to this island, and that the mainland is ten days' sailing from here.

Monday 29 October

In order to parley, I sent two rowing boats to a village. All the men, women and children of the village fled, abandoning their houses and everything they contained. I ordered my men not to touch anything. The houses resembled military tents, but were as large as those belonging to royalty; they were not arranged in streets, but here and there. The interiors were clean, with well-made furniture. All these houses are made from palm branches, beautifully constructed, except one which is very long with an earth roof covered in grass. There, we found many statues in the shape of women, and many heads like well-carved masks. I do not know whether these are ornaments or idols. Inside these houses were dogs that did not bark and little wild birds that had been tamed.

There must be cattle here, because I saw some skulls that looked like the skulls of cows.

Sunday 4 November

These people are very peaceful and fearful, naked as I have already mentioned, without weapons or laws. The land here is very fertile.

Monday 5 November

At dawn, I ordered the ship to be careened, and afterwards the other vessels, but not all at the same time so that for reasons of safety there would always be two in anchorage. Although it must be said that these people are very dependable, and we could without fear have careened all the boats at the same time.

Monday 12 November

Yesterday, a boat with six young men inside came alongside the ship; five of them came on board. I ordered them to be held and I am bringing them with me. Afterwards, I sent some men to a house on the western bank of the river. They brought me back six women, some young and some old, and three children. I did this because the men will behave better in Spain if they have women from their own land.

That night, a man came aboard. He was the husband of one of the women and the father of the three children: one boy and two girls. He asked me to let him come with them. This gave me great pleasure. Now they all seem relieved, which makes me conclude that they must all indeed be related. The man is forty or forty-five years old.

Friday 16 November

The Indians I brought with me fished some very large shells from the sea. So I told my men to examine the shells that the Indians had fished to see if there was any mother-of-pearl, which is in the shells where pearls grow. They found a great deal, but no pearls.

Saturday 17 November

The two eldest of the six boys I took from the river of seas, who were on the caravel *Nina*, have escaped.

Sunday 18 November

I have been out again with the rowing boats, taking many men with me, to plant the great cross that I ordered to be built from two large trunks and set in a visible spot cleared of trees. It was planted high up and looked beautiful.

Tuesday 20 November

I do not want the Indians that I took from Guanahani to escape, because I need to take these men with me to Castile. They are convinced that, once I have found gold, I will let them return home.

Wednesday 21 November

This day, Martín Alonso Pinzón set off with the caravel *Pinta*, in defiance of my orders and against my wishes, out of avarice, because he believed that an Indian I had sent aboard his caravel could show him where there was much gold. So it was that he left us, not because of bad weather, but because he so chose.

He has betrayed and insulted me too many times.

Friday 23 November

I sailed all day towards land, steering south with little wind. Beyond this headland there stretched out another land where, the Indians said, live people with one eye in the middle of their foreheads and others who were cannibals, and of whom they are much afraid.

Sunday 25 November

Before sunrise, I got into a boat and went to inspect a headland, because there appeared to be a good river there. Presently, near the point of the cape, at a distance of two crossbow shots, I saw a large stream of very clear water falling from the mountains above with a loud roar. I went to this stream and saw some stones shining in it, spangled with gold-coloured patches. I remembered then that at the mouth of the river Tagus, close to the sea, there was gold to be found, and it seemed certain to me that there must be gold here too. I ordered some of these stones to be collected, so that I might bring them to Your Highnesses. Looking up towards the mountains, I saw pine trees of such size and splendour that it would be impossible to exaggerate their height, like vast, slender spindles. It occurred to me that here was material for an endless store of planks and masts for the largest ships in Spain. I saw oaks and strawberry trees, and a good river, and a place for a water-powered sawmill.

On the beach, I saw many iron-coloured stones and others that some said came from silver mines, all brought down by the river.

No man who has not seen these things for himself will be able to believe what I have witnessed here, and yet I can assure Your Highnesses that I am not exaggerating in the slightest.

I kept sailing along the coast, to get a good view of it all. This whole land is covered in very high and very beautiful mountains, neither arid nor rocky, but easily accessible and with magnificent valleys. Like the mountains, the valleys are filled with tall and fine trees that it is a joy to behold.

Tuesday 27 November
From the south side, I saw a very remarkable port that the Indians call Baracoa, and from the south-east some marvellously beautiful lands, like a valley among the mountains. I saw much smoke rising, large villages and cultivated fields. For these reasons, I decided to put in at this port and to see if we could speak with the inhabitants. As soon as the ship was at anchor, I jumped into a boat to take soundings in the port and found the mouth of a river wide enough for a galley to enter it. As we navigated this river, the beauty of the trees and the coolness of the air, the clearness of the water, the birds made it all so delightful that I never wanted to leave.

Your Highnesses will send orders to build a city and fortress here, and the natives will be converted.

Here, as in all the places that I have discovered and that I hope to discover before my return to Castile, I say that if Christendom will find profit, how much more will Spain, to whom the whole country should be subject?

Wednesday 28 November

I decided to stay in the port because it was raining and overcast. The crew went to visit the land, and some of them walked inland to wash their clothes. They found large villages, but the houses were empty because the inhabitants had fled. They returned by the banks of another river, but one of the ship's boys was missing. Nobody knew what had happened to him. Perhaps he was taken by a crocodile or a lizard of the kind that populate the island.

Thursday 29 November

As it was still raining and overcast, I did not leave the port.

Friday 30 November

We cannot leave because the wind, blowing from the east, is against us.

Saturday 1 December

It is raining a lot and the east wind is still blowing.

I ordered that a cross be planted at the entrance to the port, on some bare rocks.

Sunday 2 December

The wind is still against us and we cannot leave. At the mouth of the river, a ship's boy found some stones that appear to contain gold.

Monday 3 December

As the weather was still foul, I decided to visit a very beautiful headland. I went with the boats and some armed men. I entered a river and found a small cove with five very large boats, which the Indians call *canoas*. We gained a foothold under some trees and followed a path that led to a very well-built boathouse. Within it there was another canoa, made from a single tree trunk like the others, and as large as a galley with seventeen benches. There was a forge to extract iron from peat, and next to it some baskets containing arrowheads and fishhooks.

We climbed a mountain with a flat top, where we found a village. As soon as they saw us, the inhabitants started to run away. I saw that they had no gold or any other precious things, so I resolved to leave them in peace.

But when we returned to the place where we had left the boats, we were unpleasantly surprised to discover that they were not there, and nor were the canoas. I was astonished by this because the people of this region had never showed such temerity. On the contrary, they were so fearful and cowardly that they almost always fled when they saw us arriving, and when they did let us approach, they always willingly gave us their belongings in return for a few little bells. It had seemed to me that they did not understand the concept of property and thus that they were incapable of stealing, since whenever you ask them for something of theirs, they never refuse it.

However, some Indians appeared. They were all painted red, and naked as the day they were born. Some of them had tufts of feathers on their head and all held bundles of darts. They remained at a distance, but from time to time they raised their hands to the sky and shouted. With signs, I asked them if they were praying. They said they were not. I told them that they had to give us back our boats. The Indians seemed not to understand.

I asked them where their canoes were, hoping that we could take them to leave the river and return to the ship.

So it was that something strange happened. A whinnying sound suddenly arose and the Indians fled.

I sent four men to find the rest of the crew by land, to warn them of this mishap. But for my part, I resolved to walk, with the men who remained in my company, in the direction of the whinnying noise.

We came out into a clearing that I took for a cemetery because it was strewn with standing stones, carved with inscriptions in an unknown alphabet, the letters composed of lines like little sticks, some of them straight and others leaning.

As it was getting dark, I ordered my men to set up camp, because it would have been too dangerous to find our way back on land in darkness, particularly since – having come by boat – we had no horses. I also judged it prudent not to light a fire. And so we went to sleep, my men and I, amid those gravestones, without any fear of the cold since the ground was more temperate than ever.

All through the night, we listened to the strident sound of whinnying.

Tuesday 4 December

When the sky lightened, I planted a cross in the middle of some stones. The cross was made of a soft wood, like elm. My men wanted to dig under the gravestones to see if there was any gold, but I thought it wiser to return immediately to the ship.

I walked along the riverbank with my men but the path was steep and in certain places we had to wade waist-deep in the water to avoid becoming tangled in the dense vegetation. Red-headed vultures flew above us. The whinnying continued behind us, irritating my men because it reminded us that we were deprived of our horses at a moment when they would have been very useful. I tried to distract them by pointing out pebbles that gleamed in the water and telling them that there was certainly gold in this river, something I am almost convinced is true. I promised myself that I would return in order to verify this for Your Highnesses.

But as we were struggling onwards, an arrow hit one of our men, who was killed instantly. This caused panic in our ranks and I had to use my authority to restore calm. I warn you there is no man so vile as a coward who never risks his life face to face, and you know that if the Indians find one or two isolated men, it will not be surprising if they kill them. The arrow had an iron head. After that, we were on our guard. I ordered each man to wear his helmet and to personally check that the laces of his breastplate were tightly tied.

Wednesday 5 December
As I did not wish to take any risks, we advanced carefully, clearing a path through what the natives here call *mangrove*, after a sort of tree that grows in the water. (Or at least that is what I was told by an Indian whom I took from the island of Guanahani, and to whom we are teaching Castilian so that he may serve us as a spokesman, since it appears that everyone here speaks and understands the same language.) Our progress was slow because of the river mud, but we did not suffer any further incidents. At one point, we saw the body of a man dressed like a Christian floating along the river. We couldn't reach the corpse, so we had no choice but to let it continue to drift with the current.

Tomorrow, by the grace of the Lord who watches over us constantly, we will reach the port where we left the ship, the *Nina* and the rest of the crew.

Nevertheless, the whinnying continues.

Thursday 6 December
We set off before daybreak because the men were nervous and impatient. When we arrived on the beach, all was calm: a light

breeze was blowing in the gulf; in the sky, the red-headed vultures were circling; the whinnying had ceased.

The ship was still at anchor, but the *Nina* was no longer there.

We could see a one-man canoa moving around on the water, and it was wondrous that this single man was able to stay afloat because the wind was blowing quite strongly now. We called out to him but he refused to come closer, and we had no means of reaching him without our boats. I sent two men to swim out to the ship. But they were not even one-third of the way there when some boats were dropped into the water to come towards us, and these were the very boats that had been taken from us. We saw Indians aboard, and they struck me as more alert and worldly than any of the others we had encountered up to that time. Using signs, they offered to row us to our vessel. I got in one of the boats with my men. These Indians had iron-bladed axes.

Back at the ship, I was received by an Indian whom the others called *cacique* and whom I take to be the governor of this province, given the respect that his people show him despite the fact that they are all entirely naked. A strange thing: I found no trace of my crew. The cacique invited me to dine with him in the poop deck. When I was seated at the table where I usually eat, he made a sign with his hand for his men to remain outside, and this they did with the greatest haste and the most humble marks of obedience. They all went to sit on the deck, with the exception of two older men, whom I took to be his counsellors, who sat at his feet. I was served food of their making, as if I were their guest on my own ship.

The situation was extremely odd, but I did not let my feelings show, as I was naturally concerned to represent Your Highnesses with dignity. To honour my host, I tasted each dish, and drank some of the wine that they had taken from my reserves. I tried to find out where the rest of my crew was and why the *Nina* had gone back to sea. The cacique did not speak much, but his counsellors assured me that tomorrow they would take me to the caravel. At least, that is what I gathered, since unfortunately we still did not understand their language. I also asked if they knew any places where we might find gold, because I do not think they collect a great deal of that metal here, even though I know there is a vast amount of gold in their neighbouring territories. He spoke to me of a great king named Cahonaboa who lives on a nearby island that I think must be Cipango.

I noticed that he seemed taken by a hanging that I had on my bed, so I gave it to him, along with a very beautiful amber necklace that I was wearing, a pair of red shoes and a phial of orange blossom water. He was so pleased by these gifts that it was wondrous to behold. He and his counsellors found it very frustrating that they could not understand me and I could not understand them. Despite these difficulties, I knew that they were telling me that tomorrow I would be taken back to my men and my boat.

'What great lords Your Highnesses must be,' he said to his counsellors, 'to have sent me so far without fear.' They said many other things that I could not understand, but I could see that they were always smiling.

Late that night, he retired with his people, taking with him the gifts I had offered, and left me to sleep in my bed.

Friday 7 December
Our Lord, who is the light and the strength of all those on the path of righteousness, has decided to test His and Your Highnesses' most faithful servant.

At daybreak, the Indian returned, in the company of seventy men. With many signs and demonstrations, he offered to lead me to the *Nina*. As he was pointing towards the east, I set sail and, with my reduced crew, navigated along the coast in that direction, escorted by canoes. The Indians on board the ship observed us without a word, but I could tell that they were admiring the way we were steering a ship bigger than any they had ever seen before, despite our insufficient numbers. They did not yet know that this vessel was capable of travelling further in a single day than they could in a whole week. For my part, I was at that moment far from doubting their duplicity.

The cacique led us to a village by the sea, sixteen miles distant, where, finding good anchorage, I dropped anchor in front of the adjacent beach. There stood the *Nina*, which had been dragged on to land, to the puzzlement of myself and my men. But when we wished to disembark on the beach to visit the caravel, the cacique and his men absolutely refused to leave the ship. Unwilling to waste any more time in pointless discussions, I chose to leave three men on board to ensure that the Indians did not steal or damage anything.

As soon as we reached the beach, we were joined by five hundred naked, painted men, armed with axes and lances. These Indians did not seem to act like the others, who were driven by curiosity and happy to exchange their belongings for little trinkets. On the contrary, they quickly surrounded us with as much order and efficiency as a regiment of landsknechts. Our backs were to the sea, the way to the ship blocked by canoes, and the ship itself in the hands of the cacique and his men, whom we had left on board.

Other Indians appeared, riding bareback on small horses and armed with lances, escorting a king whose horse wore a gold caparison. The animal was so proudly dressed that it was impossible to doubt the quality of its rider.

This king, who possesses a gravitas that years of experience have added to his natural authority, is named Béhéchio. He claims to be related to the great king Cahonaboa, about whom everyone here speaks. (I suppose Cahonaboa is the Great Khan.)

Not wishing to show any fear or weakness, even though at that instant our situation did not seem to me ideal, I strode forward and, addressing the king, told him in the most solemn terms that I had been sent by the monarchs of the most powerful kingdom on earth, on the other side of the ocean, to whom he must pledge allegiance, in return for which he would benefit from their protection and indulgence. But I think that the Indian who accompanied me as a spokesman told him how the Christians had come from the sky and that they were searching for gold, because this was the speech that he gave to everyone we met, unable as he was to depart from this belief, which, for that matter, had served us well up to this point.

Then I asked where my men were. At a signal from the king, the men of my crew (although I could see that some were missing) and those of the *Nina* were brought forward, all of them in a lamentable state. I showed my indignation at the visible mistreatment of good Christian men and threatened Béhéchio with the most terrible reprisals, assuring him that my masters would never tolerate such an affront. I do not know what the king understood, but he responded by raising his voice. If I am to believe my spokesman, he reproached the Christians for having abducted several Indians against their will, having torn them from their families, and having raped their women.

I assured him that it was for their salvation that we had taken those people, that we had done all we could not to separate families, and that if any Christians had raped the women of this country, it was without my consent and they would be punished. I do not know how these words were translated by my spokesman or understood by Béhéchio, but his response was to order the seizure of all the Christians he had already captured – the men from the *Nina* and those from my ship who were not with me – and to tie them up in the presence of all the others. And in the middle of the village square, in front of everybody, he had them tied to posts that had been planted there for this purpose, and their ears were cut off.

I watched, helplessly, as this cruel torture was accomplished, because the Indians were too numerous and too well armed for us to attempt any sort of rescue without certainly being massacred.

Finally, Béhéchio signalled that we should go away – myself and the group of men with whom I had arrived. I replied frankly that we would never leave fellow Christians in such a terrible situation, in the hands of heathens who understood nothing of salvation or the Holy Trinity. He allowed us to untie our unfortunate brothers, but when we tried to retake possession of our boats, his guards barred the way to the sea and to the caravel on the beach. He told me, using signs, that to return to the sky from whence we had come, we had no need of a ship.

We had no choice but to walk into the forest with our wounded, having been deprived of our horses.

There are thirty-nine of us.

Sunday 16 December

The Lord, who is wisdom and mercy incarnate, has sent us this trial but He has not forsaken us.

After wandering through the forest for a long time, we found other villages, almost all of them deserted by the Indians who are cowards and who face us only out of fear. For our salvation, they had left behind a quantity of food, as well as roundhouses where we can tend to our wounded.

Vicente Yáñez, captain of the *Nina*, is suffering terribly from the severance of his ears, as are all the other mutilated men. Their wounds are turning black and some of them have died.

They learned that Béhéchio came from the same country as Cahonaboa, and that he was summoned here by the inhabitants of this place in order to expel us. I do not know why they hate us because we have done them no wrong and I have always taken care that they were not ill-treated.

The Indians who stole the boats from us took possession of the ship with a surprise attack, killing or imprisoning all the members of the crew. The four men I sent to warn the crew never arrived. The men of the ship who survived the attack swore to me that the Indians who defeated them were very well armed.

Seeing this, the captain of the *Nina*, encircled by a fleet of canoes and fearing that his ship would be boarded, had attempted to escape, finding refuge in the port where the cacique had afterward taken us, but there he had been betrayed by the villagers. Who could have suspected such trickery from people who go naked?

I now ordered the careful construction of a tower, a fortress and a deep ditch. Vicente Yáñez and certain others are reduced to self-pity, complaining that we will never see Spain again. However, if we can gather our strength and recover our weapons, I believe very strongly that with the men who are left to me and the reinforcements of Martín Alonso Pinzón – when he deigns to remember the obedience he owes me and returns from his adventure – I will be able to subdue this entire island, which is, I believe, larger than Portugal and with twice as many people, but all of them naked and incurably faint-hearted, with the exception of Béhéchio's army. That is why I have it in mind to capture Béhéchio using cunning, in order to retrieve our ships, our weapons and our provisions.

In the meantime, it is good that this tower should be built and that it should be as solid as a fort because, for now, we have only swords, a few arquebuses and a small amount of powder.

Tuesday 25 December, Christmas Day
A terrible calamity has occurred.

The ship was still anchored in the port of the village where our unfortunate companions were tortured. This morning, one of the men I sent hunting in order to ensure we have enough to eat, came to me in a state of panic to inform me that he had seen, from a distance, the ship sailing away. The news had a devastating effect on my men, who were living in hope of recovering that vessel, as well as the other one, which is on the beach, in order to return to Castile.

Perhaps the three men I had left on board during our meeting with King Béhéchio, had freed themselves and seized the ship. Or perhaps the Indians wanted to try navigating it themselves.

To clear up the matter, we climbed up a rocky headland high enough to offer a clear view of the port.

It was true: the ship was sailing and seemed to be trying to leave the cove, but it was drifting dangerously towards a rocky bank. Whomever it was in command of the vessel, it was clear that he could not steer correctly.

The ship moved inexorably towards the rocks. Dismayed by this terrible sight, we all cried out in fright. When, at last, it crashed into the rocks and we heard the crack of bursting seams, the same fearful moan escaped our chests.

Now the ship had run aground, we would only have two caravels to sail home even if Martín Pinzón returned with the *Pinta*: not enough to bring all of us back to Spain.

Our Lord has sent me a terrible trial on this blessed day. I must not doubt His designs, however, and knowing for certain that nobody serves Him more zealously than I, He will not forsake me.

Wednesday 26 December

Mad with pain and rage at the loss of the ship, my men ran to the rocks where it had foundered, and there was nothing I could do or say to contain their fury. Finding nobody around the wreck, they went into the storeroom and took out as much gunpowder and wine as they could carry. Then, even angrier at the desolate spectacle of the smashed ship, they went to the beach where the caravel was, determined to fight. But Béhéchio's army was no longer there; so, abandoning themselves to their passion, they massacred all the villagers, down to the last one, men, women, children, with cries of 'Santiago! Santiago!', then they pillaged and burned the village. This was a reprehensible act, but in their defence I would say that the sight of that place brought back vivid memories of the torture they had suffered there.

Having sated their fury, they took as many things as they could from the *Niña*'s stores, but they did not attempt to make the caravel seaworthy again since this would have taken much time and work, and they feared the return of Béhéchio. The weapons they recovered, and particularly the barrels of wine, were greeted with cheers. On the other hand, we still have no horses.

That evening, we organised a banquet to celebrate the victory, because it was one: our situation, which seemed one of utter despair yesterday after the loss of the ship, has now steadied a little, thanks be to God.

Monday 31 December
Six of my men, who had left to search for supplies of wood and water, were caught in an ambush and all perished. An Indian on horseback rode to the entrance of the fort to leave baskets containing the heads of those unfortunate Christians.

I ordered the strengthening of our defences, because I feel certain that Béhéchio will come to us.

Tuesday 1 January 1493
Three men who went out to fetch rhubarb, which I planned to bring back to Your Highnesses, were attacked by horsemen. It is a miracle that one of them was able to escape and to hide in the mountains, where the horses could not follow.

My men are nervous because they think it inevitable that Béhéchio will come, as do I.

Wednesday 2 January

Nobody now dares leave the fort, out of fear of being ambushed and devoured, for my men have got it into their heads that the Indians eat human flesh. It is true that they are extremely cruel when they have defeated their enemies, and they cut the legs off women and even children.

I am vigilant, day and night, to the point that I cannot sleep. During the last month, I have slept no more than five hours, and in the last week I have slept only as long as three hourglasses, lasting thirty minutes apiece, so that I am half-blind and, at certain hours of the day, completely blind.

Thankfully we have seeds and animals that are well accustomed to the earth of this country. All the plants in the vegetable garden are thriving, and there are even certain vegetables that will give two harvests if they are sown, which is also true for all the fruit, whether wild or cultivated: so favourable is the aspect of the sky and the quality of the earth. Our cattle and poultry are multiplying to a wondrous degree, and it is wondrous too to see how quickly the chickens grow: they hatch chicks every two months, and within ten or twelve days the new chickens are good to eat. As for pigs, from the thirteen sows that I brought here, many are roaming the woods, mixing with the wild pigs, but sadly we cannot profit from them because of the Indians who are prowling outside.

Our last spokesman fled.

Thursday 3 January

The siege has begun. This morning, Béhéchio appeared with his army, riding his gold-caparisoned horse.

This Indian's manner of being is such that everyone can see he conducts himself like a true warrior, and that his troops are ordered in the same way – and with just as much skill – as if this were happening in Castile or in France.

Friday 4 January
We have enough water and food to withstand a siege, but my men know that the fortress is not sufficiently robust to withstand an attack.

May God, in His great mercy, have pity on us.

Saturday 5 January
From atop the tower, we can observe the movements of Béhé-chio's troops. Watching his cavalry and his regiments of infantrymen in battle order, we cannot doubt that the attack must be imminent.

But God, who has never forsaken us, sent us a miracle in the form of Martín Alonso Pinzón, because from the top of that same tower, my men saw the *Pinta* appear on the horizon.

This miraculous apparition gave us an extraordinary surge of strength and morale. We will attempt a sortie tomorrow, at first light, and with the aid of God we will reach the coast to join Martín Pinzón and the *Pinta*, or we will die fighting.

Nothing remains for me now but to recommend our souls to eternal God, Our Lord, who grants success to those who follow His path in spite of apparent obstacles.

Sunday 6 January
In the morning, we went out in tight ranks, the arquebusiers and crossbowmen in front, the wounded at the back, with our only artillery being a falconet cannon that my men had taken from the ship. We had only thirty uninjured men, but we were determined to fight until our last breath.

Outside, more than a thousand Indians were waiting for us, the cavalry in the vanguard, infantrymen behind and on the flanks, all carrying arrows, which they fired from their catapults much faster than they could have done from bows. All of them were smeared in black and painted in different colours, holding flutes, with masks and mirrors in copper and gold on their heads, and as is their custom, they gave the most terrible war cries at regular intervals. Béhéchio, on his golden horse, had set up his camp on a large hillock two crossbow shots away, and he directed his armies from there.

Some of our number had the task of waiting for the horses in open country and grabbing the horsemen's legs, since they rode without saddles or stirrups, but this was a highly perilous action and even though they did manage to put their idea into practice, almost all were killed.

Nevertheless, our arquebuses scythed down part of their cavalry and our falconet enabled us to open a gap in their ranks. We lost men, shot by their arrows and crushed by their horses, but we killed a large number of heathens, and although this wasn't the first occasion we had used our firearms on this island, the thunderous noise produced by the cannon and the arquebuses sowed confusion in the enemy, offering us a crucial respite to hurtle down the path that led to the coast (because we had built our fort on high ground).

We arrived at the beach where the *Pinta* was anchored, more dead than alive but running so hard that we could barely breathe, driven forward by the enemy's howls as if by the flames of hell, and we were already up to our knees in water, ready to swim the last few feet that separated us from our salvation – or so we believed at the time – when we saw, on the deck of the *Pinta*, standing beside Martín Alonso Pinzón, who was immobile as a statue and pale as a ghost, a man with a crown on his head decorated with parrot feathers and gold plates, his face hidden by a sculpted wooden mask, the eyes, nostrils and mouth edged with gold, his tall figure and stately bearing leaving us in no doubt about his identity and robbing us of all hope: it was Cahonaboa, king of Cipango.

I have said that Béhéchio was imposing and that we had immediately guessed his royal quality from his noble air, full of a superiority that contained no arrogance, but that was as nothing in comparison to our new arrival, whom Béhéchio himself saluted with the most abject deference, kneeling and kissing the ground.

Cahonaboa was accompanied by his wife, the Queen Anacaona, Béhéchio's sister, whose beauty and grace have no equal among the many beautiful Indian women.

As for us, poor Christians, we were disarmed and imprisoned, and our wounded were killed.

Out of respect for our ranks of captain and admiral, Martín Alonso and I were separated from our men and invited into the king's tent. Vicente Yáñez, captain of the *Nina* and brother of Martín Alonso, would have joined us had he survived the battle.

Cahonaboa, just like Béhéchio, reproached us for having abducted Indians and raped women, which they consider here to be a great crime. As admiral and leader of this expedition I was held responsible for offences committed by Martín Alonso and other mutineers, even though I had always ordered my men not to ill-treat the natives. The truth was that I had never done them any harm and had not employed cruelty towards anyone.

Whatever the Creator of all things has in store for His humble servant, I will no longer suffer the insults of malicious people of little virtue who insolently seek to impose their will against the man who gave them so much honour.

As soon as Martín Alonso and his men had reached the island next to Juana (the name that I gave to the island of Cuba, and which must be Cipango), they abducted by force four Indian adults and two young girls, hoping that they would provide information on where to find gold, but were immediately attacked by Cahonaboa's army, which was so powerful that the Christians were promptly defeated and most of them killed where they stood. So it is that God punishes hubris and folly. Nevertheless, Martín Alonso and six of his men were spared, out of the twenty-five who comprised his crew.

Of the seventy-seven Christians who departed Palos, only twelve souls remain, like the twelve apostles, and Martín Alonso.

Wednesday 9 January
For three days now, the Indians have been dancing to the sound of flutes, tambourines and singing. These festivities seem endless, while we Christians are plunged in the most profound desolation, since none can doubt that it is our defeat that the Indians are celebrating. One spectacle in particular has reopened our wounds. To entertain the royal couple, Béhéchio wished to offer a reconstruction of the battle during which our men from the fortress were defeated. To recreate this scene, the old cacique stripped us of our clothes and put them on some Indians who were to play our role, leaving us as naked as the people of this island. We also had to teach them how to fire the arquebus, and although the noise still frightened them a little, they were delighted by the thunder that they could unleash with our weapons. Horsemen were deployed around the Indians dressed as Christians, and while those men mimed terror and shot into the air, the Indians on horseback executed the most graceful arabesques. Then the men playing Christians dispersed in a disorderly retreat while the horsemen pursued them and pretended to cut them down.

Our only comfort comes from Queen Anacaona, who recites and sings poems, and even though the meaning escapes us almost completely, there is not a single Christian who is not bewitched by her beauty and her voice. Cahonaboa's wife is Béhéchio's sister, as I have said, and seems to be the subject of an extraordinary veneration by the Indians, not only because of her royal blood and her beauty, but also for her talents as a poet, which are admired by all.

Her husband the king watches all these festivities with evident pleasure, but never is his delight so keen as when Anacaona occupies the stage.

Hoping to benefit from his happy disposition, we begged him to give us back our clothing or give us death, but he refused both of those demands.

Thursday 10 January
King Cahonaboa desires to know more about the country whence the Christians came, which is why he wished to meet with me, in the presence of Queen Anacaona and the cacique Béhéchio. My words were translated by a spokesman that they had taken from Martín Alonso. The king received me wearing a shirt, a belt, a hood and a toque belonging to me, while I was naked.

So it was that I was able to tell them about Your Serene Highnesses, rulers of the greatest kingdom on earth, and also about the one true religion and the one true God, Our Lord who is in Heaven. I sought to explain to them the mysteries of the Holy Trinity, and I could tell that the queen and her brother were listening to me with great interest.

I swore to them that there is no greater honour upon this earth than to serve monarchs such as Your Highnesses, that baptism would safeguard them from hell after their earthly existence is over, and that only the true faith will reward them with eternal life.

I suggested they come with us to Castile so they could throw themselves at the feet of Your Highnesses, and I promised that they would be received with all the respect due to their rank. Cahonaboa seemed interested, above all, in our forts, our ships and our weapons, but I saw that my words had touched his beautiful wife.

Friday 11 January
Cahonaboa has departed with his army, leaving behind his wife and her brother to watch over us and the region. This is very good news, as I think they are more likely to be persuaded to free us and to be converted.

Martín Alonso does not share my opinion. He wishes to attempt an escape with our men so that we may leave on the *Pinta*, which is still anchored in the cove.

Saturday 12 January
Today, I spent a long time talking to the queen about Our Lord Jesus Christ, and she agreed to plant a cross in the square of the village where we are staying. Her brother invited me to share his *cohiba* – the name they give to those dried leaves that they burn in hollow sticks so that they might inhale the smoke.

Martín Alonso is ill.

Sunday 13 January
As the queen is a woman, I described to her the jewellery and the robes that are worn at court in the kingdom of Castile and I saw an excited glimmer in her eyes, as in the eyes of a child.

We are well fed and we sleep in hammocks, but Martín Alonso complains of pain all over his body. He says he refuses to die here and thinks only of returning to his ship.

Monday 14 January
Martín Alonso has a malignant fever and is in peril of his life. Based upon my observations, I think it highly probable that he contracted this disease through his dealings with Indian women. He despairs of ever standing upon Christian earth again.

As her name means 'Flower of Gold' in her language, I suggested to Anacaona that she become Doña Margarita.

Tuesday 15 January
The devil has seized the captain's body and mind.

While the two of us were invited, as we are every day, to eat lunch with Béhéchio (who has, until now, given us no cause for complaint, other than obliging us to go naked as he does), Martín

Alonso, consumed by his fever, grabbed hold of a knife and killed the old cacique by stabbing him in the throat. Then he forced the queen to free our companions by threatening her with his blade, made her give each of his men a horse, and escaped with all those who were strong enough to ride. The poor madman hopes to reach his ship this way. But in doing so I am certain he has doomed us all.

Wednesday 16 January
The Indians weep over their dead king. The queen, grieving for the loss of her brother, has given up all thoughts of baptism and now speaks only of vengeance. The cross she had had planted has been broken and burned.

For my part, I swear to join the Order of Friars Minor if by some miracle I ever see Castile again, although, given this succession of misfortunes, it appears that the Lord God has other plans for me. Nevertheless, I humbly beg Your Highnesses, if it please God to bring me alive from this situation, to look kindly upon my request to go to Rome and on other pilgrimages. May the Holy Trinity guard and extend your lives and your power.

Tuesday 4 March
I can now say with certainty that Martín Alonso will not betray me again.

Cahonaboa has returned carrying the traitor's head and those of the other Christians who followed him in his senseless escape. Thus perish men of bad faith.

On the king's orders, the *Pinta* has been dragged on to land. I have decided to name the bay where she was anchored until yesterday the 'Bay of the Lost Pilgrim', in view of my present condition and in memory of my gruesome fate.

There is now no question of my ever returning to Spain, and Your Highnesses should simply forget the poor madman who promised them the Indies.

Undated

After hours spent staring out to sea in the wild hope of seeing a sail on the horizon, my eyes give me terrible pain and I am losing my sight. And yet I know full well that my failure will dissuade Your Highnesses, believing me to be drowned, from sending anyone else across the Ocean Sea.

Undated

There is something else that tears at my heart. It is the thought of Don Diego, my son, whom I left in Spain, an orphan, dispossessed of my honours and goods, despite my certainty that just and grateful princes would have restored to him all of it and more, had I returned from my voyage with one-hundredth of the treasures to be found in this land of abundance.

Undated

The island of Juana or Cuba, which is approximately as long as the distance between Valladolid and Rome, is today almost entirely subject to Cahonaboa. Thanks be to the kindness of his wife, I am tolerated and I eat with their people. From them, I have learned that they call themselves Taínos, but that their king does not belong to this tribe, for he came from the Caribes, which no doubt explains his superior complexion, his natural authority, and his great ferocity in combat.

Undated

The few men remaining to me were very ill and suffering greatly. The last one died this morning and now I am alone among these savages. What other mortal, with the exception of Job, would not have died of despair already? I do not know why the Lord is prolonging my miserable existence like this.

I go about naked, like a stray dog, almost blind, and nobody pays me any attention any more. Only Anacaona's daughter shows me the kind of interest that children sometimes show to old people who tell them stories. Every day, she comes to see me so I can tell her about the great Castile and its glorious, enlightened monarchs.

Undated

It is wondrous how quickly little Higuénamota learns Castilian. She already understands it very well and can repeat expressions, to the great amusement of her mother.

In the queen's eyes, I am nothing more than a jester, fit only to entertain her daughter.

Undated

Since Your Highnesses will not be able to, as the Master of all things did not wish it, I humbly beg Our Father to save all my writings so that my tragic destiny may one day be known: how from so far away I came to serve these princes, leaving behind my wife and children, whom consequently I have never seen again, and how, now, at the end of my life, I am stripped of all my honour and goods, without cause, without trial and without mercy. I say 'mercy', but I do not mean that in relation to Their Highnesses, because it is not their fault, nor is it the Lord's. I mean those malicious people with whom I had the misfortune to surround myself, and who led me to my loss after theirs, in these godforsaken lands.

Undated

The hour approaches when my soul will be summoned by God, and while I have without doubt already been forgotten on the other side of the Ocean Sea, I know that there is at least one person who still worries about the fallen admiral, and that little Higuénamota, who will be queen one day, my final consolation here below, will be with me to close my eyes. Please God, for her salvation, let her embrace our faith in memory of Your humble servant.

Undated

I am as miserable as I say I am. Until today, I wept for the others: may heaven now receive me in mercy and may the earth weep for me. In temporal terms, I do not even have a sou for the offering. In spiritual terms, I came here, to the Indies, in the way that I have described. Isolated in my suffering, ill, waiting each day for death to take me, surrounded by a million cruel savages who are our enemies, I am so far from the holy sacraments of the one true Church that my soul will be forgotten if it has to separate here from my body. May all those filled with charity, truth and justice weep for me. I did not make this voyage to win honour and fortune; that is the truth, for in that respect, all hope was dead in me already. I came to Your Highnesses with pure and zealous intentions, and I am not lying.

Part Three

The Chronicles of Atahualpa

1. The Fall of the Condor

For we who contemplate them long after the history of the world has reached its verdict, the augurs still seem unsparingly clear. But the truth of the present moment, albeit hotter, louder and – in all honesty – more alive, often comes to us in a more confused form than that of the past, or sometimes even that of the future.

It was the solemn ceremony of the Sun, and Huayna Capac, the eleventh Sapa Inca of the Empire of the Four Quarters, had good reason to be satisfied. From the wild lands of Araucania to the heights of Quito, where he had built his favourite residence (except for his capital, for the heart of the empire was and had to remain in Cuzco), he had extended his reign as far as it was possible (or so he believed), halted only by the thick cords of the forest and by the cotton in the sky. The organs of the disembowelled llamas were still quivering and the torn-out lungs swelled with air when the priests blew into the windpipes. The carcasses of the sacrificed animals were grilling on skewers for the banquet and the guests were preparing for the toast, as protocol dictates, when a condor suddenly appeared in the sky, pursued by a squadron of small birds of prey – harriers, falcons, harpy eagles – that were beleaguering it relentlessly. And the condor, weakening, exhausted, buckling under the beaks and claws of its pursuers, let itself fall to the great square in the very centre of the ceremony, making a profound impression on all those watching. Huayna Capac stood up from his throne and ordered the bird to be examined. Immediately it was seen that the condor was ill, dying not only because of the wounds inflicted on it by its pursuers, but mangy, its body bare of feathers and covered with pustules.

The Inca and his entourage considered this event a good omen: the seers, summoned for the occasion, saw the dead condor as an augur of the conquest of a great empire situated in distant lands. And so, as soon as the nine-hour ceremony of the Sun was over, Huayna Capac led his army further north in search of new territories to conquer.

He passed beyond Tumipampa, he passed beyond Quito, and he subjugated a few new tribes in Tawantinsuyu, the Empire of the Four Quarters.

But one day, while he was following a path with his retinue, it is said that he came upon a solitary traveller with red hair and arrogantly demanded that the man move aside. It is said that his tone displeased the traveller, who refused, unaware as he was of Huayna Capac's identity. Their discussion grew heated, the red-headed man struck the emperor's head with his stick, and Huayna Capac collapsed, mortally wounded. His eldest son Ninan Cuyochi attempted to help him and was killed in the same manner. It is claimed that the red-headed traveller was a son of the Inca, fathered long before with a priestess of Pachacamac, but he was never heard of again.

So the empire fell to another of his sons, named Huascar. Nevertheless, before dying, Huayna Capac had expressed this wish: that Huascar would succeed him on the throne in Cuzco, but that he would let his half-brother Atahualpa govern the northern provinces. Atahualpa was the emperor's son by a princess from Quito, and his father had always shown him the greatest affection.

For several harvests, Huascar and Atahualpa shared Tawantinsuyu in this manner. But Huascar had a stubborn, jealous, irascible temperament. Moreover, certain lords in Cuzco were plotting against him because he wanted to ban the cult of

mummies, which he considered too costly. On a false pretext –
claiming that Atahualpa had shown him a lack of respect by
refusing to come to Cuzco to pay tribute to him – Huascar
declared war on his half-brother. To humiliate him, he sent him
women's clothes and make-up. So Atahualpa, who was loved by
his father's generals, raised an army and marched on Cuzco.

Huascar's army was the greater in number, but Atahualpa's
was led by experienced generals and their soldiers were well
trained. General Quizquiz, General Chalco Chimac and General
Ruminahui won a series of bloody battles that led them to the
very gates of Cuzco. Cavalries had made war faster and fiercer.
On the opposing side, Huascar had been obliged to command
his army himself in an attempt to stem the tide of this irresistible
advance. But he did manage to stop his brother's army on the
banks of the Apurimac river, where a great massacre took place.
Atahualpa's army took refuge in the province of Cotabambas,
where a large number of soldiers were encircled, trapped in the
savannah, and burned alive. The survivors retreated.

And so began the long pursuit to the north.

2. The Retreat

Huascar hesitated. But not for long. At first, when the outcome
of the war had seemed less favourable, he had thought of awaiting
his brother on the plains of Quipaipan for the final conflict. He
too had suffered heavy losses, and his men, although victorious,
were tired. He wanted time to put them back in battle order.
Probably, too, he was comforted by the proximity of Cuzco. The
capital of the Empire, the navel of the world, cast its benevolent
shadow over the legitimist party. But Cuzco was also the golden
dream of Atahualpa's men, its fragrant murmur exciting their

lust, and Huascar feared that this dangerous temptation, only a few arrow shots away, would resuscitate the hearts of those routed soldiers. He did not want to give the opposing army the chance to recover its strength. He still had a functioning cavalry, led by another of his five hundred half-brothers, Tupac Hualpa, so he gathered his troops and sent them after the rebels, determined to annihilate them. He even summoned the Sacsayhuaman guard from his fortress, a move that showed the true measure of his resolve: he was prepared to divert these men from their sacred mission in order to add the strength of that elite regiment to the ranks of the imperial army.

Atahualpa did not need to consult his generals – Ruminahui the stone-eyed, Quizquiz the barber, Chalco Chimac – in order to know that they could not withstand another attack. One after the other, like a pair of limping pumas, the two armies set off.

They had to cross rope bridges over rivers: the horses whinnying with fear, the oxen, the llamas, the cages of cuys and parrots, the soldiers' mess wagons, the endless retinue of the Inca (but which one?) – his slaves, his concubines, his gold and silver plates, the alpagas destined to provide him with his daily clothes – and then the wounded, who were carried on litters, like their master.

The Empire filed past, slowly. Mountain ranges extended as far as the horizon, furrowed with fields of corn and papas, but the exhausted soldiers barely looked up and those terrace farms, the pride of the Empire, disappeared into indifference. The caged parrots cawed sinister predictions and the little rodents that kept them company gave pathetic cheeping noises. Only the war dogs, with their white crests of fur, cheered up the long procession with their barking as they roamed up and down the ranks of soldiers, as if guarding them.

The shops that punctuated the Inca's route provided food for the bastard's troops. And then the state-appointed managers of these granaries saw with astonishment the arrival of a second army, which they also supplied with food, recognising the banners of Cuzco's sovereign, while, in the distance, a cloud of dust concealed the retreat of Atahualpa's rearguard.

Huascar dispatched messengers to his half-brother. The chasquis were such fast runners, and the relay postal system so well organised, that it took only a few days for the Inca to find out the news from even the most distant parts of the Empire. The soldiers took no notice of those slender couriers, and in less than the time it took for Pachamama to make the earth quake, one of them would whisper something into Atahualpa's ear and he would whisper something in return and the young man would immediately set off again and would shout out the message as soon as his colleague, ready to sprint off in turn, was within earshot, and in the space of a few relays, the response would reach Huascar. In this way, the two emperors could converse almost normally, while the Cuzco army pursued the Quito army.

'Surrender, brother.'

'Never, brother.'

'In the name of Huayna Capac, your father, cease this madness.'

'In the name of Huayna Capac, your father, renounce your vengeance.'

And the two armies were so close that the peasants cultivating corn in their terraced fields, seeing them pass, could almost believe that they were a single army.

3. The North

However, the army of the north increased the pace of their marching until they reached Cajamarca, where Atahualpa knew he could count on the garrison that he had left behind in the recently occupied city. The green valley offered the wearied men the ambiguous spectacle of columns of steam rising from the hot water springs that were the region's pride. Atahualpa, like his ancestors, used to love coming here to bathe with his father in more peaceful times. He had imagined that his men would relax in those warm pools, resting their bodies and recovering their strength, before tackling the formidable cordillera that separated them from Quito, his capital and his home. But that would only have worked if he'd managed to create a wider gap to his pursuers. As it was, he could feel the breath of Cuzco on the back of his neck. His brother's army was camped on a hillside outside the city, his white tents packed so tightly together that they seemed to cover the mountain like a sheet. The clouds of steam exhaled by the earth only added to this lunar vision.

Atahualpa descended from his litter and trod upon the main square of Cajamarca in his sandals. Around him, the men watered their horses, unloaded their llamas, set up their tents. Suddenly he felt a rush of anxiety in his throat and he decided to set off again before dawn.

In the morning, Huascar's scouts found Cajamarca deserted. The men and animals of the northern army had already begun the interminable ascent. The path was narrow, the chasm seemed bottomless, the air grew icy. The condors glided. The impassive Andes barred the way, but it was a route that the soldiers of the north knew well, having often taken it, so at last they were able to steal a march on their enemies. They passed goldmines, gorges, crevasses and pine forests. They passed fortresses constructed with Inca ingenuity atop rocky spurs. Having crested the summit, they felt the pull of Quito. Once they were home, they would be safe, they thought.

But that was to underestimate the impact of the massacres they had perpetrated among the people of the north – the Chimus, the Caranguis and especially the Canaris, for whom

Atahualpa was the cruel tyrant who had given the order to exterminate them. Had he not razed the great Tumipampa, founded by his own father, because it had taken his brother's side? The survivors saw the return of their executioners as a gift from the Sun. This was their opportunity for vengeance. A war of harassment began. The weakened Quito army suffered so many losses that the Cajamarca reinforcements were effectively wiped out. Furthermore, the energy they spent repelling the Canaris' attacks slowed them down, and the Cuzco army was able to catch up. The rearguard, led by Quizquiz, was almost entirely destroyed by the cavalry of Tupac Hualpa (brother of Huascar, and therefore also of Atahualpa, but owing allegiance to his birthplace of Cuzco).

When Atahualpa's army finally reached the valley of Quito, it was too late. They had suffered too many losses to have any hope of rebuilding their forces before several moons had passed – and that was more time than they possessed. So Atahualpa gave the order to his best general, Ruminahui the stone-eyed, to burn his city, and he climbed to the top of the highest hill – the 'heart of the mountain', as the Quitonians called it – to watch the inferno. When Huascar took Quito, he would find only ashes.

Atahualpa did not shed a tear. He set off again, heading further north, beyond the borders of the Empire. The remains of his army entered a dense forest filled with venomous animals. He had hoped that Huascar would give up following him, but he had underestimated his brother's stubbornness, or perhaps his hatred. Tupac Hualpa's cavalry nipped at his heels. Soon the glorious army of Chinchaysuyu, the Empire of the North, would be nothing but a hairless, flea-ridden old dog.

Nevertheless, the fallen emperor plunged ever deeper into the humid jungle. After the icy bite of the Andean peaks, he and his men were now assailed by oppressive heat. Not one of his remaining soldiers dared utter a word against him, but his spies reported that they were starting to curse the day they were born and to wish for death to bring their misery to an end. One after another, death granted those wishes.

Quizquiz, however, had survived Tupac's attacks. Now he was riding alongside the royal litter, guarding his monarch. Atahualpa's generals had not deserted him. They would accompany him to the edge of the world.

One morning, they thought that their pursuers had given up. But soon the sound of a war song rose in the damp air:

> *We'll drink from the traitor's skull*
> *And make a necklace of his teeth.*
> *We'll turn his bones into flutes,*
> *His skin will be a drum.*
> *And then we'll dance.*

If Atahualpa heard this, he did not show it. Under no circumstances did he ever let slip his imperial dignity.

The retreat began to resemble a strange dream. Here and there, they encountered primitive villages filled with naked men, some curious, some frightened. Some of the villagers gave them food and drink. Others were more hostile, but they had only a few bows and iron-tipped lances for weaponry and were quickly defeated. Atahualpa's men took their horses, killed their oxen, and pillaged whatever they could find. There were no shops now, but this softened the blow. Their greatest difficulty was the absence of a road. Over and over again, men and animals found themselves sinking into insect-infested swamps. A slave and then an ox were taken by crocodiles.

The court of Quito was now following the army, since it would have been slaughtered had it stayed behind, and this added another patchwork of colours to the long, tatty procession.

Finally they reached the northern isthmus, bordered to the east by the mythical sea, only ever mentioned in a few ancient

legends passed on by some surviving caravans or the lost representatives of distant tribes. So it wasn't a legend, after all. Even
amid their suffering, a few of the men swelled with pride like
explorers. Others, remembering old stories about the Red Queen,
daughter of Thunder, envoy of the Sun, raised their arms respectfully to the sky. As for Atahualpa, he paid no heed to superstitions.
He crossed the isthmus, in one last effort retreating from the
northern borders of the known world, then stopped, blocked not
by poorly armed tribes but by the fear of powerful warriors who,
in all those distant rumours, were invariably described as deeply
aggressive, with an excessive love of human sacrifices. Atahualpa
and his men, his women, his gold, his beasts, his court, at the
end of their interminable retreat, now completely cornered,
found themselves washed up on a long, sandy beach, after crossing the Andes, the swamps, the isthmus at the end of the world,
after marching further north than any Inca ancestor had even
dared to dream – not Huayna Capac, his father, nor Pachacuti
the great reformer – and now they simply waited for Huascar, for
the last, fatal conflict, which they had, ultimately, only
postponed.

But as the sovereign was thinking gloomily about the lamentable circumstances in which he would now enter the underworld,
General Ruminahui came to request an audience. Despite the
situation, and the fact that Atahualpa himself – who had
descended from his litter and now stood facing the sea – did not
smell as fragrant as usual, had dirty hair, and had been wearing
the same tunic for almost half a day; despite the fact, then, that
his monarch no longer respected all the formalities due his own
rank, probably because he was anxious at the prospect of not
being embalmed, the great general presented himself barefoot
and head lowered, with all the marks of humility required by
protocol. After all, Atahualpa still wore the braided imperial
crown on his forehead, red tassels hanging from it and a pompom

of falcon feathers sprouting from its top; this was sufficient for his father's old soldier.

'Sapa Inca, do you see those boats, out at sea?'

Without raising his head, he pointed at some little dots that were floating on the water, then clapped his hands to summon a naked man held on a leash by two slaves. He pressed down on the naked man's shoulders to force him to kneel.

'According to this man, whom we captured this morning, some great islands exist, only a few days' journey from here. Their inhabitants come here to fish and trade, aboard hollowed-out tree trunks that they call *canoas*. To judge from the provisions of fruit that we confiscated from the prisoner, those must be lands of plenty, just waiting to be picked by us.'

Atahualpa was a tall man, but his general was a giant and towered over him by a head, even when bowing. Out of habit, the emperor did not allow his expression to show whether he was intrigued by or disdainful of this suggestion.

He simply said: 'We have no boat.'

'But we have the forest,' the general replied.

And so the evacuation was organised. The valiant Quizquiz and his men held the beach. Ruminahui mobilised the remaining uninjured soldiers to cut down and carry trees, while on the beach Chalco Chimac was in charge of the boats' construction. Men were sent out on hastily carved canoes; animals and crates of gold on rafts built from tree trunks tied together by ropes of llama wool and equipped with sails cut from tent canvas. The nobility, who had never served themselves more than a drink in their entire lives, who had never dressed or even washed themselves, clumsily helped to cut, assemble and load the rafts. Meanwhile, Quizquiz's soldiers heroically drove back the attacks of the Cuzco army, and the clash of arms, the yells and hoofbeats reached the beach from the edge of the forest and mingled with the sound of the waves.

The evacuation took place. Quizquiz was the last man to embark, under a rain of arrows and insults, leaving behind him a beach strewn with corpses. The last, panic-stricken horses ran amok because they could not be fitted on to the rafts, while a few turtles, nested in the sand, had not moved during the entire battle.

4. Cuba

The sea was calm and the fleet was able to stay close together; there were almost no losses.

They landed on a white beach bordered by languid palm trees. The screeches of parrots filled the air. Pink pigs played happily in the sand and they took this as a good omen. This new country was beautiful. The air was mild. Weeks of fatigue evaporated. They sang as they climbed the snowless mountains. The peaceful rivers were forded effortlessly, and fish could be caught with their bare hands. From the heart of the game-filled forests a few people would occasionally appear, driven by curiosity. They were naked and handsome, and above all they seemed to have no hostile intentions. With the aid of a merchant from Popayan, who claimed to understand their language, Atahualpa discovered that an old queen reigned over the archipelago, which comprised three large islands – Cuba, Haiti, Jamaica – and an infinity of small islands such as Turtle Island. They marched north, without knowing why, other than for the simple pleasure of exploring this land's beauties, or perhaps out of habit, since the north had always been their home within Tawantinsuyu. In the evenings, they grilled pigs and ate the flesh of lizards. Did Atahualpa think that, here, they would be able to forget war? Perhaps. But was he even capable of peace? The series of circumstances that shaped his destiny makes that question difficult to answer. Let us say that peace did not lean over his cradle.

As anxiety ebbed from their hearts, the people of the procession returned to the old protocols: the sweepers in their chequered tunics opened a path, followed by singers and dancers who preceded the horse cavalry in gold armour, then came the emperor seated on his throne, surrounded by his guard of Yanas, his generals on horseback, the dignitaries of the court, the most eminent of whom were carried in litters – his sister-wife Coya Asarpay, his very young cousin and future wife Cusi Rimay, his equally young sister Quispe Sisa – then came his secondary wives and his concubines, the priestesses of the Sun, the servants, the footsoldiers and, last of all, the bedraggled flood of Quito's survivors. Quizquiz and his men drew up the rear of this long herd.

One day, the procession came to a halt. The men at the head moved aside to let the Inca's litter pass. Before them were forty horsemen, all naked, all armed, with painted faces and feathers on their heads. Over his shoulder their chief carried a sort of wooden stick inlaid with pieces of iron. As he did not seem disposed to let this troop of foreigners any further into his lands, the emperor had to engage in a dialogue. The chief's name was Hatuey and he served the Queen Anacaona. Lacking civilised decorum, he looked the Inca in the eyes as he addressed him, without kneeling, without even descending from his horse. Atahualpa gave his answers through Chalco Chimac. In any case, neither side understood the other's language. Somehow, though, they agreed to a meeting with the queen, in a place named Baracoa. It is likely that Atahualpa thought about slaughtering these men who were barring his passage. It is no less probable that Hatuey sensed this, for he pointed his stick at the sky and, with a noise like thunder, shot down a red-headed vulture. Panic spread through the Quito army. Old legends rushed back into memory. Voices yelled: 'Thor!' Even the giant Ruminahui lowered his head, as if the sky was about to collapse. Only Atahualpa remained impassive. The son of the Sun did not fear thunder. Nevertheless, he judged it prudent to let Hatuey depart unscathed.

In other circumstances, he would have had all those who had trembled executed, but the fallen emperor was in no position to waste men and, most importantly, had no intention of losing his best general.

5. Baracoa

When they reached the sea, they realised that the island was a narrow strip of land that could be crossed in a few days. They had not come to this country as conquerors but as fugitives and that, assuredly, was not without consequence for the fate of Cuba and the world. Atahualpa sent messengers loaded with gifts ahead of him. He offered the queen gold plates, tunics, parrots. In return, the queen received him as an old ally, to the sound of tambourines, amid games and dances, under a rain of flowers. Servants carrying palm leaves and bouquets came to meet the procession. The village had been cleared. Garlands of greenery hung from painted huts. Atahualpa's generals noticed some long houses with plant roofs and a forge at rest, with a thread of white smoke still drifting upwards from it. On the beach, surrounded by wild cattle, were the skeletons of two gigantic ships. A banquet had been prepared. The queen invited the Inca to sit next to her. Atahualpa was less arrogant than his brother and decided it would be a good idea to treat her as an equal. He himself tasted the food he was served. The queen's beauty was faded, but she had a gracefulness that pleased him.

The festivities went on late into the night and began again the next morning. The visitors from Quito were enchanted. Amid all the games and songs, however, Anacaona sent them a message: Hatuey, who was her nephew and who reigned over this part of the island, would offer them the spectacle of a simulated battle. Naked horsemen pursued men dressed in white tunics, who defended themselves with long sticks inlaid with iron. The sticks pointed at the air, and again the sound of thunder terrified the visitors. But at the end, the horsemen won the battle and – a pertinent detail – took the firearms. Observing his generals, who were trying hard to conceal their nervousness, Atahualpa saw that the message had been received. He understood that the foreigners had come from the sea, almost forty harvests before, aboard the boats that were now stranded on the beach, and that they had been defeated. The queen's daughter, Higuénamota, enjoyed telling him this story. So the Inca swore that he had come not to wage war, but as an exile seeking refuge. The people of Quito humbly asked for asylum, and the Taínos – for such was the name of Anacaona's people – graciously granted it. Furthermore, they both shared the cult of Thor, that secondary divinity of obscure origins.

6. Huascar

There is no way of knowing how long the Inca might have enjoyed this hospitality. Inaction hardly seemed to bother him, so pleasant were his dealings with the queen. In truth, what she'd told them about the foreigners from the east was completely unbelievable. He knew that the fire sticks required a certain powder to blow thunder, and that there was little or no such powder on the island, meaning that their use was strictly rationed, reserved for special occasions – and the arrival of new foreigners was undoubtedly a special occasion. He also knew that the foreigners from long ago had been obsessed by two things: their god and gold. They liked to plant crosses. They had all died.

The people of Quito abandoned themselves to the delights of Baracoa. They mixed so well with their hosts that some of them shed their clothes and went around naked, while the Taínos had fun putting on their tunics. The memory of their past trials faded and they let the present flow like sand.

But the future, though briefly hidden from view, marched ever onward.

Anacaona's spies reported that other foreigners, in all respects similar to the people of Quito – except for their superior numbers – had landed on the neighbouring island of Jamaica. Atahualpa had to inform the queen that it was his brother, come to find him, and that his intentions were not peaceful. A council gathered around Anacaona, including her daughter and her nephew, and Atahualpa and his generals were invited to attend, as was his sister-wife Coya Asarpay.

What did Huascar want? What did this stubbornness mean? Could fear of his brother's return have driven him so far from Cuzco, for such a long time? These questions did not interest the Taínos, who feared that they would suffer the consequences of this fratricidal war. Hatuey angrily told the Inca: 'Go away! To the mountains, to the sea, wherever you want!' He had to flee again … but where? Nobody knew. Atahualpa saw his generals roll their eyes helplessly. Higuénamota pointed at the sea: 'The answer lies before you.' The east … but how? Where were those lands? How far away? They were shown some maps found in the boats. Atahualpa and his people stared uncomprehendingly at the representations of a world in which Cuzco did not exist. They were incapable of deciphering the little signs written on the paper. Higuénamota had learned the invaders' language when she was a child, but not their system of transcription. Had they known how false those maps were, the invaders would probably never have agreed to take that leap into the void.

But how could they cross the sea? Again, it was Higuénamota who provided the answer: those boats abandoned on the beach … The foreigners came all the way here with them, and would have returned. The wood had rotted, though, and the boats were in no fit state to sail. Besides, they had too many people to fit on two ships, even ones of such extraordinary size. But Atahualpa's retinue included the best carpenters in the Empire. The order was given to repair the two boats and to build a third, even bigger than the others. Chalco Chimac organised his engineers, who drew up plans for a gigantic vessel, based on the models they had before their eyes and on the words of Anacaona and her daughter as they described the enormous ship that had smashed against the rocks so long ago before being swept away by the waves.

In the meantime, Anacaona's spies kept watch on Huascar. The Cuzco army was still in Jamaica and, luckily for Atahualpa and his people, did not seem to know where to search for them. The instruction was sent out to all the inhabitants of the archipelago: do everything you can to lead them astray. Huascar would find his brother in the end, but first he would waste a long time lost in these lands, and each day spent exploring a wrong island was another day for Atahualpa's carpenters. If necessary, he could be sent towards Haiti, Anacaona's homeland, to gain a little more time.

Atahualpa's men cut down trees and sawed them into planks. The women sewed multicoloured sails. The Taínos made thousands of nails, which they soaked in oil to protect them from rust. And, as if by some miracle of nature, the skeletons came back to life, like a snake shedding its skin. This slow rebirth offered hope of a happy ending to both sets of people: they had loved each other briefly, they would part ways as good friends. Of course, the departure of the Quito army would not mark the end of the story for anyone, and there was nothing to guarantee that the boats would be able to return whence they had come, nor that Huascar, out of bitterness at seeing his prey escape him once more, would not avenge himself upon the Taínos. But thanks to the hard work of the woodcutters, the carpenters, the seamstresses and the blacksmiths, the worst was no longer inevitable.

One thing was certain, however: life would not return to its old order. The world was slipping off its axis. Coya Asarpay, the sister-wife, did not want to leave, and her anxiety was shared by many of the others, despite their steadfast work. 'Brother, what is this madness?' she asked. Within her, fear of the unknown battled with fear of the known. She was terrified by the knowledge that Huascar's army was prowling around, but contemplation of the horizon did not make her shudder any less. How could anyone imagine what lay beyond the seas? Atahualpa found the right words: 'Sister, let us go and see the place from where the Sun comes.' And, aware that his people needed a leader, he ignored the protocols and addressed them all: 'The time of the Four Quarters is over. We are going to sail towards a new world, filled with lands no less rich than our own. With your help, your emperor will be the Viracocha of the new age, and the honour of having served Atahualpa will redound to your families and your ayllus for generations to come. And if we are to founder, then let it be like this. We will find Pachacamac at the bottom of the sea. But if we make it across the sea … What a voyage that will be! So let us go, now, to the Fifth Quarter!' The Quitonians, reassured and emboldened by these words, responded with a single voice: 'To the Fifth Quarter!'

However, the three ships could not take everyone, particularly since Atahualpa had no intention of leaving behind anything that belonged to him. His plates, his clothes, his animals, his food supplies: all of it had to come. After listening to Anacaona's explanations, he had decided to take lots of gold with him. Then, according to their rank and usefulness, he personally selected those who would travel with him: the nobility, the soldiers, the functionaries of the Empire (accountants, archivists, seers), the craftsmen, the women … It came to less than two hundred people, and yet even that was beyond the ships' usual capacity. He also took a few horses, llamas, cuys (for eating), and Atahualpa could not be separated from his puma or his parrots.

Just before their departure, Higuénamota came to the emperor and begged: 'Let me come with you.' Atahualpa understood that she had spent her whole life wondering about the mysterious lands from where the pale-skinned men had come, all those years before. He also saw that she would be a useful asset.

Finally, the day of their departure arrived. The Quitonians who could not accompany their emperor stood on the beach and wept. Anacaona embraced her daughter. Atahualpa, surrounded by his generals, waved farewell to the island that had welcomed him, with the feeling that he was not likely to see it again any time soon.

7. Lisbon

They sailed.

During the crossing, Higuénamota became Atahualpa's lover. The young emperor was enchanted by this woman who was old enough to be his mother and who, of her own free will, had left her homeland for tales heard in childhood that she had never been able to forget.

Together, they pored over the old maps they had found on the ship and tried to decipher them. Atahualpa's scholars had worked out how to use an instrument that enabled them to navigate using the stars, so the ship never deviated from its trajectory.

One morning, Ruminahui came to see Atahualpa in his room. The emperor was drinking akha with his mistress. Outside, white birds circled the sky, a sign that land was near. When at last it appeared on the horizon, those weeks spent in intimacy with the emperor had given Anacaona's daughter a remarkable command of Quechua (the language spoken by Atahualpa, in preference to Aymara, but with a Quito accent).

They sailed alongside the coast of these new lands. One night, just before dawn, a miracle occurred that terrified the crew: the sea began to swell, even though there was not a breath of wind. It was like a silent hurricane and it almost destroyed the three ships. How cruel it would have been to die only two cable lengths from terra firma, when everything suggested that they had reached their journey's end. The skill of the captains saved them from this tragic irony.

They entered the mouth of a gigantic river. A thick stone tower rose up, as if from the water itself, to guard the door of the sea. To their right, green hills hinted at a pleasant land. But to their left, a flooded plain suggested that the angry river had overflowed its banks. A vast white stone edifice, as long as the greatest palaces in Cuzco, ran along the shore. The birds had stopped singing. The new arrivals, spooked by their silence, did not utter a word.

Atahualpa gave the order to sail close to the tower. Its walls were decorated with sculptures of unknown animals. The crew were particularly intrigued by the head of a tapir with a horn on its snout. But there were also, carved in the stone, those crosses that Higuénamota recognised as the emblems of the foreigners from long ago. So it was that they knew they had reached their destination.

The ships continued along the shore. The strangest sights unfolded before them. Stone houses in ruins. Fires burning in the hills. Corpses strewn over the ground. Men, women and dogs wandering amid the rubble. The first sounds that they heard in this New World were the barking of dogs and the crying of children.

The river widened like a lake. The captains had to tack between the half-submerged wrecks of other boats. Finally they discovered a square so large that it was equal in surface area to the fortress of Sacsayhuaman, and across it lay ships of all sizes, with twisted keels, smashed hulls, broken masts. On the left-hand side of the square, a magnificent palace, surmounted by a slender tower, seemed to have collapsed in on itself. They disembarked.

The square, which had obviously been beautiful until very recently, was now little more than a pond. The sandals they wore sunk into the mud and the water came up to their ankles, even the imperial ankles of Atahualpa, who had decided against being carried in his litter, given the treacherousness of the drenched ground.

They encountered the dazed shadows of men, dressed in rags, moving slowly around the beached boats, staring vacantly as they dragged their feet, sometimes bumping into things like blind men, and when these ghosts saw the visitors, their faces showed no expression, no comprehension, no surprise. From time to time, a sinister creaking noise arose from the city, followed by screams that turned to pitiful wails.

Although it wasn't cold, the air bit into their flesh. The Quitonians, used to the bitter remoteness of the Andes, paid no attention to it, fascinated as they were by the desolate sights that greeted their disbelieving eyes. But Higuénamota, who had led them to the end of the world, was a Taíno. She had only ever known two seasons on the islands, one dry and one wet, both of them warm. Atahualpa noticed that her naked body was trembling. The crew was exhausted and on edge after their long voyage. He decided that they should find somewhere to rest. But where in this city of ruins could they find shelter for 183 people, thirty-seven horses, one puma and several llamas? They returned to the white building they had seen downriver – the only building, along with the tower in the middle of the sea, that appeared to be still standing.

It was a long, angular palace, with slim pointed columns like lances that seemed to act as supports, wide arched windows, symmetrical turrets, and a dome-shaped tower, the chalky stone so elaborately worked that it looked as if it had been carved entirely in bone.

It was occupied by strange-looking people: men in brown and white robes, the tops of their heads shaved, knelt on the floor with their hands joined and their eyes closed, muttering inaudible sounds. When they at last noticed their visitors, these creatures began running in all directions, like frightened little cuys, crying out as their sandals slapped against the paving stones. One, however, was calmer and braver than the rest: this man, who wore a gold ring on one finger of his right hand, approached to speak with them. Atahualpa asked his mistress if she could understand the man's language, but she was only able to distinguish a few words – '*providencia*', '*castigo*', '*india*' – amid sentences whose architecture remained obscure, if strangely familiar. She thought that her conversations with the foreigner of long ago must have been lost somewhere in the deep well of memory, and that all that remained to her were a few scattered scraps. However, the creatures, although frightened, seemed harmless. Atahualpa ordered his people to make themselves at home. The animals were brought out of the ships, and men and women moved into an enormous dining hall. Higuénamota, addressing the gold ring, said: '*Comer*'. She saw that the man had understood her. He brought them some food: a hot soup and a sort of biscuit with a crunchy crust and a soft flesh, which they liked very much, perhaps because they were so hungry. They also tasted a black, red-tinted drink.

And so the long voyage was over at last. All of them – men, women, horses, llamas – had survived the great sea. They had reached the land of the rising Sun.

Outside, the river was speckled with golden reflections. Or perhaps they were bits of straw floating on the surface.

Within this palace was a sacred place with translucent patches of red, yellow, green and blue. The ceiling there was like a spider's web carved into the stone, and even higher than Pachacuti's palace. At the far end of the building, on a raised platform that was sumptuously decorated – if not entirely covered with gold like the House of the Sun – stood the statue of a very thin man nailed to a cross. The shaved men gathered in this place for fervent devotion, which the Quitonians felt fairly sure was a sort of huaca. But who was this nailed god? They would find that out soon enough.

Yet the creatures seemed to be arguing, and the visitors knew that they were the object of these discussions.

Here and there, the shaved men were clearing away rubble. Atahualpa decided it would be a good idea to have his people help them. And so the Quitonians cleared away rubble too. For anyone from Tawantinsuyu, it wasn't difficult to guess what had happened here: the earth had trembled and opened up, and then an enormous wave had hit the coast. Atahualpa and his men were all too familiar with this phenomenon. There was even the tell-tale smell of rotten eggs in the air, brought there by an easterly breeze.

Atahualpa had chosen a sufficiently vast room for himself and his wives, where his sleeping mat had been put on the floor. He was joined by Higuénamota, who had not found anywhere to hang her hammock, and by his sister-wife, Coya Asarpay. The rest of the group took shelter under the arches of the inner courtyard. Their beasts were kept there too, and the shaved men approached these animals with fearful curiosity, having never seen llamas before. At last they went to sleep, under the watchful eye of Ruminahui, after asking for some more of the black drink.

8. The Land of the East

For all their fearfulness, the shaved men could not help being intrigued. Who were these visitors? They admired our clothes, touched our ears, and became embroiled in conjectures. The presence of the women plunged them into a state of extreme agitation, particularly Higuénamota, the sight of whom seemed to blind them like the sun, for they put their hands over their eyes and turned away whenever she passed by. They kept trying to put one of their ugly shrouds around her shoulders, but she just laughed and pushed them away. The Cuban princess wore nothing but the bracelets she had received from her mother, around her wrists and ankles, and a gold necklace that Atahualpa had given her.

Nevertheless, the shaved man with the ring – who was their chief and who seemed more reasonable than the others – having noticed that Higuénamota understood a little of their language, took her into a room where other shaved men were scratching away at squares of material covered with little black lines. She had seen them before, these talking sheets, kept in leather cases, which filled the room up to its ceiling. The shaved man with the ring unfolded one of these sheets, on which a map was drawn, similar to the ones they had found on the foreigners' ship. She realised that he wanted to know where she was from. He pointed to a spot on the map labelled Portugal. To the left, there was nothing but a vast emptiness, except for a small island situated lower down.

Quizquiz took ten men to scout the surrounding area and returned to make his report to Atahualpa: the land was completely ravaged. The city seemed very large and filled with many people. But the inhabitants were all in a daze. Nobody had even noticed the new arrivals. The river was full of fish and the land, when it wasn't trembling, seemed pleasant. As a sample of the local fauna, Quizquiz had brought back a sort of dwarfish llama that he'd found. They had not observed any birds in the sky.

Thick clouds from the north burst open and the rain put out the fires that were still burning in the hills. The Quitonians used the hospitality of the shaved men to recover from their fatigue after the long crossing. They noticed that the black drink that their hosts served them became red when it was poured into translucent cups, and this wonder made a great impression on them.

When Atahualpa judged that his men were sufficiently rested, he ordered that they should, as custom dictated, burn the remains of the food they had brought from Cuba, which they had piously kept in crates. According to protocol, they should also burn the clothes they had brought with them. However, the unprecedented situation in which the former sovereign of Chinchaysuyu found himself – in an unknown land, with no notion of its resources of alpaga or cotton (but not impressed at all by the coarse clothing worn by these people living in a palace) – persuaded him to postpone that part of the ritual.

They brought the crates from the boats. Atahualpa was carried in his litter to oversee the ceremony. He had wanted it to take place on the riverbank, where the water had finally receded. The usual pomp and circumstance were reduced due to the fugitives' meagre possessions, but the fallen monarch seemed intent, all the same, on reaffirming the prerogatives of his royal person, despite the fact that nobody had contested them. For this occasion, he had lent Higuénamota his bat-fur coat, because the air was cool. The Cuban princess stood beside him, as did his sister-wife Coya

Asarpay, while little Cusi Rimay and Quispe Sisa sat at his feet. His three generals stood to attention on horseback, axes in hand. After the dances and the songs, a woman was chosen from among the priestesses of the Sun. To the sound of tambourines, she lit the first crate. Instantly, a smell of grilled meat rose into the air, attracting the local inhabitants. They were filthy and in rags; they stared, wide-eyed, at the crates, appearing not to notice the visitors. Nobody would have dared interrupt the ceremony without an express order from Atahualpa, but they all watched the reactions of these new arrivals, who approached the crates in concentric circles. Ultimately, unable to bear it any longer, one of them thrust his hands into the blaze and plucked out a half-chewed bone. He was immediately seized by the soldiers of the guard, who were ready to slit his throat, but Atahualpa made a sign to spare him. That was like a signal for the others. The Quitonians watched speechlessly as the bestial spectacle unfolded. The crates were ripped open and the locals fought, grunting, over their contents. They wolfed down anything they found, protecting their miserable pickings with kicks and punches. Probably more out of surprise than pity, the fallen emperor allowed them to finish their meal. When they had devoured everything, down to the last cuy bone, the people seemed to wake from a fever dream. They looked up, their faces smeared with grease, and finally saw the visitors. And they froze.

Later, the scene would be immortalised in a famous Titian painting: Atahualpa, young, handsome, imperial in his dignity, a parrot on his shoulder, his puma on a leash, surrounded by his wives; Higuénamota, dressed in a gleaming bronze-coloured coat, her chest bare; Cosi Asarpay, looking disgusted; her little sister, Quispe Sisa, alarmed by the sight of the first Levantines that she had seen close up; all the Quitonians motionless in their beautiful clothes of shimmering colours and geometric patterns; the black, glistening fur of Ruminahui's horse, and the white horses, manes blowing in the wind, of Quizquiz and Chalco Chimac. At the centre of the image, a Levantine, sitting cross-legged, gnaws at a bone, his lips drawn back, in front of a horrified priestess of the Sun. Another, curious, reaches out to touch the ears of an impassive Inca lord. Still another is kneeling, arms raised imploringly to the sky. All the others bow respectfully to the emperor.

Of course, Titian wasn't there to witness the scene, and it didn't actually happen in precisely that way.

It is true that one of the Levantines wanted to touch the ear of an Inca lord, but then Atahualpa, without moving from his litter, made a sign to his guard; the men banged their lances against their shields and all the Levantines ran away like vicuñas frightened by thunder.

News of the visitors' arrival spread quickly after this. Scruffy Levantines pressed around the shaved men's palace. Quizquiz, once again, was sent on a scouting mission. He reported that their intentions, though not exactly hostile, did not seem especially friendly. So outings were limited to those that were strictly necessary. After all, the Quitonians were fine, sheltered behind those stone walls. There was an abundance of the black drink and, besides, they didn't know where else to go.

9. Catalina

Days passed: a moon, or perhaps two. The Quitonians imagined staying there until stores of the black drink were exhausted. But history has taught us that few events bother announcing their arrival in advance, a number enjoy eluding all attempts at prediction, while most are content simply to happen.

Now, it happened that the king of this country came to the palace of the shaved men. He was accompanied by a young blonde woman who was his queen, and by a large retinue of lords and soldiers. The lords and the queen were dressed with an elegance that the Quitonians had not yet encountered among the other inhabitants, their clothes cut from materials that seemed highly delicate, even if they didn't rival those of the Incas. The king, however, was dressed in a simple coat and a flat hat, both black to match his beard, and no jewellery but a necklace made of thick metal links, with – hanging from it – a red cross set in a golden ring. The queen's blonde hair intrigued them more than the king's beard. To start with, the black beard talked with the chief of the shaved men, and the Quitonians were able to see the deference with which the latter addressed the former, kissing his hands and genuflecting constantly, without ever standing straight (and yet without taking off his sandals).

Then the king signalled his desire to speak with Atahualpa.

He said his name was Joao. Hearing this, the Inca turned towards Higuénamota, because that name sounded a little like certain Taíno names.

If the bearded king was shocked by the princess's nudity, he did not let it show. He told them that he reigned over the country of Portugal and made ample gestures with his arms, apparently in reference to a vast empire, but the conversation was difficult because Higuénamota only understood a few words here and there. He used the word '*deus*' a lot, and she didn't know what it meant. Atahualpa reached his arms out westward to explain where they had come from. Joao seemed puzzled. He said another word: '*Brasil?*' But the Quitonians didn't understand that either.

A silence fell. The king spoke a few words to his wife, which Higuénamota half-understood: he asked her where he could find a translator who could speak *turc*. The queen replied graciously that he would have to wait for her brother to return victorious from his future 'crusade' against a king named Suleiman, and Higuénamota realised that she could understand the queen. So it was that, deep from the well of memory, burst forth words that she had thought forgotten: '*Hablas castellano?*'

The king and queen stared at each other, dumbstruck.

A lively conversation began between the two women.

The queen asked if they came from the Indies, Africa or Turkey.

The princess told her that she was from an island situated beyond the setting sun.

The queen said they knew a distant island named Vera Cruz where her husband's people went to fetch wood, but which they had never explored.

The princess said that she had seen foreigners who looked a bit like the Portuguese land on her island a long time ago, but that they had been looking for gold, not wood.

The queen remembered a Genoese sailor who had wished to prove that the world was round, and that her grandparents Isabella and Ferdinand had sent him west to seek out a path to the Indies. He had never returned, and since then nobody had risked trying to cross the Ocean Sea.

The princess told her that she had known that sailor when she was a little girl, and that he had died in her arms.

The queen asked if they came from Cipango and if they'd been sent by the Great Khan.

The princess told her that Atahualpa was the emperor of the Four Quarters, without mentioning the civil war that he had fought and lost to his brother.

Atahualpa knew that they were talking about him but didn't understand a word of what they were saying.

Joao seemed to understand but said nothing.

The queen said that her name was Catalina and that she came from a country called Castile.

Little Cusi Rimay touched Joao's beard and he let her.

The princess asked how big this country was, where they were.

The queen said that her husband reigned over kingdoms beyond the seas, but that her brother reigned over vast lands.

The princess knew that Spain included Castile and Aragon.

The queen told her about Italy and Rome, where a great priest lived, about Germany and its princes, and about distant Jerusalem, the city of a certain Jesus, which had fallen into the hands of enemies.

The princess asked what cataclysm had struck this city.

The queen told her that when the earth had trembled, the great river had opened in two and had thrown boats into the sky.

A mournful cry echoed outside, although nobody could tell if it was a man or an animal.

Again, Joao spoke to the shaved man with the ring. He looked anxious and spoke in a harsh voice.

Higuénamota asked the queen what the two men were talking about. She knew that they were in a temple and that the shaved men were priests. The queen explained that some of them were predicting another cataclysm and that Joao wanted to put an end to these rumours. The people here believed it was the wrath of God that had been visited on their country, and the presence of the foreigners from across the seas had only increased their fears and superstitions.

The princess asked what god they were talking about.

The queen moved her hand quickly over her face and chest, a gesture that the Cuban princess had often seen among the Spanish when she'd known them, long ago.

Then the king and the queen took their leave. They were living on the other side of the river, for fear of a disease that they called the plague.

10. The Incades, *Book I, Verse 1*

O brave men, who from distant western shores,
Thro' seas where sail was never spread before,
Beyond where Cuba lifts her spicy breast,
And waves her palms above the wat'ry waste,
With prowess more than human forc'd your way
To the fair kingdoms of the rising day:
What wars you wag'd, what seas, what dangers pass'd,
What glorious empire crown'd your toils at last!

11. *The Tagus*

In the days that followed, Atahualpa did not leave his room and had a large amount of the black drink brought to him. This interview had plunged him into a state of irritation. He had imagined conquering the New World as his ancestors had conquered the north, but now he realised the naivety of such a plan: one could not take possession of a country with fewer than two hundred men. Only a madman could imagine that. Moreover, King Joao's retinue had allowed him a glimpse of the military capacities of the men here: disciplined, well equipped, and undoubtedly good fighters if need be.

But he had to keep up his troops' morale, however few of them there were, and that meant offering them a future, something to cling to; at least the illusion of hope. Atahualpa was all too aware of the fatal effects of inaction; he knew that they must set off again ... but to where? Now they had reached this New

World, where should they go? What should they do? He couldn't steel himself to leave this stone haven so richly endowed with the black drink.

As happens to almost all of us (if we are honest enough to recognise this truth, rather than imagining that we are masters of our own destiny), circumstances made the decision for him.

They started to hear a menacing murmur, rising from a crowd of Levantines massed outside the doors of the temple. Every day, when they went out on a reconnaissance trip, Quizquiz and his men found more people in this crowd, and the noise they made grew ever louder. A few of the bolder men even went so far as to throw stones at them. Most, however, trembled as they passed and didn't dare attempt to hurt them. All the same, it was impossible to guess how long this invisible dyke of fear would hold them back, before the river of anger burst through. Higuénamota asked the shaved men what it was all about. The chief priest, who spoke Castilian, explained that the people of this country were very superstitious. They viewed the earthquake not as a natural phenomenon, as he himself believed, but as a form of divine vengeance, and they couldn't help associating this with the presence of Atahualpa's people. In Lisbon, some believed the visitors were Turks. For others, they were Indians. A small minority saw them as envoys from heaven. But the majority considered them to be demons. Even within the community of shaved men, opinion was divided.

Higuénamota asked the priest how he viewed her. The man could not help glancing at the Cuban princess's chest, hips and groin. In a muffled, confused voice, he replied: 'As a creature of God.'

Higuénamota reported this conversation to Atahualpa, who made his decision: they would leave here before the new moon.

They managed to get some food, horses, carts and *vinho* (as the Levantines called their black drink). The city's inhabitants, eager to see them leave, supplied them with everything they desired.

They left their three ships anchored near the tower in the water. The vessels were so worn out that it would have been a risk to continue sailing them, particularly as they had no idea how far this river – which the shaved men called *Tejo* – was navigable.

Not knowing where to go and having no reason to favour one direction over any other, they walked along the riverbank, as Catalina had told them it led to Castile. What would they do there? Atahualpa did not have the faintest idea. But Castile was a word, and even if it was still empty, at least it had the power of words. It could serve as their aim just as well as any other word.

On the way, they found corpses crushed by the earth, devastated villages, stricken Levantines. Reactions to them differed widely. The inhabitants of a village called Alverca regarded them as supernatural beings. In Alhandra, people begged them for alms. In Villa Franca de Xira, they were welcomed with hospitality, despite the extreme poverty of the town's inhabitants. On the other hand, they had to fight the population of Santarem, who greeted them with pitchforks and seemed possessed by an uncontrollable homicidal rage.

As the days went by, Higuénamota noticed that she found it increasingly easy to understand the speech of the Levantines they encountered.

Atahualpa knew what that meant: they had arrived in Castile. But he asked his Cuban companion not to divulge this information. They continued along the riverbank. After all, this endless wandering was preferable to being caught by Huascar or dying at sea, and since fleeing Quito his people had grown used to it.

And so they walked on, ever deeper inland, following paths and passing through villages, until they reached a town named Toledo.

12. Toledo

They found this town perched on a rocky hillock and immediately fell in love with it.

There was a stone bridge over the Tagus gorge, crenellated walls encircling the town, that temple spiking up towards the sky, and those massive palaces that looked as if they'd been placed on the mountainside by Viracocha's giant hand.

To the travellers, Toledo appeared an impregnable fortress, but seeing the Inca procession arrive, the guards on the bridge parted to let them pass without a single question.

Atahualpa's troop spread through the narrow alleys. There were numerous shops, but the town seemed deserted. They heard the distant sound of voices, however, and they followed it to a large square where all the inhabitants were gathered. Clearly, this was a special occasion.

The Quitonians were intrigued by this spectacle. Atahualpa himself, though renowned and admired for his unwavering imperial calm, even in the most surprising situations, could not hide his curiosity.

In the centre of the square, locked in a cage, stood men and women dressed in robes and pointed hats, some of them yellow, some black, with red crosses and flames painted on them. On the yellow robes, the flames blazed downward. Some of the people had ropes knotted around their necks. Each held a long unlit candle in one hand. Next to them were some black chests and life-sized dolls.

In front of them, lined around a large white cross that had obviously been put up for the occasion, were shaved men, a bit like the ones in Lisbon, listening to another shaved man give a long speech while pointing accusingly at the caged hat people.

Along one side, Higuénamota spotted the caciques: their elegant clothes and bearing marked them out. One young blonde woman resembled Catalina: she had the same mannerisms, the same look in her eyes. Sitting next to her, a bald man in a red robe had a face so lean and bony that he looked like a mummy. Armed soldiers stood behind them, apparently to protect them.

The rest of the square was completely occupied by a dense and animated crowd, listening attentively to the words spoken on the stage, and at regular intervals emitting chants, almost dancing.

Higuénamota found it hard to follow this strange speech: certain passages were in a language she didn't know, and all of it seemed rather unclear. The hat people were being asked to retract something, but she couldn't grasp what the dispute was about. Each prisoner in turn stepped forward and repeated '*si, yo creo*' to the questions they were asked, except for a few of them who were gagged.

The Cuban princess knew that this was a solemn ritual of some kind, but she had no idea what it all meant, and nor did her companions.

One young man, quite elegant in spite of the coarseness of his clothing, approached her shyly and kept stealing glances at her nudity beneath the bat-fur coat. While chants rose into the air, she questioned him about the significance of the ceremony. The shy young man took a step back, but – unlike the priests – he dared to look at her.

He told her that they were judging some *conversos* who were suspected of remaining faithful to their former religion and of *Judaising*. They could also be *Mohammedans* or *fanatics* or *Lutherans*, although they were less common in this region. Some of those on the stage were being judged for *improper remarks, blasphemy, superstition, bigamy, sodomy* or *witchcraft* (and sometimes more than one of these), but those crimes carried lighter punishments: a fine, the lash, prison or galley. The young man explained that the flames blazing downward were for those who would not be burned. He indicated one of the hat people who was accused of cooking with olive oil instead of lard. Or at least that was how she translated it to Atahualpa, although she wasn't entirely sure she'd understood the nature of that particular crime. The chants continued.

According to the young man, the judges were poisonous snakes and their mothers sold their bodies to strangers. But he respected one of them, because that man had studied in a town called Salamanca, which was completely devoted to learning and – according to the young man – contained all the knowledge in the world.

On the stage, a black cloth was removed, revealing a green cross. Then the chief judge addressed the caciques.

The young blonde woman was the queen of this country and the mummified man in the red robe was her minister.

The ceremony had gone on so long that they were distributing snacks to the participants, judges, defendants and noblemen.

Then the armed men led away the condemned people in their black robes, along with the black chests and the life-sized dolls. Intrigued, Atahualpa followed this procession. Since he had not deigned to inform his generals of his intentions, Ruminahui ordered the others to wait where they were while he went with the emperor. Higuénamota, who did not consider this order as applying to her, also followed, accompanied by the shy young Levantine.

They came out on to another square, where stakes had been set up, with rings, and faggots of wood arranged around them. The soldiers lit the first pyres, and they tossed the black chests and life-sized dolls into the flames.

Then they tied the people in black robes to the stakes.

Following a mysterious logic that escaped the Quitonians, some were strangled before being set on fire – and the shy young man explained that this was an act of mercy – but others, whose crimes were more serious, were burned alive. All of them made the same sign that they'd seen Catalina make, a hand moving quickly over the face and chest.

The Incas were no strangers to human sacrifice. Nevertheless, we could tell that Atahualpa, although he didn't want to let it show, was shocked by the sight of those bodies twisting as they were consumed by the flames, and by the sound of the dying people's screams.

The crowd stayed to watch until late that night.

The presence of the Quitonians could no longer be ignored. They were sought out and introduced to the queen.

Her name was Isabella and she was the sister of Joao, the king of Portugal. Like Catalina, though, she spoke Castilian, enabling Higuénamota to understand what she said. In truth, she was more beautiful than her sister-in-law, and more richly dressed. Her husband reigned over Spain and a distant territory that she called 'the Germanic Holy Roman Empire', which had to be ruled from the country where he was born, further to the north, and defended against a rival empire, to the east.

Her brother had written to her, warning that Indians from the west would be arriving. She wanted to offer a warm welcome to what she took to be an embassy from Cipango or Cathay, which forced her – she said, laughing – to admit that the world was round.

Atahualpa thought he could detect a certain impatience, or at least a degree of reserve, in the expressions of some of the shaved men listening to the queen's speech, and particularly in that of the mummy in the red robe. One, who introduced himself as *obispo* and *inquisidor* and responded to the name of Valverde, asked the Quitonians if they recognised the Holy Trinity. Atahualpa said he wasn't aware of it. A long silence ensued.

The Quitonians were lodged in a palace, and their animals were looked after.

The next day, they strolled through the streets, provoking only mild curiosity among the inhabitants, who were perhaps still sated and slightly drunk from the previous night's ceremony.

Amid Atahualpa's troop was a red-headed blacksmith named Puka Amaru. He noticed that the weapons made by the artisans of Toledo were almost equal in quality to those of Lambayeque. He reported his observations to Ruminahui, who put him in charge of maintaining their weaponry. Puka Amaru collected all the axes, swords, lances and star-headed clubs and took them to the local blacksmiths, who went into ecstasies over the delicacy of the ironwork. Together, they oiled, sharpened, traded. Puka Amaru very much appreciated the availability of good tools – the files, chisels and bellows were all well made – and he and his men were able to work their iron on excellent anvils. The Toledans were intrigued by the star-headed clubs. They also liked the long axes, which were similar to their own *alabardas*. In return, they offered straight swords with cross-shaped hilts and curved sabres that were like long machetes. Apart from the discovery of the black drink that turned red when it was poured, this was the first cultural exchange between the Quitonians and the inhabitants of the New World. Moreover, the black drink in Toledo was no less delicious than the one in Lisbon. The shaved men in Portugal had looked horrified when some of Atahualpa's young women had wanted to drink *vinho*, but in Toledo men and women were free to mingle.

But this harmony did not last.

One question about the *Santa Trinidad* seemed especially problematic for the local priests, who had formed a sort of council that they called *Suprema*. They showed a stubborn insistence on knowing whether or not Atahualpa believed a certain Jesus was the son of God. Atahualpa replied that Viracocha had created the world a long time ago but, for his part, he had stopped believing in Pachacama, the son of the Sun and the Moon. This response, which he had thought would satisfy them, appeared to plunge them into embarrassment, because they fell silent then and looked at one another out of the corners of their eyes.

It was agreed that the Quitonians should await the return of King Charles, Isabella's husband, who was to be informed without delay about the presence of Atahualpa and his delegation. However, the mummified priest, whose name was Cardinal Tavera, was not in favour of summoning the king for this because he had, according to the cardinal, more important business to take care of in a northern region called the Netherlands.

Queen Isabella did not share this opinion because she wanted her husband to return. She asked the Suprema, and Valverde in particular, to stop importuning her guests. This request was made with great grace, but the Suprema seemed unwilling to accede to it. The questions continued: on the number of sacraments and the celibacy of priests. Atahualpa replied that in his country, matters related to the gods were left to the priestesses. Selected women were devoted to the cult of the Sun and the service of the emperor. The entire council violently protested. In an attempt to mollify them, Atahualpa sent them a very fervent priestess from his retinue to explain how the cult worked, because they seemed extremely interested in this. They refused to receive her.

Soon, Quizquiz's men reported rumours that were spreading through the town: it was said that the visitors were, in reality, *Moros* or *Turcos*. The word *hereticos* kept turning up, and Quizquiz could tell that it was not a compliment.

One evening, an old woman came to warn Higuénamota that the Suprema had decided to arrest them all, the next day at dawn, following which they would be judged and burned as conversos. She was an old Jew who had seen members of her own family perish in the flames. She had only one son left.

Higuénamota rushed to pass on the old woman's warning to Atahualpa. They gathered with the generals and Coya Asarpay to decide on a plan of action. The Quitonians realised that something serious was going on around the different groups of believers, the Jews and the conversos, the Moorish Mohammedans, the Lutherans, the old and new Christians. They were not exactly sure what was at play behind these stories about the nailed god and cooking with lard, but they knew that the Levantines took all of it very seriously, as the ceremony with the pyres had amply proved.

A plan of action was drawn up. The Suprema had to be neutralised. So did the guards. And the queen's escort, and Tavera's. And all the soldiers in the town. In fact, they had to neutralise all the inhabitants of the town, whose reactions were impossible to predict, although the reports from Quizquiz's scouts were not particularly encouraging.

Higuénamota objected that not everyone was guilty. In addition to the old Jewish woman who had warned her about the arrest, the town's inhabitants also included potential future victims of the Suprema.

Coya Asarpay replied that since these people would be victims sooner or later, there was no point trying to save them. In fact, killing them now would be an act of mercy, if it spared them the pyres.

But Chalco Chimac remarked that these people – conversos, Moors, witches, bigamists, fanatics and Lutherans, whatever those names might actually mean – were also the Quitonians' only potential allies in this hostile land.

In that case, Quizquiz said, how do we recognise those who should be spared?

Higuénamota saw one simple means: only Christians made the sign of moving their hand over their face and chest. They did it all the time, at any opportunity, and based on what she remembered of the Spaniards she had known when she was a child, they would do it even more when they saw death approaching. Now, the people who were liable to be burned at the stake were precisely those who were accused of not being good Christians ...

In that case, said Ruminahui, they just had to spare the ones who didn't make the sign – and kill all the others.

Atahualpa decided that they should follow this rule, as far as possible.

They distributed arms and shoed the horses in secret. All of them, including the nobility, women, and children old enough to hold an axe, prepared for combat. They hadn't come all this way, they hadn't escaped Huascar's vengeance, they hadn't survived storms and earthquakes, just to end up grilled like cuys on a skewer, or strangled by hairy savages.

Just before dawn, Quizquiz gave the signal.

First they overpowered the grooms in the stables, then they killed the palace guards, and locked up the priests and caciques. The queen was confined to her room. They launched a surprise attack on the soldiers and killed a large number of them before it had even occurred to the Spaniards to defend themselves. They took the fire sticks from the corpses. Then, with all the yelling having brought the town's inhabitants out of their homes, the Quitonians charged through the streets on horseback.

It was carnage. The swords from Toledo and the axes from Lambayeque slashed and chopped without any care for profession, age or sex. They slit people's throats in their homes. Anyone who attempted to defend himself was scythed down like the others. Some took refuge in their temple, which they called a cathedral; Quizquiz set fire to it. Their nailed god was no help at all.

The shy young man who'd advised Higuénamota was caught in the attack. He sought refuge in doorways, hoping to find a hiding place in an inner courtyard, but a group of furious

Quitonians flushed him out. He fled along the rooftops but slipped and fell to the ground. He could sense death just behind him, could hear the terrifying war cries. He found himself face to face with Puka Amaru, who smashed his shoulder with a star-headed club. But the wounded young man, driven by the urge to live, managed to clamber to his feet and run away again, a hunted animal.

While the massacres continued, Atahualpa searched out the members of the Suprema. He asked them why they had planned to destroy him and his people, and they screeched and squawked while pointing to an effigy of their nailed god that hung on the wall. Some fell to their knees, as if struck down, and their bodies convulsed.

He wanted to explain to them that any god who demands that men be burned alive, whatever they might have done, was a bad god, because the bodies of the dead must be preserved in order that they might continue living after death, and that any such god did not deserve to be worshipped.

But as Higuénamota wasn't with him at that moment to translate, he decided it was simpler just to execute them. He would exhibit their heads as an example to others. The priest Valverde died uttering curses that nobody could understand.

The Cuban princess went out to make sure that the old woman who had warned her wasn't harmed. She lived with her son in a neighbourhood spared the worst of the violence, since the Quitonians had noticed that the people there didn't make that sign with their hand.

However, Higuénamota heard cries and the sound of a stampede. A bloodied figure threw himself at her feet, pursued by a pack of Quitonians led by the red-haired blacksmith. She recognised the shy young man and ordered his hunters to spare him. Puka Amaru, who objected to taking orders from a foreign princess, said that their instructions had been clear and that they had to execute them.

But Higuénamota advanced towards him until her breast was pressed against the point of his sword. To touch her was death, he knew. Reluctantly, the assailants turned around and left.

Higuénamota leaned over the young man, who was still breathing. She asked him: '*Como te llamas?*' He whispered: '*Pedro Pizarro.*' She decided that if he survived his injuries he would be her page.

In two hours, they killed more than three thousand people.

On her way back to the palace, Higuénamota was summoned by Atahualpa to serve as his translator once again. He also summoned the queen and the caciques that he'd had imprisoned, and asked them why they'd wanted to kill him; they said it wasn't them, but the inquisitors of the Suprema who had dragged them into this affair; that the Holy Inquisition was beyond their authority, and that had he been informed King Charles would never have approved such a crime.

After reproaching them for their perfidy, he set them free, and the next day, the town was full of women and children again, as if nothing extraordinary had happened.

For the two weeks that they spent in Toledo, a profound sense of peace reigned over the town and its environs; there was so much bustle in the streets that nobody would ever have guessed anyone was missing; business went on as usual. Only the heads of the priests, exhibited in the main square, served as a reminder of the recent events.

However, Atahualpa, who was responsible for his people – even if there were fewer than two hundred of them now – had to decide how to proceed. He ordered the burning of the green cross that had accompanied the inquisitors' ceremony, but thought it more prudent, for now, not to demand the removal of the innumerable effigies of the nailed god.

He reiterated to the queen and her minister Tavera his wish to meet King Charles. The queen told him that her husband had gone to defend a large eastern city threatened by the rival Turkish empire, but that messengers informing him of their presence had already been sent.

So they had to wait. But waiting, as Atahualpa knew, is a cruel mother that saps soldiers' morale, all the more so when it is linked to inaction.

Chalco Chimac remarked that it might be better not to remain in a city where they had just massacred three thousand of its inhabitants.

Quizquiz suggested that they go to meet Charles, but Ruminahui objected that while they had been able to take advantage of the earthquake in Lisbon and the disorder it had created at the time of their arrival, marching blindly into a war about which they knew nothing – neither the size of the armies in the field nor the terrain itself – and whose finer details they didn't grasp at all, held far too many dangers and uncertainties, all the more so as their group consisted mostly of civilians, albeit civilians hardened by more than a year of fighting for their lives.

So it was that they presented themselves before the queen. They had agreed beforehand that she would receive them, since they had not wanted to strip her of the outward manifestations of her royal authority until they had a better idea of how to behave in this strange land. Atahualpa wore a golden shield over one pectoral and was draped in a long white alpaga cape, an outfit that made a powerful impression on the Levantine audience, but he decided not to speak. So Higuénamota said that they had come to ask for a safe-conduct.

'*Adonde?*' asked the queen.

'Salamanca,' replied the Cuban princess.

The queen shot an anxious glance at her mummy-faced minister. Cardinal Tavera asked why they had chosen that destination. Higuénamota replied that, while they waited for King Charles to return, they wished to make use of their time to study the history and customs of the kingdom of Castile, and those of the New World in general.

'*Barbari student!*' exclaimed Tavera, rolling his eyes.

But in truth the Levantines were in no position to argue. The safe-conduct was delivered, with letters of recommendation addressed to the most eminent theologians in Salamanca.

The old woman who had warned Higuénamota came to find her again. She wanted to join the Quitonians, with her son, but also with twenty other people. She kept repeating '*Cubanos! Cubanos!*' Atahualpa, who listened to this uncomprehendingly, realised that – in the eyes of the old woman, and probably most of the Levantines they had met, including the queen and the cardinal – they were all Cubans, just like his translator. He wanted to know why these people wished to go with them. The old woman told Higuénamota that after they had left, other inquisitors would arrive, and that people like her would continue to be persecuted.

So Atahualpa received his first reinforcements, in the form of a few desperate converso families, a handful of pale-skinned and probably crazy heretics, and the half-dead young Pedro Pizarro.

13. Maqueda

Yet again the young sovereign had found, if not a goal that would make them forget themselves, at least a destination, a direction, an impetus that would unite his troops and give them the momentum and strength needed to prevent this impossible, inconceivable voyage – which had first taken them to the gates of Cuzco only to drive them far away, allowed them to touch the navel of the world before sending them to its outer edges – from tipping over completely into mere wandering, or at least to prevent the band of Quitonians from fully realising it. Because if they ever did, they would probably suspect, one after another, that they had washed up on the shores of insanity. Pachacuti's blood flowed through Atahualpa's veins, and that, perhaps more than anything else, had guided his decisions up to this point, because he had not yet studied the political philosophy of a certain Levantine from Florence, whose words would only confirm the gifts for government bequeathed to him by his famous great-grandfather, known as the Reformer.

On the way to Salamanca, they stopped at the gates of a village called Maqueda. Suspecting that rumours of the massacre in Toledo must have spread throughout the region, Atahualpa set up camp outside the village and sent two emissaries: Quizquiz, for his skills as a scout, and Higuénamota, for her knowledge of the language.

The villagers had gathered in their temple. Quizquiz and Higuénamota, who had hidden her nudity under a cape, slipped inside and witnessed a strange scene. A shaved man was giving a speech from inside a wooden box to a somewhat unruly audience. The two visitors were treated to a very different spectacle from the solemn ceremony that had led to the pyres in Toledo; this one was lacking in both pomp and gravitas.

But suddenly, a man wearing a sword on his belt interrupted the shaved man's speech and heaped him with insults. Although she couldn't follow all the details, Higuénamota understood that the man with the sword was accusing the shaved man of not being what he claimed. The two men started hurling abuse at each other until the shaved man fell to his knees inside his hut and, joining his hands and staring up at the ceiling, prayed to his god to intercede on his behalf.

Immediately, as if struck by lightning, the man with the sword collapsed on the floor. He started convulsing and foaming at the mouth. All the Levantines present were seized with terror and began yelling confusedly, begging the shaved man to lift his magic spell. He agreed to come out of his hut and he walked through the crowd to where the man's body lay jerking in spasms. Leaning down over him, the shaved man put a sort of roll of paper on his head and uttered a few words. Their meaning was obscure, but the convulsions ceased immediately.

The man with the sword, having regained his senses, hastily pledged his allegiance and then withdrew. The immediate consequence of this episode was that the crowd rushed towards the shaved man, handing him little round pieces of copper and silver. They repeated a word that the Cuban princess did not know: '*indulgencia*'.

Quizquiz and Higuénamota were impressed by the powers of the nailed god (if it really was, as they supposed, Jesus whom the shaved man had invoked to punish his detractor). They went back to report this episode to Atahualpa, who, as usual, did not look remotely concerned. All the same, he decided it would be wise to assess this threat. The morale of his troops was precarious; the last thing he needed was for it to be dented any further by potentially hostile supernatural forces. But how could he find out the truth of the matter? After the affair in Toledo, Atahualpa wished to keep a low profile, so he was reluctant to order the abduction of the shaved sorcerer. For now, he preferred to limit his contacts with the locals. Then they remembered that some Levantines had joined their group.

Young Pedro Pizarro, saved from the massacre by Higuénamota, was recovering from his wounds. In the evenings, he would tell stories about his country, which she translated for Atahualpa's wives and sisters. She went to see him and described the scene she had witnessed in the temple of Maqueda, then asked him about the source of the shaved man's powers. After listening attentively to his protector's account, Pedro Pizarro laughed softly.

'What you saw,' he said, 'is not magic. It's just two knaves who came up with a trick to con the villagers out of their money. The priest is selling indulgences. In other words, he demands money in return for bulls that he writes himself, probably in dog Latin, which supposedly allow the buyer to redeem his sins and save his soul. I'm certain that the alguazil who pretended to argue with him will get a share of the profits.'

Higuénamota translated this without understanding it. But what the Quitonians were interested in was the power of defeating one's enemies at a distance, which the shaved man seemed to take from his nailed god, and how he made the god do what he wanted. So Pedro Pizarro, who was young but not stupid, painted them a more explicit picture: 'If you go back to the village tonight, after the sun has set, you will probably see your priest in his lodging, sharing a drink with his accomplice, the two of them toasting the health of the gullible public who gave them money after witnessing their ridiculous farce.' And young Pizarro, exhausted by his injuries, added one more thing before turning over in his bed and going back to sleep: 'How many similar tricks have been played by charlatans like that on the poor simple people of this land!'

This was their first lesson about the New World.

14. Salamanca

Escalona, Almorox, Cebreros, Avila … They passed through other villages, encountered other people. It was a parade of stray dogs, beggars, men on horseback, processions of wooden crosses. By the sides of the roads, as in Tawantinsuyu, peasants working the fields raised their heads to watch them pass.

In the evenings, Pedro Pizarro regaled them with tales from *Orlando Furioso*: stories of Roland and Angelica, of Renaud on his faithful Bayard, of Bradamante and the hippogriff, and Roger, and Ferragus searching for his helmet, and Olympia grappling with Cimosco, the king of Friesland.

He told how Gradasso, King of Sericana, came to capture the Emperor Charlemagne himself, but was then defeated by Aistulf, armed with an enchanted lance: Atahualpa, who remembered his own capture by Huascar's men, then his escape, at the very start of the civil war, listened closely to this passage. Likewise, he made Pedro Pizarro repeat the descriptions of arquebuses in the story of Olympia. He wanted to know everything there was to know about culverins, falconets, bombards, because these weapons were not chimeras; the shy young man assured him that, unlike the random vengeances of the nailed god, the devastation wreaked by these machines could be controlled and timed, once you had learned how to use them. Even Pizarro himself, young as he was, had received some basic military training from his uncles and cousins. During rests, when the others in the group set up camp, he would instruct Atahualpa's soldiers in the use of the fire sticks. Quizquiz considered them more noisy than effective.

Higuénamota loved this bright young man whom she had taken under her wing. Atahualpa appreciated him for his knowledge of this country and this world. It was in this way he learned that Spain was at war with a country called France.

At an inn in Tejares, they found a little negro boy. His mother was a mistreated servant there. Pitying the child, Atahualpa's wives decided to take him with them.

Finally, Salamanca appeared on the horizon. They discovered a city whose beauty surpassed that of Toledo. Ruminahui showed the letter of safe-conduct to the local authorities, who welcomed the foreigners with a display of honours and a hint of fear. Once again, they were looked after by shaved men, a category of the population that seemed responsible for a wide range of activities: worshipping their god, making the black drink, storing and maintaining the talking sheets. They were priests, archivists, but also amautas, since they argued about the mysteries of the world and told many tales; they were also haravecs, since some of them wrote poems that followed very orderly systems of verses and stanzas. In addition to all this, they sang a lot, always in unison: slow, sad melodies, never accompanied by any instrument other than their voices. As in Lisbon, they lived in the most magnificent buildings despite apparently having made a vow of poverty.

In the doorway of one of these buildings, some students were playing a game where they had to find a stone frog hidden among the interlaced sculptures. Atahualpa, who had stopped to admire the work, did not see the frog. A blindman who was begging nearby told him: *'Quien piensa que el soldado que es primero del escala tiene mas aborrecido el vivir?'* The Inca, who had descended from his litter, did not take offence at being addressed in this way; he asked Higuénamota to translate (even though he, too, was beginning to understand snatches of Castilian now).

The beggar's words were strange: 'No writing must be destroyed or thrown away unless it is truly odious; instead, it should be shown to everybody, especially if it won't do any harm and they might get some good out of it.'

The shaved man who had accompanied them wanted to make the blindman shut up, but Atahualpa overruled him with a wave of his hand. And so the blindman was free to follow the thread of his obscure thoughts: 'If this were not so, there would be very few people who would write for only one reader, because writing is hardly a simple thing to do. But since writers go ahead with it, they want to be rewarded, not with money but with people seeing and reading their works, and if there is something worthwhile in them, they would like some praise. Along these lines, Cicero says: "Honour promotes the arts."'

And Pedro Pizarro, who had done some studying, explained in a low voice that Cicero was a very great amauti who had lived long ago.

'Does anyone think that the first soldier to stand up and charge the enemy hates life? Of course not; a craving for glory is what makes him expose himself to danger. And the same is true in arts and letters.'

And, sensing the presence of the shaved man, the old blindman turned to him: 'The preacher gives a very good sermon and is really interested in the improvement of people's souls, but ask his grace if he minds when they tell him: "Oh, what an excellent sermon you gave today!"'

The blindman burst out laughing. Atahualpa took off one of his earrings and put it in the man's hand. Then they continued their visit, while the shaved man talked about *index*, *heretico*, and *auto de fe*.

There was one thing they had witnessed that never ceased to surprise Atahualpa and Higuénamota: among the inhabitants were certain men replete with everything they needed and desired, and, begging at their doors, other men stripped bare by hunger and poverty. Atahualpa – and Higuénamota, in particular – found it strange that these poor men could suffer such injustice without strangling the rich men, or setting fire to their houses.

Pedro Pizarro knew how to decipher the talking sheets. He had got hold of a work secretly translated by a shaved man, and discreetly passed from hand to hand, and he would read extracts of this book to the Inca emperor and his Cuban mistress: 'For the nobles, seeing that they cannot resist the people, begin to have recourse to the influence and reputation of one man, and make him prince, so as to be protected by his authority.'

It was a political treatise freshly arrived from a country called Florence, and young Atahualpa, with his atavistic wisdom, sensed that this book could be useful to him in the future when he read this passage: 'Moreover, you cannot satisfy the nobles with honesty, and without wrong to others, but it is easy to satisfy the people, whose aims are ever more honest than those of the nobles; the latter wishing to oppress, and the former being unwilling to be oppressed.'

This is not to say that the young emperor was excessively concerned about the well-being of the people. He had, without hesitation, crushed the revolts of the Canaris, and those dogs of Tumbes, as he liked to call them, not to mention the ones in Toledo. But he sensed a responsibility towards his own people, this people of fewer than two hundred souls, the survivors of Chinchaysuyu. To save them, he knew that he would have to confront vast numbers of powerful adversaries, and to win this battle he would have to draw up a shrewdly political plan that used all the advantages of the terrain and a finely sharpened understanding of power ratios and balances. This Niccolò Machiavelli struck him as a rather good adviser.

Quizquiz pored over maps of the region: he wanted to know about the contours of the mountains and the valleys, the extent of the plains; he wanted to understand the nature of the rivers and marshlands. He gave a great deal of care to all this.

Chalco Chimac was being taught the discipline governing the application of laws and punishments by a famously erudite shaved man called Francisco de Vitoria.

Higuénamota was learning to decipher the talking sheets from her young protégé, who had also become her private tutor and – some said – rather more.

As for Atahualpa, he was discovering, to his fascination, the intertwined histories of the local kings.

All of them remained baffled by the shaved men's explanations of the fables contained in the thick talking case, which they quoted at any opportunity, never let out of their sight, and seemed to regard with a sort of obsessional devotion. The sacerdotal hierarchy to which they belonged also appeared absurdly complex. Nevertheless, the Quitonians understood two things: there was a place called Rome, which all the shaved men held in reverence, and a priest called Luther who got them all worked up. Even Francisco de Vitoria, who seemed wiser than most, could not hide his agitation when this Luther was mentioned. Atahualpa and his people were baffled by the nature of the disagreement, but it was obviously important because wars were being fought over it in the north.

One fable especially annoyed them: the story of a shepherd who was stripped by his god of everything he possessed – wife, children, cattle, health, wealth – because of a bet that the god had made with a demon, out of boredom or pride, to prove the piety of this miserable wretch and to show how devoted he would remain under any circumstances. This god did not strike the Quitonians as a serious being, and the fact that he ultimately restored all the shepherd's goods, wife, children and cattle (and gave him more wealth than he'd had before, as a sort of apology for the dirty trick he'd played) only increased their contempt for him. Never would Viracocha have done anything so puerile and cruel. As for the Sun, his implacable course set him far above such childish games.

On the other hand, they were interested in the ceremony of Mass. The sound of the organ struck their ears and touched their hearts. Little Cusi Rimay and Quispe Sisa, playacting as children do, learned to make the sign of the cross and said that they wanted to be baptised.

As the days passed, the shaved men of Salamanca grew more inclined than those in Lisbon had been to develop relationships with the young Quitonian women. Some of the girls became pregnant. Some of the shaved men became ill.

Atahualpa enjoyed listening to Francisco de Vitoria explaining natural law, positive theology, free will and other notions whose complexity – allied to the fact that the Inca still spoke very little Castilian – made understanding a matter of chance, and dialogue extremely limited.

Then, one day, the news reached them that Charles Quint had returned. Pedro Pizarro had told them so many stories of paladins that they were expecting to meet Charlemagne, king of the Franks, and his nephew Roland armed with his faithful Durendal. But this Charles wasn't just anybody either, as they would soon realise. His army, which was supposed to be formidable, was approaching Salamanca, preceded by rumours of its victories in distant lands. (The reality was more ambiguous, but they would not discover that until later.)

They decided that a secret delegation would be sent to meet King Charles. Chalco Chimac and Quizquiz were put in charge of this embassy, but Atahualpa would not agree to let Higuénamota accompany them: he refused to let her become this Charles's Angelica. In her place, as translator, they sent a shaved man who had begun learning the Quechua language. Anyway, the embassy was just an excuse for a scouting mission. All the same, Chalco Chimac thought it best to take Atahualpa's puma with him, along with a few parrots, just in case.

15. Charles

There were about thirty horsemen on the road. A river barred their way, so they forded it. Then the camp appeared. Large tents covered the plain. Were they expected? Soldiers in breeches stepped aside to let them through. The horses advanced into a forest of lances and flags. They were taken to see a bald man with a white beard, draped in a black fur coat, a silver chain around his neck, a ring set with a red stone on his left hand. He invited

Quizquiz and Chalco Chimac to enter a tent guarded by fourteen heavily armed soldiers. The two generals dismounted and walked inside, escorted only by their translator, their parrots and the puma on a leash.

Inside the tent, Charles Quint, surrounded by courtiers, sat on a wooden chair. He had a black beard, a red doublet and white stockings. The two visitors were struck by his crocodile jaw and his tapir nose. Chalco Chimac tried to step forward to give him the parrots, but two guards immediately blocked his path. The birds were taken away, which made the two generals think that their gift had been accepted, but the monarch had still not uttered a word, hadn't even glanced at the multicoloured feathers. The man sat with his mouth open and seemed lost in his thoughts. At his feet lay a long white dog, which he stroked mechanically. The silence lengthened, broken only by the yowls of the puma; the dog responded with a faint growl, and for a long time this was the only dialogue. The two generals stood uncertainly, waiting. At last, the emperor gave a signal and the Quitonians were handed a cup of too-pale akha that only Chalco Chimac accepted. Charles himself was served in a gold cup, which he drained in a single swallow. He wiped the foam from his lips with the back of his hand. The drink was accompanied by a roasted chicken served on a silver platter: the king tore a thigh off the bird and began gnawing methodically at it. The Quitonians watched, fascinated, as grease dripped into his beard. Then he tossed the half-eaten meat to his dog and spoke in a strange voice, so quiet it was almost inaudible. He wanted to know if, as his wife had told him in her letters, Atahualpa's men had come from the Indies across the Ocean Sea. He felt certain that they were not from the island of Vera Cruz, where the Portuguese got their wood, because according to his sister, the queen of Portugal, the men there were just cannibals and savages. While Chalco Chimac was trying to explain Tawantinsuyu and the war between Atahualpa and his brother, the monarch cut him off. He wanted to talk about his own wars against a very powerful foe named Suleiman. Chalco Chimac assured him that, if he wished it, Atahualpa and his men would go east and subdue this Suleiman. Charles Quint gave a high-pitched laugh. The men around him laughed too, but the Quitonians couldn't tell whether their laughter was indulgent or whether they, too, thought the idea extravagant. At last, Charles Quint stood up from his chair (they saw that he was only of middling height) and yelled that Atahualpa must pay for the outrage in Toledo. Emboldened by its master's anger and moved by the desire, characteristic of its species, to ape, please and defend him, the long white animal jumped to its feet and barked at the visitors. But in doing so, it came a little too close. The puma gave a deep hiss and, quick as lightning, clawed the dog's muzzle. The dog whined and backed away. Instantly, Charles stopped bellowing and knelt down next to the animal. He spoke to it in a soft voice in an unknown language. He repeated 'Sempere, Sempere ...' The dog licked its master's fingers. A trickle of blood pooled on the ground.

Chalco Chimac said that Atahualpa wished to meet the king of Spain and that he would expect him tomorrow in the main square of Salamanca, in front of the San Martin church. The white-bearded bald man protested at the incomplete pronouncement of his lord's titles, then began to list them – Emperor of the Romans, King of Spain, Duke of Burgundy – but Charles Quint, leaning solicitously over his dog, dismissed the visitors with an impatient wave.

16. Plaza de San Martin

Was he going to come? And when? Rumours spread and the inhabitants of Salamanca began leaving the city.

Atahualpa gathered his council and they concluded that the Quitonians' best chance, considering their situation – which was uncomfortable, not to say desperate – was to ambush this king of Spain. Furthermore, they had nowhere else to go, so they all agreed that they may as well stay where they were. Atahualpa recalled that he had already risked everything, on several occasions, against his brother Huascar, and that he had always somehow escaped. But nobody among his generals, his wives and his men believed that the mortal danger they faced now was in any way comparable to the situations they had experienced before. They had come to the end of the road, and that was that. The only thing left to hope for was a glorious death. The underworld awaited them.

Nevertheless, Ruminahui led the preparations. He gave Puka Amaru the task of collecting steel balls for the catapults, arrows for the bows, and all kinds of throwing weapons, with a preference for short, double-bladed axes, which, when thrown with sufficient strength and skill, could pierce the most solid armour. He set men on the roofs of houses overlooking the square and the alleys leading to it. He fitted bells to the horses to sow terror among the Levantines, then hid them in the San Martin church. He ordered all available artillery to be aimed at the enemy occupying the plain. He told his men to capture Charles alive.

Chalco Chimac wanted to believe in the possibility of a negotiated solution, but Ruminahui yelled at him: 'What do you want to negotiate? What solution are you talking about? We have nothing to offer but our surrender. And what condition can we place upon that? That we're strangled before they burn us? The underworld will not accept your ashes.'

Atahualpa knew that the time had come to inspire his men, candidly, without ceremony, without any intermediaries, because, after all, they were all going to die together, after sharing so many trials. So he spoke to them as if to companions. 'Do any of you think that the first soldier to stand up and charge the enemy hates life?' History, he told them, will record that a few men, in this far-off land, stood up to a mighty army. He had not been wasting his time in Salamanca's monasteries. He told them about Roland in Roncevaux, about Leonidas at Thermopylae. But he also told them how Hannibal triumphed against the Roman legions in Cannes. If they died, the underworld of the serpent-god would welcome them as heroes. If not, history would celebrate the 183 warriors who, by bringing down an empire, covered themselves in glory and riches. The men roared, axes in the air. Then they went to their posts.

By morning, the city's inhabitants had all fled, except for a few beggars and a handful of conversos. The stray dogs were surprised by their sudden loneliness. The silence was reminiscent of Lisbon before the storm. The waiting weighed heavy on the men's shoulders. I heard of many Quitonians who were so frightened that they pissed themselves without even realising.

In the Plaza de San Martin, the buildings were arranged in a half-moon shape facing the church, which was on the southern side of the square. The northern and western sides were closed off by stone houses, the ones on the north above arches. The eastern side was more open, blocked only by market stalls and by a tower with a dial at the top that divided the day into twelve equal parts. It was this side that worried the generals. They would have preferred a square that was completely enclosed, with narrow exits under the stone arches – as in Cajamarca, for example. But it was too late for that. Their lookouts were announcing the arrival of Charles Quint.

Infantrymen armed with long-bladed lances marched in front of the emperor, who rode on horseback with members of his court, under a large cloth canopy held up by servants on foot. On either side, in two columns, soldiers in multicoloured uniforms carried halberds and arquebuses. Horse-drawn carriages drew up the rear of the procession. In all, perhaps two thousand men. The main part of the army, which Quizquiz and Chalco Chimac had estimated at forty thousand, remained on the plain. So they would be fighting an enemy only ten times their number. Unlike in Toledo, however, where the civilian population was surprised in its sleep, this time they would be pitched against armed men ready for battle.

Charles Quint wore black-and-gold armour, and his black horse was draped in a red coat.

Higuénamota was sent, alone, to meet him. The Cuban princess had removed her bat-fur coat and advanced naked in the noon sunlight. A murmur ran through the ranks of soldiers. A shaved man who had come with the Levantine army walked towards her, holding up his talking case. '*Reconoces el dios único y nuestro señor Jesus Christ?*' Higuénamota took the leather case and, knowing the words by heart, responded: '*Reconozco el dios único y vostro señor Jesus Christ.*' Then she gave the priest an ironic look and opened the precious case. She read: '*Fiat lux, et facta est lux.*' And she pointed at the sun above their heads.

There was a whistling sound then and an arrow landed in the neck of Charles Quint's horse. Another sound followed immediately – deeper, vibrating – and the horse was hit in its head by an iron ball barely any bigger than the width of a finger. Soon the sky was criss-crossed with projectiles, all concentrated on the horsemen. The snipers, hidden on the rooftops, had been instructed to kill the horses first. They aimed at the chamfers with their bows and their catapults. One after another, the animals collapsed, whinnying tragically. Men yelled: '*Salva el Rey!*' And the guards formed a defensive square around Charles. That was their first mistake.

The second was made by the arquebusiers, who aimed at the snipers on the rooftops but, thanks to their position and the angle, could not hit any of them.

Then the doors of the church opened and the cavalry burst out, led by Atahualpa. The Quitonians' ancient equestrian traditions had made them exceptional horsemen. The timing of the attack was determined by their tactical instincts and the boldness they had forged during their odyssey. The horses' hooves rang out on the cobblestones while they encircled the massed ranks of Levantines, who in their surprise withdrew even closer, so that the arquebusiers no longer had enough space to reload their firearms. All of them were shoved uncomfortably together, entangled in corpses and horses, and since the royal guards who formed the outside line lowered their lances to protect themselves and to guard against any incursions, the whole thing looked like a gigantic epileptic hedgehog.

The horsemen had to keep riding around the Levantine soldiers to stifle any attempt to break the circle. As soon as a lancer tried to harpoon a horse to clear a way out, the next horseman had to swing a sabre at his neck. The arrows and the steel balls kept raining down on soldiers without shields, striking at the heart of the hedgehog. *'Dios salve al Rey!'* Charles Quint's generals surrounded him, protecting him with their bodies.

The Quitonians were winning, but they were running low on ammunition. The Spaniards who were still standing blew into horns taken from the corpses of their comrades to call for help. The army on the plain began to move. The situation had to be resolved, or the Quitonians were done for. They had to put an end to this quickly. So Ruminahui whipped his horse and galloped towards the lances, then launched himself over them in an extraordinary, impossible leap, landing behind the line of long blades, and the horse trampled on enemy soldiers while Ruminahui swung his huge hammer right and left, pounding the men in their armour like a chef tenderising meat.

A breach opened up and the others rushed into it. In that instant, the Quitonians were like demons, possessed by the thirst for blood. With axes they dug out a human trench that led straight the king. They had not forgotten that he was their objective, but – in the homicidal frenzy that drove them onwards – could anyone swear that he remembered the instruction to take the Spanish monarch alive?

So Atahualpa rushed over, and his horse, like the others, trampled the living and the dead. He rode into the melee, where he could just make out the king's black armour, still shining in the hot sun but sinking under axe blows, and Atahualpa in turn began slashing at everyone he saw – Levantines, Quitonians, it didn't matter any more – because he knew that his life and those of his men depended on keeping Charles Quint alive.

Charles fought bravely and the Duke of Alba fought and died beside him under a storm of swords, and the Duke of Milan fought and fell under a hail of axes, and the poet Garcilaso de la Vega died trying to protect his king from the blades that whipped the air, probing for chinks in Spanish armour, and Charles too was about to die because he fell in turn and the weight of his armour prevented him from getting to his feet again, like an overturned tortoise, so the Quitonians threw themselves at him to tear him to pieces like dogs fighting over a carcass and they chopped chunks off his armoured shell as if they were trophies. But Charles struggled – he wasn't dead yet – and he squirmed like a wounded animal and his attackers found it hard to finish him off.

At last Atahualpa was in their midst, but by that point emperors had ceased to exist, on both sides, and his men didn't listen when he yelled at them to stop, so he had to strike at them with his axe and urge his horse forward and, when he finally reached the king, he spun around and jumped off his horse and helped Charles to his feet.

The king had wounds to his cheek and his hand – the blood dripping from under his glove – and his clothes had been torn off

so he was half-naked, but Atahualpa's hand on his shoulder protected him like a magic spell: suddenly the soldiers were jolted
out of their murderous fury, their avenging arms frozen in flight.
The battle ended. The sun was still beating down on the square.
On the dial of the tower, the big hand had returned to its starting point.

17. The Incades, *Book I, Verse 11*

Nor conquests fabulous nor actions vain,
The Muse's pastime, here adorn the strain:
Orlando's fury, and Rugero's rage,
And all the heroes of th' Aonian page,
The dreams of bards surpass'd the world shall view,
And own their boldest fictions may be true;
Surpass'd and dimm'd by the superior blaze
Of Atahualpa's deeds, which Truth displays.

18. *Granada*

Some claim that in laying this ambush, Atahualpa was guilty of
great treachery, but one should consider the threats that Charles
Quint had made before the Inca emissaries about the Toledo
massacre. Furthermore, the Quitonians had been able to observe
how the devotees of the nailed god treated those who did not
share their beliefs in every detail, and this subject was so close to
their hearts that submission to their fables was the first thing that
the priest demanded of Higuénamota when they met in the
square at Salamanca.

In any case, his capture plunged the king of Spain into the deepest dejection, and the New World into a state of stunned disbelief.

Atahualpa knew that the Quitonians' survival was linked inexorably to the life of their hostage. He decided to leave Salamanca for a better fortified place.

The Quitonian procession crossed through Spain, escorted by Charles's army, which encircled it, a hostile shadow. Atahualpa and his people were like a little cuy followed by a huge puma, eager to devour it. They had to foil several escape attempts engineered from without, but were helped in this regard by the melancholic mood into which the king had sunk, depriving him of all hope and initiative.

When they came to the end of their journey, they moved into a red palace built in another age on a rocky spur by the representatives of a rival religion, who had lived there for a long time before being expelled quite recently. The Alhambra in Granada now became their Sacsayhuaman fortress.

Inside the edifice, behind the walls, was a palace that had been built especially for Charles, but where he had never yet set foot. Although construction was not complete, Atahualpa rectified this anomaly by installing the king there, along with his servants, his courtiers, his dog, and all the facilities due to his rank. His wife and his two children left Toledo and came to join him. Little by little, he shrugged off his torpor and the monarch re-emerged from beneath the shell of the broken man. To assist this process, Atahualpa offered him all the trappings of power and kept him busy with the affairs of his empire. The king was allowed to receive emissaries from all over the New World, who came to enquire about this extraordinary new situation and the political consequences it would undoubtedly provoke. Once they had seen the king, these emissaries were taken to meet the Inca. In this way, Atahualpa was able to sketch the political map of the continent, with the reigning sovereign at the centre, in his power.

Charles Quint's empire seemed almost as vast as Tawantin-suyu, if more fragmented: in the south-west there was Spain, in the north the Netherlands and Germany, in the east Austria, Bohemia, Hungary and Croatia, menaced by Suleiman, a formidable conqueror who reigned over another distant empire. In the south, close to Spain but separated from it by the sea, was a region that seemed coveted by all: Italy, a land of perpetual warfare, where the chief of the shaved men lived, the earthly representative of the nailed god. Charles's great rival for supremacy in the New World was the king of a country that cut his empire in two: France, a land whose own territory was threatened by an island to the north called England. A small confederation in the heart of the continent, Switzerland, provided soldiers for armies everywhere. Spain's neighbour Portugal was a kingdom of explorers, who sailed over the seas in search of other worlds.

At the south-west tip of Spain, a strait named the Pillars of Hercules opened towards the Ocean Sea, which the Quitonians had crossed. On the other side of this strait lay the northern edge of the land of the Moors, whom the kings had expelled from Spain forty harvests before. (Higuénamota calculated that this coincided with the Spaniards' arrival at her island.) Some of these Moors had remained in Granada, even after the defeat of their chiefs; they were called Moriscos. They lived on a hill that faced the Alhambra – Albaicín, which meant, in their language: 'the miserable'.

Outside Granada, the imperial army had set up camp in a fortified town called Santa Fe, where the Spanish court had gathered to try to settle on a strategy to deal with the crisis caused by the capture of their king.

Assembled there were the most powerful people in the kingdom, other than the king himself: the mummy-headed adviser

Juan Pardo Tavera; old Nicolas Perrenot de Granvelle, who had led Chalco Chimac and Quizquiz to meet Charles Quint in his tent; Francisco de los Cobos y Molina, his secretary of state, who wore a large red cross around his neck inlaid with an enormous ruby; Antonio de Leyva, the Duke of Terranova and Prince of Ascoli, who had survived the massacre of San Martin but who had lost the use of his legs in the battle, where he'd been left for dead. Antonio de Leyva pleaded the case for an immediate assault, but the others considered the Alhambra to be impregnable, at least while the emperor was held hostage there.

It was true that the Salamanca ambush had enabled the Quitonians to escape a seemingly hopeless situation, but it remained one of the greatest uncertainty. Atahualpa gloried in his victory and the prestige it had brought him, but he knew that its benefits would be fleeting if they were not consolidated. Soon, the element of surprise would no longer be enough, since the imbalance in the rival forces remained problematic: they were still just a handful of people against the rest of the world.

Atahualpa was reassured by the deference emissaries from all over the continent showed his prisoner: with the king of Spain at his mercy, he knew he held a precious asset. Charles himself reinforced this idea when he suggested that the Quitonians keep his two children as hostages – little Prince Philip, the heir to the empire, who was five years old, and his sister Marie, one year his junior – in exchange for his freedom. That proposal made Atahualpa laugh. Charles, embarrassed, laughed too, while glancing uneasily at his wife.

Whenever Charles received a visitor in his half-built palace, the visitor would be led to the adjoining palace, that of the former kings, where Atahualpa had taken up residence. The visitor walked through dark rooms where the motto of Charles Quint, King of Spain and Holy Roman Emperor, had been engraved in the design of a white pillar inlaid with blue ceramic: *Plus ultra*, which, in the language of the amautas of this world, meant 'further beyond', and which Atahualpa decided to adopt for his own use. Then the visitor passed in front of a long pool bordered by hedges, its water reflecting the building's arches like upside-down boats, guarded by a solid red stone tower in the shape of a crenellated cube, until finally he entered the ambassadors' suite, plunged in almost total darkness. At the end of this room, three alcoves had been dug into the wall, opening on to the plain and the snow-covered mountains of Granada, but the windows were partially obscured by blinds. Atahualpa sat in the embrasure of the central window. To his right stood the giant Ruminahui. To his left, Princess Higuénamota lay on some cushions.

After leaving the sun-drenched courtyard, the visitor would blink, dazzled by the rays of sunlight that filtered through the holes pierced in the windows, barely able to distinguish the backlit figures of the monarch and his two advisers, who appeared to him as asymmetric shadows. Above his head, a beautifully worked wooden ceiling represented the starry sky, making him feel even smaller.

Upon first seeing this room, where his ancestors had accepted the surrender of those former kings in days gone by, Charles Quint had exclaimed: 'How sad they must have been, to lose such beauty.' He had spent a wonderful time here with the queen after their wedding, their intimacy cut short by affairs of state, and he had never returned since. When he heard that phrase, Atahualpa said to Charles: 'How sad must be he who, privileged to enjoy such beauty, did not do so when he had the chance.' And he consoled him for his misfortune by showing the king that, thanks to him, Charles could savour the splendours of the palace conquered by his ancestors.

One of the first visitors was the former master of Granada, Boabdil, expelled from the palace forty harvests before, who came on the off chance that he might be able to claim something;

but the old man in the turban was given nothing and he returned to his exile, to die soon after. Shaken by this visit, Charles said to his entourage (and his words were reported to his host): 'I am the Unfortunate One.'

Atahualpa received a very young man from Florence, the city of the amauta Machiavelli, whose works he had studied in Salamanca. The young man's name was Lorenzino and he was a member of a great family, the Medicis. He seemed full of a strange passion when he exclaimed: 'Ah, if only republicans were men ...!' Neither Higuénamota nor Pedro Pizarro had any idea what this meant, but Lorenzino spoke to the Inca of tremendous palaces and remarkable treasures to lure him into complicated wars. Above all, he wanted his aid to overthrow his cousin, the king of Florence, a depraved man who tyrannised his people. Intrigued by the descriptions of this fabulous land, Quizquiz dreamed of going off to discover it, but Atahualpa – who was less than enthused by the idea of a political regime based on a sort of lordly collegiality whose authority came from the people rather than the Sun – would only agree to grant asylum and protection to the young Florentine.

A man from a German city called Augsburg had been sent by a family, the Fuggers, who were not exactly lords or curacas but who were at the head of a sort of ayllu. They were merchants who traded in gold and silver. The envoy was clothed very simply, and Charles treated him with disdain. Nevertheless, the Quitonians had noticed an odd imbalance: in Levantine society, gold and silver were not used only for ornamentation or as signs of nobility, but conferred considerable power on whomever possessed them by enabling – through the use of little round pieces of those metals – the acquisition and exchange of all sorts of goods. The Fuggers' envoy was pressing the emperor to keep certain promises that had been written on talking sheets, which were used as quipus, and explaining to him that his supply of gold and silver would be cut off if he did not keep those promises. This prospect seemed to put Charles in a very difficult position. As for Atahualpa, he smiled as he daydreamed of his Andes mountains, which were stuffed full of those metals.

An amauta, also from Augsburg, came to talk to him about the 'real' presence of the nailed god during religious ceremonies that involved drinking the black drink and eating bread. His name was Philip Melanchthon and he wore a flat hat made of black cloth. Atahualpa pretended to listen attentively because he had noticed that Charles did not like this man or his ideas and yet the king had spent a long time with him and appeared, if not exactly worried (because he had other things to worry about, given his current predicament), at least strangely preoccupied by these questions. Melanchthon was the envoy of a man whom Charles considered a demon: the infamous Luther, who had fomented a religious revolt because he wanted to reform aspects of the Christian cult and challenge certain points of doctrine, the importance of which the Quitonians found it hard to understand.

A shaved man arrived from Paris, where he had gone to study, to speak with him about the best way of countering Luther's growing influence. The new situation created by the sudden entrance of Atahualpa had somewhat altered the continent's political priorities; yet, in the eyes of the representatives of the local religion – whose fervent defender the king of Spain considered himself to be – defeating these rebel reformers in the north remained an urgent issue. Atahualpa listened with interest to the shaved man, whose name was Iñigo López de Loyola. He was a small man with a lively gaze that seemed to mingle cunning and goodness. He liked to speak about his beliefs and he did so with a clarity that helped the Quitonians increase their knowledge of the New World's legends.

The Levantines believed in a family of gods comprising a father, a mother and their son. The father lived in the sky and he sent his son to earth to save men but, after many adventures and misunderstandings, the father let his son be nailed to a cross by the men he was trying to help because they didn't recognise him. Then the son returned from the underworld and joined his father in the sky. Since that day, mortified by their mistake, the Levantines had been waiting and hoping for the son to return to earth. At the same time, they constantly prayed for and venerated the mother, who had the strange and unique gift of remaining a virgin after the father had fertilised her. There also existed a secondary divinity known as the Holy Spirit, who was sometimes confused with the father, sometimes with the son, sometimes with both. The sign that Christians made with their hands at every opportunity represented the cross on which the son had been nailed. Thus, all their actions were supposedly dictated by the desire to make up for the ingratitude that their ancestors had shown to their god when they tortured him and nailed him to a wooden cross at the top of a mountain in a distant land. The Christians had long ago been expelled from that land, but they dreamed of one day reconquering it.

The entire war with the Moors was predicated on the idea that the Moors, although they knew about his existence, refused to pledge their allegiance to the nailed god. They recognised the father but not the son. They also had different dietary habits, and a different language. Apparently this was enough to justify making war on them mercilessly for hundreds of harvests. A third tribe, the Jews, although more ancient, had customs similar to the Moors. For example, they snipped off part of the male baby's penis just after birth, refused to eat pig, and only ate other meat after it had been consecrated by their priests and killed in accordance with certain rites. (On the other hand, they could drink the black drink, which the Moors forbade.) They also did not worship the nailed god, despite the fact that he had been one of theirs. But, unlike the Moors, who had been permitted to stay after the defeat and exile of their last king Boabdil, the Jews, who had neither a king nor a kingdom, had been violently expelled from Spain unless they demonstrated their allegiance to the nailed god and renounced their old customs. Those who went through all this in order to stay, known as conversos, were mistreated and constantly suspected of remaining faithful to their former beliefs. The Inquisition persecuted and often burned them. The shaved man Loyola did not approve of this policy, or of the policy he called *limpieza de sangre*, the purity of blood that ultimately made it impossible to change from one tribe to another. 'Our Lord Jesus is not in our veins,' he said. 'He is in our hearts.'

Having learned all this, Atahualpa decided it was time to find some allies. He suggested to Charles that he should enact a law authorising the different cults to practise throughout his kingdom, then simply add to that list the cult of the Sun. Charles Quint gaped at him, apparently unable to understand what he was talking about, although Higuénamota, now very skilled in her role, had translated the Inca's proposition perfectly. Then the emperor with the prominent jaw started shouting indignantly and spitting like a llama. In the end, he simply refused.

Atahualpa was in no position to impose his decrees upon the Empire, or even upon Spain, but he told Chalco Chimac and Pedro Pizarro to communicate his proposal to the inhabitants of Granada. It created a stir in the white backstreets of the Albaicín, and all the way up to the neighbouring hill of Sacromonte, where the Inquisition had sown fear and dismay. They had begun by burning Jews. Everybody knew what that meant: soon, they would burn Moriscos. The believers in the Moors' religion, however, were unhappy at the prospect of increasing the number of divinities. 'Allah is the greatest!' they repeated ad infinitum. At first, they had no intention of extending their pantheon. However, the example of the conversos, which was close at hand (because they didn't persecute the Jews and lived in harmony with them), led them to give it more thought: hadn't the conversos been forced to adopt the rites and beliefs of their Christian masters? And also to abandon their own customs, on pain of death?

After all, 'Allah is the greatest' didn't mean that *only* Allah is great. Their motto perhaps allowed for the coexistence of their unique god with other secondary divinities.

Some of them began to regard the sun in a different light.

19. Marguerite

Imprisoned in his unfinished palace, whose very roundness seemed to him oddly ironic and bitter (though he didn't know why, exactly), Charles struggled to rise above his melancholy, but he soothed his nerves and recovered his health by playing a game similar to hnefatafl. On a wooden board divided into sixty-four squares, an army of black figurines opposed an army of white ones. The irony, in this case, could hardly escape him: the aim of the game was to capture the enemy king.

He had taught the rules to the Inca generals and, while Chalco Chimac quickly became a formidable opponent, it was Quizquiz who, when his duties allowed, spent his evenings with the emperor, playing the game over and over again and almost always losing.

One day, Quizquiz's lookouts announced the arrival of a female visitor. It was a queen, the sister of the king of France, who was coming to the Alhambra to seek an audience with the two emperors. She was accompanied by a large retinue and her litter was drawn by four snow-white horses. Her hair was styled with infinite care and she was dressed in a coat of the most exquisite texture. Her face and her Castilian were both extremely graceful, although her complexion was pale and her accent different from the people of this region.

Moreover, she spoke with Charles in an unknown language, so that none of the Quitonians could tell what was said between them. Witnesses noted, however, that Charles's face flushed crimson and he almost choked on his anger, while Marguerite (for this was the queen's name) addressed him in the coldest tone imaginable.

Nevertheless, young Lorenzino, who had not yet returned to Florence, was able to fill in the blanks: this was not the first time that the queen had visited the emperor. When Lorenzino was a child, he remembered that the king of France had lost a battle and then been taken prisoner by imperial troops. His sister Marguerite had come to Charles to plead for his release, but in vain. King Francis had finally been freed only after promising to cede vast swathes of his kingdom to the emperor.

Now, in all likelihood, it was those territories that Queen Marguerite had come to reclaim, in the name of her brother and of France.

Having discovered this, Atahualpa agreed to receive her in the ambassadors' hall.

Although he was getting much better at understanding the language of this country, he still wanted Higuénamota to serve as his spokeswoman, partly because he had more time to think while she was translating the Levantines' words, and partly because her presence was dear to him and she had always brought him luck. Her nudity also tended to intimidate his visitors.

To his right, Lorenzino had, for this occasion, taken Ruminahui's place, so that he would be able to clear up any ambiguities in what the queen was saying.

And there were plenty of those.

The queen's kingdom, Navarre, lay between Spain and France, and one of Marguerite's requests was that Charles renounce all claim to her lands.

The king of France wished to recover certain territories in the north, Artois and Flanders, which had been lost under the terms of the Treaty of Cambrai four harvests before.

He wanted the king of Spain to definitively renounce all claim to Burgundy, a region that seemed especially important to both sides.

He also claimed sovereignty over two cities in Italy, Milan and Genoa.

And then there was talk of a land called Provence and the cities of Nice, Marseille and Toulon.

None of this was very interesting to Atahualpa. Why should he care about Burgundy or Artois? What did Milan or Genoa matter to him? They didn't. Each city was just an idea. Less than an idea. A word. He hadn't even known that these places existed a year ago, a moon ago, a week ago, yesterday. Atahualpa's horizon was Andalusia: he had swept aside the claims of a certain Boabdil, who had tried to reclaim what had once been his. But he could, without any qualms, give away bits of an empire that didn't belong to him. He could toss them to the dogs – who cared! They were just dots on a map.

But equally ... why would he?

Marguerite de Navarre lowered her voice. She had understood that Atahualpa had come from over the seas, and not from the east or the south but from the west. Perhaps from the Indies or the Maluku Islands or Cipango, or perhaps from somewhere else. In any case, she knew that he was a long way from home, but that following a certain turn of events, fortune having been on his side, he now held at his mercy Charles Quint, the Holy Roman Emperor, King of Spain, King of Naples and Sicily, Duke of Burgundy. It was a remarkable situation.

She spoke in a voice that was gentle but firm. Never would Christianity accept such a state of affairs. The Pope wouldn't accept it. He would order a crusade to retake Granada, even though his relationship with Charles was not the best. The Inquisition would inevitably declare the Sun worshippers to be heretics. Ferdinand, the Austrian Archduke, would soon come at the head of a formidable army to help his brother. But the great king who came from the sea – at these words, Marguerite made a small bow – could, if he desired, count upon the support of the king of France. Hadn't Francis, her brother, made an alliance with Suleiman, the emperor of the Sublime Porte and chief of the infidels? Unlike Charles, Francis the Very Christian King had not always been a fierce defender of Christianity. Amid the religious disputes that were inflaming the north, he had shown moderation and understanding towards the Lutherans. Which led to only one conclusion: if the emperor from beyond the seas was in agreement, an indissoluble alliance could be forged between the two countries. Francis I, king of the French, offered his friendship and support to Atahualpa. Because, ultimately, who wanted the Sun as his enemy?

Atahualpa listened very carefully to all of this. The queen of Navarre's eloquence, allied to what he understood about the balance of power in the New World, persuaded him to give her everything she asked for, in exchange for the much-needed military aid. In reality, the king of France's offer was providential. But there was one major obstacle: contrary to what Marguerite wanted to believe, Atahualpa was in possession of a king but not a kingdom, and Charles, although a hostage, was still the king and emperor. He alone was in a position to cede the territories of his empire. Atahualpa already knew that no form of pressure or threat could make him give way.

Marguerite returned to France with a parrot and some promises.

The Inca gathered his council in the Court of the Lions. Coya Asarpay suggested killing Charles or making him abdicate in favour of his son, whose extreme youth – he was not yet six harvests old – would guarantee his docility. Quizquiz opposed the death of the king on the basis that it would expose the Quitonians to the vengeance of his subjects. As for Charles, why would he abdicate? He knew that his sovereignty was his best protection; without it, he would be no use to anybody. So the Quitonians were unable to satisfy the king of France's demands. With Charles alive, they couldn't give away his land without his consent. With Charles dead, they had no defence against the imperial army. As it was, the only guarantee they could make was that no offensive would be ordered against the kingdom of France.

The military question was, therefore, unresolved. They needed men to defend themselves and gold to recruit them. In the end, they decided to recall the Fuggers' envoy, who had no objection to advancing them funds, but he demanded guarantees that the Inca was in no position to provide.

So Atahualpa gave Higuénamota a secret mission. The Cuban princess must return to Lisbon. At her request, she would be accompanied by young Pedro Pizarro. They would take with them a few conversos, who – with the aid of mules – would transport several barrels of the black drink, some good swords from Toledo, some fire sticks, some talking cases, some wheat, some paintings and maps of the New World. Charles had agreed to send a message for King Joao III, his brother-in-law, bidding him, for the love of the emperor, to provide the Quitonians with a good ship and the best captain he could find. Atahualpa also gave his Cuban mistress a quipu composed of numerous threads, the arrangement of knots meticulously prepared by his personal archivist, the contents of which even Higuénamota, who had his total trust, was ignorant.

This quipu was a message to be delivered exclusively to his brother Huascar.

20. Sepúlveda

Among Charles's entourage was an amauta who had two tasks: to write the chronicle of the king's reign and to educate his son, little Philip.

This man showed an interest in the Quitonians that seemed sincere. He was always keen to talk with them, asking them many questions about their history, their customs, their beliefs, and demonstrating what appeared to be a genuine sympathy for them. So he was the first Levantine to understand where they were from and what had brought them to Spain.

His name was Juan Ginés de Sepúlveda.

He had one master whose name he often invoked, Aristotle, and two enemies whom he railed against at every opportunity: Erasmus and Luther.

In fact, this man was deceitful and so skilled at hiding his true intentions that he won the trust of the Quitonians, who sent him as an envoy to Santa Fe. His mission was to assure the Spaniards that their king was well treated, as were his wife and children, that he had lost none of his privileges except for freedom of movement, and that he would remain thus protected as long as the Alhambra was not attacked. Consequently, the king ordered the commanders of his army to make no rescue attempts.

Instead of which, Sepúlveda told the Spanish commanders that if they did not intervene their king was at risk of death at any moment, that the queen and the heir were treated so badly that they were wasting away, that they bathed in their own excrement, and that if nothing were done, this would be the end of the royal family and the Spanish monarchy.

He added that Atahualpa and his men were infidels and unbelievers, worshippers of Mohammed, demons sent from hell, heathens who knew and cared nothing about Christ, fornicators and whores who went around naked with no notion of modesty, insulting the eyes and souls of good Christians.

He also repeated what he had learned from those Quitonians who had recklessly confided in him: that their chief had been expelled from his own land by his brother, and that they were, all in all, nothing but a band of fugitives roaming the earth like Jews.

He confirmed that there were fewer than two hundred barbarians, some of them women and children, and added that – from what he had been able to observe – they barely knew how to use an arquebus, or artillery in general.

Antonio de Leyva, the cripple from Salamanca, greeted these words with enthusiasm. But the others – Tavera, Granvelle, Cobos – were more circumspect. The foreigners might be bloodthirsty barbarians, they said, but they were not immune to reason, as attested by all the reports on their actions since they arrived on this continent. They knew that their salvation was dependent on Charles's life: their hostage was valuable only if alive. So, in fact, their weakness and lack of numbers was the best guarantee of the emperor's life.

On the other hand, there were factors that argued in favour of a rapid intervention. They had to pay the troops and were short of money. Fugger refused to lend more until the situation was clarified. Meanwhile, the Swiss were grumbling, the landsknechts impatient. Already, in Flanders, Galicia and Italy, there were reports of violence, pillaging, mutiny. Nobody wanted to live through the fall of Rome again. And if the imperial army collapsed, it would give France the opportunity to attack, something that the council of Spaniards feared more than anything.

Then Tavera pronounced a name, in a threatening voice, although the others weren't sure whom exactly he was addressing: 'Ferdinand will come.' It was highly unlikely that he would countenance these delays.

And so it was decided that Sepúlveda should return to the king to spy on the foreigners and report on their words and actions. He was to prepare an escape plan for Charles or ensure that he was safe in the event of an assault being launched. When the time came, he would open the gates of the Alhambra. Until then, he would continue to pretend to be the Quitonians' friend.

21. The Incades, *Book I, Verse 20*

When Thor, the god who with a thought controls
The raging seas, and balances the poles,
From heav'n beheld, and will'd, in sov'reign state,
To fix the Eastern World's depending fate,
Swift at his nod th' Olympian herald flies,
And calls th' immortal senate of the skies;
Where, from the sov'reign throne of earth and heav'n,
Th' immutable decrees of fate are given.

22. The Alhambra

Moons passed. Atahualpa missed Higuénamota's company, but he no longer needed a translator. Coya Asarpay was expecting his baby. He spoke with Charles and practised his Castilian. Together, they drew up plans to triumph over Suleiman, reconquer Jerusalem and invade the Moors' country. Atahualpa dreamed of that southern sea that Charles called the Mediterranean. Sepúlveda explained to him the mystery of the Eucharist, and in return Atahualpa told him the story of his ancestor Manco Capac. Quizquiz played with little Prince Philip and his sister Marie. Ruminahui inspected the fortress's defences. Quispe Sisa and Cusi Rimay begged Lorenzino to take them to Italy; laughing, he promised to buy them the most beautiful dresses. They planted tomatoes in the gardens of the Generalife, on the hills above the Alhambra. Chalco Chimac watched Sepúlveda because he didn't trust him. And he was right: the Spaniard was planning his king's escape.

Charles wavered between dejection and determination. He would pray for hours on end in the Hall of the Kings in the Palace of the Lions, the very room where his grandmother Isabella and his grandfather Ferdinand had taken their first Mass after the capture of the Alhambra. It was not part of the unfinished palace where he was supposed to reside but was located in the section occupied by Atahualpa and his court. The Inca had generously granted him this freedom, as a mark of esteem and respect for a fellow sovereign.

In reality, Charles was not so dejected that he felt the need to pray for entire evenings. It was Sepúlveda's idea. The Hall of the Kings gave him access to the Palace of the Lions, which in turn adjoined the Comares Palace. Long before, the young Boabdil, held prisoner by his father in a dungeon of the Comares Tower, had escaped out of the window by sliding down a rope made of scarves tied together by his mother.

Charles would adopt the same plan. Atahualpa's men guarded him, but there weren't enough of them for such a large palace, and nobody had seen any point in guarding an empty prison.

The escape attempt failed because, on the day it was to take place, Charles was struck down by gout and could not leave his bed.

The ingenious Sepúlveda did not despair. Every morning, the gates of the Alhambra opened to let in the conversos and

Mohammedans of the Albaicín who worked in the gardens, the kitchen, the laundry and did all sorts of other non-military jobs because there were insufficient Quitonians to do all of this themselves. In the evenings, the gates would open again to let those workers leave. Sepúlveda envisioned disguising Charles and slipping him out among them. He passed along his plan to the men in Santa Fe, and they sent a detachment of soldiers to lie in ambush outside the gates; their task was to pick up the king and take him to a safe place.

On the day in question, at sunset, the two men mingled with the crowd of workers on their way home. In order to pass incognito, they were dressed in the simplest, poorest clothes and wore hoods to cover their faces. But Chalco Chimac, suspicious by nature, observed the opening of the gates every evening from the ramparts above. He recognised Charles's tapir nose as it poked out of his hood and immediately raised the alarm. 'Shut the gates!' he ordered. The king's men, waiting outside, heard this too, and charged to his rescue with cries of, '*Santiago!*' Armed Spaniards ran into the Alhambra. The Quitonians fired at them and they fired back. The workers panicked and in an instant the situation descended into chaos. Arrows and metal balls whistled through the air; men threw themselves to the ground or yelled in pain. The Spaniards, who had come as a small group to avoid detection, retreated. Sepúlveda tried to lead Charles to safety, but suddenly the king collapsed, hit by a bullet from an arquebus. Sepúlveda just had time to make it through the gates before they closed. He managed to flee with the survivors. But Charles remained within, lying on a carpet of corpses. Chalco Chimac rushed over to him. The king of Spain was struggling to breathe.

He took three days to die. Nobody understood his last words.

For the Quitonians, it was a disaster. They knew his death could not be revealed at any cost. They buried the body at night, without ceremony, in the gardens of the Alhambra, in the middle of the tomato plants. But Sepúlveda had seen him collapse and he told the lords in Santa Fe that their king had been mortally wounded and that there was now no reason not to attack the Alhambra. True, the queen and her children were still behind those walls, in the hands of the barbarians, but every good Christian's heart was now devoted purely to the need for vengeance. '*Represalia!*' he shouted.

And yet, how could they be sure that the king was dead? The Spaniards sent delegations that were all turned back. In spite of everything, they still hoped for a miracle and could not resign themselves to the death of their sovereign. Besides, the events as described by Sepúlveda and the other witnesses were so unclear that nobody could even be certain which side had fired the fatal shot. Sepúlveda swore that it came from the ramparts, but his partiality made them doubt his judgement. Not that it would really change anything. Either Charles was alive or he was dead.

The Quitonians made the most of this hesitation among their enemies to settle on a strategy. They suspected that the queen and her children would not be enough to hold back the imperial army, and that an attack was therefore imminent. Defended in numbers, the Alhambra was impregnable, but without a hostage they knew that there weren't enough of them to withstand a siege. Chalco Chimac suggested painting the corpse's face and walking him along the ramparts as if he were alive. The others praised his ingenuity, but his plan was not put into practice.

In fact, there was only one solution: they had to flee. When Santa Fe sent a final ultimatum demanding proof that Charles was still alive, Atahualpa decided that they would leave that very evening, as discreetly as possible. If they managed to reach the mountains, they might have a chance. Either way, they would take the queen and her children with them.

Barely had the last llama in the procession left the gates of the Alhambra than they had to abandon all hope of this plan succeeding. The Spanish were waiting in ambush and they fell upon them. The path to the mountain was cut off. The Quitonians were driven to the foot of the hill, where a small river flows, and the Spanish began to slaughter them there. Coya Asarpay had her first contractions.

On the other side, the Albaicín hill barred the way. They were at the bottom of a gorge and they were going to die. But the Albaicín was not sleeping. In fact, a roar arose from it and it seemed to move like the sea. Its inhabitants watched this scene: the heroic resistance of the foreigners against the Christians as they were decimated by artillery fire and the charges of the Spanish cavalry. In the white backstreets, the roar grew louder. The Moriscos repeated a sentence in their own language, a sentence that they believed had been spoken by their god: 'You will have the rulers that you deserve.' Probably, they spotted an opportunity: political, providential, emotional. Waves of men hurtled down the hillside and crashed into the melee. Where had they found their weapons? In kitchens, in shops, in workshops and fields. Perhaps they had kept them or stolen them or forged them with their own hands in preparation for just such an occasion.

The surprise attack broke the Spaniards' momentum. They were too well equipped and too numerous to be dispersed, but they yielded under the pressure, they fell back. They beat a retreat without breaking rank. But this respite was enough: it enabled the Quitonians to escape from the ravine where they'd become embroiled and to vanish into the labyrinth of white backstreets, where the Spanish would not search for them.

23. Cadiz

The Morisco revolt spread throughout Andalusia. Atahualpa took advantage of the confusion it created to flee yet again. The Albaicín was a refuge while they healed their wounded, but it was not a sanctuary where they could remain indefinitely; sooner or later, the Spanish would return. And this Ferdinand, whose army was reputedly so powerful, would come in person to avenge his brother's death.

Córdoba, Seville ... they avoided the cities now. They had left behind their parrots, their llamas, their cuys, even Atahualpa's puma, bringing only their last three hostages, the queen and her two children: all that remained, now, of the Spanish crown. Those who could ride were on horseback; there were no litters any more, only a few carts to transport the wounded. And this pathetic procession followed the sun, moaning softly, while the vultures above them – the condors of this land – squawked as they circled in the sky.

If Atahualpa had wanted simply to reach the sea, they would have headed south. But it was the west he craved; always further west he went, from dawn till dusk, without ever deviating from his course, driving men and beasts beyond their last reserves of strength, as if he were chasing the sun, as if he wanted to catch it, or reach it, or overtake it. But always the sun, Inti, his ancestor and his god, escaped him, and they arrived in Cadiz.

The city appeared deserted but in fact the inhabitants, not knowing what to expect, were all hiding in their homes, shutters closed. Sensing their mute presence, the Quitonians advanced like pumas. The temple in Cadiz in honour of the nailed god was another impressive building and some of them wanted to stop there to get some rest. But Atahualpa was fixated on reaching the port. His men began to suspect that he was looking for a ship to take him home. Some thought this a good idea. Unfortunately, the port was empty, except for a few small boats; all the ships had left. Only then did Atahualpa consent to move into the temple.

Days passed. The conversos and the Moriscos who had stayed with the Quitonians went out into the city and returned with supplies of food. One day, the son of the old Jewess from Toledo brought alarming news: a detachment of soldiers was approaching; they were searching for the Quitonians, to capture or kill them on the spot, and it was probably just the vanguard. Charles's army was on the march, and Ferdinand's too perhaps. They must flee now.

But Atahualpa didn't want to flee. The men had had enough; his sister-wife was close to giving birth. They had come to the end of the road. Everyone of a rank high enough to speak to him had told him that every hour they delayed was an error with possibly irreparable consequences, but the young Inca seemed undisturbed. He ordered Quizquiz to organise the defence of the city. Cadiz was encircled by ramparts, and they could rely on the support of all the Moriscos in the area, but if they were going to withstand a siege, why leave the Alhambra in the first place? his generals wondered. The walls that surrounded Cadiz were not comparable to the gigantic red citadel perched high on its rocks. Naturally, nobody dared say any of this to Atahualpa. Only Coya Asarpay protested, and her protests were wordless moans as her pregnancy reached its final moments.

The situation quickly degenerated. Quizquiz was able to drive back the Spanish vanguard, but then a new siege began, in conditions that were far more uncertain than before. The remaining inhabitants were hostile to the Quitonians, and the port made them vulnerable to a maritime attack. Atahualpa devoted all his attention to the port, while his generals looked after the ramparts.

And it was there, in the port, that the heaviest weight was dropped on to one side of the scales, shifting the balance of power.

One morning, when the Quitonians knew that the end of the siege was only a matter of days – or possibly even hours – away, five ships appeared on the horizon. Caught off guard, Atahualpa's people thought that they were really done for now. Only Atahualpa himself envisaged another possibility. His gaze focused on the ships' bows. And while his companions waited, resigned, for the first cannon shots, he recognised Higuénamota, Pedro Pizarro and Tupac Hualpa – Huascar's brother, and his own. That was when he knew they were saved, and that this world would be his.

24. The Incades, Book I, Verse 24

Immortal heirs of light, my purpose hear,
My counsels ponder, and the Fates revere:
Unless oblivion o'er your minds has thrown
Her dark blank shades, to you, ye gods, are known
The Fate's decree, and ancient warlike fame
Of that bold race which boasts Atahualpa's name;
That bold avent'rous race, the Fates declare,
A potent empire in the East shall rear,
Surpassing Babel's or the Persian fame,
Proud Grecia's boast, or Rome's illustrious name.

25. The Conquest

Germany, England, Savoy, Flanders … he didn't care about those places. He cared about Andalusia. Castile. Spain. Andalusia was his land, now, and he would die for her, if necessary. But not today.

The ships' holds were full of three things: gold, silver, saltpetre.

With the saltpetre, Quizquiz fed the cannons on the ramparts and dispersed the enemy. He was not attempting to defeat the Spanish army, just to send a message: the situation has changed. Your world will never be the same again. You are the Fifth Quarter.

With the gold and the silver, they could buy men. The news of the ships loaded with gold spread quickly and mercenaries came running. Many soldiers even deserted the Spanish army to join the Incas.

Atahualpa proclaimed that the conversos, Jews, Moriscos, Lutherans, Erasmians, sodomites and witches were now under his protection.

Every day, hundreds of new arrivals swelled his army and proved the truth of his proclamation.

While an emissary was sent to Navarre, another was already galloping towards Augsburg.

Atahualpa took Seville without a single cannon shot being fired. The queen and the heir moved into the Alcazar Palace with him.

He used the port in Seville to establish a maritime link with Tawantinsuyu, via Cuba. This ensured the supply of gold and silver. Fugger would now advance him as much money as he needed.

And in fact, Atahualpa needed quite a lot, because he had big plans. He summoned the Cortes and asked them to immediately confirm the child Philip as the future king of Spain, while simultaneously ratifying Atahualpa himself as regent. In this world, anything seemed possible with gold; or at least, nothing was possible without it. Gold and silver simplified everything.

The party led by Tavera and Granvelle, who had almost destroyed him, now had no means of opposing him; their claim to legitimacy had died with Charles, they had run out of gold, and their army had been ravaged by an unknown disease.

The Inca wasted no time giving Flanders and Artois to the king of France, and Ferdinand's army went off to defend his brother's provinces, leaving Atahualpa at liberty.

And now, he wished to reign. Or rather, since the Spanish crown was not exactly vacant, he wished to govern.

What had he offered to Huascar to make peace? Some black drink, some arquebuses, some wheat, some talking leaves and paintings. The idea that the world was big enough for both of them. And the prospect of new riches, in exchange for riches that Tawantinsuyu already possessed in abundance: gold and silver.

And so the Incas discovered trade, that activity that consists of exchanging goods for money.

Higuénamota had carried out her mission to perfection. She could have stayed in Cuba with her people and never returned. But she decided otherwise, out of love for Atahualpa, perhaps, although she made no mystery of her relationship with young Pizarro. More likely, it was a taste for adventure, the lure of curiosity that tipped the balance. She loved this world of passions and promises; she wanted to find out where it would lead them. And she also wanted to see Italy. In fact, she was sad when she discovered that Lorenzino had returned to his own land. At the time, she didn't know what role fate had in store for the young Florentine.

She didn't know anything about what would happen next.

26. The Incades, *Book I, Verse 74*

Has Heaven, indeed, such glorious lot ordain'd,
By Atahualpa's race such conquests to be gain'd
O'er warlike nations, and on Europe's shore,
Where I, unrivall'd, claim'd the palm before?
... Must these the victor's lordly flag display
With hateful blaze beneath the rising day,
My name dishonour'd, and my victories stain'd,
O'erturn'd my altars, and my shrines profan'd?

27. Young Manco

Tupac Hualpa had brought with him a quipu, which contained Huascar's answer to Atahualpa's message.

Huascar forgave his brother and was willing to forget his past offences since Atahualpa had renounced all claim to the throne of the Four Quarters. At his request, he was sending three hundred men and large quantities of gold, silver and saltpetre. In exchange, he expected more of the black drink, the fire sticks and the magic paintings that gave the illusion of depth. He thanked his brother for sending him the engineer Pedro Pizarro to explain these new weapons. As he could see, the Incas had managed to build their first cannons, and he had installed them on the ships that he had chartered from Cuba.

Huascar, in his infinite goodness, at the request of his brother and out of love for him, would not invade the island home of the Princess Higuénamota (in exchange for a modest tribute).

The quipu had been woven in Tumipampa, where Huascar was staying with his court, because he had not wanted to return to Cuzco, perhaps sensing that events would continue to buffet him northward (as the south was in any case barred by the savage Araucanians).

It had not been straightforward for Higuénamota to reach the emperor, but the Cuban princess had, as always, made a big impression wherever she went. In Lisbon, she had managed to obtain not one, but three ships from Joao, aided, it is true, by the fact that Isabella, the king's sister and Charles Quint's wife, was in Atahualpa's hands. Upon her return to Cuba, the Taínos, who had acquired the necessary knowledge, had built two more boats while she went to find Huascar in the heart of the Empire.

The emperor had deciphered the quipu and, impressed by the gifts that Higuénamota had brought, agreed to grant Atahualpa's requests, since the Four Quarters possessed massive quantities of the products he needed. His brother and general Tupac Hualpa had been given the mission of transporting the merchandise. After examining the maps (which they could now read perfectly) with Higuénamota, Atahualpa decided that his ships would henceforth leave not from Lisbon but from Cadiz, which was closer to Granada.

Tupac Hualpa had come with another of their half-brothers, the young Manco Capac, who had the great honour of bearing his first ancestor's name. Tupac Hualpa left again with ships loaded with weapons, wine and paintings, but young Manco Capac remained. He would be Huascar's ambassador in Seville. Or, in other words, his spy. Atahualpa diplomatically feigned ignorance of this fact.

28. The Alcazar

Seville welcomed the Quitonians in a very different way to the other cities they had visited.

That day, Queen Isabella rode a white horse and was herself dressed in white satin, a sign of mourning. Beside her, Atahualpa wore the scarlet crown of the Sapa Inca on his forehead.

The city's greatest lords – the Duke of Medina Sidonia, the Duke of Arcos, the Marquess of Tarifa – had come to meet them, along with the mayor (the curaca in charge of running the city), and they bowed collectively before the queen and the Inca.

Young Philip and his sister stood behind them, as did an army of six thousand men.

As they entered the city, Chalco Chimac and Quizquiz exchanged glances, and it wasn't hard to guess that they were remembering Charles Quint's tent in the Salamanca countryside and measuring – in the pomp and ceremony with which they were greeted now – just how far they had come.

Ahead of him, Quizquiz watched the leaps and scurries of Sempere, the emperor's long white dog, which had followed Philip during the flight from the Alhambra. The animal's snout still bore the marks of the puma's claws. When he saw the gardens of the Alcazar and found himself dazzled by their splendour, Quizquiz imagined how the big cat would have loved being here – climbing palm trees, swimming in ponds, hunting birds – and he wondered where the puma could be.

It was in those gardens that Coya Asarpay gave birth to a son. Atahualpa named him Charles Capac, in tribute to his unfortunate rival. Little Philip was allowed to lean over the cradle and to be his *padrino*. On pious Isabella's insistence, the child was splashed with water by a local priest, just in case. Atahualpa considered this patronage to be good policy. He even offered to let Isabella take him as a second husband, but she declined this proposal.

Lorenzino returned from Italy with a renowned artist called Michelangelo, whom he had gone to fetch from Rome. At first, they discussed building a tomb for Charles Quint, whose body had been left in the Alhambra, among the tomato plants. Then Michelangelo was commissioned to create a sculpture representing Viracocha, creator of the sun, the moon and the stars. Atahualpa would have liked him to paint a portrait of his sister-wife and their newborn son, but since the artist hated painting living people, the Inca had to give up on this idea. Instead, Lorenzino was sent to find another painter, who had worked for Charles before and who lived in a city named Venice. However, Michelangelo agreed to make an exception for Princess Higuénamota, and he created the magnificent sculpture of her that can be found today in the great temple in Seville, the very same temple where Charles and Isabella had been wed.

In truth, Atahualpa would have preferred to return to Granada because he liked being high up in the Alhambra, but he needed a residence with a maritime link to his homeland, and the river Guadalquivir, which ran through Seville, though not very deep and difficult to navigate for the large ships that he sent to Cuba, provided that link. Soon, the barrels of wine and flour were being rolled day and night along the quays of the port, passing the barrels of saltpetre and coca that were rolled in the opposite direction, and the crates of gold and silver sent by Huascar were unloaded as jars of olive oil, honey and vinegar (all of them very popular among the Incas in the west) were loaded into the ships' holds.

Trade boomed to such an extent that Atahualpa ordered the creation of a specific institution – known by the locals as the *Casa de Contratacion* – to administer commercial relations between

Tawantinsuyu and the Fifth Quarter. Nobody in Spain – or elsewhere among the eastern lands – was permitted to trade with the countries of the west unless they passed through Seville. The one exception to this rule was Lisbon, in gratitude for the aid that city gave to Higuénamota, without which this story would have ended very differently for the Quitonians in Spain; very differently, indeed, for the entire history of the world. Even so, a quintile of everything brought to the New World on Portuguese ships had to be given to the Spanish crown.

This was also a form of compensation to Queen Isabella, sister of Joao III, for the loss of her beloved husband.

29. The Cortes

Another compensation was the promotion of her son to the position of king of Spain.

Custom dictated that an assembly of lords, priests and merchants, from all the regions of Castile, should present their tributes to the new king. This was the Cortes, and the solemn ceremony was intimidating for little Philip. Nevertheless, in order to spare him any embarrassment, Chalco Chimac had written his speech, which was translated into Castilian by Higuénamota, with the aid of Pedro Pizarro. The dukes of Arcos and Medina Sidonia were kind enough to revise this speech and to enrich it with their knowledge of local institutions and protocols.

So it was that little Philip could ensure that he was worthy of the onerous duty he had taken on, since it had pleased God to make him king of Spain at such a tender age. The Sevillian lords, who had lent their support to the preparation of the speech, kept emphasising the fact that his father had been called to God at the age of thirty-three, and Chalco Chimac, suspecting that this information must have some symbolic importance, had mentioned it several times in the speech.

However, God had not left the little king empty-handed before such a mighty task. In his infinite mercy, he had sent him the son of the Sun, from beyond the seas, to guide and advise him.

This advisory role was difficult to conceal: whenever little Philip hesitated or lost the thread of his speech, Chalco Chimac would kneel beside him and whisper the next words into his ear, a sight that at first did not make a very favourable impression on the assembly. Then the older among them remembered that it had been the same way for young Charles and his old master, the lord of Chièvres. True, the situation had been markedly different, but ultimately not much more extraordinary, with the arrival of a young monarch who did not speak a word of Spanish. At least Philip had been born in Valladolid, not in Flanders. As for the lord from beyond the seas, he had lots of gold and seemed willing to share it.

And so the young king, inspired by his new entourage, was able to announce the first edicts of his reign.

The very first was the dissolution of the Supreme Council of the Inquisition and the complete suppression of the Tribunal of the Holy Office. Hearing the murmurs of approbation that spread through the assembly, including certain representatives of the Church, Atahualpa understood that this measure would not be unpopular.

The second edict consisted of ceding Artois and Flanders to the kingdom of France, in return for a treaty of alliance consolidated by a promise of mutual assistance. The Spanish were not interested in the northern provinces, and this news was greeted with general indifference and a small sigh of relief.

Lastly the lord from beyond the seas, Atahualpa, son of the Sun, was appointed the king's chancellor, taking the place of

Nicolas Perrenot de Granvelle, whose head now had a price on it, like those of the other rebels.

The reward offered for the head of Sepúlveda, declared guilty of King Charles's murder, was a thousand ducats.

Pedro Pizarro was named secretary of state, replacing Francisco de los Cobos y Molina, who was also placed on the list of outlaws, alongside Juan Pardo Tavera and Antonio de Leyva.

The first Minister of Cults was appointed. Atahualpa initially offered the post to Iñigo López de Loyola, but he refused, so the converso humanist Juan de Valdés, brought from Rome by Lorenzino, was given the job.

The Alhambra Decree concerning the expulsion of the Jews, dated 1492 in the ancient era and signed by Charles Quint's grandparents in Granada, was repealed.

30. Letter from More to Erasmus

Thomas More to Erasmus of Rotterdam, greetings.

You know, my dear Erasmus, how I have savoured my retirement since handing back the Seal and laying down my office of chancellor, with which His Majesty King Henry so honoured me by his incredible favour.

I have heard that you left Basel because your uncertain health led you to wish for a more tranquil life, and, on that subject, I hope with all my heart that your kidney stones are giving you some respite.

However, I have picked up my quill today, my very dear Erasmus, to beg you to help your old friend in an affair that goes far beyond my own situation and involves, I am not afraid to say, the fate of all Christianity.

I am sure that you are not unaware that it has entered the mind of His Majesty the King of England to seek the annulment of his marriage with Queen Catherine to allow him to marry Lady Anne Boleyn, and that the Pope has refused this annulment, a situation which presently makes him a bigamist in the eyes of the Church.

You must also have heard talk of this new religion which is spreading through Spain, which some call Intism *and others* Solism, *and which claims to be the religion of the Sun, according to this new lord Atahualpa, who was responsible for the death of the Emperor Charles and who is, I have heard, presently the real power behind the Spanish throne.*

Now, can you imagine what idea has struck His Majesty, my king? He threatens to convert to the Inca religion, and to force the whole of England to follow him in this folly, if the Pope does not give him satisfaction, since he has heard that under the tenets of this religion it is possible to multiply one's spouses as Our Lord multiplied loaves of bread.

Although Our Holy Father has threatened the king with excommunication, it has been for nought. His Majesty is so besotted and so obstinate he seems determined to disregard the judgements of the Pope himself.

Can you imagine a greater blasphemy? We must already defend ourselves against the progress of that Luther and his damnable heresy. And now he makes us face an even greater and more diabolical peril: those barbarian idolatries that seem to have emerged directly from Hell itself.

I beg you, dear Erasmus, to write a letter to the king to make him see all the consequences of this folly, which must end in undermining the very foundations of all true faith in Our Lord. You see, it is no longer simply a matter of combating those who strive to deny purgatory or who refuse to abstain from meat on Holy Friday. It is no longer simply the unity of our Holy Church which is in peril but Christianity itself which risks sinking into the infidelity of atheism.

In truth, the best thing you could do would be to publish a text that recalls our attachment to the true faith and condemns these impious superstitions.

Only you, my dear Erasmus, possess sufficient authority to put an end to this madness, and a word from you may set all of Europe back on the righteous path which leads to God.

Who knows? Perhaps this Atahualpa has been sent to us by God to reconcile the Church with its lost sheep, to bring the acolytes of Luther to their senses, that we may unite to defend our faith from these heathens.

You know I have always ardently desired that you should produce from your heart, the most appropriate organ to ensure the truth, a treaty that will show, irrefutably, that our faith is the only true one. I do not believe that any moment in history could be better chosen than today, and I pray that nothing will turn you away from this noble task.

Take care, Erasmus, dearest of all mortals.

From Chelsea, 21 January 1534,
To Master Erasmus of Rotterdam,
A man of eminent virtue and knowledge.
With all my heart,
Thomas More

31. Letter from Erasmus to More

Erasmus to Thomas More, greetings.

You were not wrong, my friend, when you sensed my fatigue and weariness. In truth, my body scarce leaves me in peace and it is rare that a day passes when I am not stricken by new pains.

However, out of love for you, and because you are addressing important matters that deserve our attention, I am taking the time to reply to you as diligently as I can.

First of all, I must tell you that the calumnies against me have so weakened me that I no longer have the strength or ardour necessary to enter the arena again: so much for the treaty that you ask me to write.

Furthermore, those calumnies and the loss of credit that they have attached to my reputation make me doubt that the king of England will listen to an old man who is already half-buried and forgotten and who, moreover, refused on numerous occasions the generous invitations that your sovereign sent to him.

As for the Pope, I believe that your best ally in this business and the one who will be of most assistance in your noble enterprise is perhaps that Atahualpa himself, whose name, to my mind, you blacken too hastily.

Indeed, in causing the death of Charles, who was the nephew of Queen Catherine and who threatened Rome with reprisals if ever that lady was repudiated with the blessing of the Holy Father, Atahualpa has in fact rid us of the menace that was the emperor and, at the same time, the principal obstacle to the annulment of that marriage. Once this annulment is pronounced, there is no reason why King Henry's wedding to Lady Anne may not be made official, and this act, by giving the king full satisfaction, will remove any reason for your king to desert the Catholic Church.

But beyond these considerations, I would ask you to reflect on what you wrote about this Inca and his religion. Do you truly believe it to be worse than the Lutheran heretics that you revile? And that it will harm our Church more than the rapacious monks with depraved morals whom you once denounced? True, it was in full knowledge of the cause that Luther unsheathed the sword of justice to tear apart the Church. But Atahualpa is innocent of that.

Is it his fault if the message of the Gospel has not yet reached his island, wherever it may be?

You seem convinced that the enemies of the Church are doomed to Hell, and I would not know how to prove you wrong, but remember, my friend, that Hell cannot attack heathens.

Moreover, if you really study this religion of the Sun, you will find numerous points of commonality with our own faith. Are not Viracocha and the Sun a little like God the Father and his Son Jesus, Our Lord? Is not the Moon, sister and wife of the Sun, the very image of the Virgin Mary? And the lightning that they worship ... could that not bring to mind our Holy Spirit? After all, you have often seen the Holy Spirit represented in our churches in the form of a bird, so why might it not also be imagined as a lightning bolt?

Take care, my friend, not to see heretics where there are only creatures of God. Precisely because the name of heretic is so odious to Christian ears, we must all be diligent not to wither its meaning by taking it lightly. You know that I condemn Luther for his eagerness for destruction, his warlike ardour. Well, don't you see, my friend, that I am fully in agreement with you on one point? Perhaps this Atahualpa is a stroke of good fortune, sent to bring us peace.

Take very good care of yourself, my friend, and please extend my greetings to Mrs Alice and Mrs Roper.

From Friburg, 28 February 1534,
To Thomas More, the wisest
and most fervent defender of God.

Didier Erasmus of Rotterdam

32. Letter from More to Erasmus

Thomas More to Erasmus of Rotterdam, greetings.

Once again, in your perspicacity, you have hit the nail upon the head, you who are the wisest of all wise men: our most Holy Father has suspended his threats of excommunication and finally authorised the annulment of the marriage. Now, there is nothing to prevent King Henry from marrying Lady Boleyn.

But even your astonishing sagacity did not guess what nobody, other than God himself, could have foreseen.

You might think that England is saved, since the king no longer has a motive to fall into impiety. But I must inform you that this has not changed anything, and that the danger is, in fact, greater than ever.

Can you believe that His Majesty has been struck with the idea of opening a Temple of the Sun, filled with virgins handpicked for his own pleasure? Indeed, his madness is now so advanced that he has decreed himself the son of the Sun, following the example of that barbarian Atahualpa.

I would love to share your benevolence towards that impious religion, but I am afraid that I can see no rapport whatsoever with our one true faith. And what if there were? True, the Old Testament heralded the New, as you rightly reminded me, and contained within it, most certainly, the prophetic signs of the messiah's coming. But I must ask you, dear Erasmus: even if we admit that Moses prepared the way for Jesus's coming, is that any reason to become a Jew?

In any case, I thank you for your letter to the Pope, and I have no doubt that it weighed in the balance in his decision to annul the marriage, even if this did not, ultimately, have the effect for which I was most earnestly hoping.

May God keep you, Erasmus, dearest of all my friends.

Chelsea, 23 March 1534,
To Erasmus of Rotterdam, farewell.

Thomas More

33. Letter from Erasmus to More

Erasmus of Rotterdam to his very dear More, greetings.

Did I not tell you that this foreigner, this barbarian as you call him, was a stroke of fortune for Europe? In truth, I deserve no praise for prescience in this regard, despite what you say, because it was by way of a letter from our good friend Guillaume Budé that I came to forge this opinion.

In Paris last month, King Francis received an ambassador from the Spanish crown who was accompanied by several of those Indians or Incas, I do not know how I should call them. (Perhaps they are from Persia, as the sun is worshipped in that land.) It appears that they are beings of great refinement and beauty, but also that, most importantly, by ceding large portions of King Philip's inheritance to the kingdom of France, they are responsible for the signature of the peace treaty between France and Spain. In exchange, King Francis, in his great wisdom, has renounced his claim to Milan, an act that may allow Italy, a land of incessant war, to witness finally the dawn of a durable peace.

But this is not all. In truth, I am trembling with joy and contentment as I write these lines to inform you, if you are not already aware, my very dear More, of the latest news from Spain.

Imagine that the young King Philip, following the advice of his new chancellor, has promulgated in Seville an edict proclaiming that each man is free to choose and to practise his religion throughout all the territories of Castile and Aragon! The only obligation is to celebrate the festival of the Sun twice a year. (Even the most fervent defender of Christianity must surely agree that this constraint is a light one; I hope and believe that you will be of the same opinion as me on this point.)

Do you understand what this means, my dear More, most precious of all my friends? It is the door that is finally opening into a Europe of tolerance, the very land we despaired of ever seeing, and perhaps even, if God wills it, the pathway to universal peace. May this edict of tolerance serve as an example to kings and princes, and may it by the same token disarm Luther's fury.

Do you see, dear More, the lesson to be drawn from all of this? The wisdom of a heathen, if he is guided by God, however unwittingly, can do more for humanity than a bloodthirsty Christian. After all, was not Socrates, too, a precursor of Our Lord Jesus? Would you say that Socrates and Plato were impious barbarians? Or would you, for that matter, say that the monk Savonarola, who presided over a reign of terror in Florence in the name of Our Lord, was a good Christian?

Dear Thomas, I am eager to know your opinion on all of this, and I send you warmest greetings.

From Friburg, 17 April 1534,
To Thomas More, my brother humanist.

Erasmus

34. Letter from Thomas More to Erasmus

Thomas More to Erasmus of Rotterdam, greetings.

I received your letter belatedly as I was not present at the address to which it was sent, and I beg you to excuse the delay in my response.

I wish I could share your joy and enthusiasm for the course of recent events, but alas, here in England, things have not gone as we might have hoped.

As I told you in my previous letter, King Henry has promulgated a law decreeing that he is, like your new friend the chancellor of Spain, son of the Sun.

Throughout the kingdom of England, he is replacing the monasteries and abbeys with Temples of the Sun, which are nothing more nor less than brothels run by what the most indulgent call vestal virgins but the more lucid among us call what they are: whores.

And if all this were not enough to make us ashamed and most greatly afflicted, he has demanded that all his subjects take an oath swearing that their king truly is, by the grace of God, the son of the Sun.

And that is why I am writing to you today from the Tower of London, where I am presently imprisoned, awaiting my trial and probable death sentence, having refused, as you can readily imagine, to swear that oath and lend my support to this unimaginable heresy, crowned for all the world by these incredible blasphemies.

To you, Erasmus of Rotterdam, farewell.
From London, 15 August 1534,

Thomas More

35. Letter from Erasmus to Thomas More

Dear Thomas, my beloved brother,

When I mentioned Socrates in my previous letter, it was not my intention that you should model your conduct on his by going voluntarily to your death.

I beg you, in the name of our old friendship and for the love that you bear Alice, Margaret and all your children, to swear your king's oath and say whatever else he demands that you say. What does it matter if he imagines he is the Great Turk or even God himself? You know, and we know, deep within our hearts, God's truth as it was delivered by the message of the Gospel.

What matters now is your loved ones, and the tasks that you still have to complete, and the goodness that you can still spread across this earth. These things are more important than the childish games of a capricious monarch, don't you think? I beg you, my old friend, to save your life. What is the value of an oath sworn under penalty of death? What meaning could it have before God and your conscience?

Let me remind you of a story. It happened not so long ago, and perhaps you have not forgotten it, although you were but a young man at the time. When King Louis XII, upon acceding to the throne, demanded to divorce his wife, the daughter of Louis XI, many good people were displeased, among them Jan Standonck and his student Thomas. In their sermons, however, they said nothing, other than that everyone must pray to God that He send inspiration to the king. Louis contented himself with exiling them and allowing them back into France once the divorce had been accomplished. Now, let me ask you a question: if the formidable Standonck could accommodate himself to a situation that offended his conscience, could not the good More do likewise? Beware, my friend, the demon of vanity. Have you advised your wife, your children, your friends, to follow the same path that you have followed, by refusing to swear the oath? No, of course not, because you do not want them to die, and also because you know that this oath will not imperil the salvation of their souls. Why, then, should what is good enough for them not be good enough for you? What is this vocation of martyr that has you in its talons?

I pray that God will bring you back to reason and greater humility, and I am going to write a letter to King Henry now, pleading with him to spare you.

In the meantime, God keep you, my friend, and my prayers go with you.

From Friburg, 5 September 1534,
Erasmus

36. Letter from Erasmus to King Henry VIII

To the invincible king of England, Henry VIII, greetings from Erasmus of Rotterdam.

Your wisdom is without equal, and hence I have no doubt that you will divine, O great king, the purpose of this letter. I pick up my quill today to beg Your Majesty to spare the life of our great mutual friend, the distinguished Sir Thomas More.

May I remind you that it is not so long ago that you showered him with honours, and that was not by chance. You see him today as a traitor, a faithless friend, but did he betray you when he voluntarily resigned the task you had given him? Would a deceitful conspirator really have renounced the highest office in England next to your own?

You know, O king, that our More is incapable of doing anything to harm Your Majesty, because of the love he bears you.

It is true that, where religion is concerned, his piety can be somewhat irritating due to his naivety and tendency to superstition. But cannot a grown son forgive his father as his father once forgave that son? What does the oath of a poor, powerless man matter to one so great as you?

I implore you, O wise and invincible king, to put down your mighty sword and spare the head of our good More. By sparing a man of such remarkable piety and erudition that immortality is already within his grasp, the king of England will have burnished his own glory. If you truly wish to punish him, then exile him from your kingdom, O most dazzling of monarchs, and in that way demonstrate both your power and your mercy.

As for myself, I do not doubt that these words will touch the heart of he whom I taught Plutarch when he was still a most promising child, and who now, a full-grown man, has fulfilled those promises beyond all measure.

Friburg, 25 September 1534,
Erasmus of Rotterdam

37. Elizabeth

The Seville Edict swept like a hurricane throughout all of Europe (as their world was called before it became the Fifth Quarter).

In Spain, it was logical and reasonable that the Moriscos and conversos should be the first to salute the new law, because they were its most immediate beneficiaries. Atahualpa knew that the edict made them loyal to him, though he was vigilant not to take this loyalty for granted, for he knew people and their changing moods.

In Germany, in France, in England (as the preceding documents show), even in Switzerland, wherever Lutheranism was a growing influence, wherever its followers were persecuted, wherever they fought to replace their old religion with a new, rejuvenated one (albeit fairly close to the old one in truth, recognising the same gods but wishing to pay tribute to them in different ways), the Seville Edict was greeted as a glimmer of hope in the darkness. If the dream of a world without the Inquisition was taking shape in Spain, perhaps everything could become, if not possible, then at least imaginable, including peace and harmony.

Unable to approve of it, Luther said nothing about the religion of the Sun.

The king of France, fresh from his first indulgence, did not wish to make peace with these insolent Lutherans; in fact, he felt more inclined to burn them alive.

But others, weary of massacres, called for laws similar to the Seville Edict.

Awful tales were told of men quartered alive, roasted, and eaten, in the manner of the Chirihuanas, a tribe who revolted the Quitonians. A letter from Marguerite of Navarre reported that in France, a Lutheran had his heart ripped out and devoured by a crowd of crazed Catholics, and the account of this crime, which the queen herself described as 'execrable butchery', circulated in the Alcazar, making the Incas shudder. To them, these vile acts were the consequence of an incomprehensible belief: during the rites that they carried out in their temples, the Levantines were invited by their priest to eat a small white wafer and to drink a mouthful of the black drink. But, with a contortion of the imagination that Quitonians found almost inconceivable, the upholders of the old religion believed that this was actually the blood (because the black drink looked red in the light) and the body of their god, which they thereby drank and ate.

Those of the newer religion did not want to believe this, yet they seemed to commit just as many crimes. They, too, burned men alive.

The son of the Sun did not cease to be amazed that such disputes, caused by frankly incredible beliefs, could degenerate into mortal conflicts, sometimes even within families or ayllus.

In Germany, particularly, these divisions raged, and their echoes reached as far as Seville.

A princess who had converted to Lutheranism had left her husband, the Catholic Margrave of Brandenburg, and taken refuge with her uncle, the Landgrave of Thuringia, whom she urged to promulgate the same religious liberty that was now commonplace in Europe. She sent a fine, passionate letter to Chancellor Atahualpa, expressing her admiration for his actions and thanking him for the prospect of peace that he had brought to the north (she herself came from a small country that the Quitonians had never before heard anyone mention: Denmark). Chalco Chimac suggested that his master propose marriage to her, with a view to future alliances. Coya Asarpay had to remind the general of the matrimonial rules of the New World, which even princes had to obey (with the notable exception, henceforth, of the king of England): Elizabeth of Denmark was already married, and as long as her husband remained alive, she was not free to marry anyone else, despite the fact that they were separated and their relationship broken beyond repair. In fact, what she asked for was not marriage, but troops to defend herself. She begged the chancellor to give her his protection. Since Charles's death, the shadow of Ferdinand stretched over Europe and everyone feared his wrath. Or, rather, everyone, knowing that it would inevitably strike someone down, prayed that it would be his neighbour, not himself. Elizabeth of Denmark mentioned a Schmalkaldic

League, an alliance of small Lutheran countries, but this league did not have the strength to face up to the imperial army. Ferdinand, king of the Romans and successor to his brother Charles as the head of the Empire, would soon be crowned in Aix-la-Chapelle. Elizabeth begged Atahualpa to prevent this coronation, which would be a disaster for everyone.

Nevertheless, the Inca was not at that moment really all that interested in the countries of the north or in the new emperor, because his main preoccupation was to strengthen his position in Spain.

38. Valencia

Andalusia, it was true, had been completely pacified. Ruminahui had returned to Granada to set up a garrison there. Cadiz was building ships. A Temple of the Sun designed by Michelangelo was being constructed inside Córdoba's cathedral. Seville grew richer every day, and its population multiplied, making it the greatest city in the New World. Jews flocked there, providing skilled manpower that increased the country's prosperity. Young Philip had finally buried his father's remains, transferred from the Alhambra to the splendid marble tomb built within the cathedral where he had married his wife Isabella. As promised, Lorenzino had brought back a painter from Venice, one Titian, whose merits he vaunted, and who immediately got to work on a portrait of Atahualpa as the son of the Sun. And, as ever, crates of gold and silver were carried past barrels of the black drink on the rafts of the Guadalquivir.

Despite all this, there were still two trouble spots elsewhere in the peninsula. The first was in Toledo, in Castile; the other in Valencia, in Aragon.

Toledo was home to Charles Quint's last remaining followers. Its position, perched on a rocky hillock, made the city difficult to capture. All the same, Toledo inspired only moderate anxiety in the Inca general staff: without outside aid, the rebels could not withstand a siege indefinitely.

Valencia was something else altogether. This city was the gateway to Italy via the sea: ships left from there for Genoa, and from there to Naples and Sicily, which little Philip had inherited after his father's death. Its position exposed it to the whims and constant attacks of Barbary pirates paid by the Turkish emperor, Suleiman. More than a third of Valencia's inhabitants were Moriscos, accused by the old Christians of being in cahoots with their African brothers, with whom they shared a religion and a language and, almost certainly, the desire to return Spain to its former masters.

It would be a lie to say that the Seville Edict had been greeted favourably throughout Spain, because nobody could fail to notice that its primary beneficiaries were the Jews and the Moriscos. Nevertheless, the end of the Inquisition had helped make the new laws more acceptable to the old Christians. Their attitudes were also softened by the elimination of the taxes that Charles had levied ceaselessly on his people to fund his voyages and wars. With the flow of gold and silver arriving from Tawantinsuyu, Atahualpa had no need for taxes. It was poverty that created disorder, and Spain was becoming more prosperous with each passing day.

But fear, too, created disorder. In Valencia, more than elsewhere, the Moriscos had remained Moors, and while the Christians drove back the pirates' assaults, they believed that they could feel the cold curved blade of Moorish daggers at their backs. And so a rebellious movement was born: a fraternity of old Christians sworn to resist the new laws. Curacas sent from Seville were assassinated.

Atahualpa knew that the solution to the Valencia problem was not military but political, and it would require tact and cunning. Once again, he called upon the advice of the Florentine, Machiavelli.

39. The Council

Of all Titian's portraits of Atahualpa, the most famous is probably that painted in the gardens of the Alcazar, which history has remembered under the title of *The Council*. The Inca is represented as the son of the Sun, in his scarlet crown, offering his best profile (the artist having taken care to conceal the ear that was wounded during the civil war with his brother), a blue parrot on his arm, a gold bracelet around his left wrist. He stands before a fountain, with baskets of oranges and avocados on its rim. A ginger cat sleeps at his feet. A snake is wound around his leg. In the background, palm trees rise to the sky, where the sun and the moon shine together, haloed in gold and silver. Embroidered in gold thread on the emperor's alpaga tunic is his coat of arms: one can make out the castle of Castile, the red and yellow stripes of Aragon, a falcon between two trees, and a pale purple caravel silhouetted against a setting sun, representing his voyage from Cuba. In the centre, five puma heads under a rainbow surround a yellow fruit with red pips, the symbol of Granada and Andalusia.

Further back, we can see Coya Asarpay cradling her newborn son in her arms (a New World custom that she decided to adopt), Higuénamota, naked and aloof, Quizquiz, Chalco Chimac, Manco Capac, Pedro Pizarro, Lorenzino de Medici.

Absent from the painting are Ruminahui, Quispe Sisa, Cusi Rimay Ocllo, Philip II and Isabella.

In fact, the genealogy of this picture enables us to retrace one of the most decisive turning points in the history of Spain and of the world.

For it was true that Atahualpa had got into the habit of gathering his council while he posed for Titian.

During one of these sessions, they decided on a series of measures that determined the fate, not only of a number of important individuals, but of entire countries too.

At the time, Atahualpa was only the chancellor. It was not until he made the finishing touches to the painting that Titian added the blazons of Spain on the Inca's tunic.

Ruminahui was at the garrison in the Alhambra; Quispe Sisa and Cusi Rimay were playing somewhere in the gardens; but the absence of the young king and his mother was more significant. The truth is that they had not been summoned.

After all, the Toledan rebels were supporters of Philip's father. It made sense to be wary of the son and the widow.

They resolved to send Quizquiz to lay siege to Toledo. The general was chosen for his military valour, but also to distance him from Philip; Quizquiz was very fond of the young king and had taken to teaching him to fence, using wooden swords.

Lorenzino would travel to Genoa to find Admiral Doria. The admiral's mission would be to assemble a fleet and take possession of the ports on the far side of the Inner Sea which served as the Barbary pirates' bases. Isabella would be sent to Lisbon to ask her brother Joao for Portugal's support. Higuénamota would go to Paris and seek the king of France's backing.

In parallel with this, Valencia's Moriscos would be moved out of the city. Atahualpa thought these measures likely to calm the anger of the old Christians.

However, Higuénamota remarked that it was unwise to upset their allies, and that these measures did not send a good signal to the Moriscos. Chalco Chimac proposed dressing up the deportation as a valued mission: Valencia's Moriscos would be dispatched to pacify the cannibalised German states, who were asking for our aid. They would travel through France and settle in the Netherlands, governed by Philip's aunt, Mary, where they would first ensure that Spanish sovereignty had not been disturbed by Charles's death. Manco Capac would lead them.

They also had to settle Philip's fate. Chalco Chimac's spies had intercepted letters from Ferdinand: the new emperor swore to his nephew that the imperial army would invade Spain as soon as the war with the Turks allowed. Escape plans had already been hatched with moles inside the Alcazar. The question had to be asked once again: was it possible that a dead king could be more useful than a live king? Atahualpa had his sights on the throne, and his lieutenants had given up pretending that they weren't aware of this.

Coya Asarpay, who was breast-feeding little Charles, advocated a public execution, as an example to the others.

But nobody knew how the Spanish would react to such an act. They had learned to love the father, and it was to be feared that they would support his son, particularly as the boy was not yet eight harvests old.

Chalco Chimac proposed a more discreet form of elimination, which would appear accidental. This solution had the advantage of not causing conflict with the king of Portugal, who was Philip's uncle, or his mother, or the people.

Quizquiz, though, was fiercely opposed to the idea. 'He's only a child!' he kept repeating.

But Atahualpa, who until this point had remained silent, replied: 'No, he is a king.'

And so that famous scene was produced. Titian did not understand the subject of the discussion, as it was taking place in the Inca language, which Lorenzino and Pedro Pizarro had learned to speak. But, perhaps moved by some dark foreboding, his hand had trembled and he had dropped his paintbrush.

Atahualpa relaxed his pose, walked towards him, bent down, picked up the paintbrush, and handed it back to the artist.

This is what actually happened, and not what Gómara claimed. In fact, he said many other things, too, that I think it best not to mention.

And, on this subject, I hereby affirm that what is contained in this book is very truthful. These are not old tales of Mochicas and Chimus that stretch back seven hundred harvests: these events happened only yesterday, so to speak, and they happened precisely how and when I say they did.

In any case, the question of the king's fate remained in limbo. But Philip's life now hung by a thread.

Atahualpa had great plans for reforming Spain, which he believed he could accomplish only if he was fully invested with royal power, having rid himself of all dynastic obstacles.

His advisers were taken aback: a reform? Religious? Again?

Atahualpa's response cannot be contradicted by Francisco de Gómara or Antonio de Guevara or Alonso de Santa Cruz or any other chronicler of the Fifth Quarter. He said: 'Not religious. Agrarian.'

40. Philip

There are two of them, both very little; a chaperone guards them. Their father is dead, their mother far away. They are playing at the edge of the large pond in the Alcazar, with their little wooden boats. They are dreaming of glory, of storms and adventures. Philip sees himself at the head of a great fleet. He is sailing off to conquer the land of the pirates, with Quizquiz beside him, following his return. Marie, not wanting to be outdone, says: 'First, we take Tunis. Then we take Algiers.' Brother and sister argue over the capture of Barbarossa. The chaperone, dressed in black, watches them tenderly.

A letter from Lisbon says their mother is on her way with her little brother Luis, Duke of Beja, their uncle, who is bringing them twenty-three caravels. But it is Doria, the old admiral, who excites their imagination, leading his Genoan galleys. And those funny Indians, where are they?

Quizquiz is setting fire to Toledo.

Higuénamota is sleeping with the king of France, who will send ten thousand men.

Manco is arriving in Brussels, with his Valencian Moriscos, after a long march.

Ruminahui is on his way to Barcelona, where troops are gathering.

In the cool of the palace, where King Peter the Cruel once sat on the throne, Atahualpa pores over maps and drawings, surrounded by his engineers, absorbed in vast landscaping plans for the cultivation of corn and papa in the mountains of Spain. In the south, the Sierra Nevada, which he knows well after crossing it while fleeing Granada. In the north, the Pyrenees, home to his friend Marguerite of Navarre. For a long, long time he fled; now he will build. His eyes are red, as usual.

From a window of the palace, Chalco Chimac observes the two children. His gaze is black, as is his heart.

Chalco Chimac was a terrible thing.

He goes down into the garden and whispers something to the chaperone. The old woman turns pale but does what she is bid. She makes some excuse and takes Marie away. The little girl protests, she doesn't understand, she wants to keep playing, she would even like to fight but worries about creasing her pretty dress. In the end, she gives in and follows the old woman.

Philip is not a bad child, but deep inside he is thrilled to have the pond to himself. Nobody to contest his orders. He and he alone commands the little boats. With a palm leaf picked up in the garden, he creates waves in the pond, making his toys move. The waves spread. His ships sail across the water.

He hasn't noticed Chalco Chimac behind him. His dog Sempere is sleeping peacefully.

Little Philip is light, he is leaning over the water; one hand is enough. The sound is not much louder than a falling stone. The child's cries wake the dog, which understands, and barks, helpless. The scene drags on, horrifyingly. Guards come running but, seeing their general standing motionless beside the pond, they withdraw cautiously. Then the little boy falls silent. He floats, face down. The dog's barks change to plaintive whines.

At that very moment, Isabella is sailing through the Strait of Gibraltar, happy at having seen her brothers again, at the prospect of seeing her children.

Still engrossed in his plans for agrarian reform, Atahualpa talks passionately about local crops and those little white llamas that one sees all over the Spanish countryside.

Disturbed by the unusual agitation in its pond, a swan flies over the Inca. He does not look up.

Chalco Chimac was a terrible thing, in the service of his master.

41. Tunis

Everything became easier once Philip was dead.

The Cortes of Castile and Aragon, buried in Tawantinsuyu gold, proclaimed Atahualpa I king of Spain, Naples and Sicily. For the sake of convenience, he agreed to be baptised, since the Levantines took this ritual so seriously. He was given the name Antonio, although that is not how history has remembered him because everyone, whether friends or enemies, with the exception of certain old Castilian Christians, went on calling him by his real name.

What history remembers are his promises to the Cortes. Like his predecessor, he swore that he was determined to live and die in Spain. We have seen how he kept his word.

What followed was a policy of marriages, intended to strengthen the Incas' position in Europe.

Isabella, destroyed by her son's death, did not have the strength to deny Atahualpa's request a second time; and so Charles Quint's widow became his secondary wife. The ceremony was more solemn than joyous, since she was still in mourning. In order not to deepen the bride's sadness, it took place not in Seville's cathedral – where Charles's remains now rested – but in Córdoba's. Inca pomp met royal Spanish pomp. The king of Spain placed sandals on the feet of his new bride, then llamas were sacrificed, as custom dictated. Crates of jewellery were delivered to the queen.

In happier circumstances, Quispe Sisa married Lorenzino and went with him to Italy. As his wedding gift, Atahualpa appointed the young man Duke of Florence in place of his cousin Alexander, who – having lost the support of Charles Quint – had to leave the city as the people threw stones and yelled insults at him.

Manco was promised to the daughter of Marguerite of Navarre, little Jeanne d'Albret.

Young Charles Capac would marry Marie, daughter of Charles Quint and Isabella of Portugal, granddaughter of Joanna the Mad and Philip the Handsome, great-granddaughter of the Catholic monarchs Isabella of Castile and Ferdinand of Aragon.

Toledo fell under a rain of pebbles reddened in fire like embers. Quizquiz's catapults and his endless reserves of gunpowder finally overcame the rebels' resistance. Antonio de Leyva was thrown alive from the battlements. Cobos and Granvelle were spared death after swearing allegiance to Atahualpa. Tavera refused to submit to this oath and was hanged after first being whipped. The traitor Sepúlveda was thrown into a dark cellar filled with snakes and his skin, having been peeled from his corpse, was used to make a drum that was sent to the Inca.

With Atahualpa having been baptised, the Tunis expedition was blessed by the Pope. Barbarossa's fleet, massively outnumbered, was routed and sunk. The port of La Goulette was taken after a hard, month-long siege. Atahualpa was from the north, so had never experienced the deserts in Chile; he suffered from the heat and thirst but did not let it show. Once they were in possession of La Goulette, the way was open to Tunis, where the pirate Barbarossa, named captain-general of the sea by Suleiman, had barricaded himself with five thousand Janissaries, his elite Turkish troops. His position appeared unassailable; the men were suffering in the heat and with illness, and Atahualpa was losing patience, when a slave revolt rescued him. Twenty thousand Christians, held in the city's prisons, rose up against their masters and ran to the castle gates.

Pedro Pizarro was the first to enter the city, at the head of a regiment of Moriscos from the Albaicín that had been trained by Rumiñahui. Beside him, Puka Amaru – who, after almost killing the young Pedro in Toledo, had since become his most faithful lieutenant – smashed skulls with his star-headed club. Tintoretto painted that scene, and the red-headed Quitonian found fame.

Unleashed on their former masters, the twenty thousand Christian slaves ravaged the beautiful Berber city. And so Atahualpa made his entrance into a mass grave, a city of corpses and smoking ruins. Even so, he saluted this resounding victory by yelling Charles Quint's old motto, three times over, to his troops: 'Further! Further! Further!' A huge roar echoed the words back to him.

The triumph was not total, however, because Barbarossa managed to escape. Tunis itself was of no great value; Atahualpa needed to clean up the whole Barbary Coast. The child, Luis of

Portugal, insisted that they should flush the pirate out from his lair in Algiers. Atahualpa would have liked to grant his new brother-in-law's wishes, but for reasons of his own, he did not want this affair to drag on.

With Suleiman weakened, and further preoccupied by a new war against the Persians, the pressure on Ferdinand had lessened on the eastern front, allowing him to attack in the west. Having come into possession of a kingdom, the Inca was in no mood to lose it. Moulay Hassan, a Moor who had been Sultan of Tunis before being expelled by Barbarossa, had his privileges restored in return for signing a treaty that made his kingdom a tributary of Spain. After all, Atahualpa had liberated Tunis from the Turks' yoke. The regiment of Moriscos from the Albaicín was left to garrison the city.

The fleet took to sea again and set sail for Sicily. The reception he received in Palermo allowed Atahualpa to gauge the impact of his victorious campaign. Suddenly, the Inca had become a Christian hero. A triumphal arch was built in his honour. The Pope sent his congratulations. Everyone compared him to a certain Scipio. Alonso de Santa Cruz, who had not yet become a historian but was at the time only a cartographer, had drawn a map that would be used by the painter Vermeyen for a monumental tapestry entitled *The Conquest of Tunis*. And the black drink flowed freely.

42. The Mita

Atahualpa exhausted the delights of Palermo before returning to Seville, loaded with crates of Sicilian wine.

Manco's reports informed him that the people of Flanders were extremely hostile to the deported Moriscos, and the regent,

Mary of Hungary, had not extended the warm welcome that her position as a subject of the king of Spain might have led them to expect. Then Manco had gone to Germany. There, in the Lutheran-held regions, it was even worse: following a demand from Luther himself to 'battle the demonic forces', the Moriscos were massacred, only a few of them escaping. Manco, too, was almost killed. Atahualpa merely ordered him to go to Navarre to present gifts to Marguerite, his future mother-in-law. In truth, he was still indifferent to the troubles in the north. He had not yet grasped how much was at stake.

He was reassured by a letter from Lorenzino in Florence: Atahualpa's reputation now shone so brightly in the Fifth Quarter that Ferdinand himself would not dare attack the saviour of Christianity any time soon, out of fear that he would be universally condemned and banished from Europe. That was all he wanted to know.

Finally, the Inca could devote himself to his secret passion. All monarchs, of course, are intoxicated by their conquests. But Atahualpa had understood this truth: it is more difficult to reign than to wage war. His ancestor Cusi Yupanqui had shrunk the borders of the Empire more than any other sovereign. But the name that posterity had bestowed on him reflected the nature of his legacy: Pachacuti. *Remaker of the World*.

In reality Atahualpa's ambitions went far beyond a bit of landscaping in the Sierra Nevada. His brother Huascar was sending him entire shiploads of riffraff from the dregs of the Empire – Collas, Chachapoyas, Chimus, Canaris, Caras – precisely because Atahualpa needed manpower on a massive scale. Wherever land remained unexploited – on mountainsides, on snowy peaks, on arid plains; places where nobody had ever thought to grow anything at all – he, Atahualpa, would plant corn, quinoa and papas, the last of which had become so popular in the Fifth Quarter that the French called them *pommes de terre*: apples of the earth. All these vast solitudes were covered with crops; networks of canals were dug to irrigate land that had been written off as sterile.

The sheep, those little white llamas that proliferated all over Spain, had been a parasite on the earth for far too long. Atahualpa considered them responsible for those bare, dry, dusty landscapes. He had entire flocks slaughtered. The new king of Spain did not want a population of shepherds. He wanted his nation to take root.

He created granaries. The meat of the slaughtered sheep was cut into strips, salted, dried. The grains of corn and quinoa were turned into flour. The potato tubers were frozen at night and dried during the day so that they could be conserved for several moons. Food supplies were kept in earthenware jars or buried in deep holes.

With these reserves, he would be able to feed anyone who was hungry in times of scarcity, plague or ruined harvests.

Spanish peasants began chewing coca, increasing their resistance to fatigue and providing them with added medicinal benefits. (It is true that some abused it, and they soon sank into a stupor.)

Atahualpa put an end to the system of land rent and rewarded the merchants who funded the army with loans.

He abolished most taxes and handed out plots of land to peasants, assembled into ayllus, or to already established communities such as the *comunidades*, leaving each group to divide up the work and goods for itself.

In exchange, he developed a system of chores that replaced the taxes, based on the mita in Tawantinsuyu. The peasants had to devote part of their time to work the Inca's land, as well as the Sun's (which were also owned by the Inca, as his representative on earth, although he delegated their management to the leaders of the cult). Each of these periods was marked by new celebrations that brightened the lives of the populace.

This vast enterprise of redistribution had repercussions throughout society. Many Catholic priests abandoned their nailed god and transformed their churches into Temples of the Sun in order to benefit from the new system. For the same reasons, convents were turned into houses of Chosen Women.

Craftsmen were subject to similar obligations: they had to devote part of their time to the collective effort (masonry, iron-work, bridges, canals, etc.) or to the personal service of the Inca (pottery, goldsmithing, textiles, etc.) – which, ultimately, amounted to the same thing.

Every ayllu or community had to feed, house and heal the disabled, the elderly, the widowed and the sick.

The fruits of the land belonged to those who worked it, even if there was a surplus, but the land itself did not. The distribution of land was regularly reviewed and adjusted according to need. If the population of a group fell, the land they were allotted shrank proportionately. And if the population rose, they were given extra land so that the group could feed the extra mouths. When there was too much variation between the sizes of the groups, there would be a redistribution of people. Armies of quipucamayocs kept accounts in their registers: men, women and children were so many little knots tied to coloured cords that formed the fringes of the quipus.

Here and there, people bridled against these obligations; occasionally, there were revolts, which were severely punished.

The Inca's envoys, his governors, his curacas, and even some hidalgos that he recruited specifically for this purpose, were given the task of spreading his message throughout all the villages and towns of Castile and Aragon: namely, that the lands he took were not those that the Levantines needed, but those that they didn't know what to do with, the ones they couldn't work; that the only tribute he expected from them was the harvest of these lands, which he had prepared at his own cost; that, in fact, he was giving them his own goods by distributing to them what remained after providing for the upkeep of his army and his court; that the pointless dissentions and the disputes that used to arise between them had all disappeared; that, effectively, their entire kingdom could be certain that nobody – not the rich, not the poor, not the great, not the small – would have any cause for complaint.

Lastly, Atahualpa decreed that every peasant, on his wedding day, would receive a pair of llamas as a gift from his king.

43. The Prince

However, the Inca's reign was still in its early days, and what he failed to realise was that this newness itself made him vulnerable. The son of the Sun did not command the same respect here as in his native land.

'Nothing makes a prince so well esteemed as undertaking great enterprises and setting a fine example,' said Machiavelli in his talking sheets.

The new king took care not to diminish the privileges of Spain's noble families. He distributed Golden Fleeces, a highly prized distinction that cost him nothing and possessed the advantage of binding him to whomever received it. It is true that they were few in number and had little in the way of resources, but the Spanish nobility constituted a potential source of danger, all the same, and it was expedient to keep them entertained.

Atahualpa drank down the words of this Machiavelli because he had the feeling that he was telling Atahualpa's own story through that of another man: 'We have in our time Ferdinand of Aragon, the present King of Spain. He can almost be called a new prince, because he has risen, by fame and glory, from being an insignificant king to be the foremost king in Christendom;

and if you will consider his deeds you will find them all great and some of them extraordinary. In the beginning of his reign he attacked Granada, and this enterprise was the foundation of his dominions. He did this quietly at first and without any fear of hindrance, for he held the minds of the barons of Castile occupied in thinking of the war and not anticipating any innovations; thus they did not perceive that by these means he was acquiring power and authority over them.'

So it was that the Inca had, without knowing it, walked in the footsteps of this glorious predecessor, the grandfather of Charles, whose crown he had taken, and of Ferdinand, who claimed it was his by right.

However, the next part of the text drew out certain differences, even divergences, between the two monarchs: 'He was able with the money of the Church and of the people to sustain his armies, and by that long war to lay the foundation for the military skill which has since distinguished him. Further, always using religion as a plea, so as to undertake greater schemes, he devoted himself with a pious cruelty to driving out and clearing his kingdom of the Moors; nor could there be a more admirable example, nor one more rare.'

So, what this Ferdinand of Aragon had done, Atahualpa had now undone. Yet the Inca felt closer to this man than to any other. He discovered his story with an avid curiosity: 'Under this same cloak he assailed Africa, he came down on Italy, he has finally attacked France; and thus his achievements and designs have always been great, and have kept the minds of his people in suspense and admiration and occupied with the issue of them. And his actions have arisen in such a way, one out of the other, that men have never been given time to work steadily against him.'

Atahualpa made a sign with his hand to silence the servant who had been reading to him. He had decided to attack Algiers.

44. Algiers

Admiral Doria advised him to hasten the invasion if he didn't want to expose himself to the winter storms, and the Inca followed his advice.

He waited until after the festivals of Corn and the Sun, and then – unwilling to leave anything to chance – assembled an enormous armada.

The king of France, persuaded by Higuénamota that he deserved his share of the glory, was present.

Likewise the cream of the Spanish nobility, gathered under the Inca banner.

The Pope himself sent his personal geographer, a converted Moor by the name of Hassan al-Wazzan, known as Leo Africanus for his encyclopaedic knowledge of that continent.

Atahualpa also invited whole regiments of Moriscos, to whom he presented the invasion as a liberation from the Turkish yoke, and a regiment of Jews, drawn by the opportunity to rediscover their long-banished brothers.

The armada occupied the Bay of Algiers, and soon the sun and the cross replaced the crescent on the battlements of Peñón, the island that protected access to the bay.

The Christians were worried that Barbarossa would not be there, but the pirate was waiting, ensconced behind the city walls.

Pedro Pizarro was sent to meet him and negotiate an honourable surrender. He was accompanied by Puka Amaru, in the hope that their red hair would create a complicity, but this proved irrelevant: Barbarossa's hair was actually white, and did not look as if it had ever been red.

Puka Amaru played his role nonetheless. Barbarossa contemptuously rejected the offer of surrender, showing breathtaking insolence in his response, addressed to Pedro Pizarro in these precise terms: 'Tell your master that no Christian dog has ever taken or will ever take Algiers, and that if my master was told about your plans, he'd send one of his slaves, with a few hastily gathered troops, to sweep aside your army and throw the lot of you into the sea.'

So, Puka Amaru, after listening to the translator, jumped to his feet and pronounced these now famous words: 'My master is no Christian, and you are a slave.'

Pedro Pizarro, thinking his time had come, was already reaching for his sword, ready to defend himself; but, respecting the universal rules of war and diplomacy, Barbarossa let them leave unharmed.

With only a handful of men, the pirate defended the city valiantly; nevertheless, it fell in a few weeks, under ceaseless artillery fire.

Francis I had a horse killed beneath him during one skirmish: the king of France was thrilled.

Atahualpa had first considered entrusting the city to the son of the former emir Salim at-Toumi, long ago expelled by the first Barbarossa, Oruç Reis. Following the death of his father (who was strangled in his bath), Yahia at-Toumi had taken refuge in Spain. After all this time, he welcomed Atahualpa's proposal as a blessing from heaven. However, the Inca changed his mind when he was made aware that the father had not been especially popular during his reign. It was not enough to be a Moor to replace the Turk. The second Barbarossa had an even more legendary reputation than his brother, whom he had succeeded. Atahualpa wanted to break this line of pirates in the service of the Ottoman Empire, but equally thought it wise to keep some form of continuity. So he decided to appoint Puka Amaru as governor of Algiers, presenting him to the populace as a third Barbarossa – the *real* Barbarossa. In the Berber language, Barbarossa did not mean 'redbeard' or indeed anything else, and in any case Puka Amaru did not have a beard because beards, although not unknown in Tawantinsuyu, had always been considered an anomaly and a physical disgrace, albeit one often suitable for people with red hair. *Amaru*, on the other hand, was similar to a word that meant 'red' for the local tribes. The Inca had an emblem of a red snake created for his new governor and gave him some Valencian Moriscos for his personal guard. He named Hassan al-Wazzan the vizir, to help Puka Amaru in his task (although, in fact, Leo Africanus was originally from Granada). Atahualpa thought it wise to have these countries governed by Moors from Spain, who had supported him ever since the Seville Edict, while sharing the same beliefs as the people of this land. The leader of the guard was a Morisco by the name of Cristobal, who had been the slave of a woman in Burgos, a town in the north of Spain, before joining the Inca to escape his condition.

Paintings representing Puka Amaru's exploits at the gates of Tunis were hung on the walls of his palace. And, so that everyone would understand that Algiers had a new master, the pirate he had succeeded was decapitated and his head planted on a spike on the battlements.

With Barbarossa gone, the clean-up of the coast was easy. Bougie, Ténès, Mostaganem, Oran … The fleet led by Doria seized all the Berber forts like a child picking wildflowers. For the Spanish, Atahualpa was now a *conquistador*. For the Moors, a liberator. But when the Genoan admiral wanted to ride this irresistible momentum, suggesting that they retake the island of Rhodes, further east, Atahualpa decided it was time to bring this venture to an end. He had no interest in pursuing Suleiman from the Inner Sea, preferring to leave Ferdinand something to occupy him on his eastern borders. Rhodes had no real strategic value to

Spain. From Naples to Cadiz, the route to Cuba was free for the ships of the Fifth Quarter: Atahualpa could not ask for more. Francis I approved of this decision too: in the past, inadequate preventive measures against the Turk in his war with Charles Quint had cost him dearly. Soon afterwards, the king of France would sign a trade agreement with the Sublime Porte.

45. Flanders

The story could have ended there. But humanity is a river and nothing, short of the sun dying, can halt its flow.

Ferdinand was on his way to be crowned Holy Roman Emperor in Aix-la-Chapelle.

We have said that Atahualpa was not interested in Germany, and it was true, up to that point. But then an event occurred and his attitude changed.

Mary of Hungary, regent of the Netherlands, was from the house of Austria; she was Ferdinand's sister. She was a Habsburg. She saw her brother's arrival as an opportunity to break with the Spanish crown and return to the bosom of the family empire. Anticipating a reaction from France, Spain's ally, she had levied a new tax to pay for an army of mercenaries. But the bourgeoisie of Gand, the very city where Charles Quint was born, believed they had already spent enough on other people's wars. They rose up against this new tax.

Word of this revolt reached Seville, and with it the rumour of a Habsburg conspiracy.

Atahualpa had not forgotten the harsh welcome received in the Netherlands by Manco and the Valencian Moriscos. He would have happily left Germany to Ferdinand, regarding it as a mishmash of turbulent kingdoms that weren't really governed by the emperor anyway. But the Netherlands constituted Charles Quint's Burgundian heritage and, all things considered, despite never having set foot there, he felt attached to it. The Inca decided to go there himself.

He led his army across France and into Flanders.

46. Gand

Wherever he went, he forbade his men to live off the fat of the land, which meant that his army required a colossal supply chain to keep them fed. And so the imperial army stretched out endlessly in a cloud of dust, as it had done in the days of the civil war with his brother Huascar. There were fewer caged parrots and cuys now, fewer llamas, fewer tame jaguars and pumas, but more sheep and cattle, more artillery, cannons and carts loaded down with barrels of gunpowder, and still a similar number of falcons in the sky and dogs running alongside the ranks of soldiers.

He had barracks built, warehouses that he filled, first of all, with food brought from Andalusia, some of it all the way from Tawantinsuyu.

When they arrived outside Gand, they set up a gigantic camp.

Atahualpa quickly visited all the lands that had rebelled, leaving governors and soldiers in each. Then he returned to the camp to let his men rest and, without even taking the time to change his clothes, entered the city with a reduced escort, flanked by his two generals, Ruminahui and Chalco Chimac. (Quizquiz, shaken by Philip's death, had remained in Seville to watch over the kingdom's capital.)

He and his men scaled a small fort whose drawbridge had been raised, then he led them along a deserted path lined by houses with closed shutters until they reached a large square containing one of those stone temples with a bell tower reaching into the sky. Atahualpa never ceased to be astonished by buildings with multiple storeys. Here, the stone was red, as it was in Granada, but the roofs were more pointed and crenellated. Each region had its own style, and Atahualpa liked this one.

A rudimentary canal ran through the square.

A crowd was gathered there.

The women and children went before him, holding green branches and shouting in the language of the French: 'Our only lord, son of the Sun, saviour of the poor, forgive us.'

(News of the reforms that he had instituted in Spain had reached these lands.)

The Inca received them with great mercy and told them that his deputies in Flanders had been the cause of their own troubles. He told them, moreover, that he completely forgave all the rebels; that he had been to see them in person so that they, hearing his pardon from his own lips, would be satisfied and would lose all apprehension of being punished for their sins. He ordered that they should be given everything they needed, that they should be treated with love and charity, and that all the widows and orphans of men killed in the fight against the regency should be looked after.

The inhabitants had been afraid that Atahualpa would massacre them in their houses (Toledo was still fresh in their memories), so this speech was greeted with great joy and applause. As the Inca approached the great temple, some people kissed him, some wiped the sweat from his face, and others dusted him off or threw flowers and fragrant herbs at his feet. Inside the temple, in accordance with the rites of the nailed god's followers, a ceremony was performed in his honour. Then he went to visit the city's nobility and assured them that they would not be asked to pay any more taxes. In exchange, he demanded only part of their time and their work to supply his warehouses.

Atahualpa spent three days in Charles's palace. Then he left for Brussels, to find Mary of Hungary and her council.

47. Brussels

Mary's troops were not ready: poorly equipped and badly paid, they were easily swept aside.

The members of the council were paraded naked through the city, a noose around each of their necks. The regent begged to be spared this indignity, but Atahualpa would suffer no exceptions. Higuénamota, for that matter, would not have let him.

Mary of Hungary looked like her brother Charles, but her lips were thicker, her cheeks fuller, her hips wider. Her breasts were still firm, and the Inca found her to his taste; he made her his concubine, and soon she was pregnant.

Ferdinand would have paid a ransom for his sister's return. But Chalco Chimac saw certain advantages in that union and advised his master to marry the regent. Mary would be the king of Spain's second secondary wife, after Isabella.

And so was born an heir who would be half-Inca, half-Habsburg.

A ceremony was organised in the St Gudula cathedral, Brussels' greatest temple. Atahualpa, wearing the scarlet wool crown, watched as his regent and new wife Mary knelt before him and put his sandal on his feet as a sign of allegiance. In each hand he held a golden cup filled with the black drink, and he handed her the one in his left hand as a sign of friendship. Then the Inca and his new wife drank together as a sign of mutual respect. The contents of the other cup were poured into a golden bowl to be offered to the Sun.

This scene is depicted today on a stained-glass window in the St Gudula temple, with Atahualpa's qualities listed in the language of knowledge reserved for the Levantine amautas: *Atahualpa Sapa Inca, Semper augustus, Hispaniarium et Quitus rex, Africae dominator, Belgii princeps clementissimus, et Maria ejus uxor*. It is true that the Barbary Coast, where Tunis and Algiers were located, was also known as Africa, and that the inhabitants of Brussels were known as *Belgians* because they believed themselves descendants of a tribe of that name. Those who are curious about languages will probably not be annoyed if I mention such details. May the others forgive me.

Eight thousand of the rebellion's ringleaders – those who had fought for the regent, organised the resistance or disseminated opinions hostile to the Inca's arrival – were sent from Brussels to Spain, where they were settled in an under-populated province called La Mancha.

To outshine Gand's tributes and consign the rebellion to oblivion, nine days of festivities were declared in the city. The centre of the celebrations was the Coudenberg Palace, home to the late Charles Quint and now to his sister Mary: in a state room longer than any to be found in a single Cuzco palace, next to the sloping road that the regent and the members of her council had been forced to ascend, naked, with nooses around their necks, a great ball in the style of the Fifth Quarter took place. With bitter irony, the regent presided over it beside her new husband. Then they sacrificed black llamas in the gardens and the Inca's troops paraded through the city.

At this point, I must briefly interrupt the narrative to return the reader to Seville where, day after day, ships were arriving from the Four Quarters, bringing gold and gunpowder, but also many men, come to try their luck in the New World. So, in addition to the 180 pioneers from Quito, Spain was now home to a considerable number of emigrants from Tawantinsuyu, most of whom had swelled the ranks of the Spanish army.

As commander-in-chief, Ruminahui had organised his army along lines of nationality. There could be no question of mixing the Chinchas with their old enemies the Yuncas, and even less so the Yuncas and the Chimus, given the bloody war that those two peoples had once fought; the same applied to the Quechuas, who hated the Chancas and would find it inconceivable to go into combat beside them.

So it was that the people of Brussels were able to watch each regiment march past, flying the colours of the peoples and tribes that comprised it.

The fierce Chancas, because of their distinction in battle, came first. They were followed by the Valencian Moriscos, horse-men from Andalusia, a regiment of Jews recruited from all over Spain. The Charas drew gasps from the crowd for the condor wings that decorated their backs. The Yuncas, with their hideous masks, scared those watching as they made the gestures and expressions of madmen, idiots or simpletons. They carried flutes and discordant drums with torn skins, which they used for all kinds of nonsense. As was customary, the procession ended with the mounted guard of Yanas, the Inca's elite troops, led by Pedro Pizarro in place of the absent Quizquiz.

In the wake of the parade there came songs, dances and ball games on a vast lawn in front of the royal palace. Large white swans glided across the surface of a lake.

The beer – a sort of akha, made not from corn but from another cereal – flowed freely, since it was a beverage highly prized in those parts.

Atahualpa decreed that the former constitution would be replaced by the new laws of Spain. It was proclaimed that Flanders and all the provinces of the Netherlands now belonged indissolubly to the kingdom of Spain, with the exception of the part already ceded to the king of France, including the cities of Lille, Douai and Dunkirk.

In that instant, Burgundy – as named by Charles the Bold and dreamed of by Charles Quint even until his death – ceased to exist.

Mary gave birth to a daughter, who was given the name Margaret Duchicela, after Margaret of Austria, née Habsburg, Charles Quint's aunt and Mary of Hungary's predecessor as regent, and after Paccha Duchicela, princess of Quito and Atahualpa's mother. Later, the little girl would marry her half-brother Charles Capac.

48. Germany

Germany, however, while preparing for Ferdinand's coronation, continued to tear itself apart. In Hesse, in Thuringia, in Pomerania, in the imperial cities of Strasbourg, Ulm and Constance, in the Hanseatic cities of Bremen, Lübeck and Hamburg, people believed that the Holy Roman Empire had exploited the credulity of the poor for long enough, and that if the body of the nailed god was contained in a wafer or a hunk of bread, that hunk of bread remained nevertheless a hunk of bread.

So it was that the Duke of Saxony, the Landgrave of Thuringia, the Margrave of Brandenburg, the Count Palatine of the Rhine, and all the other prince-electors of the German Holy Roman Empire, had no intention of welcoming Ferdinand, the defender of the old faith, as their returning messiah. The Landgrave of Hesse, a friend of Melanchthon's known as Philip the Magnanimous, led the Schmalkaldic League in its mission to convert Germany to Lutheran ideas, or at least to persuade the emperor to tolerate them – by use of the sword, if necessary. All of them were covetously eyeing the Church's riches, which they intended to confiscate, and plotting to strip away its excessive privileges and redistribute them more fairly.

All the same, there were limits to this revolt, and the Anabaptists – who believed that children should not have the religion of the nailed god imposed on them through the rite of baptism until they were old enough to reason for themselves – paid for this heresy with their lives. Likewise, the peasants, who had imagined that Luther was their saviour, a champion of the poor, had been massacred when they rose up demanding justice on earth as in heaven. Not only had Luther refused to support them, he'd even exhorted the princes to cut the throat of every single rebel.

Frederick the Wise and Philip the Magnanimous, those eminent prince-electors converted to Lutheranism, had accomplished this task with zeal and diligence, killing the leaders and mutilating all their followers. After that, the German countryside was filled with thousands of men without noses or ears.

The simultaneous coming of Ferdinand and Atahualpa had rekindled the embers of those past infernos.

On one side, the Lutheran princes saw the Seville Edict as an inspirational model for religious peace in Germany. They were counting on Atahualpa's arrival in his northern provinces to put pressure on Ferdinand before his coronation. They calculated that they ought to be able to wrest concessions from the new emperor who, faced with the united forces of France and Spain, not to mention the threat of Suleiman at his back, could not afford to alienate the German princes, even if they were Lutherans.

On the other side, the German peasants, having learned of the agrarian reforms that had swept first Spain and now the Netherlands, felt hope grow in their hearts once again. They saw the Inca as a new Luther, or perhaps a new Müntzer.

The souls of Germany, that strange region peopled by wild-eyed ghosts and misty visions, were more troubled than ever.

Armies of the noseless gathered silently. They remembered their heroes of bygone times, their broken dreams. They wept at mention of Poor Conrad. But they gritted their teeth, too. The names of the cutler Kaspar Preziger, of Jean de Leyde, of Jan Mattys, and especially of the great Thomas Müntzer, danced on the lips of mutilated men who, when evening fell, would tell their children terrible stories about the past. Some of those old ghosts reappeared, as if resuscitated, from the hiding places where they had taken refuge so long ago that everyone had thought them lost for ever. Atahualpa's arrival produced miracles. A vagabond wandering out of the woods claimed he was Pilgram Marpeck, the Anabaptist. The fur trader Sebastian Lotzer and his friend the blacksmith Ulrich Smid turned up in Swabia making all their old demands again as if not a single day, not a single harvest, had passed.

'Each parish has the right to appoint its own pastor, and to dismiss him if he behaves badly. The pastor must preach the Gospel, simply and clearly, with no human amendments. For it is written that we can only come to God through the true faith.' So they spoke and the thick breath of the plains lapped against the faces of those who stopped digging to listen.

'The pastors shall be paid from the great tithe. A potential surplus shall be used to pay for the poor of the village and for the war tax. The small tithe shall be cancelled for it has been invented by men, since the Lord God created cattle for mankind, free of charge.' So they spoke and the falcon shrieked approvingly from the grey sky above.

'The long practice of serfdom is an outrage because Christ redeemed all of us with his precious bloodshed, from the shepherd to the highest-placed, with no exceptions. Scripture says that we are and that we want to be free.' So they spoke and their friend the forest responded with the rustling of leaves.

'It is unbrotherly and against the word of God that the poor man does not have the right to catch game, fowl and fish. For, when the Lord God created man, He gave him dominion over all animals, the bird in the air and the fish in the water.' So they spoke and the dark forest responded with the growling of beasts.

'The lords have taken possession of the woods. If the poor man needs something, he has to buy it for double its worth. Therefore, all the woods that were not bought shall be given back to the community so that each man can satisfy his needs for timber and firewood.' So they spoke and the bark in the dry woods crackled joyously, ominously.

'The extra labour demanded of us should be considerably reduced because our kinsfolk served only according to the word of God.' So they spoke and then they added: 'The lords must not demand any extra labour without a new agreement.'

'Many properties are not worth the rent demanded. Honest men shall inspect these properties and fix a rent in accordance with justice, so that the peasant does not work for nothing because all workers have the right to be paid fairly.' So they spoke and frozen crows rained from the sky like stones.

'Punishments by fine must be amended by new rules. In the meantime, there must be an end to arbitrary punishments and a return to the old written rules.' So they spoke, but this was before Luther's betrayal.

'Many have appropriated meadows and acres belonging to the community. We want to take them back into our common hands.' So they spoke and the shadow of Atahualpa now glided above those words.

'The inheritance tax must be abolished altogether. Never again shall widows and orphans be robbed contrary to God and honour.' So they spoke, like owls hooting at nightfall.

'If any article herein does not conform to the word of God or is proved unjust, it must be cancelled. We must not establish any further articles that might be against God or bring harm to our fellow man.'

49. Little Johan

Caught between the hammer of solar heresy and the anvil of the furious peasantry, the princes were unsure what to do. Those in the north and the east, who were Lutherans (partly because they saw it as a way of confiscating the immense riches of the church of the nailed god), distrusted Ferdinand, the guardian of ancestral beliefs, opposed to any rupture with the great priest in Rome, but also their bulwark against the Turk. Nevertheless, they knew from experience that the peasants' anger went far beyond the question of communion and other points of ritual, which were only secondary issues for people living in abject poverty. And while that anger rumbled ever louder, the princes of Saxony, Thuringia and Brandenburg were left in a state of uncertainty, awaiting instructions from Wittenberg, the city in the state of Brandenburg where Luther lived.

Things were not at all the same in the west and south, in the regions of Westphalia, Alsace and Swabia, where the princes wished to end the revolt now before it grew, like a farmer drowning a litter of kittens. They paid mercenaries to clean up the countryside and the towns.

During this clean-up, some landsknechts were pursuing a gardener from Strasbourg, whom they considered a troublemaker because he went from village to village preaching the right to cut trees, hunt and fish. One day, when they thought they were about to flush him out of a farm where he'd taken refuge, they found only his wife and his newborn son. They killed both of them cruelly. The news of this vile murder quickly spread through the whole land. As the dead baby's name had been Johan, soon all the talk in the villages and farms and shops was of avenging '*der kleine Johan*. So it was that this new brotherhood took the place of the old Poor Conrad rebellion, seeking not only justice but vengeance, too.

But their anger, however legitimate, however inflamed by the crime, was not enough to withstand the halberds and muskets of the mercenaries. The peasants remembered all too well how, barely two harvests before, the head of their leader, Thomas Müntzer, had rolled in the sawdust, joining the rotting corpses of a hundred thousand of his followers in the fields.

It need hardly be said that neither Luther nor the emperor had come to their rescue. Today, though, the situation had changed.

They sent a messenger to Brussels, asking for help from Atahualpa, protector of the poor, because they knew that without outside support they could expect nothing from the Duke of Lorraine (the entirely misnamed Antoine the Good) but exemplary punishments and their general ruin.

Atahualpa was in no hurry to return to Spain. He felt drawn by a city in the east, only a single day's horse ride from Brussels: Aix-la-Chapelle, where his rival Ferdinand was due to be crowned. He knew that, as long as he stayed in Belgium, the new emperor would not dare get close enough to attend his coronation, unless he declared war on Atahualpa. But that would mean bringing his army across Germany, leaving his eastern flank exposed.

The king of Spain, prince of the Belgians, sovereign of the Netherlands, lord of the Berbers, decided to support Little Johan's rebellion, so he sent his troops into Alsace, with Chalco Chimac at their head.

Overwhelmed by the combined fury of the peasants and the Inca's invincible army, the Duke of Lorraine was promptly crushed. The city of Metz, where Antoine the Good had taken refuge, opened its gates to the assailants because the merchants and the craftsmen sympathised with the peasants' plight: their claims were reasonable, they thought, and they were 'often cut down and eaten up without cause'. Nevertheless, Chalco Chimac was unable to take the duke prisoner because the enraged peasants seized him, along with his brother the Duke of Guise, and tore them apart, before hacking them into smaller pieces and carrying their heads around on spikes.

Politics were not forgotten, however. They submitted to the Inca's representative a new draft of the old claims written long before, by their Swabian brothers. Chalco Chimac sent it on to Brussels. A half-moon later, the Inca's response arrived. I recopy here the original document, which I have before me, annotated in Atahualpa's own hand.

50. The Twelve Articles of the Alsatian Peasantry

Article 1
The Gospel must be preached according to truth, and not according to the interests of lords and priests.
Everyone may practise his religion freely, as long as he participates in the festivals of the Sun.

Article 2
We will pay no more tithes, great or small.
Agreed.

Article 3
Interest on land rent will be reduced to five per cent.
It will be abolished and replaced by a system of labour rotas.

Article 4
All rivers and lakes must be free.
Agreed.

Article 5
The forests will be restored to the community.
Agreed.

Article 6
Game will be free.
Agreed, but only during certain periods determined by the Inca, during festivals of the Sun and certain other festivals. This in order to preserve the existence of game.

Article 7
There will be no more serfs.
Agreed.

Article 8
We will elect our own representatives. The sovereign will be whomever we choose.
Refused.

Article 9
We will be judged by our peers.
Agreed, as long as the nomination of judges is endorsed by the Inca or his representatives.

Article 10
Our bailiffs will be elected and dismissed by us.
Refused. This is the prerogative of the Inca, but you are free to submit your candidates.

Article 11

We will pay no more taxes once we die.

Agreed. In each case, the deceased's family shall receive finan-
cial aid from the commune and food from the personal
reserves of the Inca.

Article 12

All the communal lands taken by our lords will be restored
to the commune.

Agreed.

51. Charlemagne

As soon as the terms of the agreement were discovered, a huge
explosion shook the whole of Germany.

The Alsatian peasants' victory encouraged the others. Now,
all over the German countryside, even the most miserable, isolated peasant knew that he was no longer alone but could count
upon a formidable, providential, quasi-divine force capable of
overcoming all princes; a force, moreover, that seemed inclined to
help the lower orders.

Indeed, Atahualpa sent his troops wherever his aid was
requested. He himself led his soldiers into Westphalia. Thus was
he able to see with his own eyes the temple in Aix-la-Chapelle
where Charles had been crowned emperor. He was able to sit on
Charlemagne's throne, to touch with his own hands that great
man's gilded tombstone. He had learned to admire and envy
Charlemagne while listening to Pedro Pizarro reading tales of
Roland, Angelica, Medoro and Bradamante. And that, probably,
was how an idea came to germinate inside the royal skull, and to

grow, day after day, like a papa sprouting in all directions in the bitter solitude of the dark earth.

Wherever they rebelled, in the wake of Little Johan, the peasants held up their emblem of a lace-up shoe and a flag in the colours of the rainbow. Atahualpa decided to take the rainbow emblem for himself. It struck him as a banner worthy of Charlemagne's empire.

52. Augsburg

The Diet was Germany's equivalent of the Cortes, except that it gathered not only the local princes and sovereigns but representatives of the Empire's cities. But these were so numerous, Germany still being a smorgasbord of tiny states, that the assemblies were attended by literally hundreds of people.

A Diet had been summoned in Augsburg, an imperial city on the borders of Swabia and Bavaria. The Inca, who was now master of all western Germany, naturally had the right to attend. But the presence of Ferdinand in the vicinity made it difficult, perhaps even impossible, for him to go there, particularly since Ferdinand now saw clearly that this foreigner had not only stolen the Spanish throne but had his eyes on the Empire too. In Ferdinand's mind, he and Atahualpa had been engaged in a fight to the death ever since the day his brother was killed, and he considered the looming conflict inevitable. And so he began massing his troops in Bavaria, which was, for him, the gateway to Germany, but also now a buffer state separating him from Swabia, which was almost entirely occupied by Atahualpa's armies.

Indeed, things appeared to be at a stalemate: Atahualpa was barring Ferdinand's way to Aix-la-Chapelle, preventing him from being crowned, while Ferdinand barred Atahualpa's way to Augsburg, preventing him from staking his claims before the Diet.

The two armies faced each other, but neither dared attack. They observed. They waited fearfully. This waiting sapped minds and bodies. Ferdinand's men, in particular, grew irritable and fell ill. But even Atahualpa's army, having fought alongside the peasants against the Catholic princes, was now weary after its German campaign.

Time froze on the Swabian plain.

It was, once again, Higuénamota who found the solution to her friend and lord's problem.

The Cuban princess wrote personally to the king of France, suggesting that he send a message to Suleiman. The message was to read: 'Ferdinand's mind is elsewhere. Vienna could be yours.'

Yet again, the Turkish army, which already occupied most of Hungary, went on the march.

Warned of this threat, Ferdinand had no choice but to quickly return to Austria and protect its capital. His army, moreover, was succumbing to a strange disease that had spread first through Spain, then France, then Flanders, and then Germany: men fell into a fever, they lost their hair, and their bodies were covered in red patches and swellings. The first symptom of the disease was a canker on the manhood, the backside or the back of the throat. At first, people had feared the plague, which swept through entire countries and killed you in a matter of days, but this particular disease was not fatal: its sufferers recovered and, although they never got completely better, the traces of the disease gradually faded. They remained weakened, however, and the whole situation was bad for the troops' morale. Ferdinand's army was relieved to finally move out. The Turk was a fierce opponent, but at least he was familiar, while these Indians from the sea appeared to have God – or the devil – on their side.

The path was clear for Atahualpa.

When he arrived in Augsburg, he immediately held talks with the most powerful man in the city, and perhaps in the whole of Germany.

In truth, Anton Fugger was so important that Atahualpa went straight to stay with him, before he had even presented himself to the Diet or the local authorities. The banker welcomed him into his vast estate, situated in the heart of the city, just as he had once welcomed his predecessor, Charles Quint. The Inca liked Fugger's palace, which was made of a sandy stone. It had a solid simplicity that reminded him of the buildings in Quito. (The truth is that he had never once set foot in Cuzco.) He enjoyed the feast that the banker had had prepared for him. And the beer wasn't bad either.

The two men had a lot to discuss.

Anton Fugger was dressed simply, if a little strangely, even by the standards of the Fifth Quarter. He wore a black coat, with a collarless white shirt visible beneath it, and a hat in the shape of a wide, soft pancake. His hair was enveloped in a sort of bag and there was something vaporous about his beard, which was thick in places and patchy in others. His hands were concealed beneath fine white gloves.

He spoke to the Inca in Italian, and the Inca replied in Spanish. But they understood each other well enough.

In reality, each man had a clear awareness of his own interests and wanted to explain exactly what he had to offer. And, above all, what he expected in return.

It was far from all the festivities, in Fugger's office, that the two men sealed the alliance which, more than any other, would determine the great upheavals to come.

In that office was a dresser with many drawers. Atahualpa, who could now read and write, recognised the names of cities on each of the drawers: *Lisbona, Rom, Sevilla, Augsburg*. Others were, as yet, unknown to him: *Venedig, Nüerenberg, Cracaf* ...

For his part, Fugger understood exactly why this man in a skirt with a feather crown on his head was sitting before him. He was here for the same reasons that had brought Charles Quint to him years before: the Empire was expensive, in two ways. First, you had to pay mercenaries to wage war. Second, you had to buy the votes of the great electors. The gold from beyond the seas was not arriving in Seville fast enough, and from there it was taking too long to reach his current location, not to mention that he then had to change it into ready cash. Fugger could advance enormous sums, which Atahualpa would swallow up in his conquest of the Empire. Atahualpa had to understand that, in exchange for his gold, Fugger would provide units of measure in the form of round coins. The Inca made a vague gesture with his hand. Money did not exist in that form in Tawantinsuyu, but he had perceived the ingenuity of this system since arriving in Spain.

Fugger explained to him the value of these coins: one florin could be exchanged for 25 chickens, 2 pounds of pepper, 21 pints of honey, 180 pounds of salt, or 10 days of work for a skilled labourer.

Atahualpa could believe it: he was going to need a lot of florins.

The Inca had listened attentively, and now he continued to sit in silence. He refused to ask the question. He knew the banker would answer it anyway.

What did he want in exchange?

Fugger poured out two glasses of the black drink from a carafe on his desk and handed one to the Inca, who accepted it without offence. The wine was from Tuscany, the region around Florence. The banker seemed proud of this. During all the years he had spent in the New World – in fact, ever since the civil war with his brother – Atahualpa had learned not to be upset by others' ignorance of the respect owed to his royal birth. So he had long before allowed people to speak directly to him, rather than from behind a veil. He had also had plenty of time to familiarise himself with the customs of the Fifth Quarter: here, he knew that offering someone a drink was a token of friendship and goodwill, a rite that generally took place between equals to celebrate a providential meeting, a special occasion or the conclusion of an agreement. It could also be a trick to poison the guest. But this German really had no motive to poison the foreigner who had made him the richest man in Europe, enabling him to definitively supplant his great rival Welser, the other banker in Augsburg, as well as the Genoese and the merchants of Anvers.

In all probability, the German had hesitated before backing the Inca. It would have been natural for him to support Ferdinand, Charles Quint's designated heir as head of the Empire. But two factors had determined his choice: Atahualpa's solvency, due to his seemingly inexhaustible reserves of gold and silver. And the prospect of new markets.

Fugger was not asking for much, really. Years before, the king of Portugal had granted Fugger's uncle the authorisation to trade with the city of Goa, in the Indies, in the distant East. Then he had withdrawn that authorisation. What Anton Fugger wanted from the king of Spain was a similar licence to be allowed to buy products from beyond the seas. The Fuggers were a family of weavers who had grown wealthy. Anton particularly wished to trade in alpaga wool, which was of higher quality than anything to be found in Europe. He also had it in mind to import rubber, which he saw as a promising investment, because the weeping wood from which this material was extracted could not be found on this side of the world.

Atahualpa agreed. He was about to clink glasses to seal the deal, as he knew was the custom, but Fugger raised a hand to suspend his gesture.

He had one more condition.

He wanted the Inca to get rid of Luther.

Atahualpa was surprised that his host should care so much about religion.

But the truth was that Luther was bad for business. The rebel priest had always vilified what constituted the heart of a banker's activities: loans with interest. And it was he, this little monk from Wittenberg, who had ruined the lucrative trade in indulgences, which Rome had extended to pay back the colossal debts racked up with Uncle Jakob.

The nephew said there was nothing personal, but he wanted Luther dead, within two moons, or their agreement would be null and void and he would suspend all payments.

With no clear idea of how achievable this part of the contract actually was, or of its potential political repercussions, Atahualpa, blinded by his imperial dreams, agreed. At last they clinked glasses, toasting friendship between peoples and the universal Empire.

The Inca left with a chest filled with five thousand florins – only a thousandth, it was said, of the Fugger fortune.

53. The Protestant Princes

Now, using force or persuasion, he had to bring to heel the German princes from the east and the south, most of whom were in favour of Luther's reforms.

Essentially, this meant the Margrave of Brandenburg, Joachim-Hector; his cousin, Albert of Brandenburg, the Duke of Prussia; the Landgrave of Hesse, Philip 'the Magnanimous'; and, most importantly, Luther's personal protector, nephew of Frederick the Wise, elector of Saxony, John Frederick, who was also known as 'the Magnanimous' (a quality apparently very common among these princes).

There was also Maurice of Saxony, John Frederick's cousin and rival, but given that he was neither an elector nor openly Lutheran, and also had considerable military resources to defend himself if it came to it, Atahualpa decided to concentrate his efforts on the others.

The Lutheran princes were faced with a dilemma. They were instinctively opposed to Ferdinand, as they had been to Charles, because, just like his dead brother, the new emperor was scornful of the religious reforms they were demanding. In fact, what they wanted was a German equivalent of the Seville Edict that would guarantee the same religious freedoms in the Empire that Atahualpa had brought to Spain.

At the same time, though, welcoming the Inca into Germany and putting him in charge of the Empire in place of Ferdinand essentially meant importing that religion of the Sun, which was not merely heresy, but – as far as they could tell – pure heathenry.

However, they were no strangers to the notion of compromise. First they had depended on Charles, and then on Ferdinand, to help them put down the peasant revolts. But, it seemed to them, Atahualpa's army would do the job just as well.

What worried them was this programme of political reforms that Atahualpa had implemented in his kingdoms, and the concessions he had made to the Alsatian peasants. Under no circumstances were the princes willing to forsake the substantial revenues that they drew from the resources of their lands and the labour of their peasants, which was the basis of their civil life, with its privileges for the nobility dating back to time immemorial. Now, Atahualpa's presence in the area risked kindling the flames of revolt, as did the hope offered by his reforms, based on the twelve articles that were secretly transmitted throughout the Saxony and Prussian countryside. There seemed something dangerously harmonious, too neat in its accounting, between

Atahualpa's plans and the peasants' aspirations. At most, the princes could envisage freeing their serfs, who were peasants that had been reduced to a state of slavery. But the very thought of redistributing land to the communes, or to anyone, struck them as absolutely inconceivable. Yet that was what had happened in Alsace, in Westphalia, in the Rhineland, in Swabia and certain provinces of the Palatinate.

So the princes who met Atahualpa were utterly bewildered, with no idea of what they should do next. Once again, the Inca called upon the cunning Chalco Chimac to lead the negotiations. The general used that crafty mix of threats and promises, that iron fist in a velvet glove, which he always found so effective in helping the other party make the right decisions.

Even so, the protestant princes remained hesitant to commit.

To put an end to these procrastinations, they suggested to the Inca that he organise a personal meeting with Luther. He would tell them which path to follow, and they promised they would comply with his instructions. That, of course, did not exclude the numerous emoluments that they would claim from the new emperor, and which Atahualpa was prepared to grant them, nor the gigantic bribes he would have to pay to assure himself of their support and their vote, and which Fugger would have to advance him.

Atahualpa gave his agreement. A summons was sent to Wittenberg, where Luther lived. The religious leader was asked to report immediately to the Diet of Augsburg in order to meet the king of Spain, the new pretender to the title of emperor, to hear his arguments and decide if they were worthy; in other words, to determine whether his candidacy was compatible with the Gospel.

The response arrived a few days later: Dr Luther thanked the honourable assembly for its invitation but regretfully declined. The monk wished to respectfully remind the gentlemen of the

Diet of a precedent that they certainly had not forgotten: having presented himself to the Diet of Worms before Charles Quint, Luther had found himself banished from the Empire, abducted by strangers in a dark forest, and had thought that his final hour was upon him. Consequently, he begged the princes, his benefactors, to forgive his refusal, and recommended everyone to God.

Atahualpa, well known and often praised for his legendary self-control, nevertheless began to manifest a few signs of impatience. So the Duke of Saxony suggested that he make the journey to Wittenberg. He would personally ensure that the Inca would be welcomed there with all the reverence due to his rank, and he would organise the meeting between Atahualpa and Luther.

The Inca instinctively distrusted this fat man with his half-moon eyes, red beard and short hair. But, after a brief consultation with his general staff, he gave his agreement. The call of the Empire was too strong to be ignored.

Among the seven electors who voted for the emperor's appointment, there were three priests and four princes. The three archbishops of Trier, Mainz and Cologne had come under his control during the war of Little Johan, which he had won alongside the peasants. So he already had those three votes. Ferdinand had inherited the kingdom of Bohemia, and the count palatine of the Rhine had taken refuge in his lands to the east after his defeat to Ruminahui's army. Those two votes were beyond his grasp. So he needed one more vote. There remained the two Lutheran electors. The Duke of Saxony and the Margrave of Brandenburg held the fate of the empire in their hands.

He would go to Wittenberg, accompanied by Higuénamota and Chalco Chimac. The other Lutheran princes would go too, to be present for that historic meeting. In fact, people would come from all over Germany, and even from Denmark and Poland, to see Atahualpa meet Luther.

54. Wittenberg

They learned a great deal during the journey. They passed poor peasants, starving families, sick children. They saw men without noses and men without ears. Some had two fingers missing from their right hand. The women did not speak or weep, they just stared out hatefully at everything around them, like cats caught in a trap, ready to hiss.

A blinded beggar held out his bowl as the Inca passed. The Yana guards wanted to kick him out of the way, but Atahualpa ordered his litter to be carried over to where the man sat. The beggar shook the bowl as if it were a bell. Staring at the Inca with his white eyes, he said: 'Compassionate God, support the rights of the poor.' He left with a gold ring and two florins.

Soon afterwards, the procession paused in the imperial city of Nuremberg, the magnificence of its buildings offering a stark contrast to the poverty of the surrounding countryside.

The rest of the journey, which included a stop in Leipzig, a city famous for its markets, provided the same sights and provoked the same thoughts. Here, noseless men; there, stunning opulence.

Finally, they arrived.

Wittenberg was a renowned centre of learning, but it looked nothing like Salamanca.

The city was populated by monks in robes, who bustled around like busy little ants, holding stacks or cases of talking sheets in their hands, carrying suckling pigs or loaves of bread or kegs of beer under their arms, and wearing wooden crosses around their necks.

The castle church was topped by a fearful tower – circular, with a crown of spikes, like the bulb of a black rose with its own stem growing up out of it – which cast its gloomy shadow over the surrounding city.

In the market square, monks rubbed shoulders with students, merchants and farmers' wives. Sheep and pigs weaved in and out between all those human legs.

The castle itself had been uninhabited since the death of Frederick the Wise. His nephew and heir offered to lodge the Inca and his men there; he sent them his cooks, whom they quickly sent back. They occupied the empty castle, then Chalco Chimac went straight to see Philip Melanchthon – Luther's right-hand man, who had visited Atahualpa long before in Granada – to prepare for the big meeting.

Melanchthon could speak many languages. The interview took place in Castilian. He was a man of unremarkable size, who smiled affably from behind his little red beard. Although prematurely wrinkled, his face wore a childlike expression that generally inspired immediate trust and sympathy. These, however, were not feelings to which Chalco Chimac was particularly susceptible. What the Inca general noticed was the intelligence that lay behind the affability.

The professor and the general clinked glasses and drank the beer that Luther brewed himself. This seemed to amuse Melanchthon, although he wasn't, he admitted, much of a beer-drinker.

The interview lasted a whole afternoon. The two men ignored the agitation of the household around them: the old servant who kept coming back to refill the carafe of beer, the students passing by to drop off or pick up sheets, intrigued by the sight of this unusual visitor whom they observed on the sly, overhearing snatches of dialogue that they could not understand.

When the Inca general returned to his master, this was the report he made: the people of this place were called 'Protestants'.

They demanded the freedom to practise their religion as they saw fit. They wanted to make changes to the way the nailed god was worshipped. They were very attached to certain rites, and dismissive of certain others. They wanted their priests to be free to marry, as they already did: Luther himself, although a priest, had a wife and children, which was theoretically forbidden, as was all carnal intercourse. They were obsessed by the question of where they would go after death and the best way of being saved; in other words, going to heaven to rejoin their nailed god (although he was supposed to return to the earth at some indeterminate date, which made Chalco Chimac worry that they might meet him) and not under the earth where the dead were burned for ever, except for one transitory place where souls could emerge after a certain time, but certainly not by putting florins in the right hands during one's lifetime.

Another question, which Chalco Chimac thought he had grasped a little better, concerned what they called good works. Should one, or should one not, do good things in the hope of obtaining salvation? The Protestants firmly believed that this was not the case, and that the conditions of their life after death were completely independent of their behaviour while alive. All good works must be accomplished in a disinterested fashion, motivated only by the example of their nailed god, and not by the desire to be rewarded for them. Chalco Chimac had resisted the urge to ask Melanchthon how, in that case, the nailed god could decide who to save and who to burn under the earth. In truth, the general was only interested in local superstitions to the extent that they could be used for his political advantage. The questions they raised and the moral problems that ensued left him cold.

The same was not true in reverse. Melanchthon had asked many questions: he was curious about his visitor's country, its customs, its gods; he had asked if they waged war, if they had slaves, if they'd ever heard of the nailed god before, if the Sun rewarded the good and punished the bad. He had seemed particularly curious about the location of Tawantinsuyu. He, more than the others, seemed to understand that the Quitonians were not Indians.

Anyway, in conclusion, this man had struck Chalco Chimac as being open to dialogue and negotiation. But he had implied that Luther was not so easy-going; that the great priest of the reform movement had a somewhat inflexible character, which, everyone agreed, was not improving with the passing of time.

The conversation had ended up dwindling into more peripheral subjects. Among other things, the red-bearded amauta had declared, after a large amount of beer: 'Augsburg is the German Florence, and the Fuggers are the Medicis of our time.' Chalco Chimac had considered this remark, made in passing, to be of sufficient interest to be reported to his master.

55. Luther

The first meeting took place in the large building that they called *Universität*, in front of an audience of a thousand people and in the presence of the Elector of Saxony.

To Atahualpa, looking down at him from a stage where he sat enthroned between Higuénamota and Chalco Chimac, Luther resembled an angry bull. The priest's words sounded harsh, like axe blows. Melanchthon translated them into Spanish. The speech he gave was rambling and incoherent, and the Quitonians had trouble following his meaning. He talked a lot about the Jews, whom he accused of terrible crimes and very much wished to harm. According to Luther, they were 'filled with the devil's excrement', and it was a sin not to kill them. At the very least, they should be expelled from Germany like rabid dogs and their houses burned.

Luther spoke on this subject without interruption for nearly an hour. Atahualpa listened in silence, impassive as ever in such circumstances (although this particular circumstance, it has to be said, was pretty much unprecedented), without betraying his total incomprehension.

Then Luther began talking about his guests, these visitors from beyond the seas.

There could be no doubt, he said, that Atahualpa and his men had been sent by God to punish sinners and purify the Church.

The Sun they glorified was nothing more nor less than a metaphor for God, and Atahualpa was, perhaps, if not the reincarnated Messiah, then at least a new prophet, or an angel sent to earth.

However, he, Luther, had also been appointed by God to bring justice to the world, and he could not remain silent. No, he could not. He had to warn the Inca: it was not good that this woman (here, he pointed at Higuénamota) should be beside him. Melanchthon had stopped translating at this point, but nobody doubted Luther's meaning, even those who spoke no German.

Higuénamota was wearing clothes, because it was colder in these lands. But clearly Luther had heard rumours of the famous naked princess. Naturally, he suspected her of being the devil's envoy. Higuénamota thought this was funny. And so occurred the famous scene, immortalised by the painter Cranach, when the princess, who had got to her feet, let her dress slip down, revealing her naked body to the astounded audience.

But while she stood proudly, provocatively, before him, a defiant smile on her lips, the spectators crying out in anger and dismay or watching admiringly, a few even laughing, Luther insolently pointed his avenging finger at the naked Cuban and barked: 'Men have wide shoulders and narrow hips. They are blessed with intelligence. Women have narrow shoulders and wide hips, so that they may have children and stay at home.'

The meeting was adjourned.

56. The Dilemma

'Kill him,' said Higuénamota.

But it wasn't that simple.

Eliminating Luther would mean fulfilling his part of the bargain agreed with Fugger and thus ensuring that the banker would furnish him with the hundreds of thousands of florins necessary to buy the votes of the two protestant electors. But it would also mean alienating those same electors, and with them all the princes who supported the rebel monk, grouped together in the Schmalkaldic League.

He did not have the military resources on hand to defeat that coalition: Quizquiz had remained in Spain with one-third of his army, to repel any surprise attacks by Suleiman or Ferdinand, and another third had been left behind to look after Belgium and western Germany.

But neither could he guarantee his election through peaceful means, since it was dependent upon both the death and the agreement of Luther.

While Atahualpa thought about this, crowds converged on Wittenberg. Throughout the country, an immense optimism was growing around the meeting between Luther and the Inca. Of course, the people had not forgotten Luther's betrayal when he renounced Thomas Müntzer and incited the princes to massacre the rebellious peasants, but they were all tantalised by thoughts of the Alsatian peasantry's twelve articles: they hoped that Emperor Atahualpa would extend his laws through the whole of

Germany. The market square and the streets of the little town were soon filled with men, women, children, and hope.

Meanwhile, Chalco Chimac had returned to Melanchthon's house to drink more beer and try to save the accord.

As a precondition to further talks the red-bearded little man had persuaded his friend Luther to apologise.

One important point of debate was the status of this religion of the Sun. For obvious political reasons, there could be no question of considering it heresy or like the religion of the false prophet Mohammed. Atahualpa's victories proved that God was on his side. In fact, the defeat inflicted on the kingdoms of the Fifth Quarter was undoubtedly God's punishment for their corruption, demonstrating once again the truthfulness of Luther's theories. That was why Luther, in his wisdom, considered Atahualpa to be an envoy of God, not of the devil, and, after reflection, would agree to see the Inca religion as a metaphor or a version of the Gospel designed for the world beyond the seas, just as the Old Testament was – according to followers of the nailed god – a collection of tales that heralded and prefigured the New.

'Like a rough draft?' the general asked.

'More like an interpretation of the same theme,' his host replied.

In that case, Chalco Chimac said, what were they to make of Luther's speech about the Jews?

Melanchthon swept the question away with the back of his hand. 'Nothing. As he's got older, he's grown obsessed with that subject. But it is merely an old man's folly and should not interfere with these debates. You just have to let him talk.'

They decided that the next meeting would take place in the castle church. Chalco Chimac returned from his visit reassured and even mildly enthusiastic. Then again, he had drunk quite a lot of beer. He faithfully reported Melanchthon's advice to his master: 'Let him talk, and agree with as much of it as you can. Then you'll have your accord.'

57. The Castle Church

Rumour had it that the great amauta Erasmus himself had made the journey, despite the fact that news of his death – in Basel, where he'd taken refuge long before to escape religious persecution – had been widely known for several harvests. That was a measure of the historical importance attached to this meeting between the century's two great reformers. But nobody could guess what its outcome might be, and throughout Germany, throughout the Fifth Quarter, even in Rome, the world held its breath.

Meanwhile, Wittenberg was in uproar. Printed sheets were passed from hand to hand: the twelve articles, with engravings and portraits of Atahualpa, Müntzer, Little Johan. The walls were covered with drawings of lace-up shoes. Pamphlets denounced Luther as 'the Stupid and Lazy Meat of Wittenberg'. Huge numbers of peasants continued to arrive. They set up camp at the gates of the city, scaring the elector John Frederick into calling up regiments of landsknechts as reinforcements, to prevent things getting out of hand. Rainbow banners fluttered in the wind next to the flag of Saxony.

In the castle church, however, everyone was on his best behaviour. Luther apologised publicly to Higuénamota. He said that the religion of the Sun could be tolerated as a metaphor for the Gospel. True, he excoriated the sectarians and fanatics outside who wanted to subvert God's order, and demanded that all participants join him in condemning their calls for violence. Without naming them, though, he made clear allusions to the twelve articles. He was ready to recognise the legitimacy of certain claims. ('At last!' thought some. 'A bit late,' said others.) He asked the princes to examine their consciences, and to yield what they could. He spent less time cursing the Jews.

Atahualpa, for his part, had agreed to reverse their roles: he had taken his place among the front row of the faithful, on a wooden bench, beside Higuénamota (who had graciously accepted Luther's apology), and they had let Luther climb into the pulpit. In other words, he was addressing them from a position that looked down on Atahualpa, an arrangement that under normal circumstances would never have been allowed. The Empire is worth a Mass, he'd said, laughing, to the elector. Chalco Chimac and Melanchthon glanced at each other uneasily when Luther began raging at the Jews again, but taken within the context of the entire speech, such mutterings were no more than a few insignificant dregs at the bottom of a glass of good beer.

The essential thing was that the principle of an agreement based on the Seville Edict seemed to be in the bag. When the meeting was over, they congratulated one another. The two electors John Frederick of Saxony and Joachim II Hector of Brandenburg were already negotiating the price of their votes with Atahualpa. (They wanted a hundred thousand florins, which the Inca did not have, for a very good reason.) Melanchthon and Chalco Chimac chatted between themselves. It seemed reasonable, just then, to hope that a text could be quickly written and signed.

We know, today, that that is not what transpired.

58. The Church Doors

On the morning of the fifth day, crows flew above the tower. Outside the entrance to the temple, where the parties were due to meet once again to hammer out the final agreement, a crowd had gathered, curious and excited. For the second time in twenty-five harvests, a list of theses had been nailed to the wooden doors, and these were being read aloud, and gradually passed on to those behind, so that a vague echo spread throughout the whole city. (The text was in German.)

Then the man appeared, preceded by a murmur, and everyone made way for him. He was a paunchy monk in a black beret; his jowly face was severe but weary, his gaze less piercing than it once was, his step less lively, but he was still an imposing man. In his presence, everyone felt a little smaller.

As the murmurs grew louder, he approached the doors that he had, for a long time, and not without reason, thought of as his. And everyone in the crowd watched as the monk's face turned crimson.

59. The Ninety-Five Theses of the Sun

1. The Sun is not an allegory of God the creator.
2. He is God the creator and the source of all life.
3. Viracocha is his father or his son, and father or son of the Moon.
4. The Inca is the Sun's representative on earth.

5. The Inca is descended from Manco Capac, the founding father, and his sister Mama Ocllo, both of them children of the Sun.

6. The Inca belongs to this lineage: that is why he is considered the son of the Sun.

7. The Inca belongs to the younger branch of the Sun's family, because Manco Capac was the younger brother or the grandson of Viracocha.

8. Consequently, the authority of the Pope, representative of the old religion, cannot be applied to the Inca, or to his vassals, or to any followers of the religion of the Sun.

9. The year 1531 of the old era is the first year of the new era, since it marks the coming of the Inca, over the Ocean Sea.

10. The earth trembled and Lisbon opened a door to the son of the Sun that nobody here will ever close.

11. The Holy Trinity imagined by Tertullian at the beginning of the old era is the imperfect allegorical representation of the Sun, the Moon and the Thunder.

12. This representation is imperfect because the Virgin Mary ought to take her place in the Holy Trinity, as an allegory of the Moon, and not the Holy Spirit. Or, if one had wished to add the Thunder to the three principal divinities, then it should have been called the Quaternity.

13. It is true that the god of Thunder can strike the earth with his hammer, but his power is far from equal to that of the Sun, to whom he owes allegiance.

14. The Holy Family is no more acceptable as an allegory of the true gods of the Sun, the Moon and their son-father Viracocha, since in the old religion Joseph is not considered a god but simply a man who is the adoptive father of the false messiah Jesus.

15. The virginal conception of the false messiah Jesus is a fable, probably invented to justify Mary's untimely pregnancy, since Joseph, her husband, was an impotent old man.

16. The Sun fertilised the Moon to create Viracocha, his brother Manco Capac and the earth Pachamama.

17. Those who claim that the Moon is an allegory of Mary, and not vice versa, must not persist in this error, because if that had been the case, the God of the Christians would not have permitted the Inca's arrival or his victories. Whereas we can see that the Inca has conquered this part of the world with the blessing of the god Sun and the goddess Moon, his ancestors, and that we were wrong about our false idols and our false messiah.

18. The true Jerusalem is not in Jerusalem but in Cuzco, beyond the Ocean Sea, situated at the navel of the world.

19. Neither the Pope nor his representatives can demand money for the redemption of sins because they do not have the authority.

20. The dying pay all debts when they die.

21. So the preachers are wrong who say that if a man buys indulgences from the Pope, he is relieved of all pain and is saved.

22. Christians must learn that to give to the poor or lend to those in need is better than to buy indulgences.

23. Christians must learn that one who sees a poor man and, ignoring him, spends his money on indulgences, will earn not the indulgence of the Pope but the wrath of Viracocha.

24. Christians must learn that, unless they have far more than they need, they should save their money instead of wasting it on indulgences.

25. All bishops, pastors and theologians who spread this message to the people will pay for their crimes.

26. When Christians are asked why their God expelled the first man and the first woman from paradise, they talk much nonsense and, seeing that their arguments do not hold water, they invent allegories based on that fable of the subtle serpent and the forbidden fruit and the corrupt woman.

27. When old Christians who eat the body and drink the blood of their own god are asked how they can practise such cannibalistic barbarity, they are surprised and do not know what to say, except for certain Lutherans who admit that their god's presence in the ceremony is purely symbolic.

28. As for those followers of Luther who believe that some men's salvation is already decided, and others' damnation likewise, with the rest of humanity doomed to wander after death in an antechamber of hell, with no account taken of their works or their actions, these men should be horrified by the cruelty and tyranny of this god who saves some men and not others, at his own whim, like the god of the Jews, whom Luther and his followers are nonetheless quick to vilify.

29. However, Luther is right on one point, when he affirms that if a virgin believes herself superior, or even simply equal, to others, then 'she is the virgin of Satan', even if Satan is merely the fruit of a Christian superstition; by which we mean that virginity has no value in itself and it should not be demanded as a prerequisite for marriage.

30. Why is it so important for followers of the nailed god that their god should be recognised to the exclusion of all others? This is a mystery that we cannot explain.

31. The nailed god may, however, serve as an example, as did Moses and other saints. But his life remains his own and does not save men, Christian or otherwise, in any way whatsoever.

32. The Sun does not demand the death of other gods. He does not require this to preserve his primacy or his power because none of those gods can harm him.

33. The Sun is not jealous; he does not choose his people; he does not save a minority of men and leave the rest in darkness. He extends his benign light over all the men of the earth.

34. In the same way, the Inca, the son of the Sun, extends his magnanimous goodness to all the men of the earth, with no exception.

35. Many are those who teach about the nailed god only to stir up emotion, to make people love Christ, to make them hate Jews, and other childish, effeminate nonsense.

36. Likewise, it is childish to believe that the father of the nailed god created the world and then, one day, sent his son to save men. Where was this god during the Trojan War? Was he sleeping? Why did he leave the Greeks in ignorance of his existence?

37. Why didn't he inform such wise men as Plato and Aristotle of his existence? Why wait so long? Were there no sinners who deserved saving, before?

38. In truth, the ages succeed one another like destruction succeeds creation, and like creation succeeds destruction.

39. The first age was the age of the first men who wore leaves as clothing.

40. The second age was the age of the second human race who lived in peace. The flood put an end to that race.

41. The third age was the age of the wild men who revered Pachacamac. They were constantly at war. It was during this period that the daughter of Thunder brought them iron.

42. The fourth age was the age of the warriors. That was when the world was divided into four parts.

43. The fifth age is the age of the Sun. It coincides with the reign of the Incas on earth. The world has grown bigger, with a fifth part, which is ours.

44. Just as the old religion was cruel and iniquitous, with its arbitrary punishments and its unjust decrees, so the religion of the Sun is fair and good and balanced.

45. Because, really, what father worthy of that name would sacrifice his son?

46. Why give men free will if it enables them to do evil?

47. Why make sinners, only to punish them afterwards?

48. Children know nothing of the nailed god until a Christian tells them his story. But they meet the Sun in their very first days upon the earth. That is why worshippers of the Sun need not be baptised, whether adults or children.

49. Paul worried that certain men might never know about the existence of his nailed god: 'How shall they believe in Him of whom they have not heard?' The Sun has no need of preachers because he shines in the sky and every evening he goes to sleep in the sea and every morning he rises above the mountains.

50. Paul again: 'Faith comes by hearing.' But faith in the Sun is not taught. All one must do is look up.

51. However, Paul sensed the truth when he said: 'The night is far spent, the day is at hand: let us therefore cast off the works of darkness, and let us put on the armour of light.' (Romans 13:12)

52. 'Him that is weak in the faith receive ye, but not to doubtful disputations.' (Romans 14:1)

53. 'For one believeth that he may eat all things: another, who is weak, eateth herbs.' (Romans 14:2)

54. 'Let not him that eateth despise him that eateth not; and let not him that eateth not judge him that eateth: for God hath received him.' (Romans 14:3)

55. For the kingdom of Viracocha is not meat or drink, but righteousness and peace and joy in the Sun, as revealed in Romans 14:17.

56. Let those prophets be gone who say to the people of the nailed god: 'death to the Antichrist!' when, according to them, the Antichrist is everyone that they are not.

57. The Sun supports the rights of the poor.

58. He gave birth to the earth so that all may taste its salt.

59. Neither the Sun nor the earth demand payment of a tithe, great or small, from anyone.

60. The earth cannot be bought or rented or loaned at interest.

61. The earth cannot be monopolised. It is divided according to each man's needs.

62. The waters are part of the earth and are free.

63. Fish belong to the river.

64. Game belongs to the forest.

65. The forests belong to the earth, which belongs to the Sun.

66. The Sun knows no serfs, he knows only men.

67. The Inca is the Sun's descendant on earth, but the Sun considers us all his children.

68. Under the Sun, Cain does not kill Abel.

69. If ever such a thing were to happen, Cain would be judged by men, his other brothers.

70. The living should not pay for their dead, or others' dead.

71. They are hypocrites, those princes who have secondary wives that they call favourites.

72. The Pope is a hypocrite too, giving his bastards the best positions.

73. The earth turns around his father the Sun.

74. The Sun is, naturally, at the centre of the universe.

75. Our Lord Jesus Christ is a son of the Sun who created men.

76. He is the younger brother or grandson of Viracocha.

77. Our Lord Jesus Christ is to the Fifth Quarter what Manco Capac is to the kingdom of the Four Quarters.

78. Nevertheless, between Jesus Christ and Manco Capac, precedence goes to the latter, since the sons of Manco Capac have come to our lands to fulfil the good news that Our Lord Jesus Christ proclaimed, and not vice versa.

79. God did not want us to go to the kingdom beyond the seas to teach the good news.

80. The Pope represents nobody but himself. He is not St Peter's son.

81. Luther was right to denounce the avarice and cupidity of the Pope.

82. Luther was wrong to denounce the peasants who called for more justice.

83. Luther was right to condemn the laziness and corruption of princes.

84. Luther was wrong to condemn the supposed perversity of the people.

85. Luther was right to see the Castel Sant'Angelo as the seat of the Babylonian whore.

86. Luther was right to see the Antichrist in the person of the Pope but he was wrong to see the Antichrist in the person of Thomas Müntzer, whose only fault was to want a better life for poor people.

87. Luther is a prophet of the end times.

88. But Luther did not see the coming of the new times.

89. The Inca embodies the new Law and the new Spirit.

90. The princes are not representatives of the Sun on earth.

91. The Inca is the sole legitimate representative of the Sun.

92. The princes are the curacas of the Inca. In other words, they are his representatives in his absence.

93. The princes draw their authority from the Inca.

94. The laws of the Inca are the laws of the Empire.

95. God is the other name of the Sun.

60. The End of Luther

Nobody ever found out who wrote the theses, although many people were suspected. Among them were Christoph Schappeler, a Swabian preacher; Ulrich Schmid, the author of the twelve articles, who was supposed to still be alive; the brothers Hans Sebald and Barthel Beham, two painters who had formerly been accused of atheism; Pilgram Marpeck, the Anabaptist; certain printers and students, some of whom had been taught by Luther himself; even Melanchthon was suspected. Had Atahualpa ordered the text to be written? Even today, there is no proof of that whatsoever.

Naturally, Luther was furious. He took this manifesto for what it undoubtedly was, at least in part: a personal attack. As far as he was concerned, there was no longer any question of an agreement. His voice thundered throughout the university, where he took refuge. It was a massive scandal.

But that is not all it was. John Frederick understood this, and immediately decreed a curfew and sent landsknechts to patrol the city.

He was wasting his time. The first riots began the day after the theses appeared. The elector's troops crossed swords with the rioters. Houses blazed. Corpses were strewn across the streets. Calls for calm from the most eminent professors had no effect. The students divided into two camps. A fire began in the university and spread to Luther's house, which adjoined it. Luther tried to take refuge in Melanchthon's house, but it is said he found the door locked.

While this was happening, Atahualpa did not intervene. His army, outside the city, received the order not to move under any circumstances. He remained deaf to the elector's pleas. The men in his personal guard did not leave the castle where they were garrisoned.

Luther attempted to flee in a cart, hidden under a load of hay, but he was captured by a gang of peasants displaying the banner of the *Bundschuh*, the lace-up shoe.

He was beaten and tortured, his eyes were gouged out, he was quartered and dismembered, and his remains were burned.

His death, though, was not enough to satisfy the peasants' anger. The Duchy of Saxony went up in flames, and so did the rest of Germany.

John Frederick, Joachim-Hector of Brandenburg and the others negotiated the civil peace with Atahualpa, who was the only one in a position to deliver it. In Luther's place, Melanchthon ratified the Treaty of Wittenberg, granting religious liberty in accordance with a duly negotiated principle: to each region, its religion. In other words, each prince would decide for his subjects, with no interference from Rome. This was not as liberal as the Seville Edict, but that was not what mattered. After being promised that they could keep certain privileges, the princes yielded to almost all of the twelve articles. John Frederick and Joachim-Hector, who effectively abandoned most of their sovereignty to the Inca, did not forget to ask for financial compensation.

With Luther dead, the money arrived from Augsburg, as promised: one hundred thousand florins each. In his homeland, Atahualpa had never learned to moderate his generosity, particularly when there were political considerations at play. He paid without haggling, because his generosity was part of his strategy. In reality, it was consubstantial with his imperial dignity, on either side of the Ocean Sea.

61. The Coronation

'Sire, since God has conferred upon you the immense grace of raising you above all the kings and princes of Christianity, to a position of power previously possessed only by your predecessor Charles Quint, and before him only Charlemagne, you are on your way towards universal monarchy, allowing you to unite all of ... Christianity under your leadership.'

With these words, the Archbishop of Mainz, Albert of Brandenburg – uncle of Joachim-Hector, who was himself the Margrave and Elector of Brandenburg – welcomed Atahualpa into the temple of Aix-la-Chapelle, beneath an immense gilded copper chandelier, at the feet of the statues of St Paul with his cross and St Peter with his key (two idols popular in these parts) to formally present him with the attributes of imperial dignity.

Atahualpa did not bat an eyelid as he listened to this plump priest with his womanly lips, soft flesh and baleful gaze acclaiming him as the saviour of the Catholic faith. Which, to be frank, seemed something of an exaggeration: not only had the Inca conquered most of the Fifth Quarter, leaving only France, England and Portugal beyond the scope of his territorial ambitions, but he had deprived Ferdinand of his Empire and driven the

Catholic king back into Austria, to face Suleiman alone and without support.

Since then, Temples of the Sun had spread all over the surface of the New World, and even the German princes – Catholics, as well as Lutherans – were starting to convert. In fact, the Elector of Brandenburg was one of them.

Consequently, it seemed difficult to justify the idea that Atahualpa had worked for the glory of Jesus Christ, their local divinity.

The great priest of Rome, moreover, had made it clear that he would excommunicate the Inca if he took the place intended for Ferdinand, his brother's legitimate heir. (Excommunication was a sort of symbolic banishment from the Catholic community, something kings did not pay much attention to.)

None of this apparently mattered to the archbishop, who had been deeply involved in the corrupt selling of indulgences, who had been among Luther's most resolute enemies, and who had sold his vote at a high price during Charles Quint's election. ('I am ashamed of his shame,' the king of Spain's envoy had said at the time.) His entire political career showed a distinct reluctance to let scruples and promises get in the way of his ambitions. Besides, as far as Albert was concerned, the military occupation of the Rhineland by the Inca's army had removed all alternative outcomes and moral dilemmas. His submission to the new master of Germany went without saying; and, unlike Charles, Atahualpa had not even needed to pay him. Sometimes gold replaces iron, and sometimes it is the other way round. For the Inca's coronation, the priest was wearing his most beautiful red robe, and his fingers were weighed down by a cornucopia of rings set with precious multicoloured stones.

The other electors, with the exception of Ferdinand, had come to salute their new emperor. They were all frustrated at having to renounce some of their prerogatives, but that frustration was mingled with relief at having avoided the worst. Luther was dead and rotting in hell with the Duke of Lorraine and his brother the Duke of Guise, while they were alive.

Melanchthon, too, attended the ceremony in Aix-la-Chapelle: that surely says enough about the extraordinary work of unification, if not reconciliation, accomplished by the Quitonian adventurer.

For a long time, the Holy Roman Empire had been a collection of divided states, with its symbolic leadership handed to the most powerful German family of the moment.

Now things had changed in both senses: Atahualpa was neither a German prince nor an abstraction. He was the Reformer and the Protector of the Poor, and those titles, granted to him by the people, were not symbolic at all: he had earned them. While he was receiving the crown, the sceptre and the globe of Charlemagne from the hands of the jowly priest, his laws were already being applied throughout most of the Empire, and even beyond, in certain regions of eastern France and northern Switzerland, where the local authorities had been forced to apply his reforms to avoid further uprisings.

The king of France had sent his sister Marguerite to represent him, alongside her son-in-law Manco.

The king of Portugal had delegated his brother, the infant Luis, Duke of Beja, who had, like Francis, taken part in the Barbary Coast campaign.

The king of England's second wife, Anne Boleyn, had been sent to Aix-la-Chapelle. (Since the first was Charles Quint's aunt, it was not thought suitable that she should come to salute his successor, given the events that had led to his death.)

The vizier Hassan al-Wazzan had made the voyage from Algiers.

Lorenzino had come with Quispe Sisa, dressed in the Italian fashion, and her beauty drew admiring whispers wherever she went.

Sitting on Charlemagne's stone throne, before this prestigious audience, while the music from the giant flutes inside the church echoed against the centuries-old walls, Atahualpa must have been thinking about his brother Huascar. He was Huascar's equal now, and he'd accomplished things that none of his ancestors, even the great Pachacuti, had even imagined possible.

62. The Empire's Ten Laws

The first and most important specifies that nobody who is exempted has to pay the tribute, at any time or for any reason. Those exempted include the Incas of royal blood, the captain-generals and their subordinates, even the centurions and their children and grandchildren, all the curacas and their kin. Royal officers employed in minor tasks do not pay the tribute during their time in office, nor do soldiers kept for war and conquest, nor anyone under the age of twenty-five, because until that age their duty is to serve their parents. Everyone over fifty is exempt too, as are all women and girls, whether single, widowed or married; anyone who is sick, until they have recovered from their illness; the disabled, such as anyone who is blind, or has a leg or an arm missing (although the deaf and the dumb are employed in jobs that can be done without speaking or hearing).

The second says that all Levantines not among those who have just been named are obliged to pay this tribute, except for the priests and servants of the Temples of the Sun, or chosen virgins.

The third, that irrespective of the motive, any Levantine may pay in lieu of the tribute through his work or by fulfilling his duty or by time spent in service of the king or his State.

According to the fourth law, nobody can be forced to work in a profession that is not his own, other than ploughing or the army, which everyone is obliged to do.

According to the fifth law, each man must pay his tribute with what his province can supply, without going to other lands in search of what he does not have in his own, for the Inca believes it wrong to ask any subject to provide what their land does not.

The sixth orders that all workers employed in the service of the Inca or his curacas be supplied with everything necessary for the exercise of their job; in other words, the goldsmith should be given gold, silver or copper so that he can work; the weaver, wool or cotton; the painter, colours, and so on. The worker must only provide his labour during the time that he is obliged to do so: two months, or three at the very most. Once this period is over, he is not obliged to work any longer.

The seventh says that all workers should be provided with everything they need in terms of food and clothing, and even cures and medicines if they fall ill.

The eighth law concerns the collection of the tributes. At a particular time, in the capital of each province, will gather the judge-receivers and the masters of accounts or court clerks who count up the tributes on their knotted cords. The knots show what work has been done by each Levantine, the jobs he has performed, the journeys he has made on the orders of the prince or his superiors, and all his other activities; all of this is deducted from the tribute that he owes. They also keep track of everything in the shops of each city.

The ninth law states that all that remains of these tributes after the king's expenses are met will be reserved for the common good of his subjects and distributed to public shops during times of scarcity.

The tenth law contains a declaration of occupations to which the Levantines must dedicate themselves, both for the service of the king and for the good of their cities and states; these works are mandatory as a form of tribute, and they must be carried out collectively, for example levelling paths, rebuilding or repairing Temples of the Sun and other sanctuaries of their idolatry, or providing anything at all for temples. People are obliged to construct public buildings such as shops, the residences of judges and governors; to repair bridges; to act as messengers or chasquis; to work the earth, to crush fruit for wine, to lead cattle to pasture, to look after farms and other public assets; to keep hostels for lodging travellers, and to be there in person to provide them with all the king's goods that they need.

63. The Age of the Papa

And so the Fifth Quarter entered a period of unprecedented peace and prosperity. And although it didn't last, it is good to remember it as an episode of happiness in the history of the New World. Besides, who knows how long that harmony might have endured, had not extraordinary circumstances arisen to bring it to an end?

Atahualpa had moved certain populations around: the poor peasants of Swabia, Alsace and the Netherlands were relocated to the most sterile regions of Spain, where he put them to work on vast irrigation works.

The peasants of Spain were sent to the cold German countryside to cultivate papa and quinoa. Soon, both of these crops were growing throughout all the regions of the Empire and beyond.

Colonies of Chancas were established in Saxony to watch over the Protestants who remained near Wittenberg.

The Inca organised exchanges of food in accordance with each region's needs: avocados and tomatoes were sent to Germany, while

German and Belgian beer was sent to Spain. The black drink from Castile was exchanged for the yellow drink from Alsace.

An accord was reached with Portugal, which yielded its territory of Brazil. In compensation, the Empire promised not to interfere in the spice trade or to block the route to the Indies via the African peninsula.

Huascar's envoys came regularly to salute the emperor in his brother's name and to find out the latest news.

Seville was the axis of the world. Lisbon prospered. The ports of the north – Hamburg, Amsterdam, Anvers – grew along with the Fuggers' fortune.

Temples of the Sun increased in number as local idolatries withered, although they were still tolerated: their existence was guaranteed by the Seville Edict in Spain and by the Treaty of Wittenberg in the rest of the Empire.

An astronomer from beyond the western borders of Germany published a theory that soon spread throughout the Fifth Quarter. It held that the sun, not the earth, was the centre of the universe. This paper was printed in the language of knowledge and distributed under the title *De Revolutionibus Orbium Coelestium*, which means 'On the Revolutions of the Heavenly Spheres'. Its success accelerated the rate of conversions. (The astronomer was invited to Seville and awarded the title of The King's Great Astrologer.)

However, spies sent from Rome travelled all over the Spanish countryside, inciting people to revolt in the name of their old Catholic faith. They recruited a veritable secret army, whose general was the priest Iñigo López de Loyola, whom Atahualpa had once met in Granada. The Inca took this threat seriously and ordered Chalco Chimac to remorselessly hunt down the members of this society, which went by the name of *Jesuits*, after the name of the nailed god whom they revered and for whom they had sworn to die.

Atahualpa was concerned by this rebellion, but not excessively. The future would prove him right in this regard, by exposing him to far greater dangers.

64. The Silence of Cuba

Suddenly, the ships stopped arriving in Seville.

At first, the change was barely perceptible: the docks were still busy, because they kept loading ships bound for Cuba. After a while, they put the delays down to storms at sea. It was a long voyage, after all. But none of the ships that left ever came back.

The people of Seville were struck, then, by the silence of the ocean. In their hearts, they all felt a vague anxiety. To start with, they feigned indifference. But soon, the question was on everyone's lips: 'Where is the gold?' Why had the gold route suddenly been cut? Every ship that went out in search and did not return intensified the unease of those on land. Gradually, the sailors started refusing to embark on a one-way voyage. The docks were deserted. Men ceased moving crates of gold, silver, gunpowder, wool, wine, coca and cohiba. The entire city grew sad on that silence.

Then a rumour arrived from Lisbon. In the middle of the Ocean Sea was an archipelago belonging to Portugal. It was said that a fleet of ships, navigated by men dressed in feathers and jaguar skins, had landed there. Later, messengers from Navarre indicated that the fleet had been sighted alongside the French coast. It seemed that there had been raids and pillages.

An official letter from Francis I, addressed to Atahualpa, expressed astonishment at the presence of this fleet in French waters and reminded the emperor of the treaty of friendship that linked their two countries.

Atahualpa also received a letter from Henry VIII: the mysterious fleet had entered the channel between France and England. The English artillery had, so far, managed to dissuade the foreigners from landing, but the king was puzzled by this threatening presence.

The Inca gathered his council. Everyone was mystified. What was Huascar playing at? Why had he cut the route to Cuba? Why would he put an end to a trade that was so profitable for both parties? What did this fleet's arrival mean? What were his intentions?

Higuénamota could not understand why her Taíno compatriots had not tried to inform her about the situation.

Ruminahui saw in these rumours all the signs of an imminent military invasion.

Coya Asarpay was certain that the old hatred between the two brothers had never died, but only lain dormant, and was now erupting again.

Chalco Chimac shared this opinion: everything suggested that the commercial arrangement was no longer enough for Huascar, and that he wanted to taste the riches of the Fifth Quarter for himself.

But the general pointed to a more urgent problem: without supplies from Tawantinsuyu, the Empire's treasury would soon be empty.

Atahualpa knew this all too well, having already received a reminder letter from Augsburg, its insolence a stark warning of the fragility of his position:

His Majesty is surely well aware of the devotion that our house has always shown in serving the house of Spain. His Majesty must also be aware that, without our aid, he would never have acceded to the imperial throne, as many of his followers could attest. Throughout this affair, we have never hesitated to take considerable risks.

Indeed, it would have been less risky to prefer the house of Austria to His Majesty's own illustrious house, and yet we would still have made excellent profits. Considering our devotion, I implore His Majesty to acknowledge the humble and faithful service that we have given him and to order that we should be paid without delay, and with the due interest, the sums that we have advanced him.

In any case, they had to re-establish contact with Cuba and, most importantly, come to a settlement with Huascar as soon as they could.

It was decided that Higuénamota would go to Fontainebleau, to the court of King Francis, leaving immediately and passing through Navarre, where she would see Manco and his mother-in-law Marguerite.

65. Letter from Higuénamota to Atahualpa

Greetings, son of the Sun,

First of all, you will be pleased to learn that your brother Manco, whom I had the pleasure of visiting at the court of the king of Navarre, is wonderfully well, and feels completely fulfilled by his marriage to young Jeanne, Marguerite's daughter, which was arranged in accordance with your wisdom. Those two are inseparable, from morning until evening, when they might be seen laughing like children in the palace gardens, and even more so, I am told, from evening until morning, when the echoes of their joy can be heard throughout the city of Pau. Nobody here doubts that Jeanne will soon be pregnant.

All the same, Marguerite is worried by the news from France because she fears a betrayal that would imperil her brother's kingdom. She begged me to bid you prove your faithfulness by recalling those ships that are floating in French waters, and she did not believe me when I assured her that you knew nothing about their provenance or their destination. No word of consolation had any effect and I left her in tears and great distress, swearing that her friend the king of Spain would never fail her or her brother.

France is full of wonders, and I was constantly thrilled by the landscapes through which I travelled on my way here, as if I were discovering this country for the first time. Moreover, their wine is excellent, if quite different in taste from the wine in Spain.

King Francis greeted me at his chateau in Fontainebleau with all the honours one would expect from my rank and his gallantry. While he waited for me at the top of a staircase shaped like two arms of a stone river flowing down towards the visitor, I was treated to music from an orchestra of fifes, trumpets, oboes, flutes and violas, and then he gave a ball in my honour in a splendid wood-panelled gallery that he has had built in his royal residence.

I must say that the people of his court are as charming as ever and it is a great pleasure to stroll in the gardens of this chateau, among women in extravagant dresses, wise men examining the sky, Italian painters and architects, and poets singing of the beauty of roses and the transience of life.

In contrast to his sister, His Majesty, as he likes to be called, does not seem particularly alarmed by news of those ships at sea near his coastline, being as cheerful and amiable as I have always known him. However, time has treated him cruelly: he has lost much of his old vigour and now walks with a limp, and he had to apologise that he could no longer invite me to dance, he who used to dance all night. Your ambassador here informed me that the king of France has a broken vein and that he is rotting beneath his lower parts. The doctors worry that he does not have long to live. Apparently he is suffering from what people here call the 'Spanish disease', and what we in Spain call the 'Lisbon disease'.

However, apart from occasional moments when his face betrays his body's pain and fatigue, he is determined not to let this show and conducts his country's affairs with the same great conviction.

On this subject, King Francis, unlike the king of England, is unwilling to make a place in his kingdom for the religion of the Sun, despite the fact that his sister is highly favourable towards it, and he persecutes all those who do not declare themselves good Christians and good Catholics.

As for the matter at hand, I have been informed that your brother's fleet finally landed on the coast of England – a country that is, as you are aware, at war with France – and consequently that is all we know. Without going into superfluous details, I told Francis about the probable origin of those visitors, while remaining evasive about your contentious past with Huascar. Nevertheless, I assured him that they were probably just lost ships that would return on their way to Seville as soon as the order was given in your name. For now, he seems content with this explanation.

May the Sun watch over your shade and protect your empire.

From Fontainebleau, 30 April 1544 of the old era,
Thirteenth harvest of the Fifth Quarter.

Your faithful princess, Higuénamota

PS: I am wearing your bat-fur coat.

66. Letter from Atahualpa to Higuénamota

Greetings, radiant princess,

I cannot thank you enough for the news you have sent me from France, and also for having undertaken this long journey for love of me and the Empire.

I have some news of my own for you. It is of the greatest import-ance, and primarily concerns you.

Here, a ship finally arrived from Cuba. Aboard it was – would you believe? – your cousin Hatuey, who told us about the events that led to the route from Tawantinsuyu being cut off.

Apparently a tribe from the west arrived in Cuba. They called themselves Mexicans.

They are fierce warriors and their intentions were hostile. They defeated my brother's troops on the island, as well as your cousin's. Hatuey managed to flee and took refuge – with all the Taínos who were able to follow him – on the island of Haiti, which is, I know, your original homeland. But the Mexicans pursued them there, and Hatuey had to hide in the mountains, where he lived like a wild animal with his unfortunate companions, until the day when they managed to procure a ship – and that is how they came to Seville.

As far as Hatuey knows, the Mexicans pursued the Incas all the way to the Panama isthmus, where a war is now raging. Huascar's troops are fighting tooth and nail, for if those barbarous hordes cross the gully, then there will be nothing to prevent them descend-ing upon Tawantinsuyu, and that would be the end of the Four Quarters.

You must inform Francis of these latest developments and tell him that the fleet he saw by his coastline has nothing to do with us.

Above all, repeat this: our friendship is such that I consider Francis's affairs to be my own, so that any harm that is done to him I will take as a personal affront. Lastly, tell him that he must act as if in preparation for the most savage invasion he can imagine.

From Seville, 9 May 1544 of the old era,
Thirteenth harvest of the Fifth Quarter.

Your devoted sovereign, Atahualpa

67. Letter from Higuénamota to Atahualpa

Sapa Inca, sun of Quito, greetings,

Yesterday, the Mexicans landed in Normandy; the news reached us in the evening. A few peasants saw them first, walking along empty beaches. Then they went into a port named Havre de Grace, and now they are following a river that will lead them to Paris.

Francis has raised an army to go and meet them. This news seems to have perked him up. Despite his pains in the derrière, as they call it here, he wanted to mount a horse and wishes to lead his army towards the visitors, and into combat if needs must. His old body is excited because he considers this an adventure that – as he repeats ad infinitum – reminds him of his dashing youth. His military chief, Anne of Montmorency, whom I used to know quite well and who was at one time all-powerful in the king's court, is no longer beside him. A red-bearded man, Francis of Guise, seems to have taken his place. The dauphin Henri rides beside him.

The court is abuzz and we are proceeding with preparations for the campaign amid an atmosphere of gentle intoxication and good cheer.

On this subject, a book is in circulation at the chateau that is delighting everyone. It is by a certain Rabelais, who recounts the adventures of a giant named Gargantua. I will have to read you a few passages when I return, because it is so comical, and has a beautiful irreverence that you will, I hope, appreciate as much as I do. After all, don't we also – we who must take care of kingdoms – have the right to relax our minds a little?

In the meantime, I bid you pray to your father the Sun to sustain us in the task that awaits us, and to lend us assistance if by chance the visitors wage war upon us. As for me, I kiss the hands of the emperor, my dear friend, as well as those of all his children, whom I love as if they were mine.

From Fontainebleau, 7 June 1544,
Thirteenth harvest of the Fifth Quarter.

Your naked princess, Higuénamota

68. Letter from Atahualpa to Higuénamota

Sun of the islands, very gracious princess, greetings,

Alarming news has come from Tawantinsuyu. The Mexicans have crossed the Panama isthmus and are advancing south. My brother Huascar's army is fighting valiantly but ceding territory. Quito is expected to be under siege before the next moon.

My brother, Tupac Hualpa, came in person to inform me of the situation. He and his men managed to descend the river that begins in the Andes and reaches the Ocean Sea via the forest. Then they sailed along the coast until they reached the country of Brazil, formerly occupied by the Portuguese, where they were able to refit their ship and, after a long journey, come to Seville. So now there is a second route linking Tawantinsuyu to the New World, although this voyage cannot be made in reverse. I have no doubt that my brother will send other ships to keep me informed of the war and its evolutions.

Tell Francis that the Mexicans are a fierce, bloodthirsty people, and that he must trust them no more than he would a fatal plague. My advice is to exterminate every last Mexican who has already set foot on French soil before they organise the bridgehead to an invasion that would then become inevitable.

May the Sun protect you and all the French people.

From Seville, 18 June 1544 of the old era,
Thirteenth harvest of the Fifth Quarter.

Your emperor who kisses your hands, Atahualpa

69. Letter from Higuénamota to Atahualpa

Greetings, Sun of the New World,

How sweet it is to be the one to bring you some good news, and how pleasant to imagine the joy with which it will be received, knowing that I am, if not the cause, at least the messenger of that joy!

Our fears, it turns out, were perhaps without foundation.

A meeting took place between Francis and the Mexicans, outside a city called Rouen.

To impress the visitors, King Francis ordered the erection of a camp so magnificent that I have never seen its like. Five hundred tents covered the plain, with, at their centre, a gigantic marquee where the meeting was to take place. That marquee and those tents were covered in gold fabric from Florence. Hunters had scoured the countryside to supply unimaginable quantities of game, in order to offer our guests a banquet of such splendour that they would never forget it. For the occasion, Francis was dressed in sparkling blue armour marked with a golden fleur-de-lys. He was accompanied by his son Henri, to whom he had entrusted the title and the mission of Governor of Normandy. Queen Eleonore and their younger son Charles, Duke of Orleans, were there too.

The Mexicans are a strong, handsome people, without that pale, sickly complexion that the French have. The men, like those from my land and your own, do not wear beards. Their chief is a strong man, of pleasant appearance, in the prime of life and of good stature, although not so tall as the king of France, who is a giant. His name is Cuauhtémoc, and he serves an emperor called Moctezuma. Under a feather headdress, he wears his hair long in a braid. His clothes are of poor quality but his jewellery is finely worked.

He says he serves a god called Quetzalcoatl, a word that means 'feathered serpent' in his language. But I also noticed that he sometimes invokes their god of rain, whom they call Tlaloc, and who is armed with a hammer just like our god of thunder Thor Illapa.

His warriors are armed with lances and round shields, and some wear a jaguar head like a helmet, as if the warrior's head emerged from the animal's mouth, which gives them a frightening appearance.

Cuauhtémoc, however, does not seem to have hostile intentions. He says he came in peace, drawn by the renown of a kingdom that crossed the seas. He asked the king of France permission to establish a trading post in this port of Havre de Grace, which is also known as Franciscopolis, in order to allow the coming and going of merchant ships between his country Mexico and France. As I write these lines, a trade treaty is close to being sealed, and should be signed without delay.

Cuauhtémoc also showed himself extremely courteous towards Queen Eleonore, whom you know as the sister of the late Emperor Charles. He also paid his respects to me with a simplicity that was highly gracious, and assured me that his people, on the other side of the sea, will not ask more from the Taínos than a simple trading post and the right of passage, and that as soon as these agreements have been made, he will send the order to his troops to evacuate Cuba, leaving only a small garrison, and to abandon all plans to invade Haiti.

So everything leads us to believe that there will be no war. It is good for all of us that these Mexicans seem so peaceful. Your empire is young; it needs to be consolidated through peace, not war. That is why I am certain that you will receive this news with the same satisfaction I feel as I send it.

I leave you with kisses and these verses by a poet from this land, which goes well, I think, with our common history, which has led us to where we are today:

How the world laughs at the world
Therefore it is in its youth.

From Rouen, 7 July 1544,
Thirteenth harvest of the Fifth Quarter.

Your old Cuban friend, Higuénamota

70. Quipu from Huascar to Atahualpa

Quito taken.
Retreating Inca army: 38,000 men.
Losses: 12,000 men.
Civilian and military prisoners: 15,000
Enemy army heading to Tumipampa: 80,000 men.
Human sacrifices: 2,000.

71. Letter from Atahualpa to Higuénamota

My very dear Higuénamota,

I beg you to transmit this message to Francis, before returning to Spain without delay, or at least to Navarre, where you will be safe: the Mexicans have not come in peace! In truth, I wasn't absolutely sure of it, but my fears were confirmed by the latest news from Tawantinsuyu. My brother Huascar sent me a message transcribed by his quipucamayocs. The Mexicans are a viciously warlike people who mercilessly execute their prisoners. The war at the other side of the sea is not over: it is being pursued into the lands of my ancestors. Quito has fallen and the Mexicans are advancing further south.

I am sending a message to Monsieur de Saint-Mauris this minute, but I do not know whether his embassy will manage to speak with the king before you do. Tell him that the Mexicans are setting a trap for him. The French must strike as soon as possible to seize the initiative.

As for you, my sweet princess, I beg you to flee at the first chance you get. I wrote to Manco to head for France with the Navarre army: he should be in Paris within ten days to reinforce the French army.

Once again, escape and save your life, my friend! May this letter reach you without delay. I know that the French roads are not as good as ours, but I am entrusting this missive to my best chasquis with the hope that it will be in your hands within seven days.

From Seville, 14 July 1544.
Your servant and friend, Atahualpa

72. Letter from Higuénamota to Atahualpa

My prince,

I do not know if a letter from you has already left Spain or if you were waiting to have more information before you replied to me. Without news from you, and uncertain what to do next, I remained with the king of France to witness the conclusion of the peace agreement.

That was a mistake.

Yesterday – on 19 July of the old era – the Mexicans, although vastly outnumbered, treacherously attacked the French camp by surprise, sowing panic and death, killing as many as they could.

At the same time, we learned that the English in Calais had launched an attack on the city of Boulogne.

King Francis, who only just escaped the Mexicans' attack, took refuge a few arrow flights away from Rouen, but must now face enemies on two fronts. There is no doubt in his mind that the

English and the Mexicans are working together. He has issued a retreat in battle order towards Paris.

It was only by a miracle that I myself was able to escape unscathed from the Mexicans' trap. Taking advantage of the confusion all around me, and of the colour of my skin, which made me look like one of theirs, I was able to run away through the battlefield, as if through a forest of lances, avoiding the axe and sword blades that hissed through the air, until I could mount a horse that had lost its rider. That was how I managed to flee the camp, abandoning the French people to their grisly fate at the hands of those Mexicans. Had I not been such an accomplished rider, I would be dead now. Instead, I am safe and sound, having joined up with the remnants of the French army, but I do not know for how long.

From Mantes, 20 July 1544.

Your unfortunate princess, Higuénamota

73. Letter from Manco to Atahualpa

Sovereign emperor of the Fifth Quarter, my brother, greetings to you,

Having set off, at the head of an army of fifteen thousand men, to rescue the king of France, I crossed a country in turmoil.

The French troops, scattered into disarray by the Mexicans' surprise attack, had taken refuge in the outskirts of Paris. The king of France must also fight against the English, who have joined forces with the Mexicans. According to the most recent reports, Boulogne will soon fall.

The French army is in great difficulty, faced with this double threat, but the situation is far from hopeless. If you were to send Quizquiz, at the head of an army of thirty or forty thousand men, I guarantee that we would be able to drive the enemy back to the sea.

Assuming that you will receive this letter within five days, I would estimate that your army should be able to reach us in about fifteen days. I am certain that we can hold Paris for that long.

From Poissy, 24 July 1544 of the old era,
13th year of the Fifth Quarter.

To my sovereign and brother,
General Manco, prince of Navarre

PS: Queen Eleonore has disappeared, and we do not know if she is dead or taken prisoner.

74. Quipu from Huascar to Atahualpa

Tumipampa under siege.
Resisting fiercely.
Inca losses: 20,000.
Enemy losses: 10 to 15,000.
Counter-offensive: 60,000 men (including 20,000 Chancas, 10,000 Charas, 8,000 Canaris, 4,000 Chachapoyas).
Artillery: 120 cannons.
Cavalry: 6,000 horses.
Battle of Quito: 30,000 losses on either side.
Talks in progress. (Generals Atoc, Tupac Atao and?*)
Truce possible.

---

* Illegible *(chronicler's note).*

75. Letter from Higuénamota to Atahualpa

My king,

If only I had received your letter in time ... I might have been able to convince Francis of the Mexicans' duplicity and thus avoid this catastrophe that has thrown us into chaos, with his army in desperate retreat.

Here, the situation has deteriorated alarmingly. The French are fleeing, pursued by the Mexicans, who receive reinforcements almost daily from Havre de Grace. The English, meanwhile, have taken Boulogne and are marching on Paris, threatening to catch us in a pincer movement.

It is said that Queen Eleonore has become Cuauhtémoc's lover and is providing the Mexicans with information on many important subjects, such as the inhabitants' customs, the topography and fauna of France, and the weaponry and tactics of her husband the king's army. Francis finds this idea inconceivable, but she is a Habsburg, after all, and will always be a Habsburg, and to my mind there is nothing inconceivable about it at all.

Manco has arrived with fifteen thousad men and those reinforcements gave us some respite, without which the French army would have been swept away – and us with it. Nevertheless, it will not be enough when the Mexicans and the English attack in concert. You alone have the means to save us. I beg you to send an army immediately to rescue us from the jaws of the enemy before they crush us into dust.

From Saint-German-en-Laye, 6 August 1544.
Your ever faithful Higuénamota

76. Quipu from Huascar to Atahualpa

Truce agreed.
Requesting end to war in Fifth Quarter.

77. Letter from Higuénamota to Atahualpa

My friend, all is lost!

Manco was killed in combat, braving the fury of the Mexicans to his last breath. He sacrificed himself to defend besieged Paris, and all his men perished with him.

We have taken refuge with the king, in his palace at the Louvre, but His Majesty is in such pain from the fistula on his backside that he can barely stand, never mind ride a horse, and remains bedridden for the greater part of each day. The Duke of Guise is leading the defence of the city with great zeal and diligence, but the situation is so bad that even a hundred times his present resources would not be enough.

You are our only hope, my prince, and we are constantly on the lookout for an army led by Quizquiz or Ruminahui or perhaps even the proud face of my emperor himself. This is what I dream about every time the anguish in my heart and the clash of arms outside fall quiet enough that I am able to sleep a little.

Son of the Sun, if we never see each other again, remember your Cuban princess.

Paris, 10 August 1544.
Your Higuénamota

78. Quipu from Huascar to Atahualpa

Peace conditional upon ceasefire in all territories.
Restoration of trade with Cuba negotiated.
10 merchant ships ready to leave.
Resources almost exhausted. Empire dying.
Chinchaysuyu and Antisuyu on verge of civil war.
Requesting immediate end to combat.

79. Letter from Atahualpa to Jean de Saint-Mauris, imperial ambassador in France

I, Atahualpa, emperor of the Fifth Quarter, hereby order you to transmit to General Cuauhtémoc without delay the expression of my friendship, as well as the assurance of my sovereign and uncondi-tional desire for a lasting peace with the glorious people of Mexico.

Please let him know that the emperor of the Fifth Quarter, king of the Spanish, has no greater wish than to sign a peace treaty with him and his master Moctezuma, and that this wish is so pro-found that, to achieve it, I am prepared to renounce my alliance with France and to free myself of all obligation for military assis-tance, or any other kind of assistance, towards the French or towards their king.

Please tell him to ensure that, if the Princess Higuénamota ever comes into his possession, she should be kept safe and treated with kindness.

I do not think I need to explain to you the importance of this embassy. I am relying on you to see it through with the diligence

*and industry for which Charles chose you, and for which he and I,
his successor, have always congratulated ourselves. The peace of the
Empire is in your hands. May my father, the Sun, be with you.*

*From Seville, 15 August 1544 of the old era,
Thirteenth harvest of the Fifth Quarter.*

*Atahualpa I, king of Spain, prince of the Belgians
and the Netherlands, king of Tunis and Algiers, king of Naples
and Sicily, emperor of the Fifth Quarter*

80. Letter from Atahualpa to Higuénamota

*My beloved princess, my soul, providential companion of all my
enterprises, who has saved me a hundred times from the most ter-
rible predicaments,*
*I hope with all my heart that this letter will find its way to you.
Listen carefully: there will be no reinforcements. France is lost.
Escape if you can. Leave Paris. Return to Spain. That is an order.*

*Seville, 15 August 1544.
Your sovereign, Atahualpa*

81. Letter from Higuénamota to Atahualpa

My prince, my friend,

*I do not know if this letter will reach you. The Mexicans are massed
around the palace and will attack tonight or tomorrow.*

*Forgive me, I couldn't abandon Francis. You know that I am
entirely devoted to you, and that is why – when you sent me long
ago to Paris to negotiate our alliance with France against Charles
and Ferdinand – I gave myself to him without reservations and
without regrets. In the dusk of his life and his reign, I do not have
the heart to leave him alone. I feel too much tenderness and friendship for this broken man, whose kingdom is disintegrating before
his eyes. If you saw him weeping in his bed of pain, invoking his god
and begging for death to take him, I do not doubt that your heart
would, like mine, be torn with pity by such a lamentable sight.*

*Outside, I can hear the drums of the Mexicans. Their war songs
are like the howling of a beast; they chill my blood. There will be a
great massacre, soon. This time, I doubt whether I will survive.*

Think of me. Farewell.

From Paris, 1 September 1544.
Your H

82. Letter from ambassador Jean de Saint-Mauris to Atahualpa

*To my sovereign Atahualpa, son of the Sun, Emperor of the Fifth
Quarter*

Sire,
*I am replying to the letter that it pleased Your Majesty to write to
me on the fifteenth day of the past month.*

*First of all, sire, I will follow up on Your Majesty's command
regarding the salvation of the Princess Higuénamota and the peace
offer to be delivered to General Cuauhtémoc.*

*But before I do, sire, permit me to inform Your Majesty of the
latest events here, which will, I feel sure, be of interest to you.*

After a week of bloody fighting, the Mexicans finally took possession of the Louvre. Following this, all combat ceased in Paris, with the exception of a few pockets of resistance in the eastern suburbs.

Notwithstanding, the Duke of Guise surrendered to General Cuauhtémoc and handed over the keys to the city. The duke, who fought with great bravery, had received a terrible wound in his face from a lance, and his scar was still bleeding as he signed the surrender. He is, at this very moment, in the hands of a young surgeon famed for his ability to perform wonders at sewing flesh and mending bones.

The king is presently being held in his apartments, along with his two sons.

His health was so poor that the doctors did not believe he had long to live. But after three fits of Tertian fever, his doctors now say that this fever will be the cause of his best health and disposition.

In compliance with Your Majesty's wishes, the life of the Princess Higuénamota was spared, amid all the other souls who passed away during that great carnage, and I personally ensured that she is being well treated, which, I hope, will please Your Majesty.

I must add, sire, that those rumours concerning Queen Eleonore have been confirmed. In fact, they did not go far enough. So it was that I witnessed the astonishing spectacle of the queen of France entering Paris on General Cuauhtémoc's arm, and since then I have seen her offering him advice and supplying him with information on local customs. There can be little doubt as to the nature of their relations.

As for the last and most difficult point, its accomplishment caused me a great deal of pain, not to mention fear, since, as Your Majesty may imagine, it was not easy, amid the confusion that reigned at the time, to convince the new authorities of my credentials. But, following your command, I delivered Your Majesty's peace proposal into the hands of General Cuauhtémoc, who has *asked me to transmit to you his salutations and regards, and to assure you of his most favourable disposition towards you. He is confident that common ground can be found, 'to the benefit of the Incas as well as the Mexicans' (these are his very words, translated by a spokesman and by Queen Eleonore herself).*

Sire, I beg the Creator to grant to Your Majesty the complete fulfilment of your highest, noblest and most virtuous desires.

From Paris, 18 September 1544 of the old era,
Year 13 of the Fifth Quarter.

Your very humble and obedient servant,
Jean de Saint-Mauris

83. Letter from Higuénamota to Atahualpa

Son of the Sun, glory of Quito, faithful ally,

Francis died today, in circumstances that I wish you to know.

Your new Mexican friends have built a pyramid in the Louvre courtyard. It is a stone edifice, quite imposing and, I must admit, rather harmonious in its proportions, composed of steps that are reminiscent of the terraces that you, the Incas, sculpt in the mountains.

I had no doubt that it was intended for some ritual purpose. I could not suspect, however, the dread task for which it was used.

You will be happy to learn that the Mexicans have their god of the Sun, too, whom they venerate with particular fervour, and who also happens to be their god of war. Isn't that amusing? Don't you find it appropriate?

It was to the Sun that the Mexicans sacrificed the king of France, his two sons, the Duke of Guise, and a hundred other members of the French nobility, including several young women whom they thought would be to the taste of their gods.

Would you like to know how they were executed?

The king, who was too weak to climb the steps himself, was carried, more dead than alive, to the top of the pyramid. After tearing off his shirt, they lay him down on a stone. Four men held his arms and legs, and a fifth held his head, then a sort of priest opened his chest with a pointed blade, plunged his hands into the incision and ripped out his heart, which he brandished aloft, to the shocked cries of the crowd. Then he put the heart into an urn and, as if that was not horrific enough already, he shoved the king's body off the edge so that it tumbled down the blood-covered steps to the bottom of the pyramid. There, some other Mexicans took the corpses away and, apparently, cut them into pieces so that their bones could be used to make jewellery or musical instruments.

O Sun, what crimes have been committed in your name!

At least Francis, the first to be executed, was spared the sadness of watching the executions of his two sons, Henri and Charles, both of whom struggled horribly on the sacrifice stone.

I know, through Saint-Mauris, that my life was one of the conditions that you insisted upon before signing your peace treaty with the Mexicans, and I am grateful to you for that, even if I am old enough not to be of interest to the gods, which would probably have spared me the king's fate anyway.

But I am sure you will understand that I no longer wish to serve on your council. In fact, to be perfectly honest, after the tragic events that have shaken France, which I was unfortunate enough to witness and in which you are not entirely innocent, I no longer have any desire to see Spain again. Naturally, I have no intention of acting like Queen Eleonore, although I do not want to cast judgement on the reasons why she betrayed her husband and her

adoptive country. I am the daughter of a queen and have only ever
served one king; I will not serve another. But today I am soliciting
your famous generosity: please let me show my loyalty in another
way. I would like to be made regent of the Netherlands, in place of
your wife Mary, who was, by your indulgence, kept in her post after
our campaign there, but who, before that, did not exactly merit
your trust.

To the sovereign of the Holy Empire, to the prince of Quito,
farewell.

Paris, 9 October 1544.

H

84. The Division of Bordeaux

It would be an understatement to say that the sudden appearance
of the Mexicans in the New World shook the political foundations that Atahualpa had so patiently constructed.

The decision to abandon the king of France had been difficult
but ultimately inevitable, and there had been no debate about it:
the Fifth Quarter could not survive without the other four. If
Tawantinsuyu fell, Atahualpa's empire would follow, like a child
suddenly deprived of its mother's breast. Higuénamota, blinded
by her attachment to King Francis, had not wanted to admit this,
just as she had refused to consider the implications for her homeland of a pact with Mexico. Cuba would recover its role as the
nexus of the two worlds. Haiti would be spared. Oil, wine, wheat,
gold and silver would be traded once again. The Taínos would
prosper. Soon, people in every country would be smoking cohiba.

Among the many consequences of the Mexican invasion, one
was the development of a coastal city named Bordeaux, which

became the capital of France. It was here that the peace treaty was signed, here that the New World was divided.

Atahualpa travelled there to meet Cuauhtémoc. The Mexican general had married Francis's daughter, Margaret of France, in order to legitimise his authority in the eyes of the French and to reign without impediments. Since tearing out the hearts of the two sons, he had nothing left to fear from the royal family, of which he was now officially a member.

Cuauhtémoc was not only a fierce warrior. He was also a skilful strategist and politician, who quickly developed a strong grasp of the local customs. He saw the advantages of converting to the religion of the nailed god and decided that the son he would have with his wife Margaret would be baptised with a Mexican name to ensure his lineage in the local history, then raised in accordance with the customs and rites of the Levantines. The custom in this country was for the king to have a variable number of secondary wives, who were known as 'mistresses', often preferred to the principal wife. Sometimes there was more benefit in being a mistress than in being a royal spouse. Cuauhtémoc kept Francis's widow, Eleonore, as his mistress.

The Waldensians – a Lutheran sect from the south of France persecuted by the previous king – were the first group to rally to the new power. The rest of the country followed unenthusiastically, but without any serious rebellions. The few uprisings that did occur were ruthlessly suppressed.

The king of Portugal and the king of England – allies, respectively, of the Incas and the Mexicans – also attended the meeting.

In gratitude for his military aid during the invasion of France, Henry VIII was officially granted the northern French coastline around Calais and Boulogne, but his other territorial claims were denied.

Navarre was cut in two and divided between Spain and France.

Portugal's inviolable sovereignty was guaranteed, and France granted it the same licence to trade with the East Indies that Spain had granted before.

The islands of Cuba and Haiti were declared free zones in the Ocean Sea, with an obligation to welcome all ships authorised to follow the three maritime routes linking Cuba to Cadiz, Lisbon and Bordeaux.

The archipelagos of the Azores, Madeira and the Canaries were subject to the same obligations, with their geographical situation making them ideal as stopover points for ships crossing the Ocean Sea. However, the Azores were ceded to France. Madeira and the Canary Islands remained in the hands of, respectively, the Portuguese and the Spanish.

England was authorised to explore other maritime routes between the Azores and Iceland, with the treaty guaranteeing it possession of all lands and islands that it might encounter in this strip of sea.

It was agreed that, in the event that a ship belonging to one of the four aforementioned nations should lose its way and take a maritime route that it was not authorised to take, its safety would be assured until it reached port, in return for the ship giving up one-fifth of its merchandise.

The treaty was sealed over glasses of the black drink from local vineyards, which had an excellent reputation. All present agreed that the reputation was entirely merited.

The last Levantines to continue resisting the foreign conquerors were gathered in an Italian city named Trento, where they organised numerous debates examining the reasons for their defeat and asking why their nailed god had not protected them. (At the time of writing, these debates are still ongoing.)

Ferdinand retired to his kingdoms in the east – Austria, Hungary, Bohemia – which still allowed him to govern a vast territory, albeit one perpetually threatened by the Turks. However, Suleiman was too preoccupied fighting the Persians to really trouble Ferdinand.

The republics of Genoa and Venice were allied, respectively, with Atahualpa and Ferdinand, but both retained their independence.

The Duchy of Milan was restored to Spain.

The Holy Roman Empire signed treaties with the Lutheran countries to the north of Germany: Denmark, Sweden, Norway.

Hatuey was named chief admiral of the Ocean Sea.

Mary of Hungary was dismissed from her position as regent of the Netherlands, with Higuénamota taking her place.

Atahualpa never saw the Cuban princess again.

85. The Death of the Inca

Peace reigned in the Fifth Quarter, which entered a period of harmony and prosperity.

One day, Atahualpa decided that he wished to see the beauties of Italy, which he had heard so much about and which had inspired so many great artists. Perhaps the emperor had grown melancholy since his Cuban princess had retired to Brussels, refusing to see him, refusing even to reply to his letters, other than those concerning the administration of the Netherlands. Perhaps he sought some entertainment to distract him from his sadness over his friend.

Lorenzino had invited Atahualpa to visit Florence many times, thus far without success, since the affairs of the Empire left him little spare time.

However, Atahualpa wrote to the duke promising that he would visit him in his famous city during the fourth festival of the Sun, in the sixteenth harvest of the new era.

The festival had become very popular here because its aim was to ward off disease, and the cities of the Fifth Quarter were often blighted by the plague, a fatal illness that decimated the peoples of the New World.

Fasting began on the first day of the moon that they called September.

Here, the bread, which they bake in ovens, is not mixed with the blood of young boys, but of young girls who have never lain with men, because, as I have said, they attach a great deal of importance to this inexperience (only where females are concerned, however; virginity is not prized at all among males). They draw blood from the young girls in the same way we do with young boys, by pricking them between their eyebrows.

Until this point, the emperor had hardly suffered from home-sickness, and some might have thought that his natural temperament had preserved him from a feeling so unsuited to the conquest of a new world. But perhaps, after all, the series of extraordinary events that had defined his life had simply never given him the opportunity. When he discovered Florence, Atahualpa felt as if he were pushing open the doors of a dream that led him back to his homeland.

Bedecked in the colours of the rainbow, the city celebrated his arrival. Perched on a chariot next to Lorenzino, Atahualpa half-listened to the Florentine's endless flow of compliments while his eyes widened in amazement at the stone palaces that, although more crudely carved, reminded him irresistibly of the Inca buildings of his past.

On the other side of the river, high up in the hills, stood a fortress that he thought could easily be Sacsayhuaman.

On the hillside were terraced gardens. Fireworks exploded above them and memories of Tawantinsuyu flashed through his mind.

But it was the Palazzo Vecchio, seat of the duke and his government, that made the strongest impression on him. He had probably grown weary of the delicate, orange-scented gardens of the Alcazar, and in this grey stone edifice, surmounted with a crenellated tower, he rediscovered the same brute expression of power that his ancestors had bequeathed him. And while Lorenzino was proudly pointing out the statues of a small king named David, which he had arranged in the grand Council hall, Atahualpa's mind was drifting from one empire to the other. After a while, he pretended to laugh for no reason and asked to be introduced to the architect of such wonders, because he was prepared, he said, to make him a golden bridge that would take him all the way to Seville. Lorenzino laughed too, since etiquette required it, but he had not forgotten how he himself had stolen Florence's greatest sculptor to please his master, years before, and taken him to Andalusia. (In fact, that sculptor had already left for Rome, but he didn't want to remember that.)

Old Michelangelo was still alive; he was sketching plans for monuments in his studio in Seville, which Atahualpa liked to visit at dusk. But the Lorenzino that Michelangelo had known then was no more. Now, the Duke of Florence went by the name Lorenzo. He was a man in the prime of life, who governed with wisdom and firmness. His wife, the Duchess Quispe Sisa, was widely considered the greatest beauty in all of Tuscany and had given him two children whom he adored. His city was the jewel in the crown of the Fifth Quarter, its glories praised by all. Lorenzo had made peace with Rome and Genoa. His sphere of influence extended as far as Vienna, capital of Ferdinand's empire. The greatest artists of the Empire clamoured to be part of his court.

In a word, Lorenzo de Medici reigned. But the will to power suffers no equals. Was Atahualpa jealous? Did he wish to reassert an authority that he imagined was threatened by the splendours of Florence? Did he wish to humiliate his vassal by making him pay for the pomp that he had laid out for his master? If so, then his conduct was reprehensible. Or perhaps he was simply asserting his ancestral prerogatives? But the mores of the Fifth Quarter were different from those of Tawantinsuyu, as the emperor should have known better than anyone.

He, too, was stunned by his sister's beauty. She had wide hips, firm breasts, olive skin. The oval of her face was emphasised by her black hair, which fell over her bare shoulders; this style had become the fashion among the Italian nobility and even among the women of the lower classes, who all imitated this sublime duchess. Her brother's senses were inflamed in a way that, it is said, they had not been since he and the Princess Higuénamota had first become lovers on the ship that crossed the Ocean Sea. He told the duke that he wanted his sister back. But Lorenzo was hardly inclined to give up his wife, even to the emperor. All the same, he knew that nobody could refuse the Inca. In all likelihood, Quispe Sisa herself was not opposed to the proposal, considering her brother's request as a great honour.

So Lorenzo had to resort to cunning and dissimulation. He pretended to accept Atahualpa's request with good grace, even claiming to be flattered. But he kept finding excuses to put it off: his wife was indisposed, or she wanted more time to prepare to receive her lord and brother. She had to fast for longer. She was waiting for certain rare essences from the Indies that she wished to use to perfume herself. The best couturiers in the city were creating lingerie for her worthy of such an occasion, so delicate and precious that it had to be sewn with the finest gold thread.

Meanwhile, Lorenzo was negotiating in secret with one of the richest families in Florence, the Strozzi – ancient rivals of the

Medici, who wanted a return to the republic. (I have already mentioned this original form of government, in which a group of nobles share power and choose their sovereign, as is the case for the doge of Venice or of Genoa.)

What did he promise the Strozzi? What foolish oath sealed this agreement? What support could they boast? Venice? Perhaps. Ferdinand? Probably not. What could they have expected from yesterday's oppressor, except the promise of another tyranny? Young Lorenzino had turned to the Inca precisely because he wanted to usurp his cousin Alessandro, a Habsburg puppet. The Pope, then? Yes, that was more likely. The chief of the nailed god's worshippers had endorsed Atahualpa's coronation against his will, and was disturbed by the growing number of conversions to the religion of the Sun. Moreover, he was an old hand at such machinations: hadn't he ordered the assassination of Doria, in Genoa, not long before this?

Lorenzo held talks with the Strozzi, the Ricci, the Rucellai, the Valori, the Acciaiuoli, the Guicciardini, and even with the Pazzi and the Albizzi, who had every reason to hate the Medici: 'That time can neither destroy nor abate the desire for freedom is most certain; for it has been often observed, that those have reassumed their liberty who in their own persons had never tasted of its charms, and love it only from remembrance of what they have heard their fathers relate; and, therefore, when recovered, have preserved it with indomitable resolution and at every hazard. And even when their fathers could not remember it, the public buildings, the halls of the magistracy, and the insignia of free institutions, remind them of it; and these things cannot fail to be known and greatly desired of every class of citizens.'

In truth, Lorenzo's political intentions were unclear, because he seemed to be moved more by personal motives. His determination, however, was no less unfailing for that. To those who hesitated, he said that it was craven to turn away from a glorious enterprise just because the outcome was in doubt.

Soon, the excitement provoked by the rebellious duke's plans gave rise to rumours. Talk of a plot reached the ears of Rumina-hui's spies and the general attempted to warn his master, but Atahualpa paid no attention. Perhaps if Chalco Chimac had been present, he would have been persuaded of the danger, because intrigues and conspiracies were his domain, not that of the old, stone-eyed general. But perhaps Atahualpa was simply so weary that he relaxed his usual prudence, his attention to signs, that animalistic survival instinct. Perhaps the Inca, the conqueror of the New World, emperor of the Fifth Quarter, sensed that his mission on earth had already been accomplished, and that it was time to bring it to an end, one way or another. No doubt this man wanted to rest, he whose destiny had been even greater than the great Pachacuti. Did he dream of a sunny retirement in some peaceful place, surrounded by orange trees, paintings, talking sheets and chosen women, where he might smoke cohiba while dictating his memoirs? We will never know.

For nine days, the festivities continued.

Jousts took place in the Piazza Santa Croce, then lots of small white llamas were sacrificed and roasted on spits, and the people feasted with the nobility, amid singing and dancing.

At night, messengers of the Sun ran through the streets, whirling their torches around their heads, then threw them into the river Arno, where the current took them to the sea, and with them all the evils that they had chased from their houses and their city.

In the mornings, the inhabitants went to Mass after only a few hours of sleep. The religion of the nailed god was still very popular in Florence, which possessed the most impressive temple in the whole of the Fifth Quarter. It was a white marble building that rose up to the sky, gleaming as if it had been cut like a gigantic jewel by the best goldsmiths of Lambayeque. Atahualpa had attended Mass the day after his arrival, but had not bothered since then, sending Ruminahui in his stead for these solemn ceremonies, which, as everybody knows, are very important to the Levantines – and particularly to the Italians. The old general accomplished his task with diligence, if without much enthusiasm.

As for the Duchess Quispe Sisa, she would usually attend Mass, to please the Florentines who went to admire her, but the succession of parties organised in honour of the emperor's arrival had made her less assiduous. Her nocturnal exertions left her preferring the chimeras of sleep to tales of the nailed god.

As he was short and rather puny, the duke had no intention of getting into a fight with Atahualpa, who was a head taller than him, with a remarkable physique. But there was in his service a highly devoted Yana, known as Scoronconcolo, who often carried out the most delicate missions on his behalf. The duke asked him if he was ready to avenge a great enemy, without revealing any details about his plan, and it is said that the Yana replied: 'Yes, sir, even were it against the emperor himself.' So Lorenzo devised a plot: he would lure Atahualpa into his room one morning, during Mass, by assuring him that his sister was waiting there for him, but in reality it would be Scoronconcolo, hiding behind a door, ready to slay him. At the same time, his acolytes would stab Ruminahui in the great temple, counting on the ensuing chaos to help them escape through the crowd. (When he greeted the old general, Lorenzo put his hand on his chest, in a show of friendliness, but in fact he was checking that Ruminahui was not wearing armour or chainmail under his mantle.) Then they would gather at the Palazzo Vecchio and call upon the city's inhabitants to rise up against the imperial tyranny, and Lorenzo would proclaim the return of the Republic.

And so it was done: during the evening banquet that followed the jousts in Santa Croce, Lorenzo whispered to Atahualpa the place and the time when he could see the duchess. He simply had to go to the Medici palace during Mass, and the duke himself would lead him to the bedroom where Quispe Sisa would be waiting for him. This was news the emperor had long been craving and he believed it eagerly. He spent the rest of the evening flirting with his sister, but without either of them ever mentioning their coming rendezvous – Quispe Sisa because she knew nothing about it, Atahualpa out of gallantry.

That evening's banquet was taking place in an immense palace that the Medici had just acquired, in the hills of Oltrarno, the neighbourhood of Florence where they had chosen to reside. When the duchess left the party, she went to bed in her new apartments, rather than travelling all across the city to the old Medici palace where she still had a room. The duke did not tell Atahualpa this, of course, because he wanted the duke to find nobody behind the door of that room, other than death.

When the party was over, the last witnesses saw the emperor walk through the palace gardens to the Belvedere fortress, which overlooked the Tuscan countryside. He dallied for a moment on the battlements, alone, admiring the sunrise. On the distant hilltops, silhouetted against the sky, pine trees merged with crenellated towers.

After such wild festivities, the city had a muddy taste in the mornings. Atahualpa went back to the Palazzo Vecchio, where he was staying, to prepare for his rendezvous. He decided to walk there, with a reduced escort, to savour the cool dawn. He crossed the Ponte Vecchio, which was starting to come to life, stepping over the bodies of drunken Florentines who had collapsed in the gutters and avoiding – more out of instinct than superstition – the burnt-out torches used to expel the city's evils that were still strewn across the streets.

At the given hour, he presented himself, dressed in a tight-fitting alpaga mantle, to the door of the Medici palace, which he recognised from its famous emblem: five red balls with a blue ball above them. The duke himself opened the door. Atahualpa bade farewell to his retinue. He and Lorenzo walked through a garden of orange trees populated by Roman statues, then through an inner courtyard of finely worked arches; together, they climbed the stone staircase that led to the private apartments, then went through a small chapel, its walls covered with tapestries of hunting scenes – Lorenzo told people afterwards that the emperor lingered in front of one of those hangings, and asked him the names of certain animals represented therein. Then they passed a corridor of several rooms before reaching the duke's. Lorenzo gave three discreet knocks, then moved aside to let the emperor pass.

The curtains were drawn, so the room was in darkness. He could just make out the outline of the bed, and perhaps a shape under the sheets, though these were in fact only pillows. Still, that shape was enough to sharpen Atahualpa's desire, and he stepped forward. Behind the door, the duke's man was waiting, dagger in hand.

He was aiming for the emperor's throat, but it was so dark that he had to operate by guesswork, and the blade only entered the shoulder. Atahualpa cried out, spun on his heels, and threw himself at his attacker. Scoronconcolo stabbed him several times in the sides, but the emperor was remarkably strong and would have strangled the Yana were it not for Lorenzo's intervention. The duke, unable to see anything, first had to open the curtains. Sunlight entered the room, exposing the furious struggle between the two men, who were now rolling around on the floor. Atahualpa was getting the upper hand when the duke, armed with a dagger, stabbed him in the back, burying the blade all the way into his flesh. The emperor had enough strength to turn around and see his murderer. 'You, Lorenzo?' were his last words, but his body, although covered with wounds, did not lie still. Atahualpa roared and attacked the duke, biting his thumb before collapsing on top of him.

Thus died Emperor Atahualpa.

Just then, Mass was beginning in the great marble temple, but Ruminahui wasn't present. The conspirators who'd gone there to stab him were bewildered. While the priest spoke to the crowd in his learned language, they wondered what to do next. Finally, after much muttering, as their fellow Catholics' songs rose up into the great dome, they decided to head for the Palazzo Vecchio. Luckily for them, the general was there. (He'd been told about suspicious troop movements near the neighbouring towns of Pisa and Arezzo.) They asked to be seen urgently, and Ruminahui agreed to receive them in the vast Hall of the Five Hundred, where the grand council used to meet, amid statues that almost all – apart from those of little King David – represented scenes of bestial lovemaking. Present were the senators Baccio Valori, Niccolò Acciaiuoli, Francesco Guicciardini, Filippo Strozzi, and one member of the Pazzi family. They surrounded the general but didn't dare go through with it because of the guards who stood at the doors of the room and who had not been made aware of their plan, which made it difficult to predict how they would react. Not knowing what to do, and keen not to awaken the general's suspicions, they pretended to warn him about a military rebellion that was being hatched in Tuscany, with the support of Rome, which was, in fact, true (they simply omitted to mention that they had incited this rebellion themselves).

So there they were, circling the general like indecisive birds of prey, when Quispe Sisa suddenly appeared, in a white silk dress. She had been surprised, when she woke, not to find her husband or her brother in the Pitti palace. So she had gone to the Dome and, not seeing them there either, had come to the Palazzo Vecchio.

Where was Lorenzo? Where was the emperor? The senators, obviously unable to answer these two questions, feigned surprise, as if they had just discovered the two men's absence. Ruminahui didn't know these men, and didn't speak Italian, but the duchess knew them well. She could sense something strange in their behaviour, something suspicious that went beyond the usual difficulties of officialdom. She heard how they stammered, watched how they hesitated, and saw fear in their eyes.

From outside came a distant roaring. The five senators, the duchess and the general listened to this sound, which grew louder and clashed with the deathly silence that now filled the hall in which they stood.

Quispe Sisa said something in Quechua to the general.

They heard the rioters proclaiming the Republic in the name of the Medici.

News of Atahualpa's death was starting to spread. It reached the Hall of the Five Hundred. The duchess turned pale. Encouraged by Lorenzo's success, the senators grew bold and tried to unsheathe their daggers, but Ruminahui was on his guard. The Inca giant grabbed the axe and the star-headed club from his belt. He smashed the skull of his first attacker, gouged out an eye from the second, disarmed the other three, and told the guards to arrest them.

Outside, the rioters, led by the Rucellai and the Albizzi, were hammering at the doors of the palace. Ruminahui ordered the doors to be barricaded. One of the ringleaders – perhaps Leone Strozzi, the senator's son, who had a youthful, impressive voice – yelled at the Incas to surrender, in the name of freedom. The emperor was dead. His troops were outnumbered. Florence was once more a republic.

They started hammering on the doors again.

Lorenzo had not appeared, but the crowd was cheering him anyway. 'Long live the duke! Long live the Republic!' they shouted. Quispe Sisa knew the customs of the Florentines, and of the Medici in particular. She had no doubt that Lorenzo and his accomplices had fomented this rebellion. In fact, most of the rioters outside had probably been bribed. Now the Strozzi son was demanding that Ruminahui be handed over. With Atahualpa dead, the conspirators had thought the arrest of his general all that was needed for them to be in control of the situation.

Lorenzo's mistake was not going to the Palazzo Vecchio himself. Had he shown himself to the people at that moment, he could have rallied all of Florence, all of Tuscany, all of Italy down to Naples. But perhaps he had been surprised, at first, not to hear anything from the temple where Ruminahui was supposed to be killed. He probably wanted to wait, to be informed of the turn that events had taken, to be given a sense of the people's reaction to his act: did he have the support of the Florentines? What he lacked now was the very audacity he had shown when he killed the emperor, and that was what prevented him reaping the benefits of the murder.

And yet, a huge crowd had gathered in front of the old palace.

Ruminahui thought about this. He was aware of the existence of a passage that connected the palace to the other side of the river, and he suggested to the duchess that they take it without delay. From there, they would flee the city, which was clearly lost, and ride to Milan. Or, if she preferred, prepare a counter-attack. He understood the duchess's conflicting loyalties. But whatever she decided, she should go with him now.

Quispe Sisa pointed at the five senators lying on the floor, two of them already dead, and said to the general – in Castilian, so the Italians would understand – 'Hang them from the battlements.' The three wounded men stared at her incredulously. 'Now.'

The rebels were hung from the top of the tower. The crowd yelled in disbelief. Then Quispe Sisa appeared on the balcony, in her white dress. Silence fell on the square. All eyes were on her.

'Florence!' she shouted, and the hoarseness of her voice surprised all those present, coming from such a slender figure.

'Florence! This is what happens to those who try to harm you!' she said, gesturing at the hanging bodies. 'Look at their faces: they are the faces of treason. Look at their beautiful clothes: paid for by your sweat and blood. What did they want, these traitors? To overthrow the Empire. Why? So they would be free to tyrannise the people. Think, Florence! Overthrowing the Empire means losing its laws. Do you want to go back to the old days, when a handful of families sucked your lifeblood? Do you want those enemies of the people to return? Do you want an end to the public shops? Where will you get your bread the next time there are food shortages? Where were these traitors during the plague? Where were their hospices for your sick? What have they ever done for your grandparents, your children? Beware, Florence, that you do not to fall for the empty words of these cannibals! I am told that the emperor is dead … killed by the duke? If that is true, then I count the duke among the traitors, and I will offer four thousand florins to anyone who brings him to me alive, so that he can be tried for his crimes. And I will offer a thousand to anyone who brings me the heads of his accomplices!' With these words, she pointed at the Strozzi and the Rucellai, whom she had spotted among the crowd. Raised voices spread through the square. The duchess continued her diatribe: 'Because if my brother is dead, let nobody here be in any doubt: it is Florence that they have killed! Live, Florence! Rise up! Jewel in the Empire's crown, do not let those greedy tyrants return! Long live the law! Long live Tuscany! Long live Florence!' Just then, a beam of sunlight pierced the clouds. And the duchess, raising her arms to heaven, gave her final exhortation: 'Long live the Empire of the Sun! Long live the people! And death to the traitors!'

The crowd roared. It swelled like a wave. The Rucellai and the Albizi were torn to pieces, and only the Strozzi son managed to escape, using his sword to cut a path to the Arno.

Satisfied that she had shifted the balance of power, Quispe Sisa went inside and told Ruminahui: 'Go to Milan to seek reinforcements.'

News of Atahualpa's murder was confirmed around noon. Quispe Sisa wrote a letter to Coya Asarpay, which she entrusted to her best chasqui, informing her sister of the situation so that she could prepare for the succession of her son, the future Sapa Inca Charles Capac.

Lorenzo fled. It is said that his wife personally furnished him with a horse and secretly gave orders that the gates of the city be opened for him. He took refuge in Venice, where he was assassinated by Chalco Chimac's spies, who threw his body into the lagoon. (There is a painting of this scene by the famous artist Veronese.)

Quizquiz was sent to Italy at the head of a formidable army to pacify Tuscany, and to protect the region from Rome's attacks. He seized the city of Bologna, which belonged to the Pope, and settled there. He became the city's governor, then the Duke of Emilia and of Romagna. From his base in those two Italian regions, he exercised great power over the whole country, and was able to protect Florence from its enemies. He married Catherine de Medici; she was the widow of Henri, son of Francis I, and she gave Quizquiz nine children.

Atahualpa's body was embalmed and taken back to Andalusia. He was mourned for a year, in accordance with Inca customs. His mummy now rests in the cathedral in Seville, beside his old rival Charles and their wife Isabella.

Part Four

The Adventures of Cervantes

1. On the circumstances in which the young Miguel de Cervantes left Spain

In a neighbourhood of Madrid, the name of which I have no desire to call to mind, there lived, not so long ago, a stonemason. He had a wife who was not only beautiful and sturdily built, but so wealthy that they had all the local judges and sergeants in their pockets.

It so happened that the stonemason had a bone to pick with a young man in his neighbourhood, who answered to the name of Miguel de Cervantes Saavedra. This boy, who was not yet twenty-five, was of handsome appearance and good education. He was very taken with poetry, his head a little over-stuffed with the plays of Lope de Rueda, and he spoke with a stutter, yet he charmed everyone who encountered him.

One day, it is said, the stonemason found his wife in the company of this young man in some nearby stable. It is not known how far their harmless fun had gone, although from reasonable conjectures it seems plain that it was quite advanced. This, however, is of but little importance to our tale; it will be enough not to stray a hair's breadth from the truth in the telling of it.

You must know, then, that the young man wounded the stonemason during a duel that probably took place under the arches of the Plaza Mayor.

Young Miguel, who was aware of the mason's social influence, fled the city in order to escape the wrath of a judicial system whose scales, he knew, were usually tipped by the weight of gold coins. So it was that he took refuge in a hostelry in La Mancha, in an attic room that showed clear signs of having formerly served for many years as a straw-loft. This was the right move, because soon afterwards news arrived from Madrid of his sentence: he was to have his right hand chopped off in public, and furthermore to be banished from the Empire for ten years.

Consquently, Miguel's only desire now was to leave Spain as quickly as possible, to escape this cruel punishment. He remained a few days longer in his attic, where an obliging female servant brought him food and other delights every night, then he left with a group of six pilgrims who were on their way to Wittenberg, eager to see the doors of the church where the famous theses of the Sun had been nailed all those years ago. These men were happy to welcome him into their company, since with his good looks they thought it likely that they would be given at least one silver réal in alms at each village they went through. As soon as he had made a double-headed staff and a pigskin knapsack, into which the female servant who was so fond of him stuffed a loaf of bread, some cheese and olives, with a bottle of wine to quench his thirst, they set out northward, towards Zaragoza.

The many books he had possessed were now reduced to the *Orisons of Our Lady* and a Garcilaso without commentary, which he carried in two of his pockets.

The pilgrims had planned to cross through France to Germany but, in an inn where they'd stopped en route to Zaragoza, they were told that this would be madness, due to the troubles in Navarre and parts of Occitania, where people were rebelling against the Mexican crown.

So, abandoning all thoughts of passing through Zaragoza, they changed course for Barcelona, where they went in search of a boat that would enable them to bypass the overland route that was barred to them. Finally, they found a knarr that was headed towards Florence with a cargo of wine, and consequently the crossing, although long, was joyful, because they spent the whole time sampling the wine's delights, and it was with unsteady legs that they staggered on to land in Italy. At that moment, young Miguel could not know that he would soon be going to sea again, nor in what circumstances.

2. Which treats of young Cervantes's meeting with the Greek Doménikos Theotokópoulos, who leads him to Venice

Florence was governed at the time by the Grand Duke Cosimo Hualpa de Medici, eldest son of the peerless Quispe Sisa and the regicide Lorenzaccio. While the Grand Duke enjoyed relative freedom to govern as he wished, the city itself and all of Tuscany were nevertheless part of the Fifth Quarter, from which Miguel had been banished for ten years, and where he would always remain under threat of losing his right hand. He thought about going to Rome and seeking refuge there, but there were rumours of troops moving towards the Holy City, which was said to be in a state of siege, so Miguel decided against undertaking such a journey. He preferred to follow his pilgrim friends to Bologna, where a Medici also reigned – Duke Enrico Yupanqui, counselled by his mother Catherine, the widow of the great general Quizquiz – then to Milan, which was still an imperial city. From there, they would reach Switzerland, where Miguel hoped finally to be free from the hungry jaws of justice, able to enjoy more peaceful days in Geneva, Basel or Zurich.

Fortune, however, decided otherwise. On the outskirts of Como, they came across a patrol of Quitonians, who had come to the north of Italy to inspect all arrivals to and departures from the Fifth Quarter. Although the Emperor Charles Capac's reign was a peaceful one, there were still many old Christians who refused to live among the sons of the Sun, and more particularly under their dominion, so that some of them sought to leave for Rome, or Venice, or Vienna (or even, for a few, Constantinople, on the basis that they preferred the laws of Mohammed to those of the heathens from the west, because the Turk, at least, recognised only one god).

His pilgrim friends had long ago converted to Intism, and around their necks they wore the little golden suns that attested to their religion, so they had no difficulty in justifying their destination. But fatal destiny, which directs, arranges and settles everything in its own way, did not wish this for young Miguel, who was discovered not only to have no little sun around his neck, but to be in possession of a Catholic book of hours, which, it has to be said, did not really back up his story about being on a pilgrimage to the Temple of the Sun in Wittenberg. As he was also unable to provide any proof concerning the reason for his journey or even his identity, they took him to be a refractory old Christian seeking to reach Vienna via Switerzland, and so he was sent to Milan with his legs in irons.

From Milan, he had to walk to Genoa, chained to other prisoners who were being sent to the galleys. The plan was for him to be put on the first ship to Spain so that the judges could clear up his case.

So there were twelve men, threaded together like rosary beads, one long chain attached to each of their necks, and their hands cuffed as well. With them were two men on horseback and two others on foot. The ones on horseback had wheel-lock muskets, while those on foot had spears and swords.

Young Miguel, whose flesh was cruelly bruised by the irons, was even more wounded in his soul, and he was lamenting his misfortune when a man came towards the small troop. The man was young and his clothes were well made, if simple in design. He was dressed completely in black and he had a ruff around his neck, a neat little beard, and no hat. A flask and a cutlass hung from his belt. When he reached the troops, he asked the guards in very courteous language what crimes had been committed by these men in irons. One of the guards on horseback answered that they were prisoners of His Majesty the emperor, and that was all that was to be said and all he had any business to know. Nevertheless, as the man with the ruff insisted on knowing more, with the greatest courtesy imaginable, and in an accent that Miguel realised was not Italian, the other guard said he might as well just ask the men himself, and they could answer him if they wanted to.

Some confessed to terrible crimes, while others piteously claimed their innocence, and others still told stories that drew laughter because they had gone about things so foolishly; one, however, who was chained more heavily than the others, provoked general admiration, and no little fear, with an account of his terrifying exploits, which I will perhaps tell you another day. But when it was Miguel's turn, he was so downcast by his ill fortune that he stuttered terribly as he spoke, so that nobody understood much of his story, but all were deeply moved: not only was his face sad, but they supposed that his story must be truly pathetic if it could only emerge from his mouth in such jolts and splutters.

While everyone was feeling sorry for tearful young Miguel, the man with the ruff shouted: 'No matter what crimes they have committed, they are all children of God!' At the same time, he grabbed the boot of the first horseman and tipped him off his mount, so that the guard landed face down on the ground. Then, with a speed that stunned all witnesses to the scene, he drew his cutlass from his belt and planted it in the guard's chest. The other guards were shocked by this unexpected action, and at first they did not react; but then, recovering their wits, the one on horseback lifted up his musket and those on foot lifted up their spears and they joined together to attack the man with the ruff. However, he had already picked up the dead horseman's musket and he fired it at the other horseman, who fell to the ground with a moan. Now, the two infantrymen, armed with spears, faced the man with the ruff, who was left with only his knife. The prisoners, spying this opportunity to free themselves, tried to break the chain that connected them. But when it became clear that this was impossible, the man who was most heavily chained threw himself at the closest guard and used those chains to strangle him. The last guard was promptly knocked out, and so it was that the prisoners were all restored to liberty, once their chains had been removed.

The man to whom they owed this providential improvement of their situations was named Doménikos Theotokópoulos. He was Greek and he introduced himself as a soldier of Christ. He asked them to accompany him to Christian territory to champion the true faith, combat the usurper and in this way redeem their sins and save their souls. The leader of the freed prisoners replied: 'Thank you, stranger, for the favour you've done us in giving us our freedom, but we've suffered too much servitude in irons to voluntarily give ourselves over to any other kind, even if it involved serving God himself. As for saving our souls, I'm afraid that our list of crimes is so long and so bad that three lifetimes wouldn't be enough. Brigands we are, and brigands we'll die. Our only honour is never to submit to any law or authority, except for that of the *bandoleros*.' With these words, the bandit bowed, picked up the still-loaded musket, hung two swords from the belt that he took from one of the guards (also taking his jacket and his boots), mounted the better of the two horses, and rode off at a gallop. The other prisoners immediately went their separate ways into the hills, and soon only young Cervantes remained: alone, friendless, a fugitive now sought by the authorities of a foreign country, leaving behind him three seriously wounded men and one corpse, he had little choice but to follow his saviour.

The Greek seemed to know the country like the back of his hand. He knew how to thwart the patrols by avoiding the busiest roads and most populous towns. He absolutely refused to go through Bologna, preferring to cut through forests and sleep under the stars. In this way, they reached Ancona, then set off for Venice, a city that – had Atahualpa never appeared in the world – would still be considered peerless: but, by the favour of heaven, and the ingenuity of the Aztecs, the great Venice has now found a city that may be compared to herself. The streets of those two famous cities, which are almost wholly of water, make them the admiration and terror of all mankind – that of Europe dominating the old world, and that of Mexico the new.

3. Which treats of the most glorious affair ever seen in centuries past, the present century or in centuries to come, and which was also responsible for the great misfortune of poor Cervantes

'The Church, the sea or the royal house.' Led by wars and destiny from Guadalajara to this Venetian tavern, where he was presently downing a few quarter-gallons in the company of his friend the Greek, the famous captain Diego de Urbina spoke those words to young Cervantes, who sat at the table with them. 'In this Spain of ours, there is a proverb, to my mind very true – as they all are, being short aphorisms drawn from long practical experience – and the one I refer to says: *Iglesia o mar o casa real.*' He broke off to swallow a mouthful of beer, and also to allow the young man time to consider the profound truth of what he'd just said. But as Cervantes did not seem to understand, he took it upon himself to explain: 'In plainer language, whoever wants to flourish and become rich, let him follow the Church, or go to sea, adopting commerce as his calling, or go into the king's service in his household, for they say: "Better a king's crumb than a lord's favour."'

Miguel objected that Maximilian was not a king but an archduke. This earned him a tongue-lashing from the Greek: 'Don't blaspheme! Besides, His Majesty is king of Hungary, Croatia and Bohemia, and his grandfather Charles Quint was king of Spain and Holy Roman Emperor. If God wills it, his grandson will regain those honours.' With that, he crossed himself and ordered another quarter-gallon.

When Miguel expressed his surprise at hearing such Catholic fervour from a Greek, who might have been expected to favour some Byzantine or Mohammedan cult, Doménikos told him how he had left his country as a very young man to travel to Italy. First, he had studied painting in Venice, then he had gone to Rome and entered the service of the Cardinal Alessandro Farnese, before joining the Society of Jesus; finally, as a soldier of Christ, he had gone into enemy territory to spy and recruit for his Lord and for the Church.

Whether because he had heard this story too many times before or because he considered it irrelevant, the captain grew impatient and, after ordering another three quarter-gallons, returned the conversation to its original subject: young Miguel's future. 'You're young. There'll be plenty of time for you to join the Church later. And you're not really in a position to become a merchant: banished from Spain and the Fifth Quarter, the route to the west is closed to you and you wouldn't be able to trade with Mexico or Tawantinsuyu. Which leaves only the most glorious path of all: a military career.' In an attempt to convince young Cervantes, the Greek added: 'Not to mention the glory of serving your God by fighting for the last defenders of Christianity, because I don't need any proof that you're an old Christian and that your blood is pure.' Hearing these grand words, the captain necked his beer and slapped Doménikos Theotokópoulos on the back, laughing loudly. And amid this burst of laughter, no longer thinking about the prisoner's words, Miguel said yes.

So that was how Miguel de Cervantes Saavedra was recruited into the army of the Archduke Maximilian of Austria.

To begin with, he found adventure, and had no regrets.

His regiment took him to Poland, to Sweden, to the Marches of Germany, to wherever there was fighting, wherever the new emperor and the old – or, rather, their son and grandson – battled over the hegemony of Europe. He adapted to garrison life, he grew battle-hardened. But it was in the Mediterranean that he would take part in the events that decided the fate of the old world.

Charles Capac had, like his father, always been conciliatory towards the Catholics. Since there were more of them than any other sect in the Empire, certainly in Spain and Italy, he was careful, as far as possible, to avoid upsetting them needlessly. His father, moreover, had made sure he was baptised at birth, so Charles Capac was officially a member of the Roman Church, although naturally he did not claim to be an old Christian or to have the pure blood that the Inquisition, now in Rome, continued to demand from its faithful. In olden times, the Catholic kings had ordered the Inquisition to supervise and verify this purity of blood, and – where it was lacking – to punish the culprits, with fire if necessary.

The Emperor was aware that Rome was plotting against him, and that Pius V was in regular contact with Austria. Charles Capac knew that the old man, despite his debonair charm, was a viper, not to be trusted. However, news of an alliance between the Holy City and the Turks caught him off guard, since he had imagined such a scenario impossible. The reports of his spies in Rome and Constantinople (the latter reporting to Genoa, where the intelligence network was the best in the Empire) were, nonetheless, categorical: they confirmed the creation of the League of the Book (referred to by certain Christian historians as the League of Writing), which represented a terrible threat to the Fifth Quarter.

That was why Charles Capac had sent troops to Rome: to make the Pope renounce this highly un-Christian alliance.

Pius V, though, saw things differently, and rather than falling into the hands of his imperial neighbour, he fled aboard a brigantine that took him to Greece, where Selim II offered him asylum and protection.

Furious, Charles Capac decided that this flight from Rome was tantamount to an act of desertion, and he decreed the dismissal of the Holy Father. A conclave was summoned, and Alessandro Ottaviano de' Medici was elected as the new Pope, taking the name Leo XI. This new Pope, needless to say, would be far more conciliatory towards the emperor.

Pius V had no intention of renouncing his title or his duty, however, and – in agreement with Selim – decreed the transfer of the Holy See to Athens, which became *de facto* the new Rome.

And so Christianity – unusually but not unprecedentedly – found itself with two popes. This was obviously one too many, and Charles Capac used this new schism as an excuse for a new crusade, the avowed aim being to bring Pius V back in an iron cage, but the real (and barely concealed) objective being to extend the Fifth Quarter into Greece, to control the Mediterranean, to drive the Turks out of Europe, and to catch Maximilian in a pincer attack.

Six months later, the two most powerful armies the world has ever known faced each other in the middle of the Mediterranean, in the Gulf of Lepanto.

On one side: the Kapitan Pasha's Turkish armada; old Sebastiano Venier's Venetian fleet; and the Austro-Croatian navy, reinforced with contingents of exiled Spaniards and Romans, led respectively by the dashing Marquess of Santa Cruz, Alvaro de Bazan, and by Marcantonio Colonna.

On the other side: the Hispano-Inca armada captained by Juan Maldonada, and Admiral Coligny's Franco-Mexican fleet, reinforced by the Portuguese fleet, the Genoese galleys of the brilliant Giovanni Andrea Doria (nephew of the great admiral), the Tuscan galleys of Filippo di Piero Strozzi, and above all the formidable Barbary corsairs of the ferocious Uchali Fartax, the Scabby Renegade.

In all, there were almost five hundred ships, including six Venetian galleasses: floating fortresses with unequalled firepower.

The battle of the four empires was about to take place, and Miguel de Cervantes – commanded by Diego de Urbino – was there. The contingent of refractory Spaniards were under the authority of the Venetians, which caused friction. But in no other group of men was the appetite for conflict so great.

Aboard his galley, Miguel was surprised to find his friend the Greek, whom he had left behind in Venice almost a year before. What had he done during all that time? In any case, he seemed eager to enter the fray.

The night before the battle, Miguel had a fever, and in the morning, his body still wracked with pain and pouring with sweat, Captain Urbino told him to stay in bed during the assault. But young Cervantes had by now imbibed the soldiers' code of honour and would not have missed the battle for anything in the world. He got up, gathered his weapons, buckled his belt, and went up on deck with the others, pushing his way forward to the most exposed position on the ship.

All the chroniclers have recounted that battle: the shock of the ships colliding, the flames, the creaking wood that snapped like bones, the bravery of the combatants, the deafening noise, the ferocious attacks, the men in the sea who were killed like tuna fish, the water turning red, the smell of death. Giovanni Andrea Doria was not his uncle's equal, and doubtless his timorous nature, at the moment when the decisive attack was launched, cost the Inca coalition victory. The Venetian galleasses fired thousands of their lethal cast-iron bullets, the lightest of which weighed twenty pounds. Coligny saw young Bourbon-Condé decapitated by one of those cannonballs. All the Portuguese galleys were taken or sunk. Maldonado was forced to retreat. But Uchali, the bold pirate, caused yet more losses among the Islamo-Christian ranks.

Cervantes' galley, the *Marquesa*, had survived the Franco-Mexican attacks, but – escaping Charybdis only to encounter Scylla – now found itself in the way of Uchali as the pirate snaked his way with demonic skill out of the trap set for him by the Christians and Turks.

The king of Algiers (to give him his full title) had just sunk the Maltese captain's galley when the *Marquesa* sailed across to bar its passage; the collision was inevitable, and Cervantes' ship would surely have been cut in two, sacrificing itself so that Uchali could be taken. But the renegade's skill surpassed even the most fanciful tales. With a feat of navigation that no witness has ever managed to explain, he succeeded in steering his galley alongside the *Marquesa*. The hulls grazed each other, and a long cracking sound was heard.

As the two vessels went side by side, the Greek leaped on to the enemy galley, a sword in one hand and a pistol in the other.

Dozens of men went after him, all proudly yelling, 'Santiago!' One of those men was Cervantes. But, to the terrible misfortune of those brave men, the Barbary galley moved away, preventing the rest of the crew from following. Now, cut off and vastly outnumbered, many of them badly wounded, they had no choice but to surrender.

Young Cervantes had been fired at by so many arquebuses during the battle that he was bathing in his own blood, with bullets in his chest and his hand.

And since, as you know, Uchali saved himself and his whole squadron, the survivors of that unfortunate assault became his captives.

All the surviving galleys from the Inca coalition gathered at Messina; men and ships alike were in a piteous state, and there was nothing to be done but sink the galleys in port. 'All the Incas and their allies who were there made sure that they were about to be attacked inside the very harbour, and had their kits and shoes ready to flee at once on shore, without waiting to be assailed, in so great fear did they stand of our fleet. But Heaven ordered it otherwise, not for any fault or neglect of the general who commanded on our side,' said the Greek, 'but for the sins of Christendom, and because it was God's will and pleasure that we should always have instruments of punishment to chastise us.'

The bad weather, the losses and damage in the Christian ranks, the Turk's unwillingness to pursue a war in the west when he was busy putting down a Tartar revolt in the Crimea ... all of this combined to create a lost opportunity.

And so the fate of Europe was decided.

When Cervantes recovered, after several weeks in a fever, his torso was completely covered in bandages, he had lost the use of his left hand, and he was in a jail in Algiers, where Uchali had brought him with the other prisoners, Turks and Christians all mixed together.

4. Of what followed young Cervantes' misfortunes

The king of Algiers refused to be separated from his prisoners, because it was his custom to ransom them. This had probably saved Cervantes' life – Uchali had spared him, even though he was half-dead – but he had little hope of recovering his freedom, given that neither he nor his family nor any of his friends were wealthy.

Cervantes and his companions had spent the journey locked in the hold, but the Greek told them that there was another prisoner who had been kept in Uchali's private apartments, so that nobody had seen him or knew who he was: they had disembarked separately, and he was not held in the jail with them but in a Moor's house, its windows overlooking the prison courtyard. As with most windows in that country, they were essentially just holes in the wall, covered with deep, dense latticework screens. One day, when Cervantes and the Greek were on a terrace of their prison, drawing on the ground with chalks that they had procured to pass the time, they happened to look up and saw that someone was observing them from behind one of those little windows.

On each of the following days, they went back to the terrace to draw, and each time they could sense a presence behind the screen.

Then, one morning, some guards came to fetch the Greek, and they did not bring him back until nightfall. On his return, he was very agitated, and he told Cervantes: 'My friend, Providence is perhaps offering us the opportunity to get out of this prison! Listen to this: I was taken into the house next door, where I was introduced to the man at the window, who is that high-ranking prisoner we used to speculate about. Miguel, you will never guess who it is! It is his Holy Father in person who is held behind that window.'

Uchali's men had indeed gone to Athens, during preparations for the battle, and secretly abducted Pius V and taken him on board the renegade's galley.

The Inca would have paid dearly to get his hands on the Pope he had dismissed, but Uchali had not informed his allies about his illustrious prisoner because he believed that Vienna would pay an even higher sum.

'His Holiness,' the Greek went on, 'asked me if it were true that I had been Titian's pupil in Venice, and when I told him that it was, and that the master had always been happy with my work, he granted me the grace and the honour of painting his portrait. But Miguel, the best is yet to come! He promised me that, in exchange for my services, he would pay my ransom and take me to Vienna with him, as soon as the gold arrives. But don't worry: I would not abandon you, alone and penniless, in this hell. That would hardly be Christian, would it? So I begged His Holiness to let you come with us, telling him that I owed you a debt and could not under any circumstances leave you behind (because it was I, after all, who brought you into this adventure, and I now consider you my brother), and so, in the end, he agreed to also pay your ransom and to bring you with us.'

Young Miguel was overjoyed by these words, and in the weeks that followed he would wait for the Greek to return from the Moor's house every afternoon, so that he could ask him how the portrait was progressing.

Even after it was finished, to the great satisfaction of the Holy Father – because it showed him as a charming man, without any of his severe manners or cold-heartedness – they had to keep waiting, since the sum of money demanded for the Pope was entirely in keeping with the dignity of his position. In other words, it was extremely high.

Nevertheless, Vienna paid, and the gold arrived at last.

A galley was chartered to take His Holiness to Venice. He went aboard with his portrait, but without Miguel or the Greek.

Had he conned the painter? Had he forgotten them? Had Vienna ultimately refused to add the price of their ransoms to the exorbitant sum demanded for the Pope? Had Uchali broken his promise? Whatever the reason, His Holiness was abandoning them to their fate, without so much as a goodbye, taking the Greek's painting with him. In the portrait, Pius raised his hand in a gesture of blessing; now, it seemed to them an ironic adieu.

Thanks to the Berber's greed, Christianity again had two popes – one in Rome, the other in Venice. But that did not help our unfortunate heroes, Miguel and Doménikos.

To add to their despair, they were informed that – since nobody had paid their ransoms or seemed likely to do so – they were being sold to Spain.

When they told their fellow prisoners this news, the men from Seville and Cadiz warned them that Tawantinsuyu was eager for manpower to work in its silver mines, the greatest of which was named Potosi, where conditions were so bad and the slaves so mistreated that they would die of exhaustion within a few years, or even months. They said that some of the slaves preferred to take their own lives. Either way, Potosi was a death sentence.

If they were sent to Seville, they might have a chance of remaining on Spanish soil, where they could serve as slaves to the Ibero-Inca nobility. Cadiz, however, was inescapably the last stopover before they were shipped to the Americas.

They were taken to the oars in a galley bound for Cadiz.

However, fate was so capricious in those troubled times, when empires collided amid the crash of oars and ships sank in storms, that it was perhaps no surprise that it should hold further surprises in store for our two friends.

The galley, transporting its cargo of spices and prisoners, sailed towards Cadiz. Miguel and the Greek rowed in silence, indifferent to the lashes of the whip, resigned to the miserable destiny that awaited them.

But as they approached the Spanish coast, the entire crew was stunned by the rumble of thunder that they heard in the distance. Why? Because the sky was cloudless and the sun was shining down on them.

And as the Barbary galley entered the Gulf of Cadiz, a murmur began to arise among the rowers. 'Drake! Drake!' Suddenly, the guards turned pale and redoubled their efforts with the whips. 'Port side! Port side! Head north!' yelled the captain, who was a son of the famous pirate Barbarossa.

But the prisoners grumbled. Miguel and the Greek were sharing their bench with a Spanish captain who had been taken prisoner long before them and whose name was Hieronimo de Mendoza. He was skinny, of course, as they all were, and he had a long white beard and sunburned skin. His gaze, however, was still full of life, and in that instant it blazed with even more urgency than usual. As his two companions questioned him, he told them that they were being raided by the famous pirate

Francis Drake. 'The sea is like an immense forest, belonging to everybody,' he said, 'where the English seek their fortunes.' Since England had been invaded by the Mexicans from the south and the Scots from the north, Queen Elizabeth had fled with as many men as could find a shipworthy vessel – galleys, galiots, schooners, frigates, fluyts, brigantines, brigs, even little fishing boats. At first they had taken refuge in Ireland, and then in Iceland. From there, the famous pirate Drake had built a fleet to raid the Atlantic, concentrating on the French, Portuguese and Spanish coastlines. That day he had once again launched a surprise attack on a coastal town, having ventured further south than ever before. Now, if the ship from Algiers did not want to find itself battling these pirates, it had to turn back to sea immediately. According to Hieronimo de Mendoza, who knew the way merchants' minds worked, they would undoubtedly try to reach Lisbon rather than returning to Algiers, as that way they would be able to sell their cargo, and would not have made the journey in vain. To Miguel and the Greek, the prospect of going to Lisbon, however uncertain, seemed infinitely better than Cadiz, because it did not doom them to death in Potosi.

But fate was no keener on Lisbon as a destination than on Cadiz. When the captain, Barbarossa's son, saw that an English galley had spotted them and was coming from the port to pursue them, he redoubled his exhortations, and the whips lashed down like rain as the Algerian guards started to panic.

But when the rowers realised that the English galley was gaining on them, they all dropped their oars in unison and seized the captain, who was on the rear fo'c'sle yelling at them to row faster, and passed him from bench to bench, from the stern to the bow, biting him so savagely that – before he had made it past the mast – his soul had already departed for hell: so great was his cruelty towards them and the hate they bore him in return.

And so, as the English sailors boarded the galley, the rowers greeted them with shouts of 'Long live England! Long live Drake!' because, for them, this piracy was synonymous with freedom. The English flag was hoisted and, after a few days in port filling up on water and biscuits, the galley sailed towards Iceland, driven forward by the lusty oarstrokes and the songs of the prisoners freed from their chains.

On the way there, however, to their great misfortune, they encountered a Scottish ship. The lookout alerted the crew with yells of 'Red legs!' (this was the English nickname for the Scots, since they wore Tartan skirts) and the rowers immediately re-doubled their efforts. This was difficult for poor Miguel, of course, since his left hand was disabled. In any case, the rowers could not prevent the Scottish ship from catching up with them and, after another violent confrontation – in which young Cervantes, despite being one-handed, distinguished himself once again with his remarkable bravery – they were taken prisoner.

They assumed then that they would be taken to Scotland, ruled by Queen Mary, and this did not seem so bad, but they were soon disillusioned: they were ordered to row in the direction of France, and the galley entered the mouth of a very broad river that could only lead them to Bordeaux.

Once again, fortune was against them. The Scots were delivering them to the Mexicans, and this – according to their bench companion Mendoza – was worse even than Potosi.

The Mexicans, he explained, were less interested in manpower than in human flesh that could be sacrificed in their barbarous rites.

So Miguel would not die in a silver mine on the other side of the world, but at the top of a pyramid in France, and his last sight would be of his own heart, still beating after it was ripped from his chest.

6. Which treats of how Providence allowed Cervantes and the Greek to escape death and how they found refuge in a tower

The port of Bordeaux was nestled in a fold of the Garonne, in the shape of a half-moon. The captives disembarked, watched by a crowd of Gascons – a rustic, debauched people who jeered at them and called them maggot-bags, an insult that did not seem to augur well for their future prospects. Cervantes kept a stoic silence as he descended the gangway amid these taunts, but the Greek, incapable of such forbearance, called them fucking goats and cursed all Christians who consorted with heathens, the French foremost among them. Hearing this, one of the Gascons suddenly raised the butt of his arquebus, and would undoubtedly have smashed it into the Greek's face, had a Mexican captain not ordered him to stop. Mendoza, walking beside them, did not find this particularly reassuring. 'They want sacrificial victims who can walk on their own two legs,' he whispered.

The docks of Bordeaux were as lively as the docks in Seville; from dawn till dusk, the air was filled with the rumble of rolling wine barrels, punctuated by the yells of the porters. The Gascons, leading their prisoners, used spears to shove these people aside as they made their way through the crowds.

They entered the fortified city through the Cailhau Gate, with its spiked watchtowers, which opened on to the square where the Mexicans had built their pyramid. When the captives saw the dried bloodstains that ran all the way to the foot of the steps, a sigh of lamentation arose from their ranks. They were led to the prison in the Chateau de l'Ombrière, where they awaited their fate with resignation: the barrels of wine being loaded on to ships heading for the New World had a better chance of surviving than they did. At least they were well fed: the jailors brought them bread and soup every morning and evening. On Sunday, ten of them were chosen to be executed, and the noise of the drums that reached them from the square petrified them all with horror. That day, all the prisoners were allowed a glass of wine. Young Miguel did not fear death, but he would much rather have died in action. The Greek yelled furious insults until he was exhausted.

One day, however, twice as many prisoners were chosen, and the sound of the drums was twice as loud. They had different guards now. Then, the next week, nobody came, and the drums fell silent. A few more days passed and the guards stopped bringing food. They could not hear a single sound from the city beyond the walls. They remained in the darkness of their cells, enveloped in silence. When hunger and thirst began to torture them, they decided to leave, whatever the dangers, so they sharpened their iron spoons and used them to saw open the doors.

When the locks finally gave, they found the palace abandoned, the guards' weapons neatly stored on gun racks, and dozens of dead rats. There were leftovers on the tables, and the prisoners devoured them. Mendoza, used to surviving in a crowd of prisoners, got hold of a chicken leg; Cervantes and the Greek, less experienced in this regard, arrived too late. But they were in a hurry to breathe fresh air again: they walked over the rat corpses that littered the stone floors.

Once outside, they quickly lost their appetite. Columns of smoke rose into the sky; a pestilential stink choked the air; crows fought over rotting human carcasses in the streets. The dying groaned as they were pushed along in wheelbarrows, and ghostly figures piled up corpses on handcarts. And, everywhere they looked, dead rats. At first Cervantes thought he was in a gigantic tannery of hell. But, in truth, there could be no doubt: it was the plague. They had to leave the city as quickly as possible or they too would die. They went to the docks, where all was chaos: guards were trying to prevent people leaving by sea. Mendoza, who had come with them, said they should head for the countryside.

They walked through the dying city. The few survivors were hastily packing their goods on to carts or the backs of mules. The luckiest among them had a horse and were able to take off at a gallop. The situation was so bad that neither the city sergeants nor the soldiers paid any attention to our escapees. But the route to the west was closed: the soldiers garrisoned at the Fort du Hâ were still watching the roads and nobody could enter or leave that way.

So they went back to the docks. The Greek knocked out two guards, or perhaps he killed them; the story is not clear on that point. At nightfall, they swam across the river, leaving the groans of the dying and the stink of the dead behind them.

For a long time, they wandered through the plains around Bordeaux. Every time they entered a village, they were driven away with pitchforks by people fearful of the plague, or by the groans and the stink, when the plague had got there before them; in either case, they prudently skirted the settlement. For several days, all they ate was grapes picked from the vine, and soon they all had diarrhoea. The three men went on the ground, wherever they happened to be, leaving behind a liquid trail.

Finally, they came to a chateau that appeared to have been abandoned by its owner. Only a handful of servants remained and at first they refused to grant asylum to the travellers. One of the servants, however, was more tender-hearted and, taking pity, offered to feed them if they would agree to leave immediately afterwards. Thus they were able to fill their bellies and drink to their hosts' health. But when the meal was over, Mendoza suddenly started vomiting. Seeing this, the servants panicked and ran away from the chateau. By dawn, Mendoza was dead and the chateau genuinely deserted. Cervantes and the Greek burned the body in the courtyard and took possession of the premises.

There were two small towers, each so arranged that it was habitable, and the two were connected by a curtain wall. One of the towers was fitted out like a retreat: it had a bed, a small chapel, modern facilities, a few trunks full of clothing, and – in the room at the top – a beautiful library containing many books; the beams on the ceiling of this room were engraved with inscriptions in Latin and Greek. As the chateau also had a well-stocked granary and a stable, in which they found a she-ass that gave them milk, the two friends decided that they would be better off here than anywhere else they were likely to find, so they moved into the tower. The Greek deciphered one of the inscriptions in his language on the library's beams: 'My wish: to live simply, without struggle.' Cervantes, who knew Latin, translated another: 'Wherever the wind blows me, I am a passing guest.'

7. Of how Cervantes and the Greek met the owner of the tower and lived with him in great harmony for a time

They were happy in their retreat and read many books. Although the Greek was not overly fond of Ecclesiastes, from which the quotation was taken, he did point out another inscription engraved on a ceiling beam: 'Wherefore I perceive that there is nothing better, than that a man should rejoice in his own works; for that is his portion: for who shall bring him to see what shall be after him?' And that is what they did – they rejoiced in their own works, lived fully in the present – during the time when they were left in peace; in other words, while the plague ravaged the region, keeping all visitors away and forcing the inhabitants of the neighbouring village (those who had not already fled the country) to stay inside their homes.

For several weeks, nobody dared go near the chateau, and their only company was the she-ass, who gave them milk, and a few hens who gave them eggs, until the day when a little man turned up in the library. He surprised Cervantes, who was reading a volume of the *Chronicles of Atahualpa*, and the Greek, who was drawing his friend's portrait with a stub of charcoal.

The man's name was Michel de Montaigne and he was coming home.

The Greek leaped to his feet, ready to fight, but Cervantes thought it wiser to explain the reasons for their presence. To do this, he recounted the adventures that had brought them there, omitting not a single detail.

Monsieur de Montaigne was a man of average height, almost bald, with a small moustache and beard, a ruff around his neck, his clothes made of the finest materials but dirtied by his long journey. Nevertheless, his gaze was clear and his manners friendly. He spoke reasonable Tuscan, peppered with Latin expressions, so that his guests understood him quite easily, and he had even less difficulty when they spoke since he understood both Greek and Spanish. He was a member of parliament and an adviser to the king of France, Chimalpopoca. When Montaigne started listing His Majesty's titles, the Greek wanted to grab a paperknife and stab his host in the throat, but Cervantes stayed his arm.

His agile mind already having weighed up all the difficulties of the situation, Monsieur de Montaigne offered to let his guests remain secretly in his tower for as long as they liked, since, while he enjoyed solitude, he had the feeling that they would be pleasant company. Neither his wife, who lived in the next tower, nor his servants would be informed of their presence. He would put cushions and blankets in his office, where they could set up a bed, and he would make sure that his fruit bowl and his carafe of wine – placed at his guests' disposition – would always be kept full.

As they had little alternative – other than being pursued across fields like hares fleeing a pack of dogs in enemy territory, a prospect that did not enchant them – Cervantes and the Greek agreed to this deal.

The office had a fireplace – Monsieur de Montaigne had sealed off the one in his library, fearing that the flames might devour his precious books – so the two friends were perfectly comfortable, particularly when they recalled that barely two months had passed since they were chained to a bench on a Barbary galley.

And so they spent their days reading, eating and conversing with their host. In the evenings, they ate supper before falling asleep, without ever leaving the tower, except occasionally, at nightfall, to breathe some fresh air and stretch their legs in the chateau gardens under the watchful eyes of owls.

Monsieur de Montaigne had a subtle mind, curious and extremely learned, which made for highly stimulating conversation. And, since our minds fortify themselves by the communication of vigorous and regular understandings, young Cervantes liked to discuss poetry, theatre and all sorts of other things with the Frenchman for the pleasure of hearing him cite, always with great pertinence, ancient authors such as Virgil, Sophocles, Aristotle, Horace, Sextus Empiricus and Cicero.

But what he liked even more was listening to their host arguing with the Greek, because this always gave rise to speeches of tremendous vigour and inventiveness. True, he also liked to devote himself to reading books from the library, but the study of books is a languishing and feeble motion, that heats not, whereas conference teaches and exercises at once.

As a soldier of Christ and member of the Society of Jesus, the Greek vehemently reproached Monsieur de Montaigne – with no consideration for his obligations to him in the current circumstances – for compromising himself with heathens and, in so doing, betraying his fellow Christians.

Young Cervantes tried to prevent his friend from going too far down this path, fearful that the Greek would offend their host and provoke him into withdrawing his protection, but he was wasting his time. Over and over again, the Jesuit returned to his obsessive recriminations: 'Damned are those Christians who consort with the infidel!' he bellowed.

Far from taking offence, however, Monsieur de Montaigne seemed to encourage these remonstrances, and even to take pleasure from the Greek's frank, unbridled familiarity. 'No belief offends me, though never so contrary to my own,' he said, to ease young Cervantes' anxieties. 'I can peaceably argue a whole day together, if the argument be carried on with method.' And, with a laugh, he added: 'In earnest, I rather choose the company of those who ruffle me than of those who fear me.' It was as if, by violently disagreeing with him, you stirred not his anger but his interest.

The Greek, it must be said, was all too ready to give his host satisfaction in this matter. One day, he would call Monsieur de Montaigne an infidel, the next a barbarian, because – in serving the usurper who had stolen the throne of the very Christian king of France – he not only worked for the advancement of those worshippers of the Feathered Serpent, but was complicit in the vile practice of human sacrifice; and no doubt he had accepted his position out of cowardice or greed, rather than a desire to champion the true faith.

To this, Monsieur de Montaigne began by reminding the Greek that the very Christian Francis I had not hesitated to conclude an alliance with the Turk against his enemy, the Catholic king Charles Quint, and consequently it seemed difficult, or at least cavalier, to reprimand him – Michel de Montaigne, a humble magistrate – for something that the Pope had tolerated in such a great king, for let us remember, while King Henry VIII of England and the rebel monk Luther had been excommunicated merely for wanting to reform the Church, Suleiman's friend had not been sanctioned in any way whatsoever. Likewise, the Pope had spared Atahualpa and Cuhautémoc from punishment, and had indeed allowed them and their successors to be baptised. And this had been wise, ultimately, given the new coalition that now united Maximilian, Pius V and Selim.

While duly taking note of this objection, the Greek changed tack. With a nod to his host's passion for ancient Greek authors, he invoked the love of country that drove the Lacedaemonians to Thermopyles and the Athenians to Marathon to resist the Persian invader.

Enchanted, Montaigne addressed Cervantes: 'You are from Castile, are you not? Did you know that Charles Quint barely knew a word of your language when he seized the Spanish throne? Not that this was surprising, given that he was born in Gand and was a German ... So in what way was he any more Spanish than the man who succeeded him? Can you tell me that?' And when Cervantes argued that Charles Quint had at least had a Spanish mother, Montaigne replied eagerly: 'And what a mother! Joanna the Mad, whose crown he stole. What a son! What a family!' Then, turning to the Greek, he went on: 'Granted, Charles Quint was Christian. Although that did not prevent him sacking the Holy City in the year of our Lord 1527 of the old era. Do you really think Clement VII cared, as he fled like a rabbit from the Castel Sant'Angelo, whether the landsknechts who were trying to kill him were Christian or not? Equally, why should Pius V care about the religion of Selim's sailors, if he is putting them – and his ships – at the Pope's disposal? What matters to me is that these foreigners from beyond the seas brought religious peace to Spain and France. You should know, Doménikos, that I personally advised Cuhautémoc, may he rest in peace, and actively took part in the proclamation of the Bordeaux Edict, which was modelled on the Seville Edict, allowing everyone to practise the religion of his choice without fear of being whipped, banished, hanged or burned on French soil. Don't you consider that an act that will be to my credit, on the Day of Judgement?'

The Greek grew heated: 'You talk about burning Christians, but what about your Mexican friends slicing open people's chests and ripping their hearts out before burning them on their pyramids? Don't you feel complicit in those heretical crimes?'

Montaigne had to agree that he could not approve of such practices but said that he was trying to persuade the young king Chimalpopoca to abolish them.

The Greek sniggered at that: 'Thankfully for us, the plague was more persuasive than you.'

To cut the argument short, Montaigne filled their glasses with wine from his vineyard and called out joyfully: 'When in Rome, do as the Romans do!'

But Cervantes asked shrewdly: 'What about when the Romans come to you?'

Then they all went back to reading their books.

One day, when Monsieur de Montaigne was absent, Cervantes looked through the window and saw a young woman in the courtyard below, feeding the hens. Although he couldn't make out her features from where he stood, he had the impression, from her figure and her bearing, that she was an elegant and beautiful lady. He thought there was something particularly gracious about the way she tossed seeds to the chickens.

Later that afternoon, Montaigne returned with a gift for the Greek: an easel and some painting materials. After observing Doménikos's drawings, the Frenchman had reckoned that he had an aptitude for painting.

And so the Greek began painting portraits of his host and his friend, as well as landscapes of the Bordeaux countryside seen through the window.

Montaigne and Cervantes watched, captivated and disturbed, as their faces seemed to emerge from the earth, mixed into clay and spread out on canvas.

But this did not stop the painter from arguing with the man whom he considered a renegade and a supporter of the new heresies. 'One must have the courage to remain on the side of the defeated,' he told his host.

Montaigne laughed. 'Isn't that what I'm doing with you?'

Then he gave this speech: 'Don't you see, Doménikos? Soon we will all be the descendants of the victors and of the defeated. The first children, the fruit of those two worlds, are already grown men and women now: our sovereign Chimalpopoca, son of Cuhautémoc and Margaret of France, is our Adam. Marguerite Duchicela, daughter of Atahualpa and Mary of Austria, is our Eve. The king of Navarre, Tupac Henri Amaru, son of Jeanne d'Albret and Manco Inca, the duke of Romagna Enrico Yupanqui and his eight brothers and sisters, the sons and daughters of Catherine de Medici and General Quizquiz, are as much French or Italian as they are Inca or Mexican. The child Philippe Viracocha, son of Charles Capac and Marguerite Duchicela, heir to the Spanish crown and king of the Romans, is our modern-day Abel. Atahualpa was our Aeneas: was Aeneas Roman? Perhaps, after all, we are the Etruscans of the Incas and the Mexicans.'

While he was listening to this, Cervantes caught a glimpse, through the window that overlooked the garden, of the lady he had seen before in the courtyard. This time, she was tending her tomato plants and pruning her avocado trees. No doubt his isolation in that tower, and the long series of misadventures that had led him there, combined to overheat his imagination. His youth did the rest. He fell in love.

One evening, when he went out into the courtyard to smoke a cohiba, he saw her appear at a window in the second tower – which was identical to his own tower – and the candlelight illuminated what was, quite clearly, the lady's apartments. Since he was in darkness and had no fear of being seen – except for the cohiba's incandescent end, which he took care to conceal in the hollow of his palm – he stood there for a long time, watching the young woman move to and fro past the window; he even continued watching long after the tower was in darkness and everything suggested that the lady had gone to sleep, until, finally, Cervantes fell asleep too, at the base of a tree.

Just before dawn, the Greek, disturbed at finding himself alone when he awoke, with no sign of his roommate, went down to look for him, to make sure that no servant or villager had discovered his existence. He found him beneath the tree, eyes closed and fists balled. First, he shook him gently, but when Cervantes still didn't wake, the Greek turned him over and shook him so hard that at last the young Spaniard stretched out and, glancing around in astonishment, said: 'God forgive you, my friend, for you have taken me away from the sweetest and most delightful existence and spectacle that ever human being enjoyed or beheld.' To which the Greek, slapping him about the face to drag him from his stupor, thought it meet to inform him: 'I suppose you're talking about Madame de Montaigne, our host's wife. Her name is Françoise.'

They returned to the Frenchman's office, which served as their bedroom, and went back to bed until the cock crowed, but Cervantes could no longer sleep and he spent the rest of the time before sunrise imagining the lady who haunted his thoughts as she lay in her bed, dressed only in a nightgown.

The next day, he was dreaming again, standing at the library window and staring down into the courtyard, hoping that he would see her appear there – the lady of his heart (who also happened to be the wife of his host) – while he listened to Monsieur de Montaigne attempt to convince the Greek that the Mexicans' beliefs were not all worthless: 'And so, like us, they believe that the world is close to its end, and they take to be a sign of this the desolation that men sow everywhere they go. Who can deny that this shows great wisdom and perspicacity on their part, Doménikos?' According to Montaigne, it was no less disturbing that both the Mexicans and the Incas believed that the world was divided into five ages, and into the lifespan of five consecutive suns, four of which had already died, and that the one shining down presently was the fifth. The details of how and when this last sun would perish, Montaigne had not yet learned. 'But in the end,' he asked, 'who are we to say that their beliefs are not as worthy as ours?'

Hearing these words, the Greek choked on his cigar. He yelled 'Blasphemy!' and retorted that the one true God had not wanted the infidels to triumph at Lepanto, proving beyond doubt his superiority over the false gods from beyond the seas, and that if it had been the one true God's will to test his children by sending them that scourge from the other side of the ocean, then it would surely also be his will to reward the true Christians with ultimate victory. 'Real Christians do not hide in times of adversity. They are the ones who ensure the triumph of the true faith! Where were you during the Battle of Lepanto, Michel? Where were you while the plague devoured your city? If God in his mercy awards us victory, as I am sure he will, you will hardly be able to say you played your part.'

Montaigne replied in firm but still friendly tones: 'I do not approve of what I see in use, that is, to seek to affirm and support our religion by the prosperity of our enterprises. Your belief, Doménikos, has other foundation enough, without going about to authorise it by events.'

The Greek, who saw blasphemy everywhere, could not let this pass. 'Michel, do you hear yourself? You said "*your* belief"!'

'What I mean,' said Montaigne, 'is that your ... the victory of which you so often speak (and which cost you both so dearly) was a fine naval battle that was won a few months since against the Inca Empire and France – under the command of the kapitan-pasha, I might add – but it has also pleased God at other times to let you see great victories at your own expense. It pleased God that Charles Quint be captured at the Battle of Salamanca. It also pleased him to help Cuhautémoc and the English defeat Francis I. It pleased God to wrest the Holy Roman Empire from the house of Austria and pass it to Atahualpa and his lineage. God, being pleased to show us that the good have something else to hope for and the wicked something else to fear than the fortunes or misfortunes of this world, manages and applies these according to his own occult will and pleasure, and deprives us of the means foolishly to make thereof our own profit.' Then, sensing that his speech was drifting towards sentiments that, to Christian ears, would make him worthy of burning, he preferred to change the subject.

Cervantes heard him cite Horace, to warn the Greek: 'The wise man ought to bear the name of madman, the just of unjust, if they should pursue virtue herself with disproportionate zeal.' He heard him condemn immoderation towards good, and the archer who misses his target by firing too far. Then he stopped listening.

Our young man spotted Madame de Montaigne walking through the courtyard and in that moment he lost all notion of time. He had the feeling that several days had passed – and perhaps they really had? – when his mind was brought back to the conversation, which had turned (he knew not how) to the subject of marriage.

The Greek did not have enough harsh words to condemn the detestable custom of sovereigns from beyond the seas to have several wives, and Montaigne, for once, agreed with him. What sovereign, other than Charles Quint, was virtuous enough to have relations only with his wife before God, without any mistresses or illegitimate children, except in the first flush of youth? Didn't the popes, too, have concubines and bastards whom they elevated to the most prestigious positions? But it was a sin before God, he agreed, to marry one's mistresses.

At that moment, he had Cervantes' full attention.

Montaigne explained the dangers of love in marital life, which should, he believed, forbid all excesses of lasciviousness, but required, on the contrary, moderation and temperance. Given that the chief end of marriage is generation, he argued, all immodestly debauched pleasures, all assiduous sensuality in love-making altered the man's seed and prevented conception.

For his part, Montaigne boasted that he visited his wife's bedroom only once per month, with the exclusive aim of impregnating her. Were he ever to surrender to amorous ardour, he had no doubt that the mutual respect and solid understanding that he and his wife shared would be inevitably corrupted. Marriage was a binding contract, he said, and no pleasure to be found in it was worth the candle of friendship.

Then he said something about women, which Cervantes felt was addressed directly to him, and which seemed to open up dangerous new horizons: 'Let them at least learn impudence from another hand.'

Life went on in the tower. Montaigne read books or dictated letters to his secretary (in these moments, Cervantes and the Greek would go downstairs to hide in the chapel), or sometimes he would go off to Bordeaux to take care of his public duties. The Greek painted. As for Cervantes, inspired by his readings, he began to write various little pieces, which he would read to the other two men in the evenings, after dinner. When night fell, he would go outside to smoke his cohiba beneath the lady Françoise's windows. Sometimes he would hear her singing a lullaby and, as if bewitched by her voice, his longing for her would deepen. The Greek, who feared that his friend would be discovered by the chateau's servants, disapproved of this folly and regularly chastised young Miguel for his imprudence.

One evening, though, unable to bear it any longer, Cervantes walked across the curtain wall that separated the two towers.

The Greek worried himself sick all night. When the young Spaniard returned, he was in such a state of exalted excitement, his hair and clothes dishevelled, his words wild and hard to follow, that his companion was frightened. Here, the author of this account must point out that he cannot vouch for the veracity of what Cervantes told the Greek; all he can do is faithfully report his words. The young man claimed that, after waiting an hour on the curtain wall, not knowing what to do, he had decided to scratch softly at the lady's door. Françoise, believing it to be her husband – for nobody else was in the habit of using that door – opened up. When she saw the young man standing there, she let out a little cry of surprise, but something told Cervantes that he was not unknown to her, and that for a long time she had been watching him smoke cohibas in the courtyard or stare up at her window. Whatever the truth of this, she begged him not to make any noise that might wake her sleeping child. There was a full moon that night, and almost as bright as day. Perhaps out of a desire to avoid gossip, or fear that someone would raise the alarm – Cervantes was not clear on this point – she let him in.

As he narrated the rest of his account, the young man became so agitated that the Greek had to beg him to lower his voice because, as incredible as it seems, this was the scene as Miguel recounted it to his friend: Madame de Montaigne fell silent and, as he hesitated, his goddess threw around him her snowy arms in soft embraces, and caressed him. Suddenly he caught the wonted flame, and the well-known warmth pierced his marrow, and ran thrilling through his shaken bones: just as when at times, with thunder, a stream of fire in lightning shoots across the skies. In the end, he gave her the desired embrace, and in the bosom of his lover sought placid sleep.

The Greek, struggling to disentangle truth from invention in this extraordinary tale, wanted to make his friend swear never to return to the other tower. But Cervantes, a smile of contentment playing on his lips, had already fallen asleep.

Another week passed. It had been five months since their arrival in Monsieur de Montaigne's tower. The young man would have liked to live there the rest of his life but, one morning, some archers bearing a warrant for the capture of two escaped prisoners answering to the names of Miguel de Cervantes Saavedra and Doménikos Theotokópoulos came knocking at the door. They found the two friends still asleep in Montaigne's office and promptly arrested them. Cervantes, dazed, did not offer any resistance, but the Greek, in a rage at being maltreated by these vile brigands, grabbed one of the archers by the throat and would have strangled him to death had not his companions rescued him.

Monsieur de Montaigne, in his dressing gown, tried to intervene, but it was no good: the two fugitives were put in chains to be taken back to Bordeaux. The Greek began yelling the most appalling slanders, accusing their host of selling them to the Mexicans, while Montaigne did his best to reason with the archers, pointing out that he was not only a magistrate but one of the prince's counsellors. It was all in vain. Walking beside the Greek, Cervantes left the tower in irons, watched by his beloved, the incomparable Françoise, who had come running in a panic with all the chateau's servants to find out the cause of the uproar. This was the first time he had been able to see her that close-up, in daylight – a sun in the sun – and it was also the last time.

8. Of how Cervantes finally crossed the Ocean Sea

The return to Bordeaux was without glory, for they were thrown in prison again, and there they stayed for a whole month, waiting – they believed – to be executed.

The morning when the guards came to fetch them, they entrusted their souls to God, thinking that their final hour was upon them. They would climb the steps that led to the top of the pyramid, where the executioner awaited them with his ritual knife, its handle decorated with a sculpted face, and that face would be the face of death, and that would be the end of them and their adventures and their earthly life, for ever.

Instead of which, they went past the pyramid without stopping and were led to the Chateau Trompette, the seat of royal power, a colossal stone spur jutting into the Garonne river, where they were told to wait in a corridor lined with gold shields.

The guards – Mexicans armed with lances, their heads covered with feathered helmets – refused to answer their questions.

After a long time, they were ushered into a vast room where an enormous iron chandelier hung menacingly above their heads.

Before them stood a man with his back to them. He wore a black beret. In front of him was a solid wood table with papers scattered over it. The man was staring out of the window, which overlooked the port. At this hour of the day (and at pretty much every other hour of the day as well), the docks were aswarm with porters moving goods this way and that.

Cervantes elbowed the Greek: he had spotted his friend's paintings, piled up in a corner of the room.

Without turning around the man spoke: 'You may thank your protector, who brought me your artworks, and God, who has granted you a certain talent.'

They could tell from the man's imperious tone that he must be an important person. And indeed he was. It was Admiral Coligny.

When he finally turned around, he gathered up the papers from the table and waved them under Cervantes' nose: 'A conversation between talking dogs? Very amusing. And that comedy of the miraculous altarpiece ... Have you read it, Monsieur the Artist? No? Let me summarise the story for you: two skilful charlatans persuade some villagers that they have an enchanted altarpiece whose treasures can only be seen by old Christians with pure blood, free of all Jewish or Moorish antecedents. Of course, it is all a trick. But what do you think happens? A miracle! Every villager goes into ecstasies of admiration over the altarpiece's supposed wonders.'

The king of France's first counsellor burst out laughing.

'Isn't that an amusing fable?'

Neither the Greek nor Cervantes dared respond. The admiral stroked the thick gold chain that hung from his neck. 'The great nations beyond the sea – the Mexican Empire, under whose protection the kingdom of France has been placed, and the western Inca Empire, which is its faithful ally, as well as ours – are looking for painters and writers, since painting and writing are two domains in which these formidable empires, for all their power, cannot yet boast of their superiority over those of the old world. You are not completely without talent, and that is why you will be leaving on the next ship, as part of the tribute that France owes to Mexico. Over there, you will be sold to the highest bidder, and you will be able to buy back your freedom, if God wills it.' Then, with a gesture, he ordered the guards to take them away. The next day, they were aboard a galley loaded with wine and men, sailing towards Cuba.

An old Spanish sailor had once told Cervantes: 'If you want to learn to pray, go to sea.' However, that crossing, which took only two moons, passed like a dream.

Our two friends met a Genevan shoemaker, a Mexican merchant, a Jew from Salonika, a producer of Haitian tobacco, and a princess from Cholula who was travelling with her jaguar.

All of them extolled the beauties of those lands beyond the sea, their infinite spaces, their generous natures, their abundant riches, and the possibilities of making one's fortune there, just so long as one did not set out with any seditious plans.

Then, one morning, the outline of Baracoa, the capital of Cuba and crossroads of the two worlds, appeared on the horizon. It was a city of palaces, palm trees and earth huts, where dogs spoke to parrots, where rich merchants came to sell their slaves and their wine, where the streets were fragrant with the scent of unknown fruits, where the naked Taíno nobility rode their Chilean thoroughbreds, wearing nothing but eighteen-row red pearl necklaces and crocodile-skin bracelets, where even the beggars resembled ancient dethroned kings, with masks and mirrors of copper and gold on their heads, where the shops were so overflowing with merchandise that, in the evenings, crested lizards ventured through the streets in search of crates that they could crack open. In that land, they spoke all languages, loved all women, prayed to all gods.

The Greek, dazzled by this torrent of colours, his nerves set on edge by this Babylonian excess, started laughing like a madman.

Looking up at the sky, forgetting his uncertain future, Cervantes marvelled at the red-headed vultures flying above him and thought that all those creatures were ghosts of this enchanted island. And so, undoubtedly, was he.

penguin.co.uk/vintage